LÉGENDE DE THORIGNY

FRÉDÉRIC DEBREU

GUILLAUME ROY
CONTREBASSE

VENDREDI
25 MAI 19H3

TAVERNE DE LA MARINE
RUE DU PONTEL
SAINT OUEN-DE-L'ÉLÉPHANT

The Resurrection of

Frédéric Debray

The Resurrection of Frédéric Debreu

Also by Alex Marsh

Sex and Bowls and Rock and Roll (HarperCollins, 2010)

'The thing about running into the road and shouting "Help! Help! Help!" is that essentially it is a cry for help...'

Alex Marsh's very funny mid-life crisis memoir tells of his doomed attempts to recreate his teenage years in rock bands amidst the unlikely environment of a village bowls team. A comic tour-de-force based on the blog once described by the *Independent on Sunday* as the work of a 'post-modern Mr Pooter'.

'Alex Marsh's charming and funny book charts his trajectory through East Anglia armed with nothing but four chords, the truth and some chickens.' Al Murray

The Resurrection of Frédéric Debreu

Alex Marsh

RedDoor

Published by RedDoor
www.reddoorpublishing.com

© 2016 Alex Marsh
Alex Marsh's website is at www.privatesecretdiary.com

The right of Alex Marsh to be identified as author of this Work
has been asserted by him in accordance with sections 77 and 78
of the Copyright, Designs and Patents Act 1988

ISBN 978-1-910453-17-9

A CIP catalogue record for this book is available
from the British Library

Cover design: Rawshock design
Typesetting: www.typesetter.org.uk
Printed and bound by Nørhaven, Denmark

With thanks to my father,
who knows his books and music

The lyrics of M. Debreu and French-language dialogue has been translated for this UK edition and appears in italics throughout the text. The lyrics are reproduced by kind permission of M. Debreu's remaining family

1

An Englishman's Home

Ted's fingers bulged like sausages. Premium sausages packed with decent meat, butcher's sausages; the sort of sausage that would crown the fullest of full English breakfasts. Weathered and cracked, they hardly brought to mind the fingers of a master craftsman, but nevertheless when the big Englishman removed the clamp and ran the side of his hand along the join, the two strips of ash lined up perfectly. He gave a low growl of approval and tossed the tool aside. It landed on the planks with a clatter.

His face was jowly, skin draped loosely across the cheeks that bridged the spaces between his bulbous nose and where somebody had haphazardly placed his ears. His hair retained a satisfactory proportion of its original black, and if, as they say, the human body shrinks as it enters its final years then it would be starting from a position of some substance. He wore a flannel shirt that bore a history of his life in stains: lacquer, wood glue and wax; Mann's Brown Ale, Jennings Bitter, Thomas Taylor Landlord. Two buttons secured it doggedly across a stomach that had seen its share of those; any advantage to his physique from his conversion to the grape was yet to make itself apparent. He did miss the real ale, as he missed the breakfasts and *Final Score* on the television, but what was the point of the lumpen expats who clustered in their enclaves across the world hoarding Marmite?

It was early; the slightest of clouds, the gently climbing orange sun, the sort of morning just designed to convince him that everything might be OK in the end and that he hadn't buggered the whole thing up.

He examined his work once more. This was shaping up to be an all right job, he thought; an all right job so far. With the glue having dried overnight, he could get on today, and soon he'd have one that he reckoned would be the best yet. He would give it to the farmer. Nodding to himself, Ted placed the embryonic instrument on the verandah and lowered his rump on to the step. A gentle gust whipped up the smell of dew and his cavernous nostrils twitched with pleasure. Looking down across the meadow, he noticed for the first time that a faint trail of flattened grass had begun to form where he had established his shortcut to the village. He had made his mark on the landscape already. The wind in the trees, the birdsong, his trepidation pushed to the back of his mind, Ted stretched his shoulders, filled and emptied those big lungs and allowed himself to bask in the beauty of the moment.

'Ted!' bawled a voice from inside.

By rights, the kitchen door should have been the item to most offend his carpenter's eye. Six planks and two wonky crossbeams fixed with irregular nails, it ill-fitted the frame, an inch-deep gap at the bottom having widened further as the wood had started to fall away with rot. At head height was an eighteen-inch square panel of glazing that he had already needed to resecure, splicing in two sticks of birch as mullions. Daisy had stretched a remnant of old net curtain across on the inside, to secure their privacy from the cows and the birds.

But it was the cottage's ramshackle nature that had most appealed to Ted, this broken-down cabin between the meadow and the woods, a cosy little nest that seemed to offer them so much more than the most luxurious of five-star hotels; certainly more so than the dated and unloved *gîtes* that he'd poked his nose around upon their first arrival.

The door was perfectly serviceable. It would be easy to fix properly, when he got the inclination. He pushed his way through to seek breakfast.

The kitchen had been finished in the same weathered off-white as the building's exterior, although the cupboards and fittings had been added and painted piecemeal in varying shades from glossy white to dirty cream. It would have been a cosy space even if it were not for the table, a slab of wood no larger than the average cooker hob. It had been set well off-centre in the room, partly to allow reasonable passage through to an interior door beyond, but mainly to shield a point on the floorboards where they had given way entirely, creating an opening to the black earth two feet below.

Daisy bustled and shuffled, circling clockwise, anticlockwise, jabbing Ted out of the way with a thin elbow. She packed the table with knives, a toast rack, jam, plates, all on a meticulous grid. Ted stepped forward and back to avoid her, dancing clumsily as he searched for a role. She slapped his hand away from the tin that held the teabags: Typhoo, his concession to the Marmite brigade.

'Where's the butter?' he said.

'In the butter dish.'

'Where's the butter dish?'

'Give me that.'

The water supply had come back on that morning; a saucepan bubbled on the hob whilst Daisy wrestled with the handle of the cutlery drawer, yanking and twisting with thin hands until the wood gave way and she could liberate a tarnished spoon.

'For Pete's sake, will you sit down and let me help?'

'In the fridge. It's in the fridge.'

'What's it doing in the fridge? You can never spread it properly when it's been in the fridge.'

Daisy glared up at him. 'It's in the fridge because someone left it in the sun; right in the sun, and it was a mess. So I had to put it in the fridge. Now give me that.'

Ted parked himself on one of the two chairs, grasping a knife and tapping idle drumbeats on the old tabletop. Distressed French pine had been going for crazy amounts as his time in the furniture trade had drawn to a close. Well this was the real thing.

3

He took a look around the room. Distressed? It was bloody inconsolable.

'You missed Mon-sure Patenaude,' said Daisy, her arm shaking with the weight as she poured hot water. 'Cheery soul. He brought post down from the farm.'

Ted's eyes shot up. 'Anything for me?'

'The bill for the gas bottles. Were you expecting anything?'

The cutlery resumed its gentle tattoo. Tap tap tap. 'Not really,' he said, concentrating on his tap so he need not meet her gaze. He would need to have a word with the farmer. Tap tap. A mug appeared in front of him, and the knife was prised from his grasp.

'What shall we do next week?' Daisy nibbled a mouse-sized corner from her toast.

'Do?'

It seemed an age before her mouth was clear to speak. 'Yes, do. What shall we do? Like normal folk when they have people to stay. They do things.'

'Well we're going to the festival.'

'That'll be one morning then. Perhaps for the rest of the time we'll sit and watch you do your carpentry. That'll exciting for them.' Daisy forced her chair back, and carried the teapot to the stove for more hot water. 'I don't know what your problem is. You like Stan really.'

Ted ran his finger around his empty plate. 'Wainwright's all right.'

'Stop your sulk then.'

'It's just his me-me-me-me-me stories and his famous friends and his that-remind-me-ofs.' Ted thought further. 'If he expects me to listen to his James Last tapes again then he's got another thing coming.'

'He's been a good friend to you, and you know it.'

'I get on with Wainwright. In small doses.'

Daisy stirred up the pot, oblivious to the boiling steam curling up around her hand. The tinny clink-clink-clink of spoon on china filled the silence between them. She turned back to him, her face set with a decision made. 'We should go out for a meal.'

'Look, let me carry that back.'

'They like going for meals.'

Ted snorted under his breath before affecting what he hoped would be a passable impersonation of the man in question. 'An accomplished dish. Not like the version Raymond Blanc cooked me of course. A bit rustic for that. Now Raymond, there's a chef, he said to me, "what do you think, Stan? My Michelin stars are up for review, do you think I need more salt in the kedgeree?" And I said to him ... '

'Have you quite finished?'

Ted looked around the room, trying to envisage an extra pair of bodies squashed in for breakfast. 'We'll go to the festival. And we'll take them to Gaston's.'

'Well that'll make a nice change for you.' Daisy seemed to have forgotten her toast as she rummaged in the cupboard. 'Gaston might know somewhere good, though. I suppose.'

'He did say they're trying to open a McDonald's a few miles down on the Saint-Martin road. We should take them there. That'd teach him.' Ted took one last draw on his tea. 'Mind you, he's probably best pals with Ronald himself.'

A breath of wind slipped in through the open door. Ted felt the air on his face and leaned back in his chair to savour the aroma of the hillside. His wife took his plate and applied a rudimentary rinse, peering at the crumbs as they were washed away by the icy water. Ted pulled himself to his feet.

'I'll go down to the café later on and ask Gaston what he thinks, anyway.'

'What he thinks about what?'

Ted pondered. 'Just what he thinks in general.' He shook his head and squeezed past his wife to the door, wiping his face with his palm as he stepped out into the sunshine.

Her voice bayed after him. 'It's not a café. It's a pub!'

It was a fraud, of course. Ted was a fine craftsman, but you needed specialist equipment to shape a guitar body, and this was beyond the scope of his new little hobby. So he had cheated. David had arranged it when times were better, ordering a small batch of semi-complete soundboxes to be sent to his father from a manufacturer. Ted had started to build up his instruments from here, adding the neck, the headstock, the frets; using the fixing, carving and finishing skills that he had built up over a lifetime.

Nevertheless, it did look good, propped there against the upright. He should know – he'd played the bloody things for long enough. Stepping in from the sunshine to the dinginess of the outbuilding, he stumbled over a chisel that had fallen onto the brick and earth floor. He chided himself for this lapse before chucking the tool on the pile of others that lay higgledy-piggledy on the side bench. One other incomplete instrument stood on a rack against the featherboard at the back of the room – Ted regarded it with approval as his eyes adjusted to the gloom. He would get round to a bit of decoration; some of that white paint in here would help. As the seasons moved on he supposed he might have to migrate into the spare room, but for now this space was ideal for his needs. Aside from two long workbenches, it contained an ancient winged armchair upholstered in what was once grey and red, tool racks, a bathroom cabinet with a cracked mirror, a standard lamp without a shade, a bicycle frame, an upturned wooden box. An exploded mess of splintered wood hung on the wall next to the stable door, a victim of Ted's first attempts to understand how a guitar maker balances the tension of the strings. The skills may have been very similar, but the instruments were a different beast to the sideboards and dressers that had put food on the table through the years.

At the very end of the front bench sat his gramophone, chunky, bakelite-bodied, a good fifteen inches square. Beside it were two piles of long-playing records. The first stood the best part of a foot tall: Django Reinhardt, Humphrey Lyttelton,

Nat Gonella, Louis Armstrong. A single Barbra Streisand album; several by Georges Brassens. Jake Thackray – now, he was bloody good. Even two discs by the Beatles, who were all right before they got too clever.

Three items alone made up the second stack. Ted lifted each of them from the workbench, examining the covers in turn, agonising over the choice ahead.

Finally he slid a thick disc from one of the sleeves. Setting the vinyl down upon the turntable, he pressed his index finger down upon the switch. The warm hum of power and a gentle crackle emerged from two enormous old speakers lodged beneath the bench.

The voice of Frédéric Debreu filled the room.

Ted carried his tools outside, his body unconsciously skipping in time with the bom-de-dom-de beat of the music. He twisted the volume knob to ensure that he would hear clearly and, when he'd fetched all he needed from the workshop, he pulled out one of the speakers as far as its wire would allow, setting it in the doorway facing outwards.

The melody drifted out on the wind across the field and towards the village, a landscape where Debreu himself had once walked. The thought of this filled Ted with wonder. 'The Pretty Goat' – it was the first Debreu song that he had ever taught himself. It wasn't too pacy. It required few vocal gymnastics. And of course those 'tra-la-las,' that glorious chorus, well – it was an attractively bilingual way in for the enthusiastic Derbyshire amateur. He had discovered that, with practice, he could 'tra-la-la' in perfect French.

And the rest of the lyrics had come, in time; haltingly and nervously at first, then in an intonation that might pass as French, and then as second nature as he had grown to understand and love these words in this language that he only hazily comprehended.

♫ *I will be here forever; said the lover, said the lover*
I will be here forever for you, miss… ♫

He paused and held his breath as the record reached that chorus, then sang along in a rumbustious Gallic baritone, air-conducting with a quarter-inch chisel. '*Tra-la LA LA tra-la LA LA tra-la la la tra-la la LA,*' he leapt to his feet, swooshing the blade through the air in wide circles. A game bird flapped, startled from the long grass. He jigged and waved his arms, oblivious to the wildlife, oblivious to his wife's stare through the kitchen window behind him. If there was one thing that might take his mind from lurking catastrophe, then that thing was the music of Frédéric Debreu. He might have heard this song a hundred thousand times before. But each time it made his big heart thump.

2

Café Gaston

The farmland spread out beyond the north-east outskirts of the village. There was a smattering of cows, some sheep, some wild chickens and acres of meadowland that surrounded the central orchards. Ted had not seen a great deal of actual farming being done; their landlord was a reclusive man who seemed ill at ease in the wide open spaces. The Patenaudes were once a big farming family, Gaston had said, but now he was the only one left. Any businessman would have surely made more of the little cottage. The local authorities seemed happy to license even the most fleabitten holiday lets, but a little investment would surely have brought in more than the peppercorn amount that Monsieur Patenaude had asked of the Englishman.

In retrospect, Ted had been fortunate.

Anyway, who was he to criticise his landlord's commercial nous? After all, the fellow had found the only old chump who saw character in the hole in the floor, who felt an affinity with the earthy nature of the peeling paintwork and rusting hinges, who saw the romance in bedding down in what might easily be mistaken for a derelict cricket pavilion back home. Faded glamour it wasn't. But he'd always said that he'd do something silly on his retirement; a little interlude of real life before he rotted away in a polite bungalow with hedges and a carport; the respectable old age that was Daisy's only remaining ambition. Well, she'd been very good about his stupid whim. She'd never ceased to surprise him. Their 'gap year', they'd laughed, when explaining it to the neighbours.

But who could have foretold how easily they'd have settled into their familiar roles? How, after that initial burst of sightseeing and exploration, she'd been content to potter around the house doing her own thing, leaving him to spend his life out and about, just as he had back in Derbyshire. It wasn't stoicism on her part; she simply wasn't that bothered about life outside her four walls. They may as well have gone to Outer bloody Mongolia.

Strolling on, he passed the junction with the track that would have been his route by car. The lane began to widen here, a surface of cracked and potholed tarmac emerging cautiously from the grass and dirt. His slapdash research had warned that the climate here would differ little from that back home, but they had enjoyed weeks of glorious weather now with the promise of more to come. Ted could already feel the heat of the sun on his back and shoulders, but this walk was never a chore. Besides, he was attempting to conserve his ancient Volkswagen Passat. A grinding, scraping noise had developed whenever he drove above a crawl: the sort of noise that garage mechanics retire on.

A few hundred yards on, he reached the first buildings on the outskirts of the village: a row of post-war apartments finished in a peach stucco that might once have been vibrant and neat. The lane was a proper road now, with a pavement on one side and cars parked up against the dusty kerb; many of them looked decades old. Ted hopped back into the road to give way to a young mother as she heaved a dented pushchair in the opposite direction. He smiled at her, but she failed to acknowledge him as she murmured chat to the infant from beneath her uranium-bleached hair.

He could hear the bustle as he turned left at the T-junction; from here it was a two-hundred yard walk along another residential street to the very centre of town. He remained on the left-hand side, grateful for the shade that the tall apartments provided. A small car hooted, veering across the centre markings as an ancient face turned to acknowledge him. Ted stared as it rattled off up the hill. Surely Casimir should have surrendered his licence years ago?

Ted paused at the crossing. He was still unsure as to his rights as a pedestrian, but the way was clear so he stepped out. The market place opened out before him.

There was no market.

Ted stared. It hadn't occurred to him that there would be no market. There was always a market.

The square was swarming with workmen. Carpenters and fixers; traders struggling under the weight of scaffold and ladders. There was barking and chatter, hammering, shouting, bursts from an electric drill. Ted lingered at the kerb and watched. A Luton van backed up at a creep; its driver leaped out and began to unload a mishmash of flags and banners. Men crowded around the tailgate and argued until somebody who appeared to be in authority started to organise them.

Ted peered across to the café. It stood on a corner plot opposite him, a four-storey building in a peeling cream stucco, its function denoted by a burgundy advertising banner for Amstel beer that ran the length of the frontage. Beneath this, two shallow awnings crowned the tables that lined the pavement; behind them the front windows had been folded back to expose the room within.

He hesitated. It was a little early for a drink. So he ventured onto the square, gazing around with fascinated eyes at the work in progress. It was only Monday, but he guessed they needed to be well-prepared for the weekend. He paused at the point where the first stalls would usually be clustered, wondering about his plans for dinner. He felt a hand on his shoulder.

'Mister Prescott!'

Gaston was a tall man, a good six inches more so than the big Englishman, although something in the confidence in which he stood before his new friend seemed to double that difference. He gripped Ted's palm and pumped it, once, twice, the Englishman catching up with the process on the third and final time, ever-awkward about throwing himself into this custom.

11

Gaston's face was clean shaven, always clean shaven as if, whatever the time of day, he had only just splashed the foam from his face. No roots were visible, but his hair was such a pitch black that it must surely be benefiting from some chemical help; it was creamed into a style that would have befitted any man of respectability from the last hundred years.

Extraordinarily, the café owner was sporting a pair of jeans. A rich, navy blue, and visibly brand new, they sat comfortably with the radiance of his familiar polished brogues. A clutch of rough threads hung from one cuff, although his shirt was as snow-white and as fastidiously ironed as anything that Ted had ever seen on him.

'I wear casual this morning,' Gaston said, flourishing his hands about his own attire. 'Come. You must help. Be part of the *preparations*.'

He helped, if this was the right word for allowing the Frenchman to chat with passers-by whilst Ted clambered up an aluminium ladder. It teetered on the cobbles outside the florist's shop whilst he stretched to fix a brass hook to the sill beneath the first-floor window. A stream of people stopped to make comments that he could not immediately translate, but the theme was clear: let the newcomer – an old man at that – do the dangerous work. Ted was content to be the butt of their geniality, and he took time to pause and smile and wave his screwdriver whilst clinging on grimly with his spare hand.

When the fixing was in place, Gaston passed him one end of a banner, a riot of children's paintings of vividly coloured flowers, happy faces and tricolours. The eyelet that had been set into the PVC slid over the hook and held, and Ted descended step-by-step to the street below. They shifted the ladder along the shop front a metre at a time, attaching hooks and fastening the banner as they went. The shopkeeper, a midget-like lady with a tremendous grey bun of hair, pronounced herself satisfied.

They moved to the building next door, a boarded-up shop.

Ted wiped his forehead with his sleeve; the perspiration had already glued his shirt to his back.

'*TOURIST INFORMATION*,' Gaston unrolled a fresh banner that featured the French words in stark capitals on a plain white background. 'The town, it takes over this building.' He indicated the sealed windows. 'Coat of paint, eh?'

Ted settled the ladder into place. 'You climb, I hold this time?'

'I hold. Just in case.' A warm summer gust erupted around the square; the plastic buntings around them crackled and fluttered.

'A pub!' That had been Daisy's accusation, and it is true that the stainless-steel bar was the first thing to meet the eyes as visitors stepped in through the double doors. But the surface was as devoted to coffee-making and condiments as it was to beer pumps; the rows of liquors and spirits that skulked on the high shelves beyond were complemented by perspex-fronted cabinets of canned drinks and pre-prepared pastries. The interior was well-kept and tidy, certainly not basic, but by no means one of the belligerently quaint artifices drooled over by the guidebooks. Ted had been relieved by this; it was a matter-of-fact place that would presumably attract matter-of-fact people. Ted was comfortable amidst matter-of-factness.

Despite this, the room did possess a certain stateliness. Much of this came from the illusion of lavish dimensions; perhaps it was the light that poured in through towering plate glass on both faces of the corner plot that made everything seem larger, elevating the modest environment into a grander scale. In fact there were only around a dozen tables in total, chalk-white tablecloths regimented around the left-hand section of the L-shaped space.

The right-hand area was smaller and more homely. A hulking old coffee machine occupied a good third of the bar, its riot of pipes and funnels like some great apparatus rescued from a Victorian railway. The two toilet doors were set into the far wall; a third door, marked *'Private'* granted access to the building above. This part of the room was home to a single table, a round slab of pine about five feet in diameter. There was no tablecloth and the surface was chipped and stained. Six chairs, none matching, were strewn around its circumference.

Ted had been shepherded towards this table on his third visit, a month or so previously. It had been mid-afternoon on a weekday and Gaston had seized upon his trade with gusto, pulling him by the arm to one of those chairs, his words laced with remorse for the belated personal hospitality. There they had got through two bottles of red together, chatting beneath the tatty photographs of village clubs long forgotten, beneath the old Pernod sign and broken lamp fitting. As afternoon passed into evening they had been joined by other regulars, happy to welcome the newcomer into their select group, speaking English in his presence in order to put him at ease, and using it with a fluency that made him ashamed. By eight o'clock he was extremely drunk; by nine he was attempting the Ronald Reagan impression that had once been so popular in the saloon bar of the Barley Mow.

Later, as he had stood swaying at the kerb outside, foggily considering which way he should check for approaching traffic, his mind kept returning to one thought. Frédéric Debreu himself had been to that café. The musician would surely have been treated as a regular, exactly how Ted had been. Perhaps he had sat in that very chair that Ted had occupied, drunk the same wine, joined in with the same easy chat. The thought had given him a joyous feeling, even as the hatchback had swerved to avoid him, the noise from its horn shrieking out into the dark. Visiting as a tourist was one thing. But following in that man's footsteps was quite another.

A beanpole teenager with a sallow, pockmarked face was polishing glasses as they entered. He wore a formal shirt and waistcoat, although there was something not quite right in both size and colour, and the effect was more awkward than smart; had Ted stepped up to look over the bar, he would have seen that the youth's black trousers only just covered the top of his socks. The boy wiped away with a slapdash mechanical action, staring into far space as he placed each glass down with a clump. Pockmark acknowledged Ted with a nod, bobbing his excessively greased hair. 'Morning, Philippe,' chirped Ted, as Gaston swept in behind him.

One other man sat some distance away. Fat, and middle-aged; fat not as Ted was rotund, but massive and shapeless, a morose and surly fat that seemed to cast rainclouds about him. He cradled a tiny espresso mug at his seat in the far corner, his arms melding into his torso under a sweat-stained T-shirt, his buttocks pouring over the edges of the wooden chair as if he were perched upon a dolls' house toy. His eyes were sunken and his despairing hair had been combed over his beach-ball scalp. He grunted at Ted across the room; Ted grunted back, as this had become the ritual between them.

'No market; everybody working. They come in earlier, take out coffee.' Gaston appeared to have read Ted's thoughts as he glided past to the gap that provided access to the bar and kitchen. 'Busy when they finish. Some wine then?' He turned and beamed. 'While I change to my clothes.'

Ted fumbled in his pocket, counting a puddle of small change out onto the bar, wondering whether these coins would ever become familiar to him. His host watched with patience for some moments before he gave a 'pssshhh' noise and whisked the pile of coins, unaudited, into the open till.

A rack behind the bar towered with black-green bottles of the local red, each adorned with a basic emerald-and-white label, some of which had been pasted on crookedly. Gaston reached past this display to select a vintage from the shelving beyond. He seemed to grasp it and remove the cork in one movement, then he swept back out into the public area conveying two glasses between the fingers of his other hand. Setting them down on the circular table, he patted his jeans by way of further explanation and darted towards and through the door beside the end of the bar.

Pockmark gave his eyes an immense roll, and set to work on a further glass.

Gaston knew his trade. Customers started to drizzle in almost as soon as he had returned; by the time they had emptied their first bottle, the young barman Philippe had work to do. He grappled with the old coffee machine, charged glasses with wine and millpond-flat lager, mooched between the kitchen and the bar with orders and plates. Periodically Gaston stood to welcome people as they walked in through the double doors. Invariably he greeted them by name: Nicolas ... Stéphanie ... Monsieur Bargeron ... Paul ... few tourists had arrived in town yet. Casimir, the ancient man who had driven past him earlier, returned. He manoeuvred himself onto the chair opposite the Englishman, waving a greying claw across the bar for a glass. Ted glanced at his watch but it was not late. They talked about the festival ahead and Casimir reminisced about those long ago, ones when he was a young man, ones when he was a boy.

'Of course they were all better then?' asked Gaston, his smile for Ted's benefit.

'No. They are still shit.'

'Hey!' Gaston had spotted one more customer stepping up to the doors. His smile widening, the café's patron rose to his feet.

The newcomer was a ruddy-faced man, squat and corpulent. He wore formal black trousers that billowed around his legs, and a jacket of giraffe-coloured chequers that might once have been the height of fashion. His grey-black hair was short in tight curls and his nose was bulbous, dotted with lumps and craters and red like the Martian surface. But his moustache dominated even this: long and deep fields of grey, so wide and bounteous that it seemed to reach the very edge of his face. He beamed from beneath this forest of hair and took a large stride into the room to exchange a hug with Gaston.

'He is the mayor,' Casimir said. 'Bernard. He is back.'

'Ah. Very important person?'

16

Casimir inclined his head one way, and then the other. 'He will say that, *oui*.'

The grip appeared to last for ever. Eventually Ted could free his hand. 'You have been on holiday?' he said as they resumed their seats, a fresh glass produced for the newcomer. 'Vacation ... *a holiday?*'

'No, no, no, no,' the mayor shook his head with great emphasis. 'Earlier yes, but not *just now*. A visit. Official visit. We work with a town that is the same size and the same industries. In the *Netherlands*. We arrange things together, like you say, you say ...' He struggled for the English word, staring into Ted's eyes for inspiration.

'Twinning?'

'Twinning!' The mayor beamed. 'We twin.'

'Not a holiday at all then,' said Casimir, arching an eyebrow in a gesture that Ted had no difficulty in translating.

'No it bloody is not.' The mayor's eyes shot up. 'No, not a holiday,' he continued in English, the warmth returning to his voice. 'We discuss business. Education. *For all of our benefit, Casimir,'* – and here he turned from Ted and gave the old man three sharp pokes in the chest. *'For all of our benefit, or for your bloody great grandchildren's benefit anyway, you old sod.* It is a very pretty town. Beside the sea.'

Casimir passed Ted a gnarly wink, his grin exposing the handful of yellow-brown teeth that remained. 'Because we have many good beaches here.'

Gaston stood. 'I help the boy for a while,' he said, before placing a hand on the mayor's shoulder and speaking in French. *'Ted here is the man I told you about. The Debreu fan.'*

More customers arrived. Farmworkers, pig-smelling in their overalls; then a pair of elderly ladies, then two burly men that Ted recognised from their market stalls. Monsieur Patenaude poked his head through the doors, drawled something across the room at Gaston and withdrew; the young mother who'd passed Ted on his way into town shuffled in shyly, peering around the room before settling in a far corner. Pockmarked Philippe was buzzing now, scowling and flustered with the extra work. His orders had become a juggling act; he scurried around the bar occasionally pausing to run his hands through his slicked hair. Gaston eased from table to table with all the time in the world, smiling, chatting, pouring. The young mother was joined by a man in a cheap suit, his top shirt button undone, his tie loose, waving and shrugging, and pointing to his watch.

The second bottle of wine had uncorked Ted's enthusiasm as he addressed his two companions at the round table. 'The thing is, because Debreu used a Spanish guitar, one with nylon strings – do you follow? The Spanish guitar – I don't know what you call it in France – is it a Spanish guitar? Well it isn't a loud instrument, but it has a very full sound. A very full sound.' The Englishman opened his arms wide to indicate a full sound, and leaned in close to ensure that his audience understood. 'And that sort of guitar was superseded, was, was made old-fashioned by pop music, when they just wanted to strum.' Ted made strumming motions. 'But it was popular then, because it was ideal for the style. The – bom-de dom-de dom-de dom-de. Do you see?'

'You have one more bottle.' Gaston leaned in between them as Casimir and the mayor nodded at the thought of the bom-de doms.

Ted placed the palm of his hand over his glass. 'No, no Gaston, thank you.'

'Fool, Ted. Philippe!'

'I'll have to pay you tomorrow, Gaston. I'll drop in with some money,' said Ted.

'Pssshhh.' Gaston held up his palms. 'Don't worry.'

'No, no Gaston. I'll come in tomorrow.'

The young couple left together, the man stepping back to allow her to sweep through the doors with a haughty stride. Philippe acknowledged his *'later'* with a morose nod before repenting and replying in kind as the customer's back disappeared through the closing door. Wrinkling his nose, the barman set off to clear the table.

'You make the guitars? Make them?' The mayor ran his finger through his moustache.

Ted lowered his eyes to the table. 'Oh well, I'm having a go. They're not very good, but I always wanted to have a go, and they're getting a bit better. Would you like one?'

'But good enough for to give to me, eh Ted?' Gaston had rejoined them, but now left his seat once more, looking over his shoulder as he went. *'Hey, Bernard – wait, you look.'* Ted's eyes followed the dapper proprietor as he strode to the door at the back of the room. Moments later, he emerged with the instrument in question, swinging it up by the neck, catching the body and holding it face-up next to the table for his companions to witness. They leaned in with interest, running their hands over the immaculate varnish, nodding at the engraved 'GD' on the headstock, squinting at the workmanship as if they were suddenly guitar experts of the highest stature. *'It is very good,'* whispered Casimir; the mayor hummed in agreement. 'Yes, good, very good.'

'They look better than they are.' Ted reached out for the guitar, force of habit causing it to settle into the playing position, body nestling on his left thigh, the neck aiming at a light fitting, those sausage fingers wrapped gently around. 'I'm a finisher really. I don't know much about acoustics, and with the quality of wood ...'

'It was a generous gift,' insisted Gaston. 'And I am grateful. I have tried to play it but – no. Simply, it is a beautiful object.'

Casimir waved a skeletal finger in the air. *'Old fashioned,'* he announced. *'Old fashioned ... craftsmanship.'*

'Craftsmanship,' translated Gaston.

Ted felt his face redden. 'Well I was a craftsman,' he said, running his finger along a string. He shrugged. 'And I'm old.'

'Play a song, then.'

'What?' Ted's head jerked in alarm at the mayor, who was staring at him without blinking.

'A song. Play a song.'

Ted addressed the table once more. 'Ah. Well I don't really do – that is, I really don't like playing in public, to other people. It is not really my thing.'

Gaston resumed his seat beside the Englishman and placed both hands around his big forearm. '*Oui*, Ted. You are brilliant.' He turned back to his compatriots. '*You will like this.*'

Ted stared hard at the top of the instrument, wondering how Gaston had so easily turned the request into an introduction. Shyness swept across him: the shyness that caught him between the horror of performing and the horror of appearing rude. He mumbled a few more words: he did not really think –

'Yes Ted, please.'

His eye fixed on a single spot on the table, Ted gave the strings a small brush, winced at the sound that resulted and used his left hand to alternately fiddle with the tuning pegs and pick quietly at strings. All the while he continued his dialogue with the furniture: sporadic, disconnected words and phrases under his breath. 'Well, I don't know – I really – no, flat, too flat – really don't like.' Grasping the neck at varying places to check the tuning that had been perfect for some time now, Ted's big hands left smears of sweat along the wood. He gave the open strings one strum, two strums, three, checking that there couldn't possibly be any other adjustment to make. Then he lifted his head and offered his audience a smile of bravado. 'Here goes!'

His eyes met the table once more and he took a breath, an audible breath, positioned his hands for a chord and began to play.

Bom-de, dom-de, bom-de, dom-de ... one-a two-a three-a four-a, his right thumb creating a steady marching bass, a quick march, one-two, one-two, his fingers dropping in a chord between each beat. He continued like this for some bars, that same guitar phrase – Bom-de, dom-de, taking steady and urgent breaths, nodding in time, fixed at that one spot on the table between them.

♫ *Marg'rite she is my long adored-for woman* ♫

The boom of his voice punctured the silence that had fallen across the café; the mayor's eyes opened wide at the 'gr' that had exploded from Ted's mouth in that first word, a 'gr' from the heart, a 'gr' exactly as his French companions would have spat it out. Gaston grinned like a child who had stumbled upon hidden sweets.

♫ *Her face it is the sunshine in my life*
I cry for her, I'd die for her, I'd have her for my own ♫

Ted felt the heat on the back of his neck. Once more, his shirt seemed to have stuck to him. The French phrases fell from him in a mumble after the energy of that first line; his eyes focused and focused on that invisible point on the table surface. Still clasping a glass and his cloth, Philippe left his position behind the bar to stand with them.

♫ *If it wasn't for the fact I have a wife* ♫

Ted lifted his head for the first time, forgetting himself in the security of the punchline and allowing his demeanour a twinkle as he sang. The mayor nodded with delight at the familiarity of the words, caught Gaston's gaze and let a generous grin spread across his face, a beam the width of that enormous moustache. Across the café, customers were looking towards the Englishman who had his back to them, their eyes boring into his big nodding head and those broad shoulders, intrigued by the musical interlude that had come from nowhere. As they watched, those shoulders seemed to rise, the head moving with more confident beats, the pace of the music increasing and the singing projecting, up from the table, up to the people around, around to the room.

Ted's head momentarily turned to his left hand as it shifted to reach for the first chord of the chorus; he then finally raised his eyes towards the faces of his audience, looking through them, locked in a faraway connection with the song.

> ♬ *So Father hear my simple cry for pity*
> *I've said my prayers and done my duty*
> *And in your wisdom and your beauty*
> *Won't you bring my Marg'rite to me* ♬

The French words of the chorus fell over each other in their crescendo, tumbling out with a snowballing joy and concluding with a little flourish as his hand beat out the interlude prior to the second verse. Casimir gave the table a slap with the palms of both hands, an involuntary gesture of enthusiasm that caused Gaston to laugh out loud.

> ♬ *This wife of mine I hesitate to tell you*
> *Is the ugliest woman God could ever plan* ♬

Gaston waved at Philippe, and with his eyes never leaving the guitarist the boy returned to the bar to pull another bottle from the iron rack.

> ♬ *If it wasn't for the fact she has a man* ♬

Philippe sloshed to the rim of the glasses, the bottle emptied between the party in four quick bursts. Ted turned to the hovering lad and gave him a nod of gratitude as his chords introduced the new verse.

> ♬ *Now her man is most unfortunately bashful*
> *And although I try to get them on their own* ♬

Verse, chorus, verse chorus and a final, repeated chorus as an encore – faster, louder, with the urgency of climax.

There was a silence, a deafening silence as Ted's big right hand muted the strings and those final words reverberated around the high-ceilinged room, the wood of the instrument maintaining a low ring until the sound finally died. The mayor and Casimir stared; Gaston grinned and grinned. In these microseconds, Ted felt the heat return to his neck, to his brow, to his body; he took his forearm and wiped it across his forehead to find the sleeve damp with sweat.

The three Frenchmen broke into applause. They were joined by others in the room. Startled, Ted looked round. Over in the far corner, the enormous man rose to his feet, slapping his paws together in delight, his cheeks and neck heaving and wobbling as he nodded his head again and again in approval.

The mayor grasped Ted's shoulders. 'Magnificent, Ted! Magnificent!' he cried as Gaston chortled at the reaction of his friends. Ted felt his face burning redder than the wine in front of him, which he grabbed and half-emptied, burying his face in the glass.

'It is very good, Mister Prescott,' murmured Philippe.

'*You see?*' roared Gaston, pulling a pressed white handkerchief from his breast pocket and dabbing at his eyes. 'Yes? *Oui? You see?*'

'*I see*,' said the mayor, nodding and nodding and nodding. '*I see.*'

3

The Invitation

Jenny turned away from the view. She had maintained an image in her mind from the films: the white cliffs, chalk-clean and proud. They would tower above her upon departure before receding into the crystal-blue horizon until home was lost from view and she was alone amidst the high seas and adventure. But there were no white cliffs here. Just the mist and the grey and the drizzle and more grey; the brutality of the industrial port; the swell of the anticipated epic movie soundtrack overwhelmed by the chug and churn of diesel in water. She pulled her anorak around her, but it had been designed for style, not warmth. Through the salt-stained glass she could see the thin and angular face of her husband addressing an unknown person. Without looking back, she stepped in.

'Course these aren't really ships, are they?' Stan Wainwright was leaning in on the counter, sermonising in that nasal voice that she had lived with for so long. 'Just floating boxes for people and cars.' He toyed with his moustache, a drooping caterpillar that he had adopted four decades earlier, fancying that it gave him an air of the RAF. 'You probably don't remember Clare Francis. The round-the-world lass. Well her sister asked me for a quote once, and we were talking and even Clare Francis hates these things. No soul.'

The ferry lurched, causing the girl in the burger concession to grab the counter.

'Funny thing is, they used to go out in seas ten, twenty times as rough as this – not too much milk please, just a little milk – and they wouldn't have thought anything of it. But now, any

24

more than this – well they wouldn't let it go out, would they?'
Wainwright gave the assistant a knowing smile to share his
confidence; the assistant finding her eyes locked in by the beaky
man, shifted from foot to foot.

She spoke. 'Two pounds ninety please.'

'Positive you won't have one, love?' Jenny shook her head, no,
her eyes alighting on a free table half way along the cabin. She
brushed a burger wrapper sideways to the edge, rolling her eyes
at the cloudy puddles of drink that lay unwiped on the red
plastic. Her husband trotted after her, spruce in his beige slacks
and polo shirt. He eased himself into a seat and wrestled with
the lid on his plastic mug. It sprayed him with coffee as he prised
it off. Wainwright scowled down at the drink.

'Not a shred of romance about sea travel now, is there?' Jenny's
words were addressed out towards the waves. She turned to her
husband, but all his attention was fixed on the errant mug.

'She's put too much milk in it. This is much too milky.'

'Just, in years gone by it would be more of an event, that's all.'

'I did tell her not too much milk.' Her husband looked up. 'You
know I don't like too much milk.'

'Well take it back then.'

'No. It's fine. It's just a bit milky, that's all. And I don't like too
much milk, which is what I specifically said.'

Jenny reached inside her handbag, searching for something
with which to wipe the table. But Wainwright had already rested
his sleeve in the spillage; he lifted his arm and peered at the dark
wet patch spreading across his cuff. His wife passed him a folded
tissue; he scrubbed away, screwing up his narrow eyes in
concentration as he attacked the stain.

The diesel and the wind peaked in volume as a man in
Bermuda shorts opened the door to the deck. 'I used to love
watching the boats when I was a kid,' Jenny said. 'I need some
sunshine. Everything looks depressing in grey.'

Her husband worried at his moustache. 'It's the economy
down south. They can't get good people on what they're paying.'
He mulled solutions for a short while. 'What did you say?'

25

'I wish it would brighten up.'

Wainwright grunted and sipped his tea with a grimace.

*

Daisy was cleaning. She changed the hand towel, she polished the basin. She scrubbed away at the toilet, her mouse-like frame squashed and cramped within the walls of the tiny room as she worked away with the brush. Satisfied at last, she folded the end of the roll into triangles, and triple-checked that there was a spare under the knitted doll's skirt.

In the kitchen, Ted ran a broom across the floor, corralling the toast crumbs and the dust that he had tramped in earlier and sweeping it all into the blackness of the hole. Setting the broom aside, he listened to the shuffling and bustling that was so audible through the paper-thin wooden walls. She had to slow down soon, she had to. He was canny enough to not interfere, but he also knew that it would be impolitic not to be seen to be contributing. He swept the floor a second time and fiddled with the net curtain on the door.

Daisy pushed her way in. 'I'll do our room now,' she said.

'Our room? Why do you need to do our room? They're not staying in our room.'

'No, but we might need to move things into our room to make some space.'

Ted held out his arms. 'Like what? And where would it go?'

'If it were up to you, nothing would ever get tidied.'

Her husband drew breath. 'I'll do it,' he said. 'I'll do our room.'

'Don't be stupid. You sweep the floor in here. It looks filthy.'

Ted took a step forward to push past his wife. 'Well give me a moment, then. I want to change my trousers.'

In the bedroom, Ted released his belt and let his trousers drop to the floor. His wardrobe was a ceiling-high box of the thinnest plywood daubed in that off-white paint; there was so little space in the room that the doors jammed up against the bed when he opened them. Reaching up to thrust his hands between two woollen jumpers, he pulled out a dark-blue folder that had been secreted there. He rested it upon the blankets, breathing hard.

David still hadn't called. One of their final conversations had included a good-natured squabble about whether Ted should purchase himself a mobile phone, lest he need to call his son from this far-flung place in some emergency. The irony that all concern was now for David had ceased to be amusing. Ted had given him Gaston's number, and no contact had been reported. He didn't know whether this was good or bad. But surely he should have received at least something by now? Ted pressed his hands together as a wave of stress threatened to overrun him. Stupid. Nothing, unofficial or official. No news was good news.

He could hear Daisy fidgeting outside. The folder was around a half-inch thick; there was no possibility of getting it out of the room unnoticed. He stood in his shirt and underpants, staring furiously at the bedroom door.

An idea struck him. Squeezing his body round the end of the bed, he undid the flimsy metal latch on the window, pushing the pane wide open. He made to reach for the folder but stopped himself, returning first to the cupboard for a new pair of trousers. Suitably attired, he repeated the manoeuvre, this time taking the folder and dropping it gently into the long grass outside. From there, he could rescue it and hide it in his workshop temporarily. He let his breath escape.

Stupid, he thought, wiping his forehead as he returned to the kitchen. 'All yours,' he said, making for the outside door. 'I'm going out for a bit.'

Monsieur Patenaude looked up at Ted over the black bags of his eyes. He was a droopy, hangdog man. Everything about him appeared to sag. His shoulders slouched with some invisible, unbearable burden and his clothes were baggy on him, as if his body had shrunk several sizes in the decades since he had first tried them on. Ted extended his arm to make the customary greeting; his landlord allowed his dead-weight hand to be shaken. The farmer could not be much more than fifty years old, but, after inclining his head to motion Ted to follow, he shuffled from the doorway with the dejection of a man for whom the end cannot come soon enough.

The kitchen was as tired as its owner, as far removed as it was possible to be from the rustic farmhouse glory promised by the style magazines. Unwashed plates and bowls sat everywhere; flies swooped and buzzed in the gloom. Ted knew that the farmer had a daughter who called in periodically; he guessed that her visits supplied the only housework that this place ever saw. He recalled his very first introduction to the place, when he had been directed up the hill by a market trader following his casual enquiry about cheap accommodation. Then, Ted had almost turned and walked straight out; had Daisy not remained in the car whilst Ted had braved the silent farmhouse then they would have doubtless moved on, never to discover the little wooden cottage that had become home.

'Thank you for the apples,' said Ted. He had pre-rehearsed this sentence and was pleased with the sound of his own French, although even as he spoke his hand creeped to his pocket to reassure that his phrase book was safely within.

Monsieur Patenaude grunted, a gruff, shapeless noise. *'No problem.'*

'Also, thank you for delivering the post. I am very obliged.' Ted nodded and adopted a smile to emphasise his gratitude. *'I – I have a request. Is it possible I come here to collect the post? Collect the post from this house. You not deliver it to the cottage.'*

'Here?'

'Yes, here.'

'It is no problem to deliver it.'

'I am obliged that you deliver the post, but I would want to collect the post from here. Pardon, wait.' Ted held up his palm, using the other hand to pull out the phrase book that was already creased and dog-eared from such encounters. 'Worry. Worry,' Ted

muttered to himself, the farmer studying him dully as he leafed through the dictionary section. 'Worry. Yes. *Mrs Prescott has worry. The post has worry for Mrs Prescott. If there is not post then she is very happy. She does not have worry. Ahhhhhh – I collect the post here?'* Ted tailed off. The Frenchman's face appeared to be set in stone.

'*OK.'*

'OK?'

'*You collect the post from here.'*

'*Thank you.'* Ted beamed in relief. '*She will not have worry. Thank you.'*

Ted ran into Gaston at the café doors, where the Frenchman was pasting up a new menu card. The market had returned to the square, bustling under the flags and pennants with early visitors for the festival.

'I brought your money, Gaston. From the other night.'

'*Oui, oui.'* Gaston dismissed him with a gesture. 'Bernard is here. He has something for you.'

'What's that then?'

'Aha!' smiled a delighted Gaston.

Ted's mouth fell open. He closed and opened it once more; his tongue started to work involuntary motions around his teeth and lips as he stared. A Frédéric Debreu record! Ted turned it over and over in his hands, agog at the cheap monochrome sleeve, the awkward portrait photograph, the track listing set in homestyle typography. He eased the disc from its yellowing inner wrapping to reassure himself that this was neither a mistake nor a joke – no – there it was, the name in the centre label, the song titles, some sentences of French that he didn't fully understand. The vinyl was thicker than many of his mainstream records from the same era; it was smudged and lightly scratched but there seemed to be no major damage.

'Where did you get it?' Ted demanded, his eyes refusing to leave his new treasure.

'It is my brother's, my older brother's.' His benefactor grinned at the other man's transfixion.

Ted slipped the disc back into the safety of its sleeve. 'I've got that one, and that one,' he said, his big index finger shaking as it jabbed at the track listing. 'But not that, nor that, nor that. These ones are all completely new to me.' He looked up at the mayor, realising that he should say more. 'Are you sure? Is he sure? This must be quite valuable to him.'

The mayor shrugged, pursing his lips, causing his moustache to ripple like a cornfield in the wind. 'To be true, he prefers the Phil Collins records.' He made a gesture at the seat beside him, his eyes beseeching Ted to calm down. 'And he has not got a *gramophone* now. Only CD.'

Ted breathed deeply. He placed the LP gingerly on the table, his eyes refusing to leave it, the fingers of one hand remaining in secure contact as he settled himself on the chair. It was extraordinary.

'Debreu, he is the old history now,' piped in Casimir, who had been watching the exchange with a quiet merriment. 'Even the people of his region, they forget him.'

'To be fair, my brother was not born here.' said the mayor.

'He is a philistine. He always was.'

'My brother is a cultured man.'

'He knows nothing. He is a philistine.'

The two men glared at each other. 'Are you sure?' Ted repeated, his fixation rendering him oblivious to their bickering.

Gaston placed a bottle of red on the table and set down glasses from his tray. The ancient Casimir poured, up to the very rim of each, his shaking hand causing wine to trickle down upon the table between the glasses, leading Ted to whisk the record sleeve away in alarm.

'It is not rare,' reassured the mayor, dabbing at the spillage with a serviette. 'Not here, anyway. There were many records; he would sell them when he played, and we saw him play often.' Beside him, Casimir nodded. 'Plus Debreu and I, we have the connection as he has the relationship with my sister. But they are thought rare because often his records were not – they were not – how do you say, they were not *distributed*? Distributed. They were not distributed for much distance around France. Overseas, not at all.'

'Well I thank you,' said Ted, finally prising his eyes away from the image of the great musician. 'It is a magnificent gift.'

Ted had not intended to remain, but courtesy demanded that he share a drink with the mayor, and this was his final chance of freedom before he was taken down to undertake the sentence of house guests. Those early tourists were beginning to trickle in from the hurly-burly of the market outside; there was a vibrancy about the café today that Ted was keen to witness from his spot in the regulars' corner.

He watched Philippe flurrying away. The boy seemed to be paying extra attention to two young ladies sat over by the window, making regular trips across to check their table, lingering over them to make conversation even as others in the rising tide of customers attempted to catch his eye. Gaston left the round table to assist, rejoining them periodically for wine and conversation.

Ted had an unintelligible conversation with the enormous Claude, as the Englishman gave way to him on the narrow stone steps that led down to the toilets. Claude was animated and poked him in the chest, in a way that appeared amiable, although Ted could not be sure. He smelled of body odour, but this seemed to mask something else; Ted's nose could not place the aroma but it verged on the repellent, a hint of rot or death. The Englishman adopted smiles, and nodded, and smiled again as Claude said something like 'aha!' Unsure as to what he had just assented, Ted mimed desperation and hurried the final few yards to the urinals. Claude returned to his seat carrying an air of satisfaction.

The espresso machine exploded with the hiss of a condemned locomotive before emitting a procession of clunking noises that shook the room with each thump. The young barman stood before it, holding his ground like a seasoned hero in the face of enemy fire; after the best part of a minute, Philippe slapped the contraption hard on top before removing a freshly filled cup from beneath the nozzle and placing it deftly on the counter before him.

'*That machine's screwed, Gaston,*' he said.

The proprietor gave an expansive what-do-you-want-me-to-do-about-it shrug before relenting and offering the reassurance of a broad smile.

'*I will fix it, Philippe,*' he said. '*Next week.*'

The mayor's voice was a boom to make himself heard above the increasing hubbub. 'What I do not understand is this.' He leaned into his fellow drinker and offered him a gentle prod in the chest, before pausing as he searched for words that would not cause offence. Ted bit his bottom lip in anticipation of a personal question, his anxious eyes studying that mighty hedge of moustache. Gaston grinned without malice at Ted's discomfiture. 'When you speak French it is – how can I say this – it is, it is not good. It is not to say that we do not appreciate you trying, no, not at all,' – and here the mayor looked round the table for support, before leaning back in his seat and spreading his arms wide to invite them all into the conversation – 'But it is, it is, not good. You speak it like the English. But when you sing the song that evening, it is like a French man singing. OK, it is with a little accent, but it is like French singing. It is excellent.'

Ted felt himself flush, and shook his head whilst he tried to formulate an answer. 'Well you see, the thing is that I've been singing those songs for years.' He drew on his wine. 'I just – just fell in love with them. Eric sent them to me, you see. My own brother; he was out here teaching. At the college – the technical college? – in Thorigny-sur-Sonne.'

Casimir's skeletal head bobbed up and down. 'We always like the English here,' he said. 'Always good times with the English. There are many English then, when the *college* is here. Many good friends. Some marriages.' He paused. 'If the *college* is not here, perhaps our English is as bad as your French.'

Ted chortled before readopting his earnest tone. 'Anyway, he sent me this tape – you know, one of the big reel-to-reel ones.' He held his hands wide to indicate the size of the old tape machines. 'It was something that he'd discovered – the first lot of Debreu songs. And I loved them; well, I'd love anything that he pointed me towards, but these were something else. And it was just when I was deciding that I might want to play the guitar better – you know, more seriously. And so I learned the songs, and I've been singing them ever since. I didn't speak a word of French when I first started; one of Eric's girlfriends wrote out some of the words and he sent them over, but I was just singing parrot-fashion, if you like, and trying to learn the notes.'

'Parrot-fashion,' Gaston translated for Casimir. *'He sings the words but he does not understand.'*

The ancient man grinned and nodded. 'Parrot fashion,' he repeated in English.

'Anyway,' said Ted, warming to his topic as the recollections filled his mind. 'So I started to get all right at doing them, just these few songs, then a bit obsessive about it. I thought he'd be dead impressed when he came back. Stupid really. There I was, a grown man, and I'm still trying to do things to impress my older brother.'

'And he is impressed?' The mayor was nodding like an eager dog.

Ted took a long swig of wine. 'He never came back,' he said.

Under pressure, Philippe darted around like a trapped hen, whisking up plates, glasses and mugs with clinks and crashes, flapping between tables with snapped *'excuse me's'*, back and forth at a scamper between bar and customer. At one point he upended a glass of Coca-Cola with his elbow; it spread in a sticky black flood across the table of a Welsh family, sending the barman fleeing red-faced for cloths and new napkins. Gaston eased across the room with smiles and apologies and fresh drinks; placing a matey hand on the father's shoulder he chatted easily in English, poking out his tongue at the children whilst his barman mopped and rubbed and reset the table.

Despite having secured his usual seat, Claude seemed put out by the extra trade; he tutted and blew air from his blubbery cheeks, rolling and shrugging jelly-like shoulders that were packed within his stained T-shirt. Philippe attempted to offer him a refill but he waved the youth away with an irritable paw, folding his newspaper abruptly and standing to escape from the humanity that so irked him. Swaying left and right, he peered across the room with piggy eyes. Finally he gave one enormous scowl and started to move, forsaking the double doors to lumber out through the closest route to the road: the large French windows that opened onto the pavement tables. Huffing and puffing, he paused to allow a tanned visitor to release the brakes on his child's pushchair to let him through.

'Well he was just one of those types.'

Ted drunk a little more, sucking in his lips and scraping them around his teeth to clear the dry residue that the wine was leaving. 'You know, he was a lot older; we were a little family from a little town; he wanted to see the world. He was always restless; he'd disappear for weeks at a time, then we'd hear from him out of the blue. So he was here, he had this temporary job; he was lodging with a colleague and their mother in her place out in the country. He wrote letters occasionally, in bursts. And then one day he just stopped writing.'

'Did you talk with the police?' The mayor leaned in head-to-head with the Englishman so he might keep his voice low.

'No, no, no! It wasn't like that.' Ted forced a chuckle, to try to dissipate the solemnity. 'It was just – well, just one of those things at the time. Eric wasn't somebody you worried about; he did his own thing. So we didn't hear, and didn't hear – but there was no real time when you thought: "well that's it then." We just lost touch. Like you do with people over the years.'

'I am sorry. It is sad,' said the mayor.

34

Ted put down his glass, wiping around the rim with his thumb. 'The story in the family was that he was having a bit of a thing with his mate's mother: the one he was staying with. That they ran off together or suchlike to avoid disgrace. He was always a bit of a rogue with the women; always had a story for you when he got back from wherever he'd been off to. But that was my own mother for you; even when he was writing from France it was always "this girl" or "that girl," so she put two and two together to make five. My mother did tend to build up tales in her mind, and they often didn't have much of a basis in fact. She never really left our home town, so she sort of imagined the world outside it. You see?'

'*Oui, oui.*'

'Anyway that was that. A few years later I was at the doctor's; I picked up a copy of the *Record Mirror* – a music magazine – and, blow me, I saw Debreu's name in the small ads at the back. So I spent a fortune importing his records from France. And here we are now.' He lifted his big shoulders in a gesture of apology. 'It's a stupid little story, really.'

The mayor raised his glass. 'You sing as a tribute. So to your brother Eric, we drink to you.'

'Eric.'

Had Ted not left the table, he might have been able to forestall the mayor's idea. But the Englishman had lumbered down to stand once more at the towering urinal, assessing the evening's intake as it sloshed down the gulley and out of sight. A lull in orders had allowed Gaston and Philippe to set up a production line at the end of the bar, pasting simple emerald-and-white stickers onto unlabelled bottles of low-grade Bordeaux. Casimir and the mayor sat without speaking at the circular table, the former picking away at his yellow teeth for scraps of sustenance, examining his crumbling fingernails with a sharp eye after each exploration. Beside him, the town's official squeezed and moulded his chin with a restless hand, gazing across the heads of the tourists as they ate and drank, an advance guard for the thousands who would be pouring in at the end of the week. He turned to the window. The forecast was good, but who would trust the forecast? They could not afford the washout of three years previously. His eyes returned to the customers, studying each in turn, picturing them as they traversed the showground, euros in hand, searching for the purchases that were right for them.

And then from nowhere a smile appeared across his ruddy face. Casimir noticed immediately, holding his finger mid-pick and regarding his companion with curiosity; it was an enormous smile, a stupid smile, a light-bulb grin that lit up his features with pleasure. Even the mayor himself was startled at this ridiculous notion that had appeared from nowhere; he suppressed a guffaw before calling in a boom across the bar. 'Hey! Gaston!'

Gaston looked up from his work just as Ted reappeared in the room, those fat fingers still tugging at the flies of his fading corduroys. The mayor beckoned urgently to both men, glee written across his face. He slapped his hands down on the table prompting them to sit, then took a short breath to compose himself before speaking.

'Ted. Listen. You make your guitars, OK?'

Ted gave a guarded nod, something about the mayor's tone telling him to be wary.

'Years ago, we have a maker of instruments at the festival. He is very popular, does the demonstrations, sells many. But he does not come any more. So maybe you have one then, eh? A stall? You bring your tools and show the visitors the local skill; you sell the finished ones? You have got more finished ones?'

Ted chuckled, but tailed off as the mayor maintained earnest eye-contact. He felt Gaston's hand on his shoulder, alarmed by the intent in its grip. 'Oui Bernard! Ted, this is the thing the tourists love. A local craftsman with his honest skill!' Gaston released Ted and paced around the table, waving his arms. 'He has made the guitars in the same way for years, as his father did before him, as his father did before that!'

Ted rolled his eyes and looked around the group; the mayor

was grinning, even Casimir was nodding in delight. Clearly something in the wine had sent the whole café mad this evening, barking mad, barking bloody mad with the stress of the weekend ahead.

'But I'm not a blooming local craftsman, am I?' Ted wrung every last drop of broad Derbyshire inflection from the retort. 'You're crackers. I knew it when I first walked in.'

'*Oui, oui,* yes. But they do not know this.'

Ted stared at the mayor, who returned his gaze with steady assurance. The mayor leaned forward on his elbows, palms together in prayer to his own thoughts; he spoke steadily as his plan came together.

'They do not know this. What you do is work and play the guitars a bit. You do not speak. You have somebody – Philippe? – to speak to your customers. Perhaps you say "*oui*" or "*non*" or "*thank you*" but nothing else. You are a quiet French peasant, who is – who is concentrating? Concentrating on his work.'

'*Philippe? I have to do the drinks tent on the busiest day of the year,*' said Gaston.

'*I will do it,*' announced Casimir. 'I will. Me,' he said to Ted. '*Edith does not need me on her potato stall. Every year she says that I am in the way.*' To Ted: 'Edith. Is my younger sister.'

'*That would be good for you. I would be embarrassed selling those potatoes,*' said the mayor.

'*There is nothing wrong with those potatoes. They are good potatoes.*'

'*They are mangy potatoes and you know it, you old sod.*'

Ted groped away to comprehend as Casimir and the mayor glared at each other, the Englishman struggling for control of this runaway train. 'Hold on, I …' he began. 'Anyway. Why doesn't he come any more?'

'You have finished guitars, Ted? That you could sell?' Gaston asked.

Ted was distracted by the direct question. 'Three.' He looked up at the patron. 'Three and a half.'

'So if you finish the half when you are at the festival, you have four guitars. To sell at – let us say – two hundred euro each. *Two hundred euro?'* Gaston glanced at the mayor for confirmation.

'Two hundred euro? Who's going to pay two hundred euro for one of my guitars?'

'You are saying that they are not worth two hundred euro? This beautiful handmade guitar that you have given me?' Gaston gave a look of mock-offence before taking a seat at the round table and adopting a conciliatory tone. 'Ted, you know, these are tourists, they are on vacation, some of them have lots of money. They look for something to take home to remember this vacation; something that is special. *A one-off.* They will pay two hundred euro, I promise. It is a very good idea. And it will be some good money for you.'

'Everybody! Come see the local guitar, made by hand by this French maker!' barked Casimir, waving his wine glass to imaginary passers-by. Behind them, the coffee machine roared with an explosion; Philippe smacked it repeatedly with his palm as it rattled and shook.

'It's lunacy,' said Ted. 'But you really reckon I could make six, eight hundred euros?'

'Oui, oui. Easy.'

Ted drummed his fingers on the table. 'Eric wrote about the festival in his letters. He made it sound grand. But ...'

The mayor stroked his moustache. 'Look,' he said. 'What we will do, so that you have nothing to lose, we will give you your stall so there is no risk. Then, if you sell the guitars, you pay us the one hundred euro fee for the stall.' Gaston glared at the mayor across the table. 'Fifty euro,' the official clarified.

Ted blew air from his cheeks. 'All right then. You're on.'

4

The Guests

'Prout. Desmond Prout. That was him.'

'Ah yes.' Ted closed his eyes and visualised Desmond Prout: slicked-back hair and a chubby, baby face; a joker with the habit of clutching your forearm as his features convulsed in a hilarity that must surely have germinated via some unimaginable horror in his infant years. It had been an hour or so now, and although Ted had enjoyed catching up, he knew the stock of anecdotes and people from the past would dry up; that their conversation was one of diminishing returns.

'A "colourful character" he thought he was. Had a son – named him "Russell."' Wainwright stared at each of them in turn, inviting them to comment. '"Russell Prout," don't you see? "Russell Prout." Like "Sprout."' He paused for a moment, lost in thought as Ted recalled meeting this poor kid; when Wainwright spoke again it was in a low tone of some sorrow. 'Which, when you come to think about it, was the action of a prat.'

They went for a stroll around the farm then reconvened, the four friends squashed into the tiny sitting room. This was less successful; as the afternoon wore on, Wainwright's enthusiasm began to exhaust every shared acquaintance and situation. Daisy and Jenny became passive observers to the ever-more obscure reminiscences about the furniture trade of decades past. Finally, the man began to tire and Jenny was able to guide the conversation around to the present day. Ted told them about the village, about the café and his new friends, about the preparations for the festival and how important it was to them all. He told them about his plan to join the locals for a day with his guitars, and how it was a big honour to be asked, although he skipped any mention of the subterfuge that would be expected of him. He explained the peculiar history of the area, talked about the lonely farm and the train of events that had led them to rent its run-down cottage, expounded upon the beauty and peace of the walk across the meadow to the village. Ted found himself becoming passionate and animated. It was a strange feeling, like being a young man once more.

Ted talked about Frédéric Debreu and his songs.

'It's a lovely one,' he promised, putting down his teacup and leaning forward so that the antique canes of his chair creaked in protest. 'There's this fellow, you see, and he visits the local monastery. And he's standing at the edge of the courtyard looking out on the monks, and he notices that one – just the one – isn't talking. You see?' Ted looked around his audience to check that he was doing the story justice. Daisy, who had heard this synopsis tens, hundreds of times previously, nibbled at a biscuit; next to her on the sofa, her knee almost touching his, Jenny met Ted's eye and nodded. Opposite him, Stan Wainwright stared into his china, before, sensing an unexpected pause in conversation, his head jerked up and he searched the faces of the others, wondering if he had missed his cue to speak.

'What?' he blurted.

'So anyway.' Ted focused his attention on the woman next to him. 'He asks the chief monk what's up with that bloke over there, the one who isn't talking. And the chief monk says this is Brother Jerard – he used to be an undertaker, and a real ladies' man. You see, what he used to do was hit on the widows and the grieving womenfolk of the family and the like, when they were all vulnerable, you know – in order to have his way with them. Which he did, in the back of his hearse.'

'Creepy man!' said Jenny.

'Be quite comfortable in there, I reckon,' said Wainwright, whose attention had been reignited by the concept. 'What with all the drapes and the like.'

'Typical man,' said his wife. 'Typical Stan, I should say. About as romantic.'

'I've brought you on this wonderful holiday, haven't I? Lavish accommodation? Honestly, Ted, she's always complaining.'

'Go on, Teddy,' prompted Jenny. She placed her hand on his knee and squeezed. Ted caught a burst of her perfume; it seemed out of place in the simple cottage.

'Well anyway, one day he hits on the wrong woman – she's at the funeral of the local baker. And this woman is married to the baker's twin brother, and the undertaker – well he doesn't know about him. So he – the brother – basically says: "play along with it, and I'll teach this bloke a lesson." And nightfall comes, and she's in the back of the hearse with the undertaker, just about to – you know. And the twin brother rises up out of a coffin, with flour on his face to make him look all pale and dead, catches them at it, and the undertaker runs off screaming and becomes a monk. He had a guilty conscience, you see.'

'Serves him right. Creepy man.'

'But the best bit is in the final verse, you see. Because the chief monk's finished explaining this to his visitor, and the visitor just turns to him and says "watch this." And then he calls across the courtyard to the monk: "Over here!" and the monk gets sight of him and leaps ten feet in the air, and runs off screaming. It's the twin brother, you see, visiting the monastery. He's made a vow never to let this man rest. Clever.' Ted nodded to himself with appreciation at the story's construction. The chair creaked and protested once more as he shifted his frame back. The silence was cut by Jenny, who gave a musical, tinkly laugh.

'Does anybody want more tea?' asked Daisy.

'Coffee be nice.' Stan waved his mug in the air and then turned to Ted, pursing his lips, his index finger exploring his beaky nose. 'It's not greatly plausible though, is it?'

'You what?'

'The story. I mean, I was thinking – if they were in the back of this hearse, then the coffin couldn't have been in there at the

41

same time – it'll have had to be outside? So I can't see that his dead act would have had that much effect?'

'Well it's only a song,' said Ted. 'A comic song. Clearly it's not meant to be –'

'Yes. I guess what I'm saying is that it works on the face of it, but when you really think about it – it doesn't really work?'

'It's just a song, Stan,' said Jenny. 'It's not meant to be real. Don't get up, Daisy, love.' She made to rise from the sofa, but Ted beat her to it, grabbing her cup from the floor beside her feet, pulling Stan's mug from his outstretched hand. 'I'll go,' he said, in a gruffer tone than he'd intended. Squeezing past the luggage in the doorway, Ted strode through to the kitchen for five minutes alone.

He woke early the next morning.

Ted unhooked the piece of material that served as a bedroom curtain and squeezed back round to bed. It was half past six, and his heart was still pounding from the anxieties that had been sent into a frenzy once more the previous evening. He pulled the blankets back over him, trying not to wake Daisy.

There was an English-language magazine on the floor beside the bed, one of those ad-heavy glossies for tourists and weekenders, the equivalent of those god-awful *Derbyshire Country Living* rags that they always had at the dentist's. Jenny had acquired it on the journey, and had saved it especially, passing it to him as they had all prepared for bed, as if it were some secret token between them. He reached for it, hoping to take his mind elsewhere.

The magazine was folded open at an article extolling the undiscovered charm of the region here. Debreu was mentioned in passing, two paragraphs about this 'local idol' whose refrains were 'ever-cherished by young and old'. It summarised two of the musician's works – 'The Vengeful Widow' and 'The Pretty Goat' in breathless, exclamation-mark scattered prose. It was drivel, of course. 'Impossible not to come across some legacy ...' they'd written. It meant nothing, and he wondered whether the

42

author had ever been within a hundred miles of this place. But they were right about those two songs, they were bloody right. Debreu's greatness had reached a peak there. The perfect combination of simple, flawless melodies and those sublime words. He rested the magazine on his knees and hummed to himself.

♫ *Tra la, la tra-la-la*
La la la la la
Tra la, la tra-la-la
La la la la la ♫

It was wonderful. But even as the music left him he felt those dark thoughts return.

There was a faint stirring beside him. He glanced at his watch: it was ten past seven. Hauling himself from the bed, Ted pulled on a shirt and padded through to the kitchen in order to boil water. No sound came from behind the door to the back room. Ted set out cups, rinsing the glasses from the night before as he waited for the saucepan to heat. He rested the wet items on the draining board: two petrol-station crystal goblets and two cloudy half-pint jars, one of these embossed with the Bateman's Brewery logo.

Returning to the bedroom, Ted found that Daisy had turned over, her eyes shut fast, the lightest of snores coming from her. He placed the cup on the tatty doily that adorned the bedside table and eased himself back under the covers, keeping a sitting position so that he could look across the meadow, hoping that the view would occupy him. He could see sporadic movement in the hedgerow that bordered the next field – a hare perhaps. Ted strained to see further as his wife's drink grew cold.

At a quarter-past eight there was a muffled commotion from the kitchen: a crash, a yelp and an oath, followed by a succession of 'shhh' noises louder than the incident itself. Ted heard the front door being eased shut and then a bang as somebody checked that it was properly closed. His inclination to investigate was low.

It was no use, he would have to read the letter again.

Ted pulled the blankets to one side once more. Reaching into the secret place in which he had stashed his folder, Ted pulled out the envelope that he had collected from Monsieur Patenaude late the previous evening. Taking a final look at his sleeping wife, he slipped from the room.

He blinked as he entered the kitchen. Somebody had moved the table across the floor. Shaking his head, he lowered himself into one of the chairs before changing his mind and rising again, pacing on the spot as he examined the envelope in his hand.

Ted's hands shook as he reopened the flap, glancing over his shoulder at the interior door as he pulled out a single sheet.

The letter wasted no energy on niceties. There was the name of the financial people in a typeface that was both black and bleak, as if the stationery designer had been briefed to wring every crumb of hope from each recipient of his creations. Underneath this, they had written the name of David's business and the words 'in administration', and then just two more lines of text, 'Thank you for your correspondence, which we acknowledge. We hope to reply to you within 28 days.'

That was it. Stupid. Why had he needed to read that again? As much as he stared and stared at the paper, that was all it said. He could feel his hands trembling, and for the first time it occurred to him that these peaks of stress must be doing terrible things to his body. He breathed, breathed again, consciously counting and timing his inhalations to try to get things under control. The physical reaction scared him, even as it burnt itself out to leave only background unease. Things would be all right. They had to be all right.

There was a chattering noise from outside. He stuffed the paper into the envelope and thrust it under his armpit.

"Allo 'allo! Not interrupting anything are we?' Wainwright poked his pointed head around the door with a clumsy comic stealth, his eyes making exaggerated movements over Ted's underpants and bare legs.

Jenny pushed the door open from behind her husband and shoved him in. They both wore crimson anoraks, pristine from the camping shop; the dew on their walking boots was the only clue that the footwear had ever ventured outside.

'Just getting dressed.' Ted backed to the interior doorway. 'You carry on.'

'Thought we'd go for an early morning constitutional without waking you.' Wainwright reached for his bootlaces. 'Get the kettle on, Jenny, love.'

'There isn't a kettle. You have to boil the water on ...'

Ted closed the bedroom door on them, turning his back to it to collect his thoughts. He should talk to Wainwright, however painful it might be.

Daisy was perching on the edge of the bed, fiddling with her blouse, frowning but patient as the buttons slipped from her hands. 'You should have woken me up,' she said, not looking up at him. 'It's almost gone breakfast time.'

Ted slipped the envelope back into his wardrobe. 'Why on Earth would I wake you up? What's the hurry to – look, let me help you with that.' He made to squeeze around the end of the bed.

'I'm perfectly capable, thank you.'

'Yes, but it would just be easier for me to ...'

'Just get your own trousers on, thank you. You look like a labourer.'

Ted decided not to argue. His trousers were draped across the top of the chest of drawers; he grabbed them and wrestled, grunting as he pulled them up his legs and over his ample rear. Through the crack in the window came the distant noise of a chainsaw starting up; Patenaude must be cutting logs up at the farmhouse. He had promised to give him a hand in exchange for some fuel for the burner. 'What do you mean a labourer anyway?' he asked. 'Don't labourers wear trousers in your world, then?'

'You know what I mean.'

'Funny sort of labourer.' Ted stuffed his shirt tails into his trousers before fixing his belt. 'Well I'll see you in there.' He plodded from the room.

'You see, what I tried to do was to move this table,' explained Wainwright, waving an arm to demonstrate. 'What I reckon is that if that dresser goes over there, and you're able to shift this a foot or so to the right, then you'd buy yourself another square yard or so of space in here.' Ted looked up at his friend, then at the table, then at the backs of the two ladies who were jostling each other at the sink, Jenny rinsing with nimble hands, Daisy dabbing at the cups with a tea towel. 'But I hadn't realised that you've got a bloody hole in the floor!' Stan waved his arm. 'Almost broke my ankle!'

Ted leaned back to peer under the table and give the hole a glance. 'Well you know. It helps air circulate.'

'Why don't you just get a bit of wood and replace the plank? I mean, I suppose the rest of the floor is rotting as well, but at least you wouldn't have an actual hole?'

'Well I like my hole. It adds character,' said Ted. 'You know. I like the lived-in look. Rustic, if you like.'

Stan gazed at the big man. 'You always were a strange bugger, Ted,' he said.

Having scribbled a shopping list and sent his guests down the hill to explore the market, Ted's plan was to occupy himself by preparing for his role at the festival. Six – perhaps eight hundred euro? It would be a lifeline, more so than his new friends in the café could have possibly realised. But even if those earnings were a pipe dream, he was keen to make a good fist of it; the faith that the townsfolk clearly had in him had been touching. At the very least the day might be fun, although he suspected that the dubious presentation of his nationality might meet with some disapproval from Daisy.

Ted gathered his tools together, packing them into a leather bag, scuffed and shabby, just the sort of accessory to reinforce his role as some peasant artisan. Considering this further, he delved back in to retrieve his new pair of pliers, putting in their place a set that was so rusted away as to be unusable. He then started to seek out materials, rummaging through the shoe box which held the second-hand machine heads and tuning pegs that he'd acquired, then collecting together oddities of timber that he might strew around his pitch to create the impression of a living workshop.

Frédéric Debreu accompanied him, the voice from decades ago familiar and warm. The mayor's gift had lived up to all his expectations and more. To his especial joy, one of the tracks had turned out to be a different version of a song that was already known to him. It appeared to have been recorded live in a small club or bar setting; the technical sound quality was desperately poor, but did nothing to lessen Ted's thrill at hearing the preceding crowd chatter, the rowdiness of the singalong and then the burst of applause and cries of appreciation as the final note rang out. This was Debreu the real-life figure, not just some genius in the history of music and song, but a real man who played to real people in real places – places in this new neighbourhood of his. Both the mayor and Casimir had seen the musician play several times; he wondered whether any of the claps on this record came from their own youthful palms. Ted stepped across to the gramophone and watched the disc as it spun, hypnotised by the revolution of the badly faded label. It truly was an extraordinary present; that its donor seemed to value it so little nonplussed him.

The following track – named as 'The Duck' – was already becoming familiar, the mid-tempo melody and comfortable bom-da-bom-da rhythm lodging in his head. He would sit down in the next few days and properly listen, scribbling down what he could decipher of the words, which seemed to be about a man comparing his lover to a wild duck. The vocal had a typical crescendo and inflexion on the last beat of each line – it was so 'Debreu' that it might have been written as a parody. In contrast, there was a tricky-sounding guitar bit between each verse, a run up and down the neck atypical of the singer's uncomplicated style; he would have to master this in the fullness of time.

But there was no time like the present.

Ted fetched his guitar and set it on his thigh, reaching for the arm of the gramophone to set the needle back two minutes or so. This time he listened intently to that musical bridge, his focus on the sound of the chords and the likely shape of the fingering, shifting the needle back once, twice as he concentrated. It was a diminished chord, he realised on the third run-through; his left hand fell naturally into the shape required, holding down the strings in a likely combination. Lifting the needle entirely, Ted tried it; it was close but subtly wrong. Encouraged nonetheless, he experimented with the chord in different positions, plucking lightly at the strings until he was sure that he was in the right place.

Replacing the needle down upon the old vinyl confirmed his breakthrough. The next hurdle was the run of notes that followed. Even his most loyal fans would not consider Debreu a virtuoso on the guitar, and the Englishman was confident that he would find the key. Reaching across once more to his archaic hi-fi, Ted switched the control from 33 revolutions per minute down to the 16 mark. The turntable petered to a crawl, the obsolete setting transforming the singer's voice into an impossibly bass slur, drawling painfully across the slowed-down music as the verse inched towards its conclusion. But the change in pace brought clarity to the bridge section when it came; Ted needed only two plays to comprehend what Debreu had done, realising with admiration that a combination of hand-shifts and pull-offs meant that the whole phrase was playable without once changing the shape of his fingers. He flicked the gramophone off and played the brief section in its entirity, over and over until it flowed and all awkwardness was gone. He then pulled his hand from the neck and replaced it in the shape of a simple A-major chord – the opening of the song.

Bom da-dom da-dom da-dom da-dom – his fingers and

thumb hitting that rhythm that was so familiar from other songs, the rhythm that he could play in his sleep.

'Heer swoire je tay vu o bor doo lack ...' The words exploded forth in Ted's own bass baritone. It wasn't quite there; maintaining that rhythm he repeated the line, increasing the hiss on the word 'soir' and adding a firm, mannered emphasis to the end of the line as Debreu was wont to do.

'Hier sssoir je t'ai vu au bordu lac ...'

'Hiersssoir je t'ai vu au bord du LAC ...'

Ted was still sat there twenty minutes later when he realised that he was being watched. Jenny had two shopping bags at her feet as she leaned on the doorway. How long she'd been there, he didn't know. Ted halted mid flow and fiddled with a tuning peg, his face reddening. 'Hello,' he said.

'Don't let me stop you. It sounds wonderful as always, Teddy.' She gave him the most comforting of smiles.

Ted rested his instrument against the workbench. 'I'm done anyway,' he said. 'Did you get everything?'

'Just about. You can't move in town – it's packed. Come have some lunch.'

It was time. Time to ask for help. The thought of laying himself open to Wainwright turned him hot and cold, but for David's sake he couldn't bottle out now. Ted braced himself as Daisy and Jenny laid the table with buttered bread, with cheese, meat and pâté. Squeezing past them with murmured apologies, he stooped to reach into the cubbyhole underneath the sink, pulling two bottles from amidst the bleach and washing-up liquid.

'Here you go, Stan,' he said. 'The last two from England. The very last two. Have a final beer with me on the terrace.'

The other man took one bottle, peering at its label. 'Brown ale's not normally my thing, but I'll gladly have one if there's nothing else.'

Grinding his teeth, Ted took the two half-pint glasses from the drainer and the men edged through the door onto the verandah. The wooden railing was chunky enough to act as both table and leaning post; they stood side by side, elbows on the rail, looking out across the deep green meadow grass that waved in the late afternoon sun.

'How long have we known each other, Stan?' asked Ted when they had both savoured initial gulps of the sweet liquor. Hoping his voice had sounded natural, he kept his eyes on the field, on the hedgerow, on the sky.

His friend pursed his lips and tapped the woodwork with his index finger as he thought. 'Well, it must be – no, let's work this out. I started at Flood's in 1962; just before Christmas it was, so almost sixty-three. Then it was – what – only six months or so, maybe even less when you came along, because I was still seen as the new lad there, even though I was doing well, like. But then there was you, and then there was Barney Donohoe a week or so later – you remember Barney?' Wainwright shook his head gently, smiling at the recollection. 'But it would probably have been a few more weeks before we got to know each other proper, what with me being out on the road a lot. So I'd say – well, that would be all of fifty years. Roughly, anyway.'

'It's just that I've never been great at business and legals and the like.' Ted's tone changed and he heard the next words as if they were spoken by another man. 'I might've got myself in a spot of bother.' He flushed. Stupid, he was stupid.

'Fifty years. Yes, that's right.'

A pigeon emerged from the oak that overhung the hedge, beating away with a tremendous flap, disturbed by something that neither man could perceive. They watched its chaotic progress into the air before it recovered its composure and swooped to the next field.

'You see the thing is that ...'

'Barney Donohoe. Big chap, very sandy hair, red face – think his mother was Irish, or his father or whatever. Think it was his mother. Good worker, very willing, but absolutely no attention to detail. Not a lot up top. Always smiling though, he was.'

'I remember Barney.'

'Always had a smile on his face. That's why the girls all fancied him. Which was his undoing in the end.'

Ted studied the label on his beer bottle, picking away at its edges with his fingernails. 'Stan, you're better than I am around business and the like. I ...'

'Caught him in the drying room with one of the typists.' Wainwright let loose a guffaw, banging his glass down on the wooden rail.

The trace of a smile crossed Ted's face as he found himself caught up in the memory despite everything. 'No,' he said. 'It wasn't the drying room. You remember there was a small store just for bits and pieces, next to where all the hangers were? It was in there.'

'You know what? You're right. I wonder what happened to Barney?'

Ted turned to his old colleague, opened his mouth to speak, and then closed it again. Lifting his glass to his mouth, he drained it in one, holding its base high aloft to catch the precious final trickles. 'Who knows?' he said, running his tongue round his lips. 'Come on. Let's go get something to eat.'

Ted held open the door, standing aside to let the other man pass. He lingered for a moment in the doorway, looking in at Stan Wainwright fiddling clumsily with a dining chair, at Jenny and Daisy tucked in at the neatly laid table.

'Hurry up then,' said Daisy, waving a friendly hunk of bread at him.

Ted stepped in and pulled the door shut with the softest of clicks.

5

The Festival

The American gripped the wheel with both hands as he pulled out to overtake. He'd been given a baby car – all the rental company had been able to supply – and although he'd been happy with its very European air, he was yet to acclimatise to its dimensions. He urged the little engine past his target, a mud-strewn truck that he had been tailing for some miles along the winding road, giving it as wide a berth as he could without mounting the verge on the opposite side. Roy raised his eyes to the rear-view mirror before drifting back to the right. He eyed the truck through his wire-rimmed spectacles as it receded, before switching his gaze to the empty road ahead. 'Thank you,' he shouted to nobody in particular. This was more like the France that he had envisaged.

Paris had disappointed him.

He had been disappointed, in turn, by his own disappointment. He considered himself to be a worldly and urbane man, certainly by the standards of his professionally redneck circles. Granted, he had been awed by the great cathedrals, and the streets of Montmartre had both intrigued and delighted him. But he had not found himself in the big city frame of mind.

Instead, the throngs, the noise, the crazy drivers had oppressed him; he had been seized by the urge to flee from the tourist spots, to seek space and solitude off the beaten track. After his second and final business meeting he had accepted that sticking around would be futile and personally counterproductive. It was his fault, not Paris's. Perhaps he would return one day when he was a bit less ...

When he was a bit less whatever it was that he was feeling at the moment.

Flying home had not appealed. There was too much unpleasantness to face until his wife finished moving her things out, and it would have negated the point of arranging those face-to-face meetings with the Europeans; the meetings that could just as well have been conducted over the telephone, or via email. He would doubtless be pulled up upon this at the next board meeting.

Nevertheless, he'd arranged a few days of vacation to follow on from the business trip. So he had packed his bags, taken a cab to the station and, on a whim, boarded a train to the city of Rennes. There, he had checked himself in to a budget hotel and wandered the streets aimlessly, enthralled by the historic architecture and feeling more comfortable with the calmer pace. He had found this car and had made a plan: to have no plan.

The hotel had boasted a grubby lounge area. Before setting out in the evening to find some food, Roy had lodged himself on a vinyl armchair and flicked his way through a pile of tourist brochures and magazines that had been abandoned on the coffee table.

One newly delivered glossy had caught his eye, and he had skimmed the English text for some sort of inspiration. He had read an 'introductory editorial' that made heavy use of the exclamation mark, and then had skipped some pages to peruse a piece about a winery. The article had clearly been written by somebody who knew even less about wine than the American. There were advertisements for guided tours, for 'attractions' – not what he was after. There were craft centres – he would have been happy to see a craft centre, but he would rather have stumbled across one via serendipity than headed for those 'traditional artisans' that employed suspiciously professional advertising.

Picking a fresh page at random, Roy had jumped to the middle of an article and read:

Although a manageable car journey away, the tiny region of Lower Thorigny could be a world away in physical and social character. Even by the standards of this predominantly rural part of France, a visit can feel like a step back in time! Partly this stems from geographical and political oddities – the river Sonne which skirts the region was rebridged in only one place after the second world war, and the hilly and rocky terrain that comprises much of the landscape is suitable only for small-scale farming. To cap it all, the main autoroute should logically pass directly through the region, but unexpectedly takes a south-bound turn at the forest of La Sombre, this being a result – indignant locals are prone to claim – of a corrupt national planning official in the pocket of a neighbouring region's commercial interests!

'We follow our own path here!' the locals boast. They are proud of their independence, of their very isolation. Their attitude is perhaps best symbolised by one man, a musician who ...

He had skipped the next few paragraphs. Some greasy fragments of pastry were stuck to the photograph on the next page, a wide-angle shot of an unremarkable section of countryside. He had read on.

Whilst the landscape is charming, organised tourist attractions and places of great historical interest are thin on the ground, with the notable exception of the small and delightful market town of Mailliot le Bois, which is worth a detour, offering a quaint introduction to authentic rural living.

Roy drank in the scenery as he drove: the cow-strewn hillside that meandered down to the highway on his left; the flatter yet semi-wild pastures on the other side, enclosed in squares by drab granite walling. There was a tiny stone cottage in the far corner of an approaching field. He speculated: who could live there? What did they do? A cowman, a shepherd, a labourer? The nearest town was several miles away, and there was no visible access or parking space for a car. A hunter? Did they have hunters here? A vacation let, maybe.

The American sucked his top lip in speculation as he passed by, turning his head to catch a fleeting glimpse of a forest-green front door. Even at that distance, he could tell that it could be no more than five feet from top to bottom.

Roy had no way of knowing that it was the same front door that a portly English guy had knocked upon two months previously, jittering from foot to foot in his nervousness that the cottage may not be as empty as it appeared; wondering what on Earth he might say should the bolts be drawn back and a face appear to query him in a foreign language; sheepish at his fleeting thought that it could be his own missing brother who might appear. Where, embarrassed at his own relief that neither of those scenarios had come to pass, the Englishman had tucked a note amidst the cobwebs in an alcove under the porch canopy, each awkward word having been painstakingly transcribed from a well-thumbed phrase book.

The little dwelling was well behind him now. Roy smiled inside at his own romantic notion of its rustic occupant. It was the twenty-first century, even out here; it was probably some PR guy or internet designer. The traffic was picking up now, which puzzled him; he had understood that everybody would be on the main tourist routes at this time of year. Everybody appeared to be headed in the same direction as him. Some of the cars were packed high with what looked to be camping gear. Vacation traffic, he surmised, although – unless the magazine had been hopelessly wrong – his destination was no tourist haven. A single vehicle whizzed past in the opposite direction: a dented pick-up with a large dog poking its head through the passenger window. Its long ears flailed around in the breeze, its face a picture of enthusiasm and delight.

He drove on, joining a steady line of cars. The fields became rockier, the land less cultivated; a mile onwards the road joined up with a broad boulder-strewn river that ran in parallel beside them, the flow running against their direction of travel; clear, clear water brought from the hills beyond. The road began to head uphill and the riverbed became a shallow gorge; tarnished metal barriers had been erected to protect the tired, the drunk, the distracted. The traffic began to slow. As the gorge deepened, Roy could see the water no more, just the far side of the bank, craggy and torn where land had slipped into the ravine. A forest clung tenaciously to the hillside, casting long and cold shadows from the setting sun.

The road continued to rise and dip before, two miles further on, the snaking traffic was queueing to turn right at a junction. Roy activated his indicator as he edged forwards, one eye on the crash-damaged signpost that pointed the way across the fifties pig-ugly river crossing.

He felt the urge to pull over, which he did, slipping out of the line of cars to come to a halt on the hard shoulder half-way across the bridge. Leaving the engine idling, he stepped out and walked to the edge to lean on the railings.

The cry of a wader bird; the flapping of strong wings. Even above the steady noise of the traffic he could hear the sound of the river, the swoosh between the great boulders below, the breeze in the firs ahead. The railings had once been painted white; they were less than a metre high and could be easily vaulted – what a beautiful place this would be to end things here and now. The thought alarmed and intrigued him. Being at one with this landscape, of somehow embracing those ancient rocks, that cool, clear, pure water – it filled him with an enormous longing for simplicity in his life. Finally, he had discovered the France that he had expected.

Roy circled his shoulders around and around, easing the aches in his back. He drew in a long mouthful of air; he felt its freshness buzzing around his body. He was losing his mind again; things had gotten all too much. Shaking his head to clear his thoughts, he turned his back on the river scene and returned to his car.

Ignoring the temporary *'festival'* signs that were diverting the traffic towards various set destinations, Roy abandoned his car at the gateway to a field and walked, following the noise of people. The village centre was teeming, but unlike in the city, this crowd was joyous and welcoming. He studied the bunting and decorated shop fronts. If this were not to be the quiet backwater that he had expected then it was at least full of good-natured charm.

'Lucky, lucky, very lucky,' said the lady behind the desk, running her finger down pages of handwritten lists attached to her clipboard and poking in triumph as she reached a gap in the right-hand column. The tourist information bureau seemed rudimentary to Roy – they weren't kidding when they said that this place had yet to catch up with the modern world. 'Some people cancel just now. Here.' She turned the clipboard so that he could read the address. 'I telephone.'

'Thank you. *Thanks*.' Roy paced the room, pulling leaflets from a trestle table and sliding them into his jacket pocket. Across the far wall was a tatty map of the region; he stood before it to recapture his bearings. Although there was nothing shown that he could not have gleaned from the road atlas, the scale of the coverage allowed the local geography to sink in. It was not quite 'one way in, one way out' as the magazine had implied, but the main road across the river to the west was the only route that led anywhere to speak of. To the north, the river changed course to cut them off; the nearest major settlements to the south and east appeared to be so distant that a circuitous route via that main road would surely be more efficient than the tiny lanes that meandered in their direction. Roy memorised the names of some of the further-flung towns. As the lady spoke on the telephone, he strolled back to the window and looked across the square. Yes, it was a very pleasant little place.

'OK!' beamed the lady behind the counter. She scribbled a map for him: five lines of biro across the back of a leaflet. Fifteen minutes later, he had found the place.

Roy set down his briefcase and overnight bag, kicked off his shoes and lifted himself on to the bed, sinking in to sheets, absorbing the freshness of the pillow that billowed around his head. He stretched his body from head to toe, testing its suppleness, working away the aches. He had left his second suitcase; he had intended to return to the car to collect it, but couldn't find the will to tackle the two flights of stairs. He couldn't conceive of any thieves around here, and any bad guys would be welcome to items within. They could take the lot – the car as well – they could joy-ride it into the river and leave him stranded here for good, with no transport, no product samples, no meetings hanging over him. If he leaned out of the window far enough, he might be able to unlock the vehicle with the electronic key and leave it free for any kid who fancied a thrill.

He did stand up to open the window, raising the blind to admit the evening sun and that air. And there he stood for some minutes, looking across the red-tiled rooftops to the woods and hillsides, breathing in the odour from the pines, entranced by the faint sounds of happiness from the town square.

*

All week Ted had sensed the excitement of something big. But he was amazed at the scale of the transformation as he stood in the fields at just gone seven o'clock in the morning.

It was as huge as the mayor and Gaston had claimed; as his brother had described it in his letters. Every trader, every worker in the town must be here, along with those from villages across the region. They were building a city of tables and tents in the dew. All around him was the sound of construction: chatter, hammering, hoisting, men calling across to each other; the beep-beep of vans reversing; yapping dogs; children delighted by this sudden new playground.

Wainwright had taken one listen to the noise coming from Ted's Volkswagen before insisting that they travelled in his own car. They left this and picked their way through the emerging avenues of stalls. The dead centre of the field had been roped off to provide an arena. They paused here whilst Ted scanned the area for some clue as to where he was expected. 'The opposite side to the fairground,' Gaston had told him, so they headed that way across the grass and dried cowpats.

'There we go,' said Ted as he spotted Casimir's wiry arm held aloft. His pitch appeared to be at the edge of this field, in front of a rusting old gang mower that had been cordoned off with fluorescent tape. Nicely out of the way, he thought. As he turned to Wainwright he felt a hand on his shoulder: the mayor, grinning from ear to ear with the thrill of the moment. They hugged – the Frenchman effusively, Ted growing ever-more awkward when Wainwright started to snigger at his discomfiture.

'You will like this, Ted,' said the mayor as they walked.

To the Englishman's embarrassment, Casimir appeared to have completed most of the preparations without him. Two poles had been driven into the ground and held in place by nylon guys. Between these stretched more of that bunting that was adorning the market place: red, white and blue pennants, sun-faded yet somehow bursting with cheer. A low table and an armchair had been secured for Casimir's benefit; a larger trestle was situated behind, which Casimir explained was for Ted's tools and equipment. Draped across the grass was a canvas banner, on which was daubed the words 'Finest local potatoes.'

'You stay here – I'll go get your stuff,' said Wainwright.

'No no,' said the mayor, 'you must look first.' He took the corner of the long banner and lifted it; the decrepit Casimir scuttled to the far end and did likewise. Together they held the canvas aloft, revealing the stencilled writing on the reverse.

'Édouard PRESCÔTE: GUITARS'

Ted scratched his chin whilst Casimir scrabbled with a ball of string, threading one end through an eye-hole on the banner.

Wainwright, whose attention had been diverted by activity elsewhere, turned back to his friends. His eyes seemed to bulge as he thrust his head forward to read and reread; the pointy tip of his chin sagging to his chest before being retrieved by the smirk that swept across his face.

'Ha!' he barked, switching from the sagging banner to Ted, then back again, then back once more. 'Hahahahahahaha!'

The two Frenchmen pulled the banner taut, knotting the strings to fix it in place above their heads. A small breath of wind caught the back of Ted's neck but there was no chill to it; Ted's eyes looked past the banner to the blue, blue skies beyond. It was going to be a scorcher.

The festival opened at nine, although many scores had arrived far earlier. They surged through the gates to install themselves in the front row at the show area or to catch the very best deals from the traders. The children sprinted towards the fairground, fighting to be the first on the waltzer and dodgems. A few people made immediately for the bar.

Ted worked away, lurking at the back of his pitch as the trickle around his stall became a steady flow. He said nothing and he caught nobody's eye. Wainwright had driven back to the cottage in order to return later with their wives. Surrounded by the clamour of the French crowds, Ted felt very alone.

By ten o'clock, the atmosphere had calmed. Casimir explained that the early-birds were a species apart: the fanatical bargain hunters, the obsessive livestock enthusiasts, those for which this would be their one big day out for the year. They would sell no guitars to these types.

Ted swiftly found himself in awe of Casimir's energy. The man must have been eighty at the very least. His limbs were gnarled and wiry, his twig-like legs protruding from a pair of yellowing tennis shorts that were brief to the verge of obscene. His remaining hair was unkempt and straggly where it creeped out from beneath a decades-old cloth cap; his skin was parchment-thin and his face gaunt, although his features exploded into animation as he spoke and smiled. The sun was beating down but it didn't seem to bother him; he hopped eagerly around the visitors, greeting tourists with a wink, chatting to locals, catching up with old friends who had stopped by to wonder what he was doing with the guitar maker. When the footfall slowed he would scuttle over to Ted to check that he was comfortable, see if he wanted anything. Rarely did he avail himself of the armchair provided for his rest.

In contrast, Ted sweated and puffed as the day grew hotter. Even the light effort involved in sanding down a guitar neck seemed like tough physical labour as time wore on. Ted also steered clear of his own chair, but purely out of embarrassment at the tirelessness of his companion. He threw it wistful glances as he stretched out his arms to relieve the aches that were enveloping his shoulders. He was regretting his part in this stupid facade. He could be working his way around the eateries, perhaps indulging in a small glass of wine. Not toiling away like a performing monkey, contravening every trade descriptions law in the book.

That was until he sold a guitar.

It was an English couple. They had walked past the stall once previously; the wife had kept tugging at the man's arm and cajoling him on. A late birthday present for her partner; he had always wanted to play. Ted glowed crimson in shame as he listened to the man struggling through a halting, Anglo-French conversation with Casimir, even as he admired the ancient's compelling patter. At one stage, Casimir turned and made a big, flourishing gesture to the man behind him, 'He, he is the maker!' Ted could only nod dumbly before burying his face back into his work, hoping that his taciturn response was not interpreted as rudeness.

'Two hundred euro!' Casimir exclaimed when the couple had departed clutching their trophy. 'Two hundred!' He waved the money at Ted, fanning the notes with matchstick fingers, his grin seemingly extending past the side of his face and beyond his ears. Even his ruined teeth seemed to be dancing in glee. Despite himself, Ted found himself jumping up in excitement. With a little hesitation, the pair exchanged an awkward high five.

Daisy and Jenny were almost upon the stall before he spotted them, emerging from a small crowd that had gathered to see some wood being turned. They strolled towards him, Daisy in a Sunday-best blouse and trousers, Jenny in informal pastels: light-orange shorts, a deep-yellow short-sleeved shirt. Ted noticed how much younger she looked than his own wife, despite the fact that there must have been only five years or so between them. It was the aura about her: they were a generation apart. But then Jenny was on her holidays, and holidays did that to people. He welcomed them with a booming *good day!* spreading his arms and beaming. Casimir bowed to the ladies in extravagant courtesy.

'Good day! How's it going, Teddy?' asked Jenny.

Daisy said nothing. Her head had jerked up, gawking over Ted's shoulder at the lettering that hovered above him.

'What the buggering blazes is that?'

Ted turned his head to look, as if he had no comprehension as to what might conceivably be the source of her incredulity. It would be wrong to say that keeping things from her had become second nature over the past month, but talking through the finer details of his presence here had seemed to be an unnecessary complication. He read the banner back to himself – it really had been very nicely painted. When it came down to it, it had just seemed simpler to say nothing and to let her find out for herself; the nuances of reason would have got lost, and there had been no point in stirring things up unnecessarily before the event. The tone of her response confirmed to him that this had probably been the right approach, and that his explanation now needed to be worded carefully. He turned back to the newcomers, nodding in sage appreciation at what he had discerned from the words on the banner.

'He is a Frenchman!' Casimir beamed at the ladies. 'He pretends!'

Jenny snorted as Ted shot the wizened old fool a murderous look. 'What it is –'

'For to sell to the tourists,' said Casimir.

Ted shrugged his shoulders before adopting a watery smile.

'Well, ooh la la,' said Jenny.

Daisy frowned, staring at her husband, her mouth and jaw working soundlessly as if she were chewing sour gum. She was clearly still trying to work this through in her mind. 'This is Casimir,' Ted said, to fill the silence. He gave his companion a thump on the back, relishing the impact as his fist caused the old man to stagger forward.

'Ooh la la. Nice to meet you, Casimir,' said Jenny.

The stream of potential customers dwindled as lunchtime approached. He could hear the distorted voice of the PA as an event drew the crowds away towards the central arena. After checking – with some obvious concern – whether Ted would be safe left on his own, Casimir scurried off to share a few words with his sister; Ted downed his chisel and parked himself in his companion's armchair, grateful not only for the physical rest but for the opportunity to pause and to be himself for a period. It was a short respite, however; no sooner had Ted's body achieved a cushioned equilibrium than he saw a familiar body lumbering over, fixing him with eager eyes. Ted rose to his aching feet to meet the man from the bar.

'It is here, for you,' blurted Claude, holding out his plastic shopping bag. As he spoke he nodded and smiled, expectant like a child. Ted raised his eyebrows and looked down at the offering, scrutinising it with wary eyes. The bag was crumpled and faded; it had clearly been years since its liberation from *Intermarche*. Claude nodded once more, his jowls bouncing and rippling like water in a pond. 'For you.'

'*Thanks*. Thank you.' Ted took the gift with hesitation. His own chubby hands appeared thin and bony in comparison with his benefactor's; standing next to Claude was a fine way to achieve a trim figure. The bag's handles were greasy with sweat. Ted reached in and pulled out something heavy and furry.

'It's a ... weasel!' He said, staring at the object in his hands. 'A weasel?'

'Weasel, *oui,*' Claude confirmed with a delighted grin. Ted held the object up to his eyes and examined it closely, turning it around and peering, trying to adopt the manner of an expert in stuffed weasels. The animal had been frozen into an action pose, mouth ajar to display a cruel set of teeth, its head angled to the left as if it had spotted some tasty prey. Claude had done a pretty good job, Ted admitted to himself. The weasel's feet had been glued or tacked to a weighty block of wood, which had been polished and lacquered on all sides. Ted turned it over to read the writing etched onto a brass-coloured strip. 'Weasel. For Ted.'

'Thank you. That is – generous,' said the Englishman.

'I do the *taxidermy,*' explained Claude. 'I do it every – every Saturday, Sunday. I have *taxidermy* – there.'

'A stall?'

'*Oui.* A stall. There.'

'It is very good. I will display it. In my house.'

There was a short silence. The mound of Frenchman shifted his bulk from foot to foot, seemingly eager to hear more; Ted furiously examined the animal once more, searching for further words to say. 'Very good,' he repeated eventually. 'Very good.'

This seemed to satisfy the other man, who burst into life with explanations and detail about the process of animal preservation, reverting to garrulous French in his enthusiasm. Ted, reduced to nodding and grunting as he struggled to follow, realised with concern that he was walking a line between showing polite interest and finding himself the recipient of a constant trickle of mounted dead wildlife. Still nodding, he searched over the other man's shoulder for Gaston, for Casimir, for anybody who might provide an interruption. Finally, to Ted's relief, Claude asked him to do his Ronald Reagan impression as he had in the bar.

'Ah – fellow Americans – today, I have signed legislation – we bomb Russia tomorrow!'

'Ha ha. Is very good! Is very good!'

Tapping his wristwatch with his blob of an index finger, Claude jerked his head towards the direction of his own stall; Ted nodded with understanding.

'Who the hell was that?' asked Wainwright, who had glided in to the side of the pitch.

Ted turned, clutching his animal and giving his big shoulders a weary shrug. 'Just a neighbour,' he replied. Sinking into the armchair, Ted looked down the rows and rows of fellow traders and braced himself for the afternoon ahead.

6

Édouard

Roy's lodgings were at the very top of the cliff-like rise to the north of the market square. The winding route down gave him a view across town to his destination for the day. He had been expecting something bigger than a village fair but this was on a different scale entirely. Roy looked down upon the ocean of stalls and tents; the jagged rows of parked cars; the fields of trucks, livestock transporters and RVs. The village was heaving with tourists as he jostled his way along with them through the square towards the festival fields, edging past the shops and businesses, many shut up for the day, their owners presumably heading the same way. Clearly he'd struck lucky to get that cancellation; the town had hardly seemed geared up for tourists, and every room for miles around must have gone.

Roy edged forward amidst the jumbling funnel of people impatient for admission at the desks. Through gaps between them he could see the parade of beefy, sun-stained women processing each visitor. How much would they take on the gate? His financial mind gave up as soon as it had begun. Lots. Lots and lots. When his turn came, he was fitted with a plastic wristband, his arm almost paralysed by the attendant's ferocious grip. Roy was surprised at this modern touch, but then chided himself at his assumptions. Why would they not have wristbands at such a big-deal event? He was waved on by a man in a hi-vis waistcoat; he was tall and surly and muscular, although those ladies looked as though they could handle most types of trouble. 'Clack' went the turnstile, and Roy was inside.

The event that had looked so substantial from afar became next to overwhelming at eye level. Roy was not a systematic person but he realised that some form of strategy would be needed to give him the best chance of seeing everything. He turned left, deciding to walk the lanes of stalls one-by-one, browsing at his own pace. He paused briefly at some clocks, their faces set into varnished slabs of tree stump. With glee, he realised how much his wife Laura – sophisticated, old-money, culture-snob Laura – would have hated this city of folksiness. Strolling on, he saw paintings: good paintings and very bad paintings, he saw jewellery and beads, he saw a man, bare from the waist up, sculpting mighty logs with a chainsaw. And then the wind changed and the smell of frying onions hit him, drawing him away from his carefully charted course and over towards the next field, and the food.

He skirted the crowds that were packed around the central ring to be entertained by a sheep demonstration of some kind. The bleating of the animals was punctuated by barked instructions on the PA system; he guessed that even the natives might struggle to comprehend through the boom and crackle. The din mingled with the hubbub of the spectators, with bursts of music, the rumble of portable generators, the stabs of that chainsaw. As he walked on, the people behind him began to clap and cheer; the voice on the PA worked itself up into a frenzy. Roy was striding now at the behest of his stomach. A head-massage lady tried to waylay him; he demurred with an amiable smile. He passed a man selling giant garden pots, daubed in vibrant and garish glazes applied with a child's sense of colour-matching. Next, there was a simple stall, a fellow making acoustic guitars; he was deep in conversation with an enormously obese man, although as Roy passed by, the stallholder raised his head and seemed to make some sort of pleading eye contact with the American. Roy hurried on.

He could have browsed the food stalls for an hour, the choice and variety was so great. But his hunger was unendurable. He would be in the vicinity long enough for another meal; he'd be able to spend time exploring the variety later. He made a beeline at random for a pretty-looking pitch, an open-fronted tent of forest-green bedecked with clusters of balloons. Here, an eager young man beckoned him towards three immense cauldrons, bubbling and steaming, filling his head with impossible aromas as he bent over each one to inhale. He chose what he understood to be a rabbit stew; the chef ladled it into a polystyrene bowl and hacked off a generous chunk of loaf as accompaniment. Selecting a plastic spoon from a very unrustic catering pack, Roy cast his eyes around the vicinity for the best place to sit and eat. There were free benches available there, just there, right outside the wine tent.

*

A few merciful cotton-wool clouds drifted in after lunch. New to this game, Ted had packed himself neither a drink nor a snack. Casimir had fetched bottles of water earlier, and now Wainwright, having been apprised by Ted of his plight, arrived back at the stall with baguettes, three plastic glasses and an uncorked bottle of red wine.

'He said pay him later.' Wainwright tapped the side of his beaky nose as if he were party to a great secret. 'When I told him who it was for, like.'

'Who? Gaston?'

'Haven't a clue. Spotty kid; run off his feet; not coping well.'

'Ah. Yes. He's a good lad.'

Ted and Casimir held the glasses whilst Wainwright poured, sloshing the deep red between each of them until a stream of black sediment slid out and the bottle was done. Casimir, noticing the residue, wrapped his skeletal fingers around the bottle and twisted so that he could see the emerald and white of the label. He muttered something under his breath.

'What's that?' Wainwright looked between the men.

'I think Casimir means to say that he is very grateful for the wine, but perhaps the vintage may not be the best,' said Ted.

Wainwright frowned, his rat-like eyes darting over the bottle. 'I'm sure he told me this was the local wine,' he said, an explanation that prompted an explosive hiss from the old man. 'He gave it to me especially. Although to be honest I can't remember seeing any vineyards on our way here.'

Ted lifted his glass and swigged, grimacing at the acid-assault on his lips and tongue and following up with a hurried gnaw at one of the baguettes. The roll was overflowing with a cheese that would have been soft and crawling even before a morning in the sun; its sweetness mingled with the wine to create a sensation in his mouth that was unexpectedly pleasant. Ted took another sip to make sure – no, it was perfectly acceptable. 'Cheers,' he said, his cheeks still packed out with bread.

'Is it rough?' Wainwright asked. 'I would have got one of the other ones if I'd known this stuff was rough.'

Ted chewed away, taking a third quaff, and then a fourth. 'Well you'll know for when you get the next bottle, won't you?' he said.

The afternoon was racing by. Ted reflected that there was nothing quite like a nice glass of wine or two to lubricate the work of the everyday bogus French guitar maker. He sanded his wood cheerfully, drawing on the safer Côtes du Rhône that had been brought as a follow-up, finding that it made his role-play feel more natural; easy, even. No wonder actors were always pissed, he thought. This was the third bottle, but of course the earlier ones had been shared between the trio. Well, just the two of them for the past hour, after Wainwright had been sent packing following a disastrous interaction with a potential buyer.

Daisy and Jenny returned at just after four o'clock, tutting at the 'Édouard Prescôte' sign just as they had earlier; Jenny with a twinkle, Ted's wife with dangerously pursed lips, glaring through narrow eyes at Casimir, who she seemed to be holding responsible for the nonsense. Wainwright followed several paces behind, adopting an exaggerated tip-toe and making his nose-tapping gestures once more.

'Can I stay here, Ted?' he hissed. 'Please? These two want to sit down and drink tea. They've found somewhere that'll do English stuff for them.'

'Sit over there and don't talk to the customers. Or anyone.'

'Oh thank you. You've saved my life.'

'You've sold some?' said Jenny, checking over her shoulder for potential eavesdroppers.

'All four! I sold all four! One this morning and the rest after lunch.' Ted reached into his back pocket and felt the wodge of notes stuffed in against his rump. He allowed his hand to remain there for a moment, stroking the money in wonder. Four! It was beyond all his expectations. And it all stemmed from that kick-start that David had given him.

'It is because he has excellent guitars and excellent guitar seller,' said Casimir, thrusting his face towards Jenny and blessing her with a beam of decayed brown and yellow.

Ted wrapped his arms around the old man in a bear hug. 'A team! What a team!'

'It's because –' began Stan from the armchair at the back of the pitch.

'Quiet! No talking!' Ted turned to him. 'No talking or you're gone.'

'Give over.'

Ted and Casimir held on for appearances' sake until all but a handful of stragglers remained in their vicinity. The vendors around them were packing up their remaining stock. Then the pair started towards the food stalls. The mayor joined them on the way, his walk a swagger, a beam cemented across his face.

'Thank you, Casimir,' said Ted as he swung his bag of tools. 'Thank you.' The wine was working through his system nicely. He could do with a pee.

'No problem, Ted. It is fun. More fun than selling the potatoes. I should have retired from that since ten years.'

'You should have retired from that since forty years,' said the mayor.

'I have been wasted selling those potatoes. I am the best at selling in this town.'

'You must be if you got people to buy those potatoes.'

Casimir exploded in a splutter of dribble, waving his limbs angrily at his old friend. The octogenarian made to stalk off between two gazebos, but caught his foot in a guy rope and overbalanced, falling with windmilling arms in a crotchety heap. Chortling at his loss of dignity, the others helped him to his feet as he cursed and complained in an outraged staccato. Casimir was still muttering as they passed through the avenue of abandoned stalls that took them to the makeshift food and drink court, a place that was most definitely still open for business.

*

Roy had napped in the meadow, a clover patch his pillow, his hat pulled down over his face. A passer-by might have seen him there, noted the bottle resting in the grass beside him and leaped to a conclusion that was quite wrong; although he had enjoyed an afternoon drink in the side field, taking himself away temporarily from the crowds and the noise, his sleep had been one of deep relaxation, not the wino's sprawl that it must appear.

He pulled himself to a sitting position, stretching away the aches from the concrete-hard ground; flapping his right hand vigorously to restore his circulation. Still blinking away sleep, it took him a moment to register that the light was all wrong. Dusk was drawing in. Looking across to the site, people were drifting out; the noise in the air was of automobile engines. He looked at his watch. Three hours! He had slept for three hours.

Reaching for the bottle and searching around for his plastic glass, he saw that he'd contrived to flatten it as he slept. Momentarily thrown, he hesitated before pulling the loose cork and raising the bottle to his lips. The wine was warm and acidic, but right for the occasion, so right. He sat and finished it at his leisure, watching the people as they swarmed from the festival site towards the parking lots, the cars, trucks and RVs queueing

71

to leave, the packs of children full of the thrill of a late bedtime, a gang of men heaving trashcans onto the back of a pickup. Ants in the distance, observed from his position as king of the field. This hobo life would suit him, he thought.

When he finally stood, it was with one particular thought in mind: that he would very, very much enjoy a little more of that wine. The little café in the village had been dark that morning; it was unlikely to have opened now. A late bar here was his best chance.

*

Now Ted was drunk, and fully aware of the fact. A half-century of exploring the effects of various alcohols had taught him to recognise the tipping point: the time to stop and go home if he were ever going to. Tonight, he didn't care. His gusto from the day's achievements, the sense of reward well-earned, the sheer bonhomie of the villagers and the occasion – he would feel rough tomorrow, but no matter. Besides, Gaston was pretty pissed as well. The mayor was all but pie-eyed. Casimir was legless, big Claude was blotto. Wainwright was nicely smashed. Look at them, Ted thought, as his fond gaze swept around the gathering of new friends and neighbours. Tanked. Plastered. Brahms and Liszt – that was a good one. Brahms and Liszt.

Philippe was OK. Sensible lad. He'd been nursing the same bottle of Amstel for a good while, picking at the label with his fingernails, occasionally stopping to perform some service for Gaston, wordlessly and without a smile. Ted's eyes rested on Daisy and Jenny. They were good as well, sat there catching up on old times, taking sporadic sips of a white wine from a bottle that had sat between them for hours. Quite right too. Good girls. His smile fell. Poor Daisy. Let her enjoy the moment.

Ted pressed his own glass to his lips and drained the little that remained. It snapped him out of the maudlin thoughts that had threatened to emerge. Now was not the time to think of that.

'Would you like, ladies, one more bottle of the vino bianco?'

Wainwright posed the question with an urgent tone, planting his elbows on the table between them and switching his glance from one to the other, like a man engrossed in a tennis match. Daisy lifted her palm and shook her head; Jenny offered him a reassuring smile. 'I think we're quite all right, love. But thank you.'

'It's just that I understand that they might be about to shut the bar. So if you would like another bottle of wine then say now, otherwise you might not be able to get one.'

'Don't worry, love. We're fine.'

'OK. I just thought I'd check.' Wainwright turned and retreated four deliberate steps, before swinging round as an afterthought. 'If you change your mind and decide that you did want one after all,' he fixed them with a stare, 'then I'm sure we can do something.' The beaky man made his nose-tapping gesture, but no response was forthcoming so he retreated once more. Jenny watched him as he tottered.

She said nothing for a while. The sea of canvas as dusk turned to dark, the laughter and calling-out as the vendors packed away, it brought to mind an army camp in a war film. 'Did Ted change when he retired?' she asked, her eyes fixed towards where her husband was now holding court. Some men had started a bonfire on the edge of the gathering, throwing on pallets and boards and debris from the stalls; the flames danced high in the clear air. Even from this far, Jenny could feel its warmth on her face. 'You know. Lose it a bit?'

Daisy pulled her cardigan around her. 'Apart from bringing me on some fool's trip here and being lured into the life of a con-man's moll?'

'You have to admit that was quite funny.'

'I do not. You'd think a man would grow out of letting bad influences lead him. I don't mind a bit of mischief but I don't like lies.'

Jenny looked away to hide her smile. She took a sip from her glass before speaking again. 'Is it lonely?'

Daisy angled her head as she chose her words. 'I'm happy

doing my own thing.' She shrugged. 'He's all right. He was a bit of a lost soul in his last year at work. I'm hoping that coming here will make him properly happy. Lay his ghosts, if you understand what I mean.' Her voice suddenly grew firm. 'Even if he is going to be done by the Fraud Squad, or whatever they have over here. Perhaps you should join us? Mine and yours – they can burn off all that energy together.'

'Can you imagine? Stan?' Jenny watched her husband as he held court amongst a trio of bemused-looking traders. 'It's nice to see you again, love. It really is.'

As far as Ted could ascertain, Marie was quite the loveliest looking human being that he could ever remember seeing in his life. Well, the honour either went to her or her sister. It was strange how he hadn't properly noticed before. He looked from girl to girl to girl, before something twigged inside him that he ought to make some sort of response for the mayor's benefit.

'Oh – er – delighted to meet you properly,' he said. 'I'm Ted.'

'Édouard.'

'Yes. *Oui. Édouard. Enchanted. I am highly enchanted to meet you.*'

'That is very good,' replied Celine, the older of the two, her perfect lips, natural and devoid of make-up, blessing him with a smile that punched him like a steam-hammer in his old and drunken heart. *'And you, Mr Prescott. It is clear you have had a good day.'*

'Tell me. Have you ever wanted to play the guitar?'

'Ay! Ay! Ay!' A cry from Gaston interrupted the exchange, the interjection allowing the mayor to drop the forced smile that he was increasingly wont to adopt when his daughters were out in public. *'Ladies and Gentlemen! Excuse me! Quiet! Ladies and Gentlemen, we regret that the bar is now closed to the public. Thank you and enjoy your visit to our town. Stallholders and workers are welcome to remain; some drinks are now on the house for a job well done. We will work no more today. Philippe – take over the serving, please.'*

74

A smattering of applause greeted Gaston's words, rising to a cheer as Philippe stepped forward to be presented with a corkscrew by his bowing boss. The youth blushed as much as his complexion would permit, staring at the grass in his self-consciousness and with the realisation that there would be no relaxing wind-down for him, that his feet were destined to ache for hours to come. Removing the tricolour apron that he had donned as a tourist prop for the day, Gaston tossed the garment onto a heap of empty cardboard boxes and refuse before sweeping a bottle of red from the makeshift bar. Stepping forward with his trophy, the host attempted to pour, gazing with incomprehension at the bottle as nothing happened and then sheepishly calling for the return of his corkscrew.

'Ted! Play some songs!'

The words seemed to exist on another plane to the big Englishman, as if they were coming to him in a dream, or as the imaginary voices that he'd understood mad people heard. 'Play some songs!' He raised his glass to his lips yet again, but the mantra continued, nagging at him to rouse him from his stupor. 'Ted!' Somebody grabbed and held his shoulder and he snapped into realisation, appreciating with horror that his lack of awareness had allowed this cry to take hold and to spread; that his tormentors were encircling him, fixed upon a request that could not now be quietly shrugged off. 'Ted! *Oui!*'

'I ...' He tailed off and gaped around with the bewilderment of a man falsely accused by the mob. Beside him, Casimir's bony arm was holding aloft the guitar that Ted had presented to Gaston all those weeks back, a guitar that had appeared just like magic here in this field, spirited in from the town by some malevolent power. Ted shot acidic looks at the wrinkly traitor who was prancing around grinning like a monkey with a fresh banana; he then rained missiles down upon the café owner, who returned the look with a guileless shrug.

'Go on then, mate.' To Ted's surprise it was Wainwright who snapped him out of it; Wainwright who hated to be anything other than the exclusive centre of attention; Wainwright who was urging him to step forward to perform his French songs; this lowbrow little Englander who'd once tried to entice him along to Val Doonican at the Assembly Rooms. Ted gaped at his old colleague and utterly lost the thread of his resistance. With the drink keeping his nerves at bay, all he was left with was that small, secret feeling that he had never admitted even to himself: the very, very tiny excitement at having been asked.

'One song then,' he heard himself replying. 'But I shall want more wine.'

A ragged cheer rang out around the stallholders.

If you want to divert attention from yourself, get a volunteer from the audience. He'd seen comedians do it, on the television and in shows at their local theatre. Performing seemed to be partially an art and partially a box of tricks. One song, he'd said. And they'd loved it.

Celine's frame was slim and as light as a mouse; Ted could perceive no weight from the bottom that nestled amongst his big thighs. With his shirtsleeves pulled up and his arm wrapped around her, the touch of the girl's mohair sweater against his bare skin was sensual and hypnotic. Ted breathed in the light smell of perfume. Her short bob of raven-black hair was shaved at the back to meet the warm flesh of her neck; he fixed his eyes there, studying its perfection.

Clang! Celine took a downward strum at the guitar, but Ted's left hand had slipped around the neck and the chord was ruined. The crowd laughed at her disapproval and embarrassment, the mayor maintained his fixed grin. At the makeshift bar, Philippe glared across at the Englishman.

'Oops! Now that was my fault.' Ted shaped the chord once more with his fat fingers. 'Try it again. Once with the thumb and then a big old whack with your hand.'

'In French, Édouard!' shouted Casimir.

'Édouard! Édouard!' The villagers set up a chant.

'Oh. Uhhh – oooh la la! Jouer le guitare!' His response prompted loud laughter.

Celine tried once more. Bom-ching in a perfect E chord. 'Again! *Encore!*' urged Ted. *'Encore!'* Bom-ching, bom-ching, bom-ching. The audience roared its approval. Ted could see that flawless neck redden slightly; three or four strums later and Celine hopped off his lap, bolting into the safety of the crowd to a chorus of boos.

At the edge of the circle, Wainwright was speaking intently to her sister, oblivious to the further glares of the young barman. 'And Ken Adams; he designed all the sets you know, the well-known hollow volcano and the like. Anyway, he and his wife were at dinner with Sean and the lovely Mrs Connery. And next thing I knew, Mrs Connery was on the telephone to me enquiring about a sideboard!' Wainwright's hand squeezed Marie's shoulder, oblivious to the incomprehension etched on the college-girl's face.

'You are friends with Sean Connery?' she said.

Jenny pushed away her unfinished glass and patted Daisy on the arm. 'I think it might be time to make a move,' she said.

'Édouard! Édouard! Another song!'

Ted held up his palms toward the voice in the crowd. 'No, no,' he said, settling the guitar back across his leg.

'Might take some time.' Daisy pursed her lips.

♫ *Forty years of marriage to a faithless lying hound*
A smile it passed across her lips as he passed in the ground
'I'll pay him back, I'll pay him back for being such a beast'
She chucked the soil unto the pit and copped off with the priest ... ♫

An accompaniment emerged as Ted played – clapped hands, slapped thighs, bashed tables – anything to augment the steady beat of Ted's right hand. A trio of men started to dance; they were given a clear berth as they twirled around each other and crashed into the trestle tables. Casimir twirled his walking stick around his head with dangerous bravado; Celine glided amidst the crowd like a señorita, brandishing imaginary castanets above her head. The crowd roared along with the chorus.

At the very back, around the edge of a canvas tent, appeared an American.

The booming voice had been intriguing from a distance; up close it was captivating as it danced around the language that was so exotic to him. Spellbound, he eased closer through the pack of villagers.

♫ *She goosed the judge, she groped the clerk in passion-driven fury*
Outraged the public gallery and tampered with the jury ♫

'Excuse me. I'm sorry.' Roy knocked into the mayor as he sought a gap in the crowd.

The official turned to him. *'Ah. This is closed, sorry. We are the vendors only.'*

But his words were interrupted. Gaston's interest had been piqued by the transatlantic accent. He leaned in with a smile of hospitality. *'Forgive me!* You are welcome here. Still open to sellers and Americans. Sellers and Americans only.' A shadow crossed Gaston's face. 'You are American? Not Canadian?'

'I'm American, yes.' Roy felt his hand being gripped and shaken.

'You have a drink?'

'I don't, no.'

'Ah. An American without a drink!' Gaston thrust an empty glass at the newcomer as the mayor withdrew with a cordial nod. Without taking his eyes off Roy, the café owner waved in Philippe's direction.

'Thank you,' said Roy, reaching into his trouser pocket.

'No, no. There is no charge. We take no more money tonight.'

'On the house! Thank you! I think I may have found heaven here.'

'Ha! Philippe!'

Philippe slouched across and surrendered his bottle to Gaston's outstretched hand. Roy recognised the boy from the café, but his thank-yous went unregistered. Raising his glass to salute his host, Roy took a swig, his throat now oblivious to the sandpaper tannins.

'This is great,' he said, gesturing with his head towards the guitarist.

Gaston, whose eyebrow had shot up on the misapprehension that the wine was the source of such appreciation, let his face relax. 'Yes! Very good. Very, very good.'

'He is a seller also? He has a proper hoedown going.'

Gaston beamed. *'Oui,* yes. His name, it is Édouard. Édouard Prescôte. He is our maker of guitars. The instruments are very fine.'

'His playing's pretty fine, also.' Roy turned from his new companion, his gaze once again fixed upon the big man playing and singing. His head was already bobbing along with the crowd's beat; the fresh injection of alcohol prompted his free arm to follow suit and then settle into a genial back-and-forth marching action. 'Dah-di-dah-di-dah-di-dah,' he half-chanted at Gaston. 'First-rate music, sir!'

'You know, it is why I love very much the Americans. Here, people do not call me "sir." Philippe, the boy, he calls me many things; "sir" never. So I say to you, *cheers,* good health, we drink to the Americans and to you, our honoured guest. Good health!'

'Good health, sir. Good health.'

♫ *So Father hear my simple cry for pity*
I've said my prayers and done my duty
And in your wisdom and your beauty
Won't you BRING MY MARG'RITE TO ME! ♫

Ted's flourishes had become progressively more dramatic as each song had climaxed. This time he held his clenched fist aloft as the mob before him roared and whooped, although the theatrical rush deserted him almost as soon as the gesture was complete, sheepishness flooding his face as his arm began to wobble and he rushed for the succour of his tuning pegs. Plucking idly at a handful of open strings with his right hand, he leaned down to the grass for more wine, but he had kicked the bottle over, presumably in that over-energetic final chorus. His eyes scanned the crowd, searching in the flickering light of the bonfire for a friendly face. Catching Celine's attention, he lifted the empty bottle, pointing repeatedly at it for new supplies.

Ted half-stood, but that didn't go so well, so he let himself drop safely back down once more. He opened his mouth with a sudden intention to explain something in French about the song he was about to play, but his words deserted him and he was left gaping at a cluster of faces peering at him out of the dark. After a beat, his breath left him in an ambiguous 'beeeyaaahh' type sound; he flapped his arm at his audience to let them know that whatever it was that he was about to say was triflingly unimportant. He gave a little cough to clear his throat, then coughed, and coughed once more to make sure. Suddenly all was silent aside from the crackle and spit of the fire. Ted could feel the fear galloping towards him again. Before it could overcome him, his fingers came to the rescue by plucking out the introduction of 'The Pretty Goat.'

The mayor barked along, his jacket bursting across his stout body as he held up his arms in solidarity with the crowd. Beside him, Roy's empty glass allowed him to perform the full marching-on-the-spot actions. By the second chorus, the American had grasped the tune; with immense gusto he joined the singalong, his rasping tones soaring along with the melody of the mob.

> ♫ Tra la, la tra-la-la
> La la la la la
> Tra la, la tra-la-la
> La la la la la ♫

Gaston returned with a new bottle, took Roy's glass from his hand and filled it to overflowing.

'You have been introduced now?' said Gaston, as the whooping died down and the mayor pushed his own empty glass towards the café owner. 'This is Bernard Claveyrolat, our mayor. Bernard, I introduce you to Roy Young, the very polite American. He is the new big fan of Édouard.'

'Ah! Édouard, yes, yes. *Delighted, Monsieur Young.* I apologise that I did not welcome you when you arrived.'

'Please don't mention it.'

'You sing with a good voice,' said the mayor, pumping Roy's hand. 'These are the songs of Frédéric Debreu, a man who was a legend to us.' He grinned as he tapped his own throat. 'Songs that are good to sing.'

That magical guitar started up again: a slower, mournful melody. The three men fell silent as the warm baritone drifted across the air. Roy fixed his gaze once more upon the big man who had the crowd so spellbound. The American's head bobbed slowly up and down. The music was simple, so simple, and yet it had a depth that seemed to go on forever. Its language, its nationality was unimportant; it was so much like the music that he had been brought up on as a child; the music that had kindled his love affair with those great country artists. The ones who had come before everything had turned plastic.

'There's nothing like this in the US now,' he said.

'Pardon, monsieur?' Gaston frowned at his new companion.

Roy turned to the café owner and shrugged. 'The bluesmen. The original country singers. The ones that grew up on the small farms, up on the mountain, way back. The ones that sang from the heart. They have that thing inside them.'

'Oh *oui, oui.* I have heard this.'

'Well all I'm saying is that I'm glad that at least they live on in France.' Roy turned back to the performance, stretching his neck this way and that, bobbing up on tiptoes, keen to see as much as he could.

Gaston's grin returned as he worked it out; wider and broader so that it threatened to explode from both sides of his face. 'Édouard, *oui!* Yes!' he exclaimed. 'You have hit the nail there!'

Roy risked taking his eyes off Ted for one moment to glance back at his new companion. 'It'd be great to speak with him,' he said.

Gaston forced his features to rearrange back into normality, then melded them into a look that he hoped was suitably regretful. 'I am sorry. Monsieur Prescôte is a man of little words, Monsieur Young –'

'Roy. Please call me Roy.'

'Roy. Monsieur Young. I will tell Bernard what you say.' Gaston patted the mayor's arm. 'Monsieur Young. He admires our *chansonnier*. He says he is like a French singer of the blues.' Gaston glanced sideways at the American and angled his head; a nod in return confirmed that he had interpreted correctly.

'Eh? Ha! That is good! Yes!' said the mayor. 'Good!'

There was a cheer as the song ended, then a bigger wall of roars and whoops as Ted lifted himself unsteadily and held his guitar aloft.

'He has the audience in the palm of his hands,' said Roy

'Yes, yes,' said Gaston. 'Édouard – he is very popular in the town. In the region! Like the country singers of America. He lives in a very small house – of wood, what do you say?'

'A shack?'

'That is it. Lives in a shack, on the hill.'

'Like a hobo?'

'Ha! Hobo, yes. No electricity.'

Roy's attention was now focused on the café owner, so he failed to spot the mayor's eyebrow shooting skyward; the official brought his glass to his lips to cover his expression.

'There is something unique about guys like him, you understand?' Roy said.

'You know music, *Monsieur?*'

'I'm a Nashville man. I know music.'

'Ah! You know music very well!'

'I do. But this is – just to come across somebody out of

nowhere. It's exciting, you understand. You're his friends. Do you think I might speak with him?'

Without a word, Gaston placed his arm around the American's shoulder and shepherded him to a quieter patch of ground. The mayor hesitated for the briefest of moments, then joined them to form a huddle. Grabbing a new bottle from a nearby table, Gaston refilled their glasses one by one; somehow it was understood that no talking would take place until this ritual was done.

Gaston took a long drink, swilling the wine around his mouth, deep thought etched across his face. 'I am afraid, Monsieur Young,' he said eventually, 'that Monsieur Prescôte is of not many words. He plays and sings, *oui*. But talks, *non*. You are fortunate, however, as I do the management for him for when he plays. So I ask: what can I do for you, Monsieur Young?'

The mayor took another hasty drink, then wiped his moustache, leaving the back of his hand across his mouth for safety.

'He has a manager?' said Roy.

'Sure, I am his manager.'

'His manager,' blurted the mayor, adding a vigorous nod before hastily replacing his hand lest the American look too hard at his quivering lips.

But Roy was lost in his own contemplation. The anxiety, the stress, the anger; the feeling of being lost, of wondering where his life had gone and where it was headed; the cruddy lawyers' letters, the constant pressure and questioning about figures, about sales, about return; the creeping expectation that he should consult accountants before he could wipe his own ass. That weird compulsion that had gripped him on the bridge over the gorge, the tranquillity of his rented room; the unsullied homespun honesty of the day's event, the warmth and the unsought hospitality of his new friends. The jolt that he'd felt inside when hearing that man's songs; just a guy and a guitar and a big heart, just like it used to be; the primal roar of the people in the crowd who had clearly been touched just as he

83

had. The clarity, the oh-so-rare clarity of a simple decision that he might make; a throwback to how he used to operate before the corporations had finally sucked in what was left of his heart and soul.

Roy studied the mud and grass around his feet, taking in the shadows that danced in the light of the bonfire, then raised his head to speak with a confidence that startled him even as the words left his mouth. 'What I'd really like would be some recordings,' he said.

A lifetime's mask of poise and assurance deserted Gaston for the briefest of seconds as he stared at the American. Then he let his shoulders fall. 'Ah. You see, I am sorry but Édouard is a very simple man. You see he does not record his songs.' He glanced at the mayor for support as he recovered his aplomb. 'We try, Bernard, we try, but you know – when we put the tape recorder in front of him, he is like – woah! What is the machine that sounds like me? He is terrified!'

'Very simple man,' confirmed the mayor, nervously picking at his moustache.

Roy held out his arms. 'Listen. You could persuade him? If I funded it, would you try to persuade him?'

'*Pardon?*'

'Some funds. Arrange for him to record three or four songs, if I pay for it. Nothing big-deal. Him and his guitar: I know people who would love to hear it.'

'Well, I am certain we could help him to overcome the fears.'

Roy felt something overwhelming him. He was suddenly dog-tired. 'Could we sit down?' he said.

The only light now came from a smattering of lamps and the gentle glow of the bonfire. All but the hardcore drinkers were beginning to edge away, staggering across the field towards the village, a handful swaying away in the direction of the car park to take their chances on the road. Daisy and Jenny rose, pulling their jackets around them, their breath condensing in the chill air.

'The café is your main business?' said Roy, as he accompanied Gaston back to their table.

'Yes. There we have shows from my artistes,' said Gaston. 'We move the tables, the chairs.'

Roy pulled a business card from his back pocket. 'You will email me?'

'Email, yes, yes.'

The two men shook hands. Roy exhaled from the very depths of his lungs. He ran his hand across his stubble in the hope that his mind might clear once more. From his seat, the mayor stole a glance at Gaston, but averted his eyes at once lest his own facade should crumble. Instead, the official worked his top lip, jiggling his great moustache up, down, left and right as he waited for the American to break from his reverie.

'I should say "hello" to him at least,' said Roy eventually.

Once more, Gaston brought forth that air of great regret. 'I think you are too late, Monsieur.'

Suddenly alert, the American scanned the sparse crowd, but the musician was nowhere to be seen. 'Oh.'

'Never mind,' said Gaston, placing a hand on his shoulder. 'It is late, and he has a walk of kilometres through the fields to his shack.'

'Without electricity,' added the mayor. 'Or water.'

7

The Morning After

Sunday morning was brutal.

Ted curdled in a mess of perspiration and pain, submerged in that very particular wallow of despair that only an excruciatingly grim hangover can provide. He drifted in and out of consciousness, shivering with each panted breath, but even the moments of slumber provided no respite from the hammering behind his eyes. The nausea was remorseless, washing across his body in tides whilst providing no indication that heaving up his guts might provide any relief. Daisy looked in on him mid-morning, screwing up her nose and edging across the room to struggle with the window, but otherwise he was left to his misery. Intermittent recollections of his triumph amongst the townsfolk might have cheered him, but with them came vivid memories of the taste of the wine, and these nudged his stomach closer to the brink. He had a picture of being bounced around in the car, powerless to lift himself from his sprawl across Wainwright's knees as they had bumped up the uneven track home. But there was nothing after that. He had evidently made it through the kitchen to his bedroom. And somebody had undressed him down to his underpants.

He pulled himself from his bed to pick at some late lunch, poking bread around his plate whilst trying not to rise to the gibes at his expense. He could not even summon the energy to glare at Wainwright. For such a scrawny man, a fellow well-known as a lightweight throughout the inns of the High Peaks, an embarrassment after the second pint, his old colleague was invariably chipper on the morning after. Ted could not ever recall seeing Wainwright with the hangover that the man so richly deserved.

They took a stroll around the farm as evening approached, returning to dig out the Scrabble set. But there was no dictionary, so there was no means of challenging Wainwright's zealous contributions. The four went to bed early, Ted in disgust at his wasting of a precious day.

Monday, however, was sweetness and flowers.

He had sprung from his bed with vim; he had nodded along with rapt attention to Wainwright's military travel plans. He had chortled with gusto at the witticisms about driving on the wrong side of the road; the very same witticisms that had been so spirit-sapping just a few days earlier. He had bashed his old colleague on the back with enthusiasm when the talk turned to when they might have their next reunion. He had shared a long hug with Jenny.

And then they had gone.

Ted cruised the rooms, weaving and dancing about the space, their squashed cottage suddenly a mansion. Daisy's knitting needles clack-clacked away as she regarded his pirouettes through long-suffering eyes. She had still not forgiven him for the little deceit at the festival. He blessed her with a grin; a big, dopey, freedom-loving grin. She pursed her lips into a threatening 'O' shape. His smile widened and he bounded from the room once more, through the kitchen, across the verandah and on to the grass, spreading his arms out wide and waltzing about the meadow, a fat old man from Derbyshire acting out 'The Sound of Music.' He tapped his fingernails on the lounge window to get her attention, and then grinned once more, directly at her, challenging her to maintain her stony facade. Finally, her face cracked and Ted skipped back to the front of the cottage breathless and happy, parking himself on the steps to take a good, long listen to the silence.

Without the burden of house guests, Ted threw himself into guitar-making. His confidence had soared after the festival, and reflection on its events had caused him to look at his handiwork with fresh eyes. It was true that his instruments were the work of a beginner, an amateur. A master luthier might wince at the woods that he'd chosen; at the mix of compromises and guesswork that he'd been forced to employ. But, in all, the things were rather nice. They were handmade and had some character about them. Their sound was a little colourless, but it was good enough for the average strummer, and certainly no worse than you got from the cut-price things they churned out in the Far East. Ted spent an afternoon etching an intricate seascape design into a scratchplate, scraping away with the point of his very smallest chisel until his eyes forced him to yield to the diminishing light. What if he'd started thirty years ago – how good would they be by now? He felt a very small pang of regret, which prompted a droll smile at the irony. Of all the things that he might currently regret.

He made fruitless trips up to the farmhouse, hoping for news of David. And he found himself dwelling upon something else: that he had never heard back from his note; the timid speculation that he had left at Eric's last known address. Ted chided himself that he should have never have expected to; that it had been a hundred-to-one chance. Yet he realised that he was crestfallen that his flight of fancy had been just that; that in Eric-terms his visit here had been such a non-event. As he worked in the late afternoon sun, wood shavings gathering around his feet, he tried as best he could to probe his own feelings. What was he really after? His memories were of his brother as a young man, but Eric would be well into his seventies now; he could be infirm; he could well be dead. Deep inside, was Ted secretly hoping to find some new family out here? Well one of those was enough; more than enough at present. He had told himself that the chance to dig around would be a by-product of his presence – he had not consciously come here with thoughts of happy family reunions in mind. And yet he could have picked a dozen more convenient parts of this country in which to indulge his silly little retirement whim.

That evening, Ted re-examined the bundle of banknotes, pulling them from the envelope that had been secreted amongst his socks and underpants. Daisy maintained a stream of caustic remarks as to their origin as he counted the notes in piles on the kitchen table. He set aside fifty euro to pay the mayor, then, after deliberations, the same amount again to offer Casimir. It had occurred to him that the tax authorities might want a cut; he had brushed this away. Law-abiding all his life, and look where it had got him. He counted out a further eighty for his wallet, and pushed some more into a drawer. He walked up to the farm with the remainder, to buy a little more time with Monsieur Patenaude.

*

He took the car out the next morning, turning up the music to mask the grinding and scraping from beneath him, skirting the village centre to visit the cheap mini-market that squatted amongst the industrial units on the edge of town. He spent the afternoon tidying his workshop, for the first hour as a genuine attempt to organise his things; for the remainder as an excuse to lose himself in his records. It was a full week before Ted set foot in the café once more, striding in on a morning ramble, still troubled but healthy from seven days of abstemiousness.

*

Casimir laughed. He laughed and laughed, head thrown back towards the ceiling, his scrawny neck exposed and juddering as his decrepit lungs struggled to maintain an air supply. He clutched the edge of the table so tightly that his pallid fingertips glowed red. His wheezing and hooting filled the room; it echoed around the stucco and the big glass windows, causing the handful of other customers to stare in curiosity and bewilderment. Eventually the cackles became less frequent, the old man remaining frozen in his pose, eyes glued towards the light fittings as his muscles finally gave up on their thin heaves. Released from this manic possession, he let out an enormous and audible sigh, a cross between a whistle and a 'whooooo,' gave three deep breaths and rejoined the two men at the table.

Ted glared at him.

'It is good,' said Casimir. 'It is good!' His shoulders started to twitch once more; he repeated the phrase over again as he struggled against a secondary attack.

Gaston raised an enquiring eyebrow. It took Ted a moment to notice.

'No!' the Englishman repeated. 'No. No. No.'

Behind the bar, Philippe prepared coffee. The machine was behaving itself this morning, perhaps conscious of the increasingly intense batterings that the sallow youth was wont to deliver. He delivered cups and a small jug of cream, then lingered, hopping from foot to foot, keen to be part of the developments.

'Come Ted,' urged Gaston, rising to his feet and patting his breast pocket. 'Are you not curious to know how the American would price the music of a French singer of the blues?'

Ted flapped his palms. 'He must be some sort of bloody halfwit!'

'A little bit curious?'

'No!'

'I do not blame him. You are very good Mr Prescott.' Philippe dropped his eyes to the floor, surprised at his own intervention; Ted could not resist smiling at the boy. The coffee was robust; he rolled it around his mouth before raising his voice once more.

'I mean, what was he thinking of? What were you thinking of?'

'He is very determined, Ted. He first tries to give me an American cheque. I say "sorry, no use to us." But the *credit card machine* is still at the bar, so we go to use that.'

'Well cancel it, or whatever you do.'

'Ted. Ted.' Gaston's face flooded with gravitas as he dropped his voice into a dead baritone. 'Ted, you think that you are no good and that you are just, what, messing? And I tell you that you are good, and Casimir and Bernard – who both saw Debreu himself play – tell you that you are good, and the customers say that you are good, and even Philippe who knows nothing says that you are good. And then this American, who is from Nashville – Nashville! – the town where the people all know music, he says that you are good. And you say "no" because you know better? Eh?'

Ted averted his eyes from the inquisition, the Englishman finding new interest in the detail of the yellowing ceiling. The silence was too much. Finally he had to mutter to fill it. 'Well I can't take his money. I just – can't.'

Gaston took the folded slip from his pocket, holding it aloft between the men. 'He gives you this money to record yourself singing. He has heard you singing. He likes your singing. He wants to pay you to sing once more.'

'But I'm not who he thinks I am!'

'This is not what he is asking. He is not wanting to be your wife. He wants to hear you sing and play the guitar.'

Ted looked about helplessly. Casimir and Philippe were staring at the small piece of paper in Gaston's hand, hypnotised as he brandished it about their faces.

'Let me show you how much,' Gaston said.

The Frenchman paused, and then, taking the silence as assent, meticulously unfolded the slip, presenting it to them with two solemn hands whilst nodding his head very, very slowly.

It took Ted a moment to focus. 'Bloody hell,' he breathed.

Ted was surprised when he was joined at the urinals. He had never seen Gaston use the public facilities before, assuming that the Frenchman popped into his apartment whenever he needed to pee, undoubtedly retiring to a pristine-white bathroom with fragrant soaps and laundered towels.

'I am sorry we laugh,' said his friend. 'It is, very surely, a big compliment to you.'

'For goodness sake don't apologise. It was – it is – funny in its way.'

'No, we are tactless. I think you have your problems.'

'Ach.' Ted fastened his trousers and turned for the sink.

'Ted, you know if I can help?'

The Englishman rinsed his hands under the single tap, keeping his back to his friend.

'To be honest, Gaston, I don't really want to talk about it at the moment if that's not being rude.' Ted shook his hands free of water, for longer than he needed. 'Things have just gone belly-up.' He ran the towel across his hand and turned as if to say more, but contented himself with a hopeless shrug of the shoulders instead.

'No, no, no.' Gaston shook his head; he had not been offended. 'It is money?'

'You could say that.'

'But selling the guitars? This American's money? You do a recording very cheap, there is an OK profit for you?'

'Yes, well. The guitar money won't last long. And that extra would have been welcome, believe me. But not enough.'

'Not enough? You have no money?'

Ted looked the Frenchman directly in the eye. 'I think I've lost everything, Gaston.'

They exchanged places whilst Gaston washed his own hands, returning to the soap dispenser twice during the operation. Ted stood motionless by the door, taken aback by his own impetuousness and struck with a wave of fright about the conversation that he could not now avoid. The cellar room seemed cold. He could feel himself shivering.

The Frenchman broke the silence. 'I have money I could lend? If it would be of assistance?'

'I couldn't repay you, Gaston. No income, no assets.'

'You will have to go back to England?'

'Not quite as simple as that.'

Ted cast his eyes around the small chamber, at the walls, the floor, the urinals, anywhere but at the Frenchman looking round at him from the sink. His hand worried away at the door handle, turning it open, closed, open, closed. He spoke again. 'Sorry. I didn't mean to be abrupt. You're trying to help.'

'No, no.'

'The wife doesn't know, you see. Things are a bit complicated.' Gaston's shocked expression precluded any need for a reply, so Ted continued to speak. 'Our son's had a bit of trouble. Money trouble. I helped him out, but – well – good money after bad. Daisy – well, I'm not telling her until I know things are all right with him. Which is why I keep asking you if he's rung here.' Ted gave a terse and mirthless chuckle. 'Business as usual, if you get me.'

Gaston reached for the towel but withdrew, shooting a look of distaste at the the laurel-green rag. He shook his hands vigorously then appeared to consider wiping them on his trousers, before angling out his arms to one side so that there might be no danger of drips soiling his clothes.

'You could repay me for a loan if I have work for you?'

The question caught Ted by surprise. 'Do you need another barman?'

Gaston shook his head. 'No, not a barman. I have ideas. Bernard also, he has ideas.'

'Mmm.' Ted studied the Frenchman's face, trying to read his expression.

'Perhaps it will not solve your problems, but some money comes to you from the blue today. A start?'

'I know. I know that.' Ted's voice was a mutter.

'Perhaps it is like an *omen*? Maybe you will think about it?'

The Englishman pushed open the door. 'I will, Gaston. I will.'

8

The Celebrity

'You're in one of your moods,' said Daisy, not looking up at him. And she was right, although she could not know why. Too restless to remain at the kitchen table, Ted stomped about the cottage with his toast, drifting between each tiny room to gaze at nothing in particular. The window in the second bedroom was jammed ajar; he shoved it outward with his palm and then slammed it back in, again and again until it forced itself into the frame. Flecks of paint showered from the ceiling. He brushed them from his hair with a scowl.

'Don't drop crumbs!' her voice called.

Ted returned to the kitchen. 'I can't find my bloody mug.'

'On the side.'

'Where?'

'There.'

His remaining tea was tepid; he sloshed it into the sink and rinsed the mug under the tap.

'I'll be outside.' He clumped out into the morning dew.

*

David had opened a bar. Not an unassuming, locals' haunt like Gaston's, but something shiny and expensive in a city centre; a 'brasserie', he had called it. Ted had visited twice, each time agonising over what to wear; each time making an avuncular effort to savour the expensive Far-Eastern lagers before gushing over-fulsomely about the minimalist dinners that had been presented to him on blocks of wood. Outwardly, Ted had been cheerfully sanguine about not being the young fashionable type towards which the place was aimed. His unease had been well buried, but it had been in there somewhere; a whisper that David was not this person either.

But what could he have done when his son had come to him for help? To expand; that was the first time; a property next door that was going for a song. David talked of knocking through into it, sorting out his profit margins by trebling his potential covers at a stroke. What could his father say, this old blockhead who'd lived his life in the cocoon of the regular weekly wage; who'd never run so much as a jumble sale stall in his life? That he should inspect the figures? That David should find himself a proper business partner? That he had a gut feeling that his son wasn't up to it?

That had been the first time. The second time had been when the taxman had come calling.

*

He needed something mindless to occupy himself, so he cleared a large space for firewood on the far side of the cottage, in a spot where it might be shielded from the worst of the weather. He had a batch to collect from his agreement with Monsieur Patenaude, and he walked up to the big house to borrow the farmer's wheelbarrow. It was as rusty and as useless as he had anticipated. He loaded it up as far as he dared and set off back with his first batch, hoping that the fresh air and sunshine might lift his spirits.

He'd said too much to Gaston. His own blurting had surprised him; clearly he'd been bottling things up for too long. He was certain that he could rely upon the urbane Frenchman to be discreet. But this was not the problem. Ted's recklessness had cost him the one thing that had kept him going for the previous weeks: his capacity to retreat into denial.

Ten quid? Twenty? How much had he thought that he might make from the daft American when he had so righteously waved Gaston's entreaties away? Selling his guitars had given him a windfall, but how far would the last of that get him? He wrestled with the barrow, fighting to prevent his load from pulling him sideways down the hill, a fat useless chump with pride for brains.

But surely that pride was a good thing? He struggled to order his thoughts as he stacked the logs. The reason he was tying himself in such knots was to protect Daisy. And Daisy valued pride above all other virtues. Pride and honesty, and doing the right thing; a clean house, a polite tongue, the iron belief shared by her generation of decent working-class women that riches came a distant second to respectability. Nothing that he could greatly disagree with himself, in fact. But Gaston's argument had been persuasive. A little extra cash, there for the taking. He battled the idea as he stacked the logs, disgusted at his own weakness.

The barrow-load made a meagre pile; he turned to double back to the farm. Business as usual, that's what he'd told Gaston, and that was the nub of it. If he could maintain business as usual then David would ring, he could open up to Daisy, and everything would be resolved one way or another. Or the official receiver people would write again with more positive news. He focused on the squeak-squeak of the wheel as he tramped back and forth between the cottage and the farm, consciously emptying his mind of everything but the hypnotic sound. This worked until the wheel hit a rock and jammed solid, oblivious to all his attempts to free it with his hands. Swearing at the contraption, he dealt the wheelbarrow a vicious kick before heaving it around and taking himself backwards step-by-step for the remaining hundred yards, dragging the good-for-nothing machine up the hill behind him. The locked wheel cut a long farrow in the grass and the dust. Reaching the outhouse that listed in a shambles against the ivy-strangled gable wall, Ted dumped the barrow with a clatter. He trudged back down to the cottage to shower.

Shoving open the door, Ted found the kitchen stuffed to bursting point with the paraphernalia for marmalade-making. The glass jars that had been accumulating in crates under the verandah had been rinsed and set out over every surface.

Mountains of oranges, lemons and grapefruit were piled in a pair of wooden crates on the table, which had been shifted to one side so as to sit directly next to the stove.

He stood in the doorway, staring. 'Eh? When did that lot arrive?' he said.

'Evie, whatshername.' Daisy flapped her hand in the direction of the farm. 'His daughter brought it up in her car. She helped me get it in while you were playing with your wood.'

'I didn't see her?' Ted took a hesitant step forward and selected an orange to examine. It was soft, over-ripe.

'Well you'll see her in a minute. I said you'd drop her by some money when you got back.'

'You did, did you?' Ted grabbed at his wife's bony shoulder as her foot strayed too close to the exposed hole in the floor. 'Mind out, for Christ's sake! Why did you move the table?'

'So that I wasn't going this way then that way then this way then that way all the time.' Daisy rummaged for a knife. 'She says there are two big pans up at the farmhouse that I can use. I said you'd get them when you took the money.'

'At least let me put a board or something down.'

Daisy halted her bustling and turned to her husband. 'Or,' she said, looking up at him and poking a finger so that it sank into the folds of his midriff, 'you could just mend the floor. You know. Mend it. So it was like a proper floor. Like they have in proper houses.'

Ted retreated to the doorway. 'I'll get something to put over it,' he muttered.

He collected the two pans from the farmhouse. They were aluminium, dented and lustreless, and of such a vast diameter that they would clearly not both fit side-by-side on their tiny hob. His conversation with the farmer's daughter was unsatisfactory, involving lots of nodding and smiling gestures; heaven knows how Daisy had placed her order for fruit. He left a twenty-euro note with her and was not offered change. Then he loped back down the hill, swinging the pans, one in each big paw.

Daisy took them with a grunt, turning her back on him as he stood in the kitchen doorway, a spare part in the morning's activity. Taking the hint, he forsook his shower, contenting himself with splashing palmfuls of water on his face from the kitchen sink. Murmuring apologies as he squeezed past the production area, Ted grabbed his wallet from the bedroom, tiptoed back through the kitchen and set off down the meadow.

The skies were as clear as they had been, but there was an air of September coming from somewhere – a less vivid blue above, perhaps, or the faintest emergence of bronze in the hedgerow. The weather would turn soon, surely. Perhaps he should practise lighting the burner. He should certainly make sure the flue was clear – it wouldn't take much of a stray spark to destroy the wooden cottage in moments. How the place had survived the Heath Robinson electrical supply he would always wonder.

On first sight, the end-of-season feeling seemed to have touched the market also. There was none of the hubbub to which Ted had become accustomed, even in the weeks before the madness of the festival crowds. As he approached, he wondered what it would be like here in the winter, empty of even the small number of committed tourists and weekenders that had made it their business to seek out this backwoods place.

He had not stopped here to shop recently, and to his astonishment his arrival was greeted with brio from the stallholders. Many of them had been the last to abandon the festival site, staggering away with glazed eyes and hoarse throats from the impromptu concert by the big Englishman who had bellowed out those timeless songs from around the campfire. They thumped him on the arm, they raised their thumbs aloft, they addressed him with a twinkle as 'Édouard'. It dawned upon Ted that he had become some sort of celebrity. He was embarrassed by their attention, but it also filled him with a joy that well and truly dispelled the remnants of his bad mood. He realised that, however long this lasted, his status here as the curious outsider was well and truly over.

The bonhomie prompted him to risk his French. A routine developed: he would comment on the weather, compliment the produce, enquire *'how much is that?'* then ask the stallholder to repeat his answer; to slow down; to repeat once more. For once he persevered, determined not to retreat into the comfort of gestures. If people thought him a buffoon then so be it. His purchases were reckless, but his recent earnings might be his final chance to keep up appearances. His final acquisition was a rabbit-and-onion tart; it would make a fine supper for the weekend. Business as usual, although his wallet was now much thinner.

There was an iron bench at the edge of the square, on the far corner from Gaston's café. Ted lowered his rump onto this, resting his bags at his feet and reaching for his handkerchief to mop his forehead. Behind him the apartment buildings clung to the hill, their painted facades cracked and peeling in the face of the sun. Glancing at his watch, Ted saw that it was coming up to two o'clock. This explained the hunger inside him. He'd been carrying around a loaf that had been irritating him with its excessive and inconvenient length; it had wobbled about under his arm as he walked. A good solution seemed to be to wrench off an eight-inch chunk and eat. Ted rummaged about within his cheese purchases to find the soft one – the one that looked to him like brie; the stallholder had called it something that had already slipped his mind. He unwrapped the parcel with difficulty; the cheese was already oozing in the warm air, plastered to the paper, pulling itself into a formless stringy shape, a gluey near-liquid that would need to be scraped rather than cut.

Ted broke the bread lengthways with his big fingers, rested the two halves on his lap and attempted to fill the sandwich by wiping the cheese-paper against the loaf. Finding this unsatisfactory, he had a brainwave and reached down into his back pocket for his wallet, lifting his buttock to allow himself access, careful not to tip his lunch upon the cobbles. Scrabbling past old membership cards and receipts, his fingers alighted on his useless credit card, which he pulled out and wiped with the side of his hand. It proved ideal for spreading cheese. Ted sat humming as he watched the market from afar.

> ♫ I've made my choice
> Just an artisan, my tool my voice
> I have met the people from every region
> The world is my village, France is my family
> The earth my bed
> For wherever I go
> I long for my Thorigny bread ♫

Bread and cheese on a sunny day; not a bad meal. A blue van reversed at a crawl into the square in front of him, the driver leaning from the open door as he looked back and shouted something. The vehicle's path drew Ted's eyes across to the café. He had been planning to buy water from the pharmacy, but the thought of a quick one was certainly attractive, even though the rest of the goods in his bags could do with seeing the inside of a fridge.

Ted dismissed the thought as soon as it entered his head. Household shopping was one thing, but he could not justify splashing out on lunchtime drinks. Besides, he was unenthusiastic about subjecting himself to Gaston's interrogations again so soon. Chewing at his bread, he had another idea. He would do a little reconnaissance of one of his brother's old haunts: go see the college, perhaps, or drive to Saint-Ouen or Maubette, towns that Eric had written home about in his free-and-easy tales of drinking, dancing and girls.

Ted brushed crumbs from his trousers with a sweep of his paw. It would be good to do something positive again; to get out there and properly look for that years-old trail. But even as he stood and turned from the town square, a shopping bag in each hand, he could feel gloom enveloping him once more.

The kitchen was in disarray. Pots were lined up on the table, newly labelled with spidery handwriting, but fruit was strewn across the worktop and the floor; a pile of washing up sat in the sink; a milk carton lay on its side.

'Is that you?' Daisy's voice was calling from further within the house.

'Is that who?' Ted edged through the room to the interior door. In the sitting room he found his wife in one of the ancient winged armchairs. Her bare foot was raised, nestled by a cushion that she'd perched atop the magazine rack. She looked pale in the light from the single window, although she fixed him with a look that challenged him to pity her.

'What happened to you then?' He strode over, trying not to look concerned.

'I twisted my ankle, didn't I?' Her voice was contemptuous for a moment, before settling in to ruefulness. 'Knocked a jar onto the floor, then trod on it. Silly.'

'Is it swollen?'

'It's tender.'

Ted cradled her foot in his big hands. The swelling around her ankle was red and hot; no other damage was evident, although Ted examined the area as a man with no mechanical knowledge might expertly kick a car tyre. Resting it back upon the cushion, he looked down at his wife, her frame dwarfed by the back and sides of the winged armchair. She had always been small; suddenly she looked old.

'You daft thing,' he said.

Taking a second cushion, he eased her shoulders forward so that he could slide it down behind her back. Happy that she was comfortable, Ted bent to untie his laces, easing off his boots and nudging them to the side of the room with his toe. 'Have you taken anything? Any painkillers?'

'No.'

'Well you need some painkillers. Paracetamol or something. That'll make the swelling go down as well. And I'll get you some tea.'

'There's no milk. I knocked it over.'

'Black coffee, then.'

But on investigation, Ted discovered that the medicine chest was empty of anything helpful. Sore throat sweets, plasters; old containers of iron tablets, anti-diarrhoea drinks, stuff for athlete's foot. There was a crumpled box of ibuprofen, but every tablet had been pressed out of its foil. He returned to the lounge.

'I'll drive back down and get some proper stuff,' he said. 'Get some milk as well while I'm there.'

'Don't on my account.'

'Well we need the milk, and I can get you some pills. And they'll have some spray or suchlike. For the swelling.'

'But you've already been down there once.'

'You think you won't be able to manage without me?'

Daisy folded on his trump card. 'Don't be stupid.'

He parked in a side street and hurried to the pharmacy. The lady inside was helpful and welcoming and understood his carefully enunciated English explanation; she listened with sympathy before selling him some painkillers and a spray that boasted an image of a heavily muscled sportsman. Thanking her, Ted strode off back to his car.

The Volkswagen got him halfway up the hill.

The scraping had been noticeably worse from the moment that he'd pulled away from the cottage, although his preoccupation with Daisy's mishap had allowed him to ignore it. But from the moment that he turned the ignition key and stuttered off, edging through the square and on to the road home, he knew. 'Come on, come on,' he muttered, as the levelled surface gave way to the potholes. He could sense some mechanical force struggling against the power of the engine, as if the rear axle had been attached to an enormous length of elastic. Attempting the incline of the farm track had been insane, but Ted clung to his optimism that the problem might simply go away, grinding his teeth and chuntering as his body was shaken and rattled even as he climbed at a crawl. Finally, as the car dragged itself into the right-hand bend that would take him round a grove of young ash trees, something beneath him clanged and cracked with dreadful finality, and the car simply trailed to a dead stop, the air filled with the screams of engine revs as the power unit severed all connection with the drive wheels.

Ted reached for the handbrake and sat gasping in air, clutching the wheel with sweat-drenched hands, all his energies fixed in a battle to control the agitation that he could feel engulfing his body. He needed a car here; what would he do without a car? Whatever had happened was terminal, he was sure about that, or at least it would require inconceivable amounts of money to fix. He thought of what he'd spent at the market, of David, of the letter, of things back home, all the while gripping the wheel tighter and tighter, his eyes alternately wide open and tightly shut, his whole body trembling as the engine chugged away unevenly and finally stalled to a halt.

It was ten minutes before he released the key and climbed from the driver's seat, turning to lean on the bonnet with both hands whilst he collected his thoughts. The Volkswagen had met its final moments on a wider part of the track, so there was no pressing need to attempt to move it. What about him personally? The panic attack – if that's what it was – had shocked him. It had all gone on too long now.

Ted began the remaining ascent on foot. The gradient already seemed to be steeper than usual; he had undertaken this hill once already today, and his legs and lungs were keen to remind him.

He was almost at the oak tree when his shoulders sagged, and he turned one hundred and eighty degrees to return to the car for the milk and medication that he had left sitting in the boot. Daisy was dozing in the chair when he finally reached her; he poured himself a mug of water and flopped into the sofa, past caring about dealing with the mayhem in the kitchen.

Whilst her swelling had cooled after a night's rest, the same could not be said for Daisy's temper. She railed as Ted propped her up to drink her tea; she snapped at his gentle enquiries about her comfort. Sharp remarks followed the discovery of a burnt edge on her toast; Ted knew, from her running complaints as he semi-carried her to the sitting room, that he was in for the long haul.

He washed up and packed the unused jars into their plastic crate, lugging it outside and scrabbling around on his knees as he jammed it back in the space underneath the boards of the verandah. He shifted the kitchen table, removing the board that he had used as a temporary cover for his beloved hole. He brewed more tea, daring his wife to pass comment on its colour and quality, and they sat for a while in an unspoken truce.

Ted had not felt strong enough to mention the calamity of his drive home, and he had little compulsion to revisit the horror now. Instead, he fetched her knitting and rinsed the cups once more, a brooding frown set upon his face as he swilled them around under the stream of icy water.

'Are you all right if I go out for a bit? To get some things?'

'All right? Of course I'm all right.'

'I'll make you a sandwich before I go. In case I'm not back by lunchtime.'

'I'm perfectly capable of making a sandwich.'

Ted clenched his fists in exasperation. 'To save you hobbling to the kitchen.'

She pursed her lips. He prepared the food anyway: slices of salami set into more of that protracted baguette. He almost made the mistake of asking one more time whether she was all right, but checked himself, covering the plate with a tea towel and setting it down alongside a mug of water. 'I'll see you in a bit then.'

'Good bye.'

Ted left the room and sat lacing his boots in the kitchen. Pulling the kitchen door shut, he trotted down the steps, started across the meadow and then, on impulse, turned and made for the farm track that would take him down the long way.

No miracle had happened. His car was still there where he had left it. Anyway, who would ever move it if he didn't? Ted snarled at the abandoned wreck as he passed, kicking up dust with morose feet. At the bottom he made the usual right turn. Then he walked on, to the village, to the café, to see Gaston, and talk.

9

The Shrine to Frédéric Debreu

'Because it would kill her, Gaston, it would!' Ted pounded the corner table with his fist, causing the mugs to leap and rattle and clank. Dimly, it registered that the background noise in the café had died down. Looking around, he saw that customers were turning to stare. Reddening, he dropped his voice once more. 'Well not actually kill her, you know. But –' His companion waited whilst Ted groped for words. 'She's always worried about David. I just want to hold off until the lad's properly back on his feet and I can give her some hard facts. Then I'll talk to her, of course. I'll have to talk to her eventually because she'll be wondering where all the bloody money has gone. But when he's got a job, and a proper place to live, and I can answer all her questions about that and not leave her desperately worrying. Then I'll talk to her. Then.'

'How long?'

'You tell me?' Ted waved his arm towards the telephone in the corner. 'Days, could be weeks, could be bloody months at this rate. I've left enough bloody messages for him, but –'

'You are yourself very worried for him?'

Ted blew air from his cheeks. 'He'll be OK. In the big scheme of things. He's young. I reckon he's just avoiding us; he can't face speaking. Which is daft, but I'd probably feel the same. Of course I'm worried about him. But not in the way she worries about him.'

Gaston probed Ted's story, asking simple, direct questions in a way that undermined the Englishman's periodic attempts to back away from his uncomfortable honesty. He gave a benign smile at Ted's insistence that the letter from the receivers offered a glimpse of hope. He listened with patience as Ted posited that something would probably turn up.

Casimir edged his way through the double doors, observed that the pair had shunned the communal table, and put two and two together, toddling off to the regulars' area with a tactful nod of the head. Philippe sidled along the bar to fill him in.

'Three months.' Gaston's voice was decisive, firm.

'Three months?'

'I have money for you for three months. You pay me back with work you do for Bernard and I. To add to the American's money also, which you must take. After that –' Gaston shrugged. 'After that, who knows? But you do not tell her for three months. You do your "business as usual."'

'But the American ...'

'His *transaction*, it has completed. I decide as your manager that I will not cancel it. You record some music, I will send it to him.' Gaston patted his heart. 'To make sure my conscience is clear.'

Ted nodded dumbly.

'I have faith in you,' said Gaston, as he stood to end their summit. 'I am sorry that you perhaps do not. But we had a problem. Now! We have a solution.'

Ted reflected upon Gaston's generosity as he lingered at his seat in the corner. He was a good sort, there was no doubt about that. There had been a time, during the first days of Ted's arrival, when he had worried about acceptance by the locals. True acceptance, that was. Not the calculated welcome that a community like this might give to the tourist, but a genuine arm round the shoulder and a round at the bar. Well, he'd been in trouble and these friends had rallied round. This place had become a proper home.

There was some vagueness about the work that the café owner and the mayor might have for him. Ted had a suspicion that there wasn't any, or at least none of any consequence; that this had been a ruse to prompt him to accept help whilst retaining some dignity. If this was the case then they were being doubly generous. Gaston's money would buy him the leeway he needed. If he was careful, he and Daisy could live in a state that might just pass for normality until the time was right to face up to everything.

'It's bananas. Tell me I'm bananas.'

'No, no, no.' Gaston's voice was warm and reassuring.

Back at the big round table, at his newly-rightful place with the café's regulars, Ted felt an aura of comfort about him as if he had awoken from a bad dream. It was the drunk American, the crazy out-of-the-blue windfall that had prompted all this. Gaston was right, he thought, as he twirled his coffee around his mug. They would have to fulfil their side of the bargain, however wrongly conceived. He would have to record a few songs, which would presumably mean going to some sort of studio. Five hundred euro so that some pissed and sentimental Yank might have a bogus souvenir of his holidays! He could feel a giggle rising from within as he thought of it, a silly, immature, childish giggle. He blinked twice, to try to regain some perspective. Just ten minutes earlier he had felt fraudulent, almost criminal at the decision to which he had committed himself. Now he was sitting there like a schoolboy in assembly who'd got away with breaking wind. A grin erupted across his chops – he could suppress it no longer.

'There we go,' he said, holding his mug aloft in a toast. 'A new job, and my first ever record deal. Sixty-whatever, and I'm a professional musician.'

'You are a pop star, Monsieur Prescott!' called Philippe.

'Some pop star I am, at my age, lad. Hate performing, can't dance.'

'You will not have to dance, Ted,' said Gaston. 'As your manager, I will protect you from having to dance.'

'But I always did fancy myself as a bit of a ... "recording artiste."' He pronounced the two words with heavy affectation. 'Funny how things turn out.'

Gaston rose to his feet, purring greetings to an elderly couple as they shuffled towards a far table. 'Stay for some wine, Ted. I will pay. To celebrate.'

The Englishman shifted his chair back. It scraped on the tiles, the sound reverberating around the room. 'Thanks. I want to get out for a bit,' he said. 'You know. Time to think.'

'A walk in the fields?'

'Have to be, won't it?'

Gaston made a quick movement with his arm. Ted saw a flash of silver between them; out of instinct he thrust out a hand. He caught the keys automatically in his big palm; he gave Gaston a startled look.

'You have my car. I do not need it today.'

Ted wandered out into the square, ambling around the village in the sunshine, an old pop star who couldn't dance. The lady in the bank recognised him and smiled; he wondered if this was his post-festival fame, or whether she knew about the postscript, whether his deal with Gaston had got halfway round the bloody town in the time it had taken him to walk the five hundred yards. No matter. He nodded his head and managed a hearty *thank you very much* as he left.

The gauge was almost on empty. Ted drew into the petrol station, searched for the release for the fuel cap and then stood awkwardly beside the car for an age, trying to work out what it ran on. The motorist queueing behind him stepped out to help, studying the label on the cap then tapping the diesel pump; a few minutes and some halting apologies later, Ted was on his way.

He set off for the main road. Gaston's car was spotless; showroom-fresh with a pervasive smell of leather. The engine was smooth and quiet and he could slip between gears with a nudge of the finger. Well, whatever he could get on his budget wouldn't be a tenth as nice as this. Ted wondered how little he could get away with. It would be an old banger, for sure. How long could he get by without one if, as Gaston had implied, he might have the regular use of his new employer's? Determined not to dwell on his problems on what felt like a day of resolution, Ted put his foot down. The surge from the engine gave him a youthful thrill. It had been a while since he had driven anything like this. It occurred to him that he should have made some enquiries about insurance.

There was little traffic as he crossed the gorge and swung right. He tried the radio, but he could not understand the gabbling DJs, nor could he find any music to his taste. So he sang:

> ♫ *Tra la, la tra-la-la*
> *La la la la la*
> *Tra la, la tra-la-la*
> *La la la la la* ♫

A record; he was going to make a record! Was it too early to start thinking about which songs he might do? They would be limited to a handful at most; he should perform the ones that he knew inside out: 'Marguerite,' 'The Pretty Goat,' 'The Forger.' But would this really be best? Surely the key to all the great albums was pacing and dynamics; painstaking track selection; an instinct for the perfect running order. What about 'The Lovesick Clerk?' Perhaps he should –

Ted found himself spluttering out loud at this big-shot star giving off airs in the rear-view mirror. He would take copies of the recordings, of course he would. But one little vanity project hardly made him Barbra Streisand. He just needed to choose those songs with which he was most comfortable, making doubly sure he had the words right so that he wouldn't bugger it up. The Widow, 'The Vengeful Widow.' That would be the one to start off with. Hit 'em between the eyes.

> ♫ *Let us not begrudge this ancient widow her revenge*
> *They say the one laughs longest who is laughing at the end*
> *No, let us not begrudge this ancient widow her revenge*
> *They say the one laughs longest who is laughing at the end* ♫

Forty minutes or so later, he'd reached the borders of Saint Ouen-de-l'Eléphant. Eric had written postcards to him from this town; even after many years he could picture his younger self chuckling at his brother's reference to the unusual name ('no elephants here!'). Ted passed through the outskirts, through the rows of prefabricated commercial units. The structures were undistinguished and identikit, but nevertheless fascinated him as an outsider discovering a new land. Towards the old centre the streets became medieval, the buildings a jumble of zigzag tudor beams, topped with roofs that scrambled up at those crazy angles that he still found alien and peculiar. He spotted a gap between the parked cars and drew up alongside, but Gaston's vehicle was unfamiliar; as he contemplated reversing in he found himself with cold feet. Instead he continued in a circle until he saw a more reassuring 'P' sign.

A couple were emerging from an alley just ahead of him, the man weighed down by bulging shopping bags in each hand. Ted strolled in that direction and found that the passage took him through to another cobbled street just six or seven feet wide, a slender canyon between tall rows of apartments of unfriendly stone. A further alleyway led on directly opposite and on a hunch he made for this, crossing the empty road in three strides, passing between the buildings and on through an archway flanked by two iron gates. They hung open, sagging from rusted-away hinges.

Ted found himself in a formal square that huddled in the broad shadow of a tremendous gothic church. The view seemed to strike a chord within him, although memories are tricky things: the blackened stonework and fantastical decoration above him might have been familiar – was it the image from one of those postcards years ago? Or had he merely seen something similar elsewhere, in a guidebook, or on television?

Try as he might, he simply could not remember.

But his brother had been here, he was sure of that. He racked his brain, but everything had been so long ago. Had it been a special place to Eric, or had he merely dropped by on day trips, as Ted was doing today? On a whim Ted climbed the steps to the church's great door. The stones beneath his feet were steep and worn at the edges, displaying, as he noted with satisfaction, a proper French attitude to health and safety. At the top he hesitated for an instant. He hadn't been inside a church for many years. It had probably been half a century, if you discounted funerals and weddings. Fleetingly, he felt a ridiculous sensation of anxiety that somebody he knew might spot him and laugh. Here, hundreds of miles from home, and as if there were anything wrong with looking round an old church anyway. Feeling foolish, he stepped in to the silent gloom.

What he saw took his breath away. Gloom? In brilliant contrast to the darkened and shadowy exterior, the walls, the columns, the immense vaulted ceiling had been hewn from a clean and creamy marble that caught and reflected the light from a procession of soaring arched windows. These towered from a base in the gallery forty feet above him, and must have reached up forty more, the scale of the design calculated to make any mere worshipper puny in comparison. At the far end of the aisle, the base of the main tower formed a focal rotunda, the clear glass making way to vivid blues and purples that cast washes of colour in all directions.

Ted stood with his back to the door, the craftsman within him humbled. Then, self-conscious once more, he took a few hesitant steps forward and parked on the end of the rear-most pew. If anything, this felt more awkward. He tried to adopt an air of reverence, which he knew was inconsistent with his secular gawping at the architecture. How could he feel at peace here when he was such a profane interloper? He tried to summon forth thoughts of Eric by which he might create a formal moment of remembrance and respect. But nothing came.

There was a small gift shop beside the church. Thinking that he might find a bench somewhere and write a shortlist for his record, Ted went in and picked up a biro and a pocket notebook adorned with the symbol of the cross. At the till, the assistant – a dapper elderly man – asked in English if Ted had visited the museum, pointing through the open door and across the square at what appeared to be a house of some ecclesiastical origin, tall, thin, with meagre arched windows. Ted had no great wish to investigate this cheerless-looking building and its presumed collection of provincial curios, but the man left his position and followed him to the exit. Ted could feel him watching as he left. The Englishman felt compelled to honour his throwaway agreement.

The museum had tall double doors that had not seen paint for many a year; only the left-hand one was open, and this stood ajar by mere inches. Ted fought the urge to look back to see if the shop assistant was still monitoring him. He stepped inside cursing his own cowardice then had to wait for his eyes to adjust; there was no repeat of the unexpected brilliance of the church. The decor and fittings of the rooms seemed to have been chosen to suck the light from the air, to milk the hope from any casual visitor who may have stumbled in off the street. A silent, severe woman appeared from a door marked 'Private' and sized him up through wire-framed spectacles. She wore a full-length chequered skirt of browns and more browns; her cardigan was beige; her mousy hair was tied up in a clip. Ted gave her what he hoped was a friendly nod, and made a pointed look of interest as he stared into a display case.

The three rooms on the ground floor held old photographs and paintings of the area, civic documents and what he took to be historical 'finds'. His footsteps echoed as he walked; he found himself on near-tiptoe so as not to disturb the ghosts that such a building must surely harbour. Climbing the sheer flight of stairs, he took in agricultural antiquities, needlework and tapestries, craftwork and a sheep that appeared to have been born with two heads. The curator stalked him from room to room, maintaining her distance but watching him, dogged and determined. As quickly as seemed decent, he ascended to the top floor. Here, he discovered a recreation of a nineteenth-century schoolroom and a collection of unusual kitchen implements. He made what he hoped were convincing grunts of appreciation to appease the woman; she had now assumed a vantage point halfway up the stairs, checking on his progress through the open doorways, her angular arms folded in a resolute barrier across her sheer bosom.

It was in the final room that he found it: a ceiling-high display cabinet that froze him in his tracks. 'Well bugger me,' he found himself muttering as he ogled the contents within. 'Bugger me.' He could feel his big old face reddening with excitement; he took a pace forward and pressed both hands onto the dusty glass.

Pinned up in neat rows were papers full of scrawled writings and crossings out. A beaten and abused guitar hung from a wire beside them. There were black-and-white photographs, a poster, handbills. The display was a shrine; a monument. The legacy of the life of Frédéric Debreu.

It was a struggle to make himself understood. The curator seemed to understand very little English. For his part, Ted's agitation had caused his own rudimentary linguistics to desert him; with shame he realised that he was starting to raise his voice like the worst of the English abroad. But surely somebody in such a professional position should have some small knowledge of the major tourist languages? Ted waved his arms as the woman maintained a stare of sub-zero sentiment, as if this interloper in her museum was attempting to explain why he had just urinated in the agricultural records section.

'Frédéric Debreu!' he blustered. 'Debreu!'

It took some time for Ted to quell his exuberance and collect his thoughts. He spent a minute standing silently, nodding his head like an idiot; the woman maintained a safe distance but did nothing to provoke him. Finally, Ted regained the focus that he needed to formulate a sentence, and the two began a conversation of sorts.

The exhibits were, indeed, a tribute to Frédéric Debreu. The musician had visited the town many times to play. He had a girlfriend or girlfriends here – the woman pronounced the words with distaste – and regularly used their apartments, or those of their fathers, to write and compose. Being for much of his life of no fixed abode, he would leave notes and lyrics everywhere. His guitar had been found by a fan; other fans had collected the cuttings and memorabilia. The town was very proud of him and maintained the exhibits as a shrine. So proud, Ted noted, that they were here, fading and unadvertised on the top floor.

As she recounted her tale, the lady started to use progressively more assured English. Ted surmised that he had misjudged her and that her stern facade masked an echo of his own shyness of looking foolish in a foreign language. She continued to radiate negligible warmth, but perhaps this was just her way; it was hardly a job for the naturally ebullient, stuck here in this dingy building with one visitor every blue moon. She finally climbed the last of the stairs to join him, presumably conceding that the Englishman was no longer considered a physical threat. Ted told her that he was a musician, that he played Debreu's songs, that he would like to study the lyrics. Without answering, she unclipped a set of keys from a fastening on her skirt then slid past him in her flat sandals and reached for the lock.

It was more than Ted could have ever hoped for. Without the barrier of the old glass, the items leaped into the living world. Ted leaned in so that his nose almost touched the exhibits. The poster was an original, cheaply printed in black and white, tatty and near-torn on the fold, a real-life advertisement for an event that had taken place in this town: the artist, the café venue, the date of 3 April 1969 picked out in glorious sixties Monotype Grotesque type. The handbills were similar: sporting a variety of design styles but a uniformly budget-conscious production, they told of shows in that and the following decade, always clubs or cafés, always cheap – occasionally free – ticket prices. A couple of them sported what Ted took to be beer or coffee stains. The photographs were a mixed bag. There was the 'official' portrait of Debreu, which Ted recognised from his own record sleeves, but there was also a collection of informal snapshots that were more interesting: Debreu on stage, Debreu posing in front of venues, Debreu with various fans and admirers. And then there were the papers. The material was cheap and yellowing; the ink had faded to an insipid grey-blue. But they were the songwriting genius's own words, in his own handwriting, a jagged scribble in a random mix of upper- and lower-case letters. None of the song lyrics had titles but he recognised the first two immediately; a third was totally unfamiliar to him. Some were near-perfect, with no crossings-out, others were a mess of rewordings and interjections as the writer had grappled for the perfect word or phrase. Ted's eyes darted from item to item, in awe of this astonishing find. The only jarring note was the guitar. Ted could see immediately that it wasn't the instrument Debreu held in the photographs; whilst both bore similar bashes and scrapes, the instrument before him sported a smaller headstock and simpler detailing around the soundhole. Ted wondered if the museum had paid for the exhibit. He decided not to say anything.

The curator jabbed at his arm with a finger and gestured towards the base of the cabinet. The lighting was so bad that at first he struggled to see what the lady might be indicating. Then he twigged. Beneath the floor of the display itself there was a six-inch plinth of dark wood reaching down to the floorboards. Stooping to look, Ted realised that what he had taken for a straightforward wooden panel was in fact a drawer that ran the whole width of the cabinet; its two brass handles that were set fully three feet apart were so tarnished that they all but disappeared in the shadows of the room. He grunted as he pulled on them – there were no runners; the drawer was set directly onto the floor. Creaking and scraping echoed around the chamber as its dead weight jarred across the boards.

Ted gave a little cry of delight. More papers, dozens upon dozens of them. There had clearly been too many to mount and display. He reached in and, sensing no hostility from the exhibits' guardian, clasped a handful and leafed through fifteen or so sheets of bone-dry, yellow paper. Some pages contained just a line or two; there were a couple of sheets that were completely blank. Nevertheless even in this small sample there were three song lyrics that appeared complete.

'Could I have a copy of these?' he asked at last.

The curator pursed her thin lips. There was no photocopier at the museum, she explained, and items must not be removed from the building. Ted nodded his understanding. With her permission he would copy them down himself, he said, in his new notebook. This solution appeared to be acceptable. With a single nod, the curator turned and left him to his task.

Ted spent the rest of the afternoon transcribing. With no chair to hand, he had set himself gingerly on the wooden floor, working through each paper one by one. It was a slow job. Debreu's handwriting reflected what little Ted knew of his life: chaotic and wayward; the crossings-out and insertions rendered some words illegible, and Ted's French was not up to making educated guesses. After an hour, he realised that he would have to be more disciplined; he would have to stop pausing to marvel, to guess at translations, to remember exactly how each line was sung on record. The curator returned, padding remorselessly up the stairs to bring him a mug of hot coffee. He thanked her extravagantly for the unexpected hospitality, even though the black liquid smelt of rusting metal. She said nothing, offering the merest hint of a nod before turning to retreat to her den.

He put his pen down in the late afternoon. He had ploughed through only one third of the papers, but his wrist ached from scribbling and his eyes were struggling to keep focus. Ted's frame tottered as he rose from the floor, his thighs and knees struggling to readjust to the balance and weight of normal posture. He steadied himself by grasping the edge of the display case, shook his head to encourage the slowly returning circulation and made for the staircase.

The door marked *'Private'* opened before he had a chance to knock. 'Good,' said the curator, examining her visitor. 'I close now.'

'Thank you again,' said Ted, pulling the notebook from his jacket pocket to show her. *'Thank you. Thank you very much.* I will come back.'

The silence that he received in return was interrupted by bells; the church opposite was sounding five o'clock. The chimes were flat and mournful, accentuating the cheerlessness of the corridor and the diminishing afternoon. Ted turned to leave, suddenly alarmed. He had lost track of time and left Daisy all day, wrapped up as he was in his own obsessions. What sort of a carer was he?

'You stay in the town?' The abrupt small talk surprised him as he grasped the door handle.

'No,' he swivelled his head to respond. 'I live ... I am going home now. But thank you again. *Thanks.*'

'Oh.' The woman gave him the slightest of shrugs and turned once more for her refuge.

There was a succession of slow lorries on the main road out of town, and it was almost seven before Ted hastened through the doors of the café, jangling Gaston's keys in his hand. There was no sign of the patron but Philippe was in his usual station behind the bar. He seemed to flinch upon seeing Ted; the boy kept his eyes to the floor as the Englishman handed over the keys and asked for his thanks to be conveyed. Ted was secretly relieved; he owed Gaston a drink for the loan of the car, but his concern for his wife was mounting. Casimir was sat alone on the round table with a bottle of wine that looked near-empty; the old man said nothing, but raised his glass and treated Ted to a peculiar, knowing grin. Ted nodded to him, gestured to his watch and left the building to traverse the village square at a trot.

A bizarre sight greeted Ted as he reached the top of the meadow, huffing and sweating from his haste. One of his first tasks upon their arrival here had been to run a washing line from the awning of the verandah to a pole that he'd planted a short way into the meadow. Now, it was semi-adorned with laundry, and his wife was hopping and stumbling from item to item, shirts and tea towels draped across on her shoulder, occasionally grabbing at the line to save herself from overbalancing.

Ted halted to take a breath. There was a chill on the evening air. 'What the blooming hell are you doing?' He tried to roar the words, but his lungs failed him and they came out as a succession of panted syllables.

Daisy looked round, one tiny slippered foot upon the other, her short arm stretched fully as she clutched the safety of the cord. 'I'm bringing the washing in,' she barked back, thrusting her face forwards to meet his stare head-on. 'What does it look like?'

Ted summoned the energy to stride forward, kicking at the longer grass that grew immediately around the little house. 'For Gawd's sake, why don't you let me do that? And why did you need to do washing anyway?'

'Well, I waited. And I waited. And then I waited some more.'

'I'm sorry. I've been tied up.'

'Help me then.' Ted was surprised by the capitulation, although Daisy's tone was a demand rather than a request. He started to unpeg items, before realising that it would be better to assist his wife to the house first. She took his arm without protest.

'How long did it take you to peg that lot up then?' he asked.

'Ages.'

Despite his fatigue, Ted could hardly feel her weight as he guided his wife across the grass. 'You wouldn't guess what I found today. Hold on – I'll tell you when we get in.'

Setting Daisy on a chair on the verandah, Ted finished retrieving the items, placing the pegs in a small net that hung from the shabby woodwork. When this was done, he unclipped the line from the pole, winding it around a pair of nails that he'd driven into the upright.

'Your friend Gaston's boy came over,' said Daisy. 'He fixed the washing line up for me.'

'Philippe? I saw him just now. He didn't say anything.'

'Well you weren't here, so he left a note.'

Daisy was hauling herself from the chair when she heard the explosion from the kitchen. Edging her way along the railing towards the doorway, her eyes widened to see her crimson-faced husband stomping back and forth as best he could within the confines of the little kitchen, slamming his palm against the chairs whilst he swore at the air and brandished the scrap of paper that the French boy had entrusted her with. Later on, she would gather it from the waste bin and wonder what 'concert arranged, signed – manager' meant.

10

Ric

The boy was in a quandary. The leather biker's jacket, or the hipster look? He tried both, dithering in his attic room, striking poses before a chipped full-length mirror as he studied each wardrobe in critical detail.

'Philippe!' Gaston's voice echoed in the stairwell.

'Oui, oui.' Biting his lip, he settled on the jacket, a frayed and scuffed cast-off that he'd been thrilled to find within his means on the secondhand stalls. Besides, it made a better combination with the mock snakeskin shoes that were too big for him and that protruded out from beneath his drainpipe jeans like canoes. He had a grotesque spot threatening to erupt on his chin; it would be today of all days, and there was no time to deal with it without making things worse. Fuming, he massaged palmfuls of wax into his straw hair then hastily rinsed his hands in the basin as his boss called once more.

Casimir was behind the bar, munching on a toasted sandwich between hefty shots of *la goutte*. Philippe edged past, noting that the disgusting old man had already trodden slices of tomato into the floor. No prizes for guessing who would be clearing those up. Gaston should have closed for a few hours rather than pandering to this geriatric volunteer.

But Marie was there! Sat in the corner in a snug purple mohair top, her big doleful mascara eyes buried in her book. This was more than he could have hoped for. Gaston must be waiting with the car outside. Absent-mindedly tousling his hair, Philippe sidled up, then stood awkwardly as she affected not to notice him.

'You be OK this afternoon with the old man in charge?' he finally said, giving a contemptuous flick of his head towards the bar.

Marie looked up from her pages. 'I am sure I will be OK.'

His heart galloped as he caught a smell of her perfume. 'It's just that with that coffee machine, you do the wrong thing and – boooooom!' Philippe threw out his arms in what was planned as an explosive gesture, but caught the back of a neighbouring chair with his flying knuckles. The impact made him blurt a cry of agony; he flapped his left hand furiously to make the sensation go away.

'Oh.' Marie's eyes returned to the paperback. He craned his head to see the title, blinking away to clear his watering eyes.

'It's just that me and Gaston, we are going to the recording studio.'

'A-hmm.'

Philippe tousled his hair once more and picked at his teeth with a thumbnail. 'Well anyway, I'll see you later.'

'See you.'

Philippe turned and made for the double doors. Casimir shot him a tickled look as he passed, raising his bottle in a salute that he combined with a leery wink. The boy ignored him as he strode past, maddened by the feeling of blood rising around his sallow neck and face.

*

'Will you just sit down for one single second? I can't concentrate.'

Daisy was back at her place on the sofa, her foot raised whilst she fumbled away with two knitting needles.

'Sorry.' Ted parked himself on a chair, stood up again, sat down, stood up and walked to the kitchen to check that his guitar was still there, patted his trouser pocket for the notebook, returned to the lounge, hovered, then sat down once more.

'You've got ants in your pants.'

'Sorry again.' Ted had fully expected to feel nervous about the recording session, but Gaston's imminent arrival was also gnawing at him. The two men had not spoken since the row at the café, when he'd barged through the doors to demand what that note about a concert had meant. It had been a risible confrontation. Gaston's easy manner and calm demeanour had thrown cold water upon Ted's huffing and puffing. The Frenchman had soothed him and understood and offered him a glass of wine. Ted had declined, on the back foot immediately, apologising for his manner, and Gaston had told him that no apology was necessary; Ted had been glad that no offence had been caused. And then they'd talked very briefly about the opportunity that Gaston had heard about. They discussed the date and the time, and the suggestion that Ted could be part of a mixed bill in a very small setting, as a favour to a friend of a friend who was looking for performers, and as a very easy way that Ted might help the café owner.

Ted had assented to a coffee as he had tried to get across just how terrified the idea of playing in front of people made him, and why this would be so different from the previous times that Gaston had seen him pick up a guitar. Even as he had talked, Ted had found himself in a prickly sweat at the thought, picturing these people – even just the handful of fellow Debreu enthusiasts that Gaston had spoken of – watching him with the expectations that came with a paid ticket.

There had been no pressure from the Frenchman for him to change his mind. Yet Gaston had looked so crestfallen at his own insensitivity to Ted's wishes that they had found themselves discussing the practicalities of how the Englishman's nerves might one day be overcome; whether – in general terms – it was good for a man to stand up to his own fears and insecurities; how it was a shame that there were no other performers keeping alive the flame of Frédéric Debreu, this man who had meant so much to the region.

And then he had walked obediently home, having consented to take part, on the condition that Gaston would bring along enough supportive friends to give him some lifeline of comfort, and that he could have a skinful first. The disagreement between the two men had been resolved there and then, and if he was beholden to Gaston for the Frenchman's financial generosity then by no means had he been asked to feel it. So why did he feel that their relationship had changed?

'What are you doing?' Ted blurted out the words, suddenly aware that Daisy was on her feet and progressing limp-by-limp towards the door, clutching on furniture as she went.

'I need my sewing box.'

'Let me get it. Christ alive, will you sit down?'

'I can manage!'

'Will you –' She was at the doorway now, so that he could not push past her. For an instant he thought of physically grabbing his wife, hauling her back into her chair, nailing her down if needs be.

'No, I cannot.' He clenched his fists, glaring as she dragged herself the short distance to the kitchen door. 'I can manage. Besides, your friend's here.'

His uncertainty about their meeting had been silly. The café owner was his usual self; if anything he was going to great lengths to put the Englishman at his ease. He lounged beside Ted in the back seat whilst Philippe drove, the boy clenching the steering wheel in both hands whilst thrusting his head forward to peer at the track ahead.

'OK Philippe, this is what the plan is,' said Gaston, when the vehicle had reached flat tarmac. 'You are to make sure Ted does not worry for anything. If he wants drink, you get him drink. If he wants to eat, you get him that. If he wants strings for the guitar, or sweets for the throat, you get him that.'

'Why can you not do that?' Philippe braked rather too hard as they reached the junction with the main road.

'I am the manager. I am there to manage. I advise; I talk with the producer. You are there to make him not worry about anything. If he needs the toilet you hold it for him.'

The car lurched to the left. 'That won't be necessary,' said Ted.

'I am serious, very serious,' said Gaston. 'We pay the studio for the afternoon, just one afternoon, for less money. We waste time, we get less done. He is not relaxed, he plays less well, he has to do songs again, we get less done.' Gaston turned to Ted. 'You are relaxed?' he demanded.

'Well, relax-ing.'

'Here.' Gaston produced a hip flask. 'To make you relaxed.'

This town was unfamiliar to Ted. Philippe slowed the car as they passed through the outskirts, another mishmash of prefabricated industrial and warehouse units. As the commercial belt gave way to dense housing, Philippe took a street map from the door pocket beside him and, balancing it on his lap, peered from road to page and back again as he crawled through the down-at-heel residential area. Ted tensed as the youth scrutinised the street signs through his side window whilst the car drifted to the centre of the road. Eventually they turned in to an estate of 1960s mid-rise apartments. Philippe pulled over, scepticism written across his face. Even the unflappable Gaston was taken aback.

'This is it?' he said.

Philippe shrugged and indicated the name of the block in front of them. Gaston stared across before pulling out his mobile phone and scrolling through to dial a number. A brief conversation in French followed whilst Ted stared pointedly out of the window.

'How much less money was it then?' he asked, as Gaston pocketed his phone.

They decided to walk, having waited several minutes in a rank-smelling foyer for the lift. Gaston went first, his conviction recovered, bounding up the concrete steps in his spruce jacket and trousers. Ted trailed him, hauling his ample frame one step at a time, pausing at each floor and half-landing to catch his breath and mop his brow with his old handkerchief. Philippe came last, climbing gingerly in his outsize shoes, Ted's guitar in one hand, Gaston's briefcase in the other. Clearly Gaston needed to relax also. The 'studio' was apparently on the eighth floor. On the sixth, even Gaston paused to rest.

Three girls were descending the flight above them. Punks, Ted thought, although he guessed that there was probably a different word these days. The trio wore tattered crop tops, tartan skirts and boots; one had outrageous blue spiked hair and bore a Yamaha keyboard slung over her shoulder; the instrument had been plastered with stickers and graffiti.

'We are in the right place, eh?' said Gaston to Ted as the girls passed them without a word.

A moment later they heard a chorus of snickering and a laughed cry of *'screw you!'* Ted looked down to see Philippe two flights behind, scuttling away from the girls, his head buried in the flapping collars of his jacket. Shaking his head sadly, the big Englishman steeled himself for the final ascent.

The front door was a solid wall of wood. There was no window, no letterbox nor any form of knocker or bell, just the dull brass disc of a Yale lock. The surface had been painted, but many years ago and in a single slapdash coat; in places the grain showed through the thin and greying emulsion. The door frame was chipped and bashed, its edges knocked away in several places. Gaston rapped hard with his knuckles; the noise he made was pitifully soft and dull and could not possibly rouse anybody within. Nevertheless, a bolt was drawn just as the Frenchman was reaching once more for his mobile; the door opened by inches then held fast with a 'clunk' as a trio of security chains engaged. An eye peered through the gap via black, thick-rimmed glasses. Its owner was jabbering in machine-gun French; it took Ted a moment to realise that a phone conversation was taking place and that the words were not addressed to them. They could hear the chains being released and the door swung inward. The man beckoned them through with a jerk of his head. As they squeezed past into the hallway, Ted saw that the door had been reinforced on its inner side with a thick sheet of metal. Forcing it shut and fumbling with his free hand to replace the chains, the man nodded once more, this time towards a door on Ted's right. The big Englishman edged through.

He'd expected some form of lounge, which it was, partially – there was a small sofa and a coffee table adorned with a half-empty pizza box. But opposite, behind a coppice of microphone stands, was a desk with two big screens and a computer; next to this was a keyboard on a stand, and a tower of black hi-fi type boxes that Ted took to be recording equipment. Thick wires snaked everywhere; across the floor, up the walls, into those black boxes. A long fluorescent tube provided light; the window had been blocked off with another slab of sheet metal.

Rather self-consciously, Ted eased himself down onto the sofa. Its cushioning had long gone, so much so that his bottom was almost at floor level before it found some support; he looked up helplessly, a fat man trapped in a bucket. Gaston remained on his feet, out-of-place in this shabby environment, his nose twitching at the reek of stale food.

Philippe entered last, catching the neck of Ted's guitar against the door frame as he sized up the contrasts of technology and torn wallpaper.

'*Rock and roll,*' he muttered.

The man's name was Ric. He joined them once his conversation was finished, making kissing noises into his phone as he entered the room. He chattered with enthusiasm as he cleared space, hauling the microphone stands to one side and unplugging cables that would evidently not be needed for the afternoon's activities. The pizza box was moved with apologies. They learned that the 'studio' was his – or partially his, and partially the credit card company's; that he had once wanted to be a guitarist but had realised that he was a better listener than a player, and that he had more interest in producing. Now he hired himself out to whoever wished to record. ('*Cheaper than others due to the facilities,*' he explained with a wave of his hand.) He sometimes helped local bands for nothing if he liked their music; he had a small regular source of income from an audiobook company (*'not interesting, but pays my bills.'*) Perhaps his recordings would land him a job in a commercial studio; perhaps one of those local bands would be discovered and would remember him. Perhaps.

Ted listened to Gaston's translation, disarmed by the producer's lack of conceit. Then, having dashed across the corridor to boil water for coffee, Ric turned to the Englishman, pulling up a wooden chair to face the artist floundering in the upholstery, posing him questions via Gaston about his music, his background, whether he had ever recorded before. Ric nodded his head vigorously at Ted's responses, which grew less apologetic as the Englishman started to grow in confidence. The producer thanked Philippe – the youth had been ordered by Gaston to finish making the drinks – and explained that he was there to listen, not to direct; that he understood that Ted might be nervous and that he should relax; that he would be making a simple, no-frills recording that could nevertheless be brought to life with some subtle adjustments on his equipment. If one of his producer's tricks was to put his subjects at ease then it had worked on Ted in spades – so much so that when the Englishman was asked to dry-run a song, he positively beamed as he puffed and squirmed himself up from the settee. For all the run-down surroundings, Ted realised that this was a far better environment for him than anywhere large and formal.

Ric faced the wooden chair to the wall and motioned Gaston and Philippe from the room. Ted took his guitar from its case and sat with it, fiddling with strings and tuning pegs until he was satisfied with the sound; plucking and strumming random chords and shapes. The ease was suddenly gone now the conversation had ceased and eyes were upon him. In a cheap frame on the wall before him was a photograph of a dark-haired girl on a sandy beach. Ted centred his vision on this. The sea was a deep, wonderful blue; a holiday-brochure blue. The Caribbean, perhaps, or one of the Greek Islands.

'*OK?*' asked Ric from his position beneath the boarded-up window.

Ted drew breath. 'OK,' he said.

The Englishman leaned forward, his right arm poised over the strings.

'I'll start with an easy one,' he said.

'Easy one, *oui*.'

'OK.'

'*OK.*'

There was an odd expression on the girl's face, as if she had been startled by the photographer's approach. She wore a white T-shirt and the briefest of shorts.

> ♫ *My brush, it's just a brush, it's just an ordinary brush*
> *My palette plain, my canvas cheap and rough*
> *My talent with the pencil it is nothing but inept*
> *My genius, my artistry is making them accept*
>
> *Although the law may misconceive*
> *It is no crime if you believe*
> *Although the law may well lament it*
> *It is no crime if you're contented*
> *Bom bom bom, bom bom bom*
> *Bom bom bom, bom bom bom* ♫

'Wow,' said Ric, as Ted bowed his head.

They recorded five tracks that afternoon – more, the producer told them, than would normally be attempted even for an experienced singer. Ted glowed at the compliment; he was pleased with himself, dead pleased.

Granted, he had practised and practised, and the serendipity of finding those historic lyrics had both helped and inspired him. However, deep down he'd been terrified that he simply would not be able to perform, that he'd stumble over the words, that he'd bugger up take after take after take, ruthlessly exposed for what he was – a stupid Northerner having a stab at the songs of an alien culture. Even his embarrassment at hearing his own voice played back at him had been more than compensated for by the reaction of Gaston and even Philippe. As the playback reached the second verse, the producer started fiddling at his computer keyboard and the music seemed to leap into three dimensions. Ric said that he was very satisfied; he would ideally like an hour's break before listening again afresh to do his polishing. He would send the tracks by email, a CD in the post if they liked.

'Mister Prescott, smile!'

'Get away!' But Ted beamed as Philippe clicked away with the camera on his phone. He was still brimming with elation as the barman drove them home. The day had crowned something off for him: the re-emergence of joy in his life following the battering and bruising of recent weeks.

He had been ungrateful in having a go at Gaston. His friend had done a perfect job of arranging the afternoon: the right studio, the right surroundings; Ted had fulfilled their obligation to the mad American whose dispensation could now be honourably set against Ted's debts. He stole a glance at the café owner, who was pressing his mobile phone to his ear as he tried to get hold of Casimir. Ted might well have been loath to accept Gaston's patronage, but if he was to become an employee once more then he suspected that the Frenchman wouldn't make a bad boss. The little musical evening wasn't greatly his bag, but Gaston had subsequently made noises about teaching him the basics of bar work, and mentioned again the possibility of a formal venture with the mayor. It had been a short retirement, Ted reflected, but needs must.

'Nothing,' muttered the café owner, screwing up his face.

The car surged ahead as Philippe pressed his absurd footwear to the floor.

Gaston had become increasingly agitated about the non-response from the café, yet had insisted upon dropping off Ted before he went to investigate. At the Englishman's bidding, they left him on the lane, beside the gap in the hedge at the foot of the meadow. He would relish the calm of the walk up through the field, a chance to relive, once more, the day just gone.

He hoped the old galoot Casimir hadn't wrecked the place. He'd probably just got trolleyed and left the phone off the hook. As Ted pushed his way through the brambles, he marvelled how that for a strange and unexpected few hours on a September afternoon, his cares had floated away. David's absence; what the future might hold for him and Daisy: it was all abstract; too massive to comprehend. Whereas the little silver disc that was forthcoming, it was a thing, a real thing that he could hold in his hand; an achievement that he could share with his friends, with Daisy, with his son. Perhaps even Eric might hear it one day, those five timeless songs to which his brother had introduced him all those years ago.

His workshop came into view as he reached the ridge of the hill. He pictured the stack of records on the bench. Jake Thackray, Neil Diamond. Barbra Streisand and Georges Brassens, Humphrey Lyttelton, Frédéric Debreu, the great Frédéric Debreu. Well he had joined that list now; he was on that pile; in his own small and silly way, he was one of them.

Ted laughed out loud as he skipped past the outbuilding, bounding up the steps to the cottage. He paused at the kitchen door and turned, gazing out across the meadow to the fields and hills, down upon the village, Debreu's Thorigny Fields framed in the orange sunset. He'd nailed those songs; grabbed them by the throat; got them in the bag and made them his. Now he had to do the same thing in front of an audience. It wouldn't be a breeze, but with today's triumph behind him, what could he possibly be afraid of?

11

The Return

Celal had worked at the hotel for three weeks now, and had reached the conclusion that the hospitality industry was not for him. Having drifted across Europe fuelled by casual work and petty theft, it seemed clear that self-employment was his destiny. Being barked at by sweating Germans and stiff English; treated like a little kid by the fat Greek owner with the personal-hygiene problem; forced to be polite to jerks and being told to go screw himself by the African chambermaid who'd pushed him away with loathing and disgust – no, it was not for him. Celal stalked the corridor with a face like sour milk, stooping to shove free tourist papers into the draught-friendly gaps under the door of each room, little caring when this scrunched up and tore them.

At the door of room thirty-two, he paused mid-shove. An odd noise from within had caught his attention. A grunt, or a snort. No – a grunt, and then another grunt – a man. And a moan, a low moan, a woman's moan. Grunting and moaning – definitely. There were people in there. A couple. Doing it.

Breathing harder, the sharp-faced figure let the ad-sheet slip from his fingers. He crept to his feet and eased his head forward to press his ear against the door. Grunt, grunt, grunt. The noise from the man was steady, rhythmic. 'Mmmmpphhhh' – another moan. Celal felt some awkwardness in his trousers. It was the Scandinavians, he was sure. He had seen them at breakfast the previous day, well-dressed and looking comically out of place in a dump like this; him in his tailored suit, with his finely trimmed beard of silver; she, much younger, with flowing, white-blonde hair and the shortest of pencil skirts. She was a prostitute, she was obviously a prostitute. The woman's voice cried out, the sound unmuffled by the paper-thin door. She was enjoying it, the tart, the slapper! She was loving it!

A clanking from the end of the corridor jolted him back to awareness; the cleaners were starting their rounds. Celal's face flushed at the thought of their mockery should they find him eavesdropping. He cantered in the opposite direction, his mind lingering on thoughts of the blonde girl being serviced on the double bed, perhaps on the floor. The youth's heart was now beating swiftly at the image. As he reached the next door, he had an idea. Ditching his newspapers in a heap outside a laundry cupboard, he hastened along to the fire door. Pushing through, he found himself in an unused lobby and thence to the grim courtyard onto which those rooms faced. He skipped past the window of room thirty-six; room thirty-five was closed due to a flood; rooms thirty-four and thirty-three were unoccupied. This one would be room thirty-two, and there was a gap in the draped curtains, THERE WAS A GAP IN THE CURTAINS! He took a breath, a deep, deep breath and held it there – first consciously, and then because his mind was too tied up to remember to continue breathing. He could feel his hands quivering; the pumping of his heart was near-unbearable.

Now oblivious to discovery, or humiliation, or the sack from a job that he despised, Celal shuffled forwards, screwed up one eye and pressed his face directly against the cold and weather-stained glass. It took his vision a short while to adjust and enable him to focus on the bed, so it was a full half-second before he staggered back. The wind exploded from him, his jaw slackened and shoulders fell, his paralysed young brain attempting to process a vision that would stay with him for the rest of his life.

Jenny lifted herself to a sitting position within the bed, reaching down for the duvet from where it had half-fallen onto the carpet.

She pulled it over her legs and tummy, leaving her breasts exposed. Stan Wainwright did not reply; lifting a bath towel from the floor, he draped it over himself, awkwardly lifting his bottom as he drew it underneath, wrapping it tightly so that he could trot to the bathroom without his wife catching an embarrassing glimpse of his retreating privates.

'I need to check the screenwash before we leave,' he called from the en-suite, safely shielded from view as he dabbed away with toilet paper. 'One of the jets was low. I don't want to be on the motorway and not be able to clean the windscreen.'

Jabbing a thin finger at the button to flush the toilet, Wainwright re-parcelled himself and emerged back into the bedroom to find his white underpants. The act of donning them without dropping the towel required a wriggling agility that caused him to struggle and mutter, but Jenny seemed to be unfazed by the performance, staring at the ceiling with no expression.

'We can always pick some up at a garage,' Wainwright said.

With his pants safely in place, the thin man dropped his towel and cantered across to the dressing table for his remaining clothes. His progress was interrupted by a beeping from his trouser pocket. Lifting his carefully folded slacks, he took his phone and examined it, not recognising the number that had popped up, his mind working methodically through potential senders before he went on to press the button.

'It's the lad from that bar,' he said. 'Daisy's had an accident.'

*

Every muscle in Ted's body ached from the rusting and squeaky camp bed that the farmer had lent him. He had taken himself into the spare bedroom on the first night, in order to allow Daisy to spread herself out in as much space as possible, and to ensure that he didn't roll on her leg in the night. But now that spare room was occupied once more by the Wainwrights, the good Wainwrights, who had driven back across the country to answer his cry for help.

He tried to blink himself awake, but the exhaustion was too heavy-set to brush aside. His eyes were tender and sore; his head was both painful and woolly, as if his thoughts were clumping around amidst a thick fog. How much sleep had he managed? Two, three hours? His mind had been clear enough as it raced with worry: that the doctors had glossed things over; that they had misdiagnosed; that they had missed something significant. Worry about the practicalities of looking after her. And guilt, that he should have been firmer, that somehow he could have forced her to be a bit more sensible; to rest and not to flit around like she was in her bloody twenties again.

Ted cursed himself as he peed to the sound of the cockerel bellowing up on the farm. He cursed himself as he padded into the kitchen to start the tea ritual, as he pulled the curtain aside to check the weather, as he stumbled over Stan sodding Wainwright's sodding canvas shoes that had been discarded in front of the fridge. He pushed open the kitchen door; the chill, dewy air hit his face and he cursed himself once more.

Jenny had been calm and sympathetic and reassuring; Stan full of the excitement of crisis, keen to make Ted aware of how lucky it was that this had happened before their return home, adamant that changing their itinerary had not been a problem whilst keen to impress upon the household that their plans were now in tatters. Even as Jenny had fixed them some supper, made up the beds and assisted Daisy in some unspecified women's task, Ted had felt like bashing his fat head against the wall as he recalled his panicked assent to Philippe's suggestion that he contact his English friends. Philippe! The clueless youth with his cock where his brain should be had been worried about this stupid old bugger not coping on his own.

In a grimly strange way, it had been a good day for Monsieur Patenaude to give him the new letter. The cheerless farmer had stopped by on his cycle back from town. Ted's panic, his uselessness, the practicalities and the questions – there hadn't been the time to indulge in anything but a matter-of-fact acknowledgement of the confirmation from the legal people:

that things were concluded, final, that was it; that he had lost their money; their future was settled now and there would be no option but to accept and to get on with it. Even if there was a 'helpline' to ring in case of any queries. This sanguinity had lasted until the tumult had died down, until he was sat with her late into the night, her face grey, her chest barely moving with each breath, as tiny as a doll in the hospital bed. 'Sorry, I'm so sorry.' He had murmured the words as he had cradled her hand, tears welling in his eyes at his stupidity and his betrayal, repeating over and over as she slept, oblivious to the crushed shell of her husband beside her.

The backlash of anger had hit him the following day, as she had reclaimed her wits from the haze of the strong painkillers, and he had begun to cautiously believe the reassurance of the doctors. He'd had to force himself not to rail at her pig-headed idiocy as he wheeled her from the hospital to the taxi. He'd kept it in check whilst he focused on being grateful for the procession of friends and neighbours – yes, even the Wainwrights – who had been so helpful. Well this was another day, and, however unfairly, his appreciation for his house guests was plummeting once more. Ted lashed out with his foot, sending one of Wainwright's shoes flying across the tiles.

Minute bubbles started to rise from the base of the saucepan; he set out four mugs on the table then turned away and pulled open the kitchen door. He stood in the chill of the doorway, trying to breathe regularly, his bare toes poking across the threshold onto the damp wood outside. The cockerel wailed once more.

He willed himself not to go through the told-you-sos once more as he fumbled with the pillows and bundled Daisy upright so that she could sip her tea. He had told her to be sensible, told her to rest. He had told her and he had told her and he had bloody told her. His anger melted at her grimace of pain as he moved her legs. How could somebody that small and feeble be so stubborn?

Well, she would have to bloody rest now.

He donned his boots to walk down to the village. He needed air, and solitude, and sanity; he needed to escape the four walls as they edged inexorably inward. His pretext was that they needed supplies: bread and milk and whatever else might occur to him on the spur of the moment. Jenny seemed to understand; she headed off Wainwright's offer to drive him by insisting that her husband was needed to help make a practical list of Daisy's needs. Ted was impressed by the psychology. He caught her eye as he reached for the door. She returned his gaze and he looked away, flushing.

As he was about to leave, Ted hesitated then swung round to return to the bedroom. Daisy was dozing, and registered nothing as he reached for the hidden folder. Pulling it down, he concealed it within his jacket. He padded back through the kitchen making non-committal 'won't be long' noises.

Gaston's apartment was antiseptic and well-ordered, all sparse and modern in contrast to the fading grandeur of the bar. Ted studied it whilst he was kept on hold by the automatic switchboard. Had there ever been a Mrs Gaston, he wondered? The café owner had never spoken of his personal life. The only woman about the place was Mme Kerharo, who did the cooking, and she was about 103. The place was certainly kept tidy, but perhaps it was simply never used. After all, the Frenchman's day-to-day front room – his space for living and entertaining – lay the other side of that connecting door.

The 'helpline' was as helpful as Ted had envisaged. They asked his name and some questions for security, although he had no idea what he had left to secure. The lady was polite, and sounded genuinely sorry, but could do nothing. Having dialled the number with no expectations, Ted felt no slump of disappointment. He had simply needed a human being to tell him what was clear amidst the gibberish of the legal letter: that he was a nobody; that his relationship with his son counted for nothing; that his money had been just lines on a page; a drop in the financial ocean that had been pissed away in a business that nobody had understood.

He felt strangely at peace as he emerged from the apartment. He'd once read of folk who had experienced a wave of serenity upon hitting rock bottom; perhaps this was happening to him. But it didn't feel as if he'd lost everything. He'd not lost Daisy, although they'd had a scare; she would be herself again before too long and they'd get through this together. And – after insisting that she was unable to discuss anything other than his own situation – the lady had taken pity on his entreaties and looked through her computer files. David had spoken to their office the previous week. No, she could not reveal his contact details. But this meant that he was … well – that he had not disappeared completely. Ted would hear from him soon. He surely would.

In this state of semi-awareness, it took him a few seconds to grasp that something was amiss in the bar. Gaston and the mayor were sitting at the round table exchanging no words, the mayor cradling the ample flesh of his chins in both fists, propping his morose face, with his elbows on the table. There was no sign of Casimir. Shaking his head to clear his thoughts, and registering once more the rampaging spiderweb of cracks that engulfed the plate glass of the ruined front windows, Ted wondered whether the old man might have been banned.

Philippe pushed past him on to the stairs. 'Piss-stained one-horse town.'

Seeing the Englishman in the doorway, Gaston rose, adopting a smile that was far from his usual easy beam. 'You OK Ted, the call is done?'

'Thanks Gaston. I just needed to speak in private, that's all.'

Ted made a show of reaching for his trouser pocket and producing some coins, which Gaston dismissed with a wave of the hand. Then, placing his palms together and exhaling sharply, as if to expel bad spirits, the Frenchman seemed to claw back his old facade. Within two strides he was at the bar. 'Wine, Ted,' he said.

'Can't. They're expecting me back.'

'Oui, go on. We need wine, I think. All of us.' Behind him, the mayor gave a grunt. Ted visualised the trudge up the hill and the situation that awaited him at home.

'All right then. Thank you.'

'Philippe!' Gaston beckoned at the youth, who had re-entered with a pile of clean napkins.

Ted stepped across to the table. He had never experienced the café as anything other than a joyous place. He momentarily despised his friends for picking this particular moment to forgo their usual supportive camaraderie. Disgusted by his selfish thought, he pulled up a chair. 'Is everything all right? Have you had some bad news?'

The mayor smiled without mirth. 'Bad news, *oui,*' he said.

Gaston resumed his seat, waiting for Philippe to pour wine, which the boy did without a word. 'The little airport at Pontcerf, it was to expand,' the café owner said, drumming his fingers on the table as he spoke. 'It would take international flights, you understand, the EasyJets. Now, it will not happen.'

'It is the interfering European Community! They bloody interfere!' exploded the mayor, making Ted leap in surprise and causing wine to flood down his chin and on to his shirt front. 'The European Community,' the official repeated, the momentary pause whilst he translated to English drawing the sting of his fury. 'They wish to interfere in our decisions. French decisions, *commune* decisions.'

Ted tried to picture the airport concerned. He had driven past it a few times; an aerodrome he'd have called it. In fact it was little more than a field, used, he had presumed, for hobbyists and the occasional internal jaunt. 'Was it important?' he asked, embarrassed at the fatuousness of the question as soon as the words had left his mouth.

The mayor blew air into his cheeks clasping his hands together as he sought the words to explain. 'Some tourists come here, OK. Some with the second homes also, they do the journey. But there are other places more easy. If there is the airport near the region then the British take the empty houses. They come into town, they open their wallets, they spend, we have businesses, we have jobs.'

'Ah. I'm afraid I don't have much of a wallet to open.'

Gaston gave Ted's shoulder a pat. 'You are a valuable resident and employee. One of us. Look. Look at this place. I am OK. I have the regular customers, and we are busy at some times with some tourists, but we are also not busy some of the time.' Ted's eyes followed Gaston's gesture; the bar was empty apart from his companions and one elderly man nursing a coffee and a newspaper. 'I have Madame Kerharo who cooks well and who is cheap, and I employ Philippe because I promised his poor father and,' – his voice rose to a shout, directed at the youth leaning on the bar – *'because nobody else would employ him because he does not set the tables quickly enough!'* Philippe hastened to distribute his napkins.

'We survive,' said the mayor. 'But, but, but! You see it with your eyes. People, they leave because there is nothing here. The young people, to go to the cities. All to go to the cities. Why stay? Marie and Celine, they are clever. They go to the city, they have good jobs, good husbands. Why stay?'

'In your dreams, boy,' Gaston called across the room.

'They move the *college* to Paris. Paris!' The mayor spat out the word. 'And our country, it has changed. The farming, the industry. There is no point to this town now unless there are the tourists. Without the tourists it becomes just a shit town that was important before. Me, I do not want to be mayor of a shit town that was important before.'

'I'm sorry,' said Ted. 'We have those in England as well.'

*

He pulled the blankets over his wife, letting them rest with delicacy as if their weight might crush her ribs. Plodding to the kitchen for a mug of water, he could hear the Wainwrights fussing and bickering in the spare room. He bumped into Jenny as he made to cross the tiny corridor back to Daisy; they danced awkwardly before Ted backed himself against the wall to let her squeeze past, her body pressing against his as she went through. She giggled. Her nightdress smelt of wild flowers.

Placing the drink on the table next to the bed, he pulled the door shut and perched on the edge of the bed. It strained and sagged with his bulk.

'How've you been today?' he asked.

Daisy raised her eyebrows to consider this. 'Well, apart from not being able to walk, and having to have everything done for me, and being carried from room to room, and being talked to like a halfwit child, I'd say I'm fine.'

He ground his teeth. 'No, how are you really?'

'I'd say I'm really fine.'

Ted let it rest, casting his eyes about the room in silence, letting his feet absent-mindedly fidget a drumbeat against the floorboards.

'You won't be able to come when I play,' he said.

'I'll be with you in spirit.'

Ted dropped his voice. 'Have you mentioned anything to them about it?' He gestured with his thumb towards the wall that separated the two bedrooms.

'Them?'

'Stan and Jenny.'

'Why are you whispering?'

'What?'

'Why are you whispering?'

'Because of them.' Ted hissed the final word. 'They'll still be with us.'

'What?'

Ted's shoulders sagged. 'Because although I hate doing things like that, I was hoping that it would be some sort of nice evening of Freddie Debreu fans, and it won't be if I have Derbyshire's bloody Ronnie Scott there.'

'Who?'

'So I pulled Brian Epstein aside and said "there's this band from Liverpool you ought to check out. There a bit rough round the edges but show potential. And then Mick Jagger's mother's sister –"'

Daisy's eyes were almost closed. 'Will you give that a rest for once in your life?'

Ted picked at the dirt under his fingernails. 'I'm sorry you can't come, love. Really sorry. I thought it would be a bit of a night out for you. A treat.'

Ted reached across to stroke her hair. The thought of playing without her moral support did not faze him. She wasn't one to mingle and had old-fashioned ideas about women in bars; even in full health, she'd have given him extra things to think about on an evening that would be nerve-racking enough as it was. But being able to share this odd little experience had been one of its few attractions. It had kept him positive about the prospect, even as the impetus he'd gained from the recording studio had begun to fade.

'I'm sorry, too. You'll be very good, I'm sure. They all enjoy your playing.' Her mouth hardly moved as she smiled, but the faint squeeze that she gave his hand told him everything.

Ted gave a scornful tut, trying not to reveal his pleasure. Wishing her a good night, he rose and padded through to the living room to set up the camp bed.

They tried to take Daisy for a walk the next morning, but the hospital-issue wheelchair was no match for the meadow grass, and when they turned round to attempt the track it was clear that the bumps and potholes would be ruinous for her bones, even had they not first pitched her head-first into the dirt.

She muttered and groused as they retraced the hundred or so yards to the far side of the house, Ted hauling the chair backwards as delicately as he could. He parked her on the patch of shorter grass where the washing line stood, and went with Wainwright to fetch chairs from the kitchen so that they could all sit together in the sun.

'You almost shook me to bits.'

Wainwright patted her good knee. 'You were loving it.'

Ted pointed up the meadow towards the farmhouse. 'Stan, there's a broken barrow in the outhouse up there. If you stick Jenny in that, well, we could organise a race.'

Jenny pulled a face of mock-indignation. Daisy exploded in a torrent of irascibility. The men roared as she aimed a finger at each of them in turn, before her own face cracked and she joined in with the laughter.

She asked for a nap after lunch, and they left her on the sofa to take a walk. Ted took them to the very top of the track, then forked left into a field that was home to a dozen or so bedraggled Friesians. The gate was riddled with corrosion; he had to lift and drag it to one side, the hinges having fallen away to nothing. The cattle followed them with dull eyes as they passed through, Jenny wallowing in the sun and scenery, Wainwright hopping and dancing, his gaze fixed to the grass lest his hiking boots should be sullied by the outrage of a misplaced cowpat.

Ted heaved the gate back into position and jogged to catch up with his friends. The circuit they were taking was familiar, but the dynamics of the threesome seemed awkward and alien in a way that he could not put his finger upon; without Daisy, Ted felt somehow estranged from these people whom he had known for decades. They clambered over a low stone wall into a second field, this one free of livestock, and tramped up through the long grass to the brow of the hill. The wind hit them as they reached the top, but the gusts were refreshing against the warmth of the afternoon and the exertion of their climb.

'Isn't it beautiful?' Jenny lowered herself to the ground, stretching out her legs as she sat and drank in the view of the village that nestled in the hollow amidst the woodlands. Ted nodded as he followed her gaze, picking out the snaking roads, the terracotta rooftops, his eyes searching for the places that were familiar to him. He parked himself down beside her.

'I can see why, well – you know,' she said.

'Ach. Lots of bloody gorgeous places over here, or that's what they say, anyway. This one just seemed a bit more real.'

'What, because of your Eric?'

Ted shrugged. 'Not greatly. But – I mean, yes, in that I'd not have heard of it otherwise, and never would have found it.' He picked a clover leaf and toyed with it between his fingers. 'Same with the Debreu connection, if you like. Which was Eric's fault anyway.'

Wainwright scuffed away some rabbit droppings with the toe end of his boot and joined them on the grass. He glanced his head towards a thin copse a hundred yards or so along the ridge. 'What are those – ash trees? They look like ash. Good firewood, that.'

Ted pointed down the hill. 'No idea who owns the land, but you can walk down there to the woods then come into the village from the north,' he said. 'It's about a mile and a half. More to the point, a mile-and-half downhill. Don't want to lose too much weight.' He patted his belly. 'But normally I just turn round and follow the wall. It takes you back to the track, about halfway down.'

'It must be odd, though. Thinking that he still might be around here. Eric, I mean.'

Ted turned to Jenny, but she was looking at him with such intensity that he turned away again, flustered. 'To be quite honest, well I suppose it's something I've thought about, and I've had a bit of a root around, but it's not something that's really haunted me, if you get my drift. It's just – well, he's like someone from another world, now.' Even as he spoke, Ted thought of his trips out: to the isolated cottage on the main road, to the town named after the elephant. A melancholy descended upon him at the realisation that these forays had led to nothing; he was suddenly more affected now, sat here on this windy hilltop, than he had been at those places themselves. Well, his mind had been churning with everything else. 'It would be good to see him again.' His voice was almost a murmur.

'You've got no sign of that dieback on them. That's good.'

'What?'

Wainwright pointed his finger at the copse. 'The ash dieback disease. It wilts the end of the leaves first, before the tree goes. There was a TV programme on it before we came away.'

'No idea. Perhaps they don't have it here.'

Wainwright shook his head. 'No, it's all across Europe. If you don't have it here then you're lucky. Funny thing was, one of the experts that they interviewed on the programme, just a young lad he was, but he knows all about fungal diseases and what have you, in plants. Well his parents live just about a mile away from us, in the big houses on the edge of Bakewell.'

A strong gust blew dust up around them, causing Ted to shield his eyes with his palms. Jenny rose to her feet. 'Come on. I'm getting chilly now.'

The noise of a car drew Ted's attention. He had risen early the next morning, pulled on his clothes and slipped outside with a view to a much-needed rehearsal prior to Gaston's evening. It had been the first time that he had picked up his guitar for some days, and he had struggled to get his fingers going. He had felt furtive, sneaking out like this, and this in turn had made him self-conscious, even in the familiar comfort of his workshop. Another fitful night on the camp bed had not helped his concentration, and his clumsy hands and wavering vocals had piled on the conviction that he had made a dreadful mistake in agreeing to play for the café owner's friends. He forced himself to complete his song, stumbling over the words to the final verse. Too fast. He had started the introduction too fast.

Stepping into the daylight, he saw Gaston's car parked by the oak tree. But it was Philippe who he found in the kitchen, a mug of tea being prepared for him by Jenny. The boy mumbled his thanks as the older woman fussed over him, his eyes alighting upon the Englishman with gratitude.

'Morning!' Ted eyed the teapot; he had forsaken his early-morning cuppa in his eagerness to get going. 'Is she awake yet?'

Jenny shook her head and reached for a new mug. Wainwright appeared in the kitchen doorway. 'Bonjour! Bonjour, mon-sure barman!'

Jenny handed Ted his tea. 'Philippe says that you're going to be playing at a show?'

'I am very sorry Monsieur Prescott,' mumbled the youth as they walked back to Gaston's car.

Already, Ted was contrite at the furious tone that he had used on the hapless barman, and the succession of belligerent gestures that had gone sailing over Wainwright's head. 'No, no.

Not your fault. I should have warned people to keep quiet.'

Philippe pulled open the door. 'Gaston, he asks if you can come to the café this morning to help with the damage from when the old man is in charge. But not if Missus Prescott is bad.'

'No, no. He's the boss now. I'll be there.'

The barman turned the ignition key, but hesitated, looking up at the big Englishman through the open window. 'Mister Prescott, the show that you will play tomorrow, when you describe it to your friends ...'

Ted peered down into the driver's seat, suddenly on full alert. 'What?'

'Uh – you are talking about small, but it is a big club, you know, Mister Prescott.'

Ted leaned forward, his face filling the window, his breath scalding the young barman's cheek.

'How big, exactly?' he growled.

12

Django's Club

'Supportive friends,' had been his condition to Gaston, and the café owner had agreed to close for the night so that Ted might have his circle around him.

But Stan Wainwright?

His nerves had been intensifying from the very moment that he had released the reluctant Philippe from his inquisition. A big club: that was what the lad had said; Gaston had told him the opposite, although perhaps this had been Ted's own inference; he could not remember the actual words that had been used. Agitated, he had undertaken a further rehearsal session in the workshop. It had been desperately unsatisfactory. He could not seem to recapture the natural flow of these songs that he'd been playing for decades; even when he got through one with no mistakes it had seemed wooden, as if he were a newcomer sight-reading from printed music. The interruptions didn't help: Jenny asking if he wanted tea or coffee; Wainwright poking his head round the door to 'om-pom' in a monotone along with the choruses.

Why could he not get to grips with this pressure? He had managed to relax for that recording session, and that had been in the most unnatural of circumstances. It was the product of that day in the shabby studio that kept his self-belief from deserting him entirely. Philippe had brought the CD that had arrived in the post, a nondescript silver disc with Ted's name scrawled across the reverse. The only player available had been in Wainwright's Mercedes; they had carried Daisy across and listened in there. The five songs had leaped at them with the joy

147

of their performance, fighting their way through Ted's trauma, offering a glimmer of hope that he might be up to the task ahead. Even Wainwright had been complimentary. 'Is this you, you old bugger? Naah – it's not you.'

He thought back with a renewed admiration at how Gaston and the producer had put him at his ease, and even if the café owner seemed to have pulled a fast one with regards to how he had described the evening ahead, Ted could still have some optimism that his friend wouldn't simply leave him to sink or swim. Gaston would have to use all his powers to free him from this mental straitjacket. That, or he was going to have to have a hell of a lot to drink.

Ted gave his wife the lightest of kisses on the forehead, his knees protesting as they cranked him down to the level of the sofa.

Her face was tired, but she gave him a half-smile. 'I won't say "break a leg,"' she said.

'Thank you. I'll try not to.' Ted held on to the upholstery, wobbling as he squatted. He held his position for some time, partly to spare his joints the pain of rising, partly unwilling to let go of this final bit of security for the evening.

She seemed to read his thoughts. 'I'm glad you've found people to do your music with. I always said you should. Go on now; you'll be fine.'

A nasal voice called from beyond the doorway. 'You coming then?'

In the kitchen, Jenny handed him his coat. She had refused to join the men on their evening out, despite Daisy's insistence that she could cope on her own. 'Don't have too much wine again,' Jenny said. 'Or if you do, keep still this time when I'm getting your trousers off.'

Ted avoided her eye.

It was picking up the guitar that set him off. It felt like an alien device in his hands. He replaced the instrument on its stand before grasping it once more to weigh it up, to check that it was what he thought it was. Slowly, with infinite care and prevarication, he nestled it in its soft case, pulling the zip closed tooth-by-tooth.

Wainwright thumped him on the back. 'Ready then?'

'Where is this bar anyway?' The beaky man panted as he trotted half a pace behind, Ted having decided that the best way to overcome the apprehension was to mask it with a steely bullishness. 'And who are these other musicians you're meeting?'

Ted marched grim strides through the grass, his fist clenching and unclenching, swinging the guitar back and forth in its case. Keeping his eyes firmly to the floor, Ted tried to betray nothing but matter-of-factness as he relayed an updated explanation: that they were off to a club, a big club, a club that would be paying good money for him to play, up there, on a stage.

'Ha!'

Ted had known that the laugh was coming.

'Hahahahahaha!'

The big man strode on.

'You brown your pants playing for two men and a dog in a pub!'

Ted grunted responses without turning his head as Wainwright fired delighted observations at him. He quickened his pace as they reached the ridge and the meadow began its downhill slope. The pair were almost jogging as they reached the bottom of the hill.

'What do they use for rotten fruit and veg over here anyway?'

Ted put in an extra-long pace to ensure that he reached the gap in the hedge ahead of his companion. He had hacked back the undergrowth when he'd first discovered the shortcut, but that had been back in May, and the prickles and thorns and barbs had gradually reasserted themselves. Ted edged himself through in the manner that he'd practised many times before, squeezing in his shoulders and elbows. He held his guitar case out front as an additional shield.

There was a yelp from behind him as Wainwright became ensnared. Ted indulged himself in a grim smile and strode on towards town.

Ted had never seen the café dark like this of an evening. The men mingled on the pavement as they waited for Casimir, Ted hopping from foot to foot in his tension, Wainwright complaining in loud and deliberate English about the cuts and scratches on his arms. The old man arrived eventually, careening across the square in his worn-out Ford, the beaten-up hatchback coming to rest face-on to the café, one wheel up on the kerb. Its driver beckoned towards the passenger door. It was Wainwright who responded to the wizened hand, opening his arms and smiling as if he were greeting an old friend; he took a moment to demonstrate his wounds before fumbling for the seat belt. Ted looked to the heavens in gratitude that he would be spared his fellow Englishman's company for the journey ahead.

Philippe was to drive their car. It was important, Gaston explained, for the manager to be able to take a drink with the concert promoter. There was a brief argument about this, which Ted failed to follow. The decision was not overturned and the boy stomped around to the driver's seat. As the artiste, and the fattest of the quartet, Ted was given the passenger seat. The mayor and Gaston settled in the back. The car leaped away, Philippe stamping on the throttle, the bump and thud of tyres across cobbles raising the noise level even in Gaston's well-insulated motor. Above the din, Ted could still hear his heart.

Ted had not previously spoken about his discovery of the exhibits in Saint-Ouen. Keen to keep his focus away from the forthcoming performance, he brought up the topic as they crossed the river, explaining how Debreu's papers had helped him to newly understand the musician. He was surprised when his throwaway remark led to an interrogation that became heated. The mayor was evidently ignorant of the museum, although it had hardly appeared newly established. The official prodded the Englishman repeatedly on the shoulder as he ranted from the back seat about other towns stealing an association with Debreu. Would Paris set up a museum because Debreu's father once went there by bus? Ted was taken aback and found himself defending the curious little institution, pointing out that the Debreu display was all but incidental to its purpose, a small corner of the very farthest room. This seemed to mollify his inquisitor, who apologised for his passion, brushing away imaginary fingermarks on Ted's shirt. Ted was gracious in response. It was good for him to see at first hand how much the great singer meant to the village. And the exchange had eaten up a solid five minutes that he might otherwise have spent brooding. The car lapsed into silence, which was not so good.

Ted's plan was to be humble. There was a clear danger in an Englishman presuming to present these quintessentially French anthems. Ted figured that if it was made very clear to the audience how much the music meant to him then he might be forgiven the small matter of nationality. He had no qualms about sucking up to the crowd; his enthusiasm would be genuine, and his sincerity would come across. To that end, he had scrawled a few words about each song. He had had no time to translate to the French, but had figured that if he kept it very simple then some in the audience would have enough English to at least catch the sentiment. 'This song is about a man who is in love with a woman who he cannot have. It has a wonderful chorus.' If this ate up some of his time on stage then so much the better.

He had performed one single gig in his life. It had been fifteen, possibly twenty years previously, at a fête in aid of the local church. Some neighbours had talked him into it; they had framed the request so that he could not possibly say no. Daisy had encouraged him. She was into all that village community malarkey at the time. They had installed him at the edge of the lawn, beside a trestle table from which old ladies were serving tea and scones. There may have been a couple of dozen people sat eating and drinking, none paying any special attention to the reluctant troubadour in their midst, although they had clapped politely at the conclusion of each song.

He remembered that he had been taken aback by his own nervousness. He had always known that he was bashful about playing to people, but this had been the first inkling of actual fright. It was stupid; silly and stupid. He had completed the engagement, smiling weakly as the vicar had thanked him in his speech, referring to Ted for some reason as 'our own John Denver.' It had been an interesting experience, but the following year he had deliberately booked their summer holiday to coincide.

He thought of all this as the car surged towards La Croix de Jouance. It was beginning to get dark and the butterflies were churning in his stomach.

'I have this for you, Ted,' said Gaston, 'for your souvenir.' Leaning forward, the café owner passed a sheet of paper over Ted's shoulder.

Ted peered, holding it close to read. Philippe reached up and switched on the courtesy light without a word.

The sheet was a handbill, from a club called Django's. A souvenir indeed. Four shows were listed, with dates and the names of the artists appearing. He scanned the page for his own name.

'SEPTEMBER 19 – Édouard PRESCÔTE, guitar. The songs of Frédéric Debreu.'

Philippe kept his eyes on the road ahead.

It took Ted some moments to realise the implications.

'The audience want to see Édouard,' explained Gaston, in the face of the tornado that followed.

Ted jabbed his thumb onto the seat belt release so that he could turn round to give the café owner the full benefit of his broadside. His face bulging with agitation, he thrust the handbill directly into the Frenchman's face. 'For pity's sake! For pity's sake!' he clamoured. 'What the bloody hell are you doing?' He stared at his friend with wild eyes, Gaston's calm demeanour only serving to further enrage. 'I mean, for the – the bloody ...' He took a deep breath as he tailed off into a homicidal glare.

'Ted, it is not a big deal, no, no. You do the show as Édouard, they pay the money. It is the deal. Debreu, his songs can be sung only by a Frenchman.'

Ted continued to boggle, panting hard and fast, not trusting himself to respond.

'This is true,' said the mayor, breaking his diplomatic silence. Ted's head twitched further round. They were in this together.

'But we're not going to get away with ...' he spat.

'It will be no problem,' said Gaston. 'It is a good audience. There will be some English there, the tourists. Mostly French. It is a place of class, not rough.' Philippe slowed the car as they approached a crossroads. *'Left here,'* Gaston murmured to the driver. *'Maybe half a kilometre down, at the old slaughterhouse.'*

'Stop the car. Stop the bloody car.'

'We cannot let them down, Ted. All the arrangements.'

'I have cancelled my cards game,' confirmed the mayor, nodding in solemn agreement. Ted stared at him with incredulity; even Gaston shot his companion a sharp glance. The interjection caused Ted to lose his thread; he felt his broad shoulders rise and fall as his lungs regained their composure and he struggled to pick up the momentum of his thoughts once more. It was too late. He heard the scrunch of gravel as the young barman pulled in to a car park. They came to rest in a far corner, away from the brightly lit concrete building that was presumably the club. There was silence as Philippe killed the engine, then a second scrunch as Casimir's vehicle drew in beside them.

'They'll lynch me when they find out,' breathed Ted.

'They will not find out. How will they find out? You say

nothing. You sing in French like at the festival and at the café. And you are good at singing. Very good.'

'Very, very good.' The mayor's head bobbed up and down in the half-light.

Gaston placed a reassuring hand on Ted's forearm. 'Ted, the owner of this club; he will become a man of importance if his business is a success. I try hard to solve your problems. I am now to disappoint him?'

Ted went cold. A newly horrible thought had struck him.

'Wainwright. You really think he'll play along with all this guff? Eh?'

'Do not worry, Ted. Casimir, he will explain to him on the journey.'

Philippe appeared at the passenger door, pulling it open for Ted before withdrawing at pace to a safe distance. The Englishman climbed from the car, tottering slightly as his feet met the ground. Wainwright was already standing on the far side of Casimir's little Ford, leaning across the roof with folded arms and a monstrous grin across his pointed face.

'Ha! Haha!' he chortled. 'Hahahahahaha!'

Django's smelt of paint and new carpet. The party trooped into the bar area, Gaston striding ahead, Ted stumbling as if in a trance, Philippe bearing the guitar and Gaston's briefcase, keeping a cautious distance from the pair. Outside, the mayor and Casimir had remained in order to doubly impress the sensitivity of the situation upon Wainwright, whose bearing had approached hypermania. The bar was not full; there were perhaps thirty people gathered there, but the low ceiling and stark acoustics made the room echo with chatter. Adding to this, a steady rumble of noise came from a set of double doors opposite the main entrance. Ted couldn't stop himself; he veered across to peer through.

Within was an old industrial space; no amount of redecoration could hide that. The pipes and ducting had been painted the same beige as the walls, with the steel girders that supported the ceiling emphasised in a dull burgundy. In contrast to that of the bar, this ceiling was thirty feet high or more, lending the room the air of a vault and making the circular tables that dotted the floor seem microscopic. There were probably fifty of these, about one-quarter of them already occupied by drinkers.

'It's bloody huge!' Ted swung round to confront Gaston, who had followed him to the doors and placed an arm around his shoulder.

'Sh! *Non, non!* Shh!' His companion quelled him with a stare. Ted shook his head and muttered something, but turned back to his peep-hole, drawn by the inescapable horror within.

He tried to collect his thoughts. Ted had been envisaging some sort of formal auditorium setting, with seating facing the stage. But with all those tables – might it be that the performers would be there to quietly complement a night's eating and drinking, rather than to be the focus of events? Could this provide a crumb of reassurance? Beneath his panic, he could feel some sort of fight-or-flight reflex kicking in. He was beginning to calculate. There was a second bar area to the right of the inner room; many people were clustered around this. Presumably this facility would remain open whilst the musicians played? That would mean that there wouldn't be dead silence as a backdrop? On the opposite side to the doors was the stage, an area raised waist-high that could easily accommodate a large jazz band. The whole space seemed horribly over-lit. Ted's eyes darted from side to side. A man trotted up some steps onto the stage, carrying with him a bunch of electrical leads. He looked like a dwarf up there.

Ted felt a pat on his shoulder. *'Édouard, meet Monsieur Richepin.'*

Monsieur Richepin was a stubby man in his late forties. He wore a formal black jacket over simple T-shirt; his hair was gelled into a broom of dark spikes. Ted felt a strong grasp on his hand; he allowed it to be shaken whilst he looked at the floor, at the walls, at the ceiling, at his own arm.

'*Édouard! Monsieur Prescôte! Frédéric Debreu, oui, oui!*' The promoter spoke with a voice of slick bonhomie, as if he had just arrived from presenting a phone-in competition on local radio. Fortunately, it was a statement that Ted could easily understand and that mercifully did not seem to warrant a proper answer. 'Mmmmph,' he said instead, nodding in a way that he hoped would come across as amiable.

Gaston clasped both men by the arm. '*Philippe – bring Monsieur Prescôte's things.*' And then, to the club's owner, '*Excuse us – we're going for a cigarette.*'

'*OK,*' said Richepin, before turning back to Ted. The Englishman's heart sank. '*You are on first, as you are new to the club. You have around twenty minutes – an encore if you are going well, or finish at fifteen if they are booing you.*' The promoter gave him a chuckle to indicate a joke; Ted responded in kind, although he had not even attempted to follow what had just been said. '*You go on at eight.*'

'*At eight,*' echoed Gaston, looking at his watch and making a show of drawing Ted away.

'*I'll leave you to it,*' replied the promoter. '*Thank you, Gaston. Édouard.*'

'It is very simple,' said Gaston, as the three of them loitered at the side of the building, Gaston and Philippe leaning on the wall, Ted pacing and circling. 'I will do all talking. You go on to the stage and prepare, then I will go on to the stage with you and speak the introduction.' Ted looked sharply at Gaston. 'A brief introduction. Brief. So. You do not talk between the songs, you bow at the end. You do only twenty minutes as you are new – a newcomer. You stop in fifteen minutes if – if it does not go so well.'

Ted nodded automatically. 'So four songs will do it,' he heard himself say.

'Four songs. Good. If they like you, they will ask you to do an encore also.'

'Encore. Right.'

'And now I suggest we have wine to steady our nerves.'

Philippe shrugged at Ted as Gaston started towards the bar.

'What's French for "encore?"' Ted called after the café owner.

'It is *"encore"*.' Gaston turned, confusion etched across his face. 'Ah. You joke with me. That is a good sign.'

Ted said nothing.

They found Wainwright, Casimir and the mayor at a corner table. A half-dozen Amstel beers and two bottles of red wine sat between them. *'From Richepin,'* said the mayor to Gaston. *'For the Prescôte party, with his compliments.'*

Gaston beamed. *'Get yourself a coca-cola, Philippe,'* he said. The boy departed with a scowl.

Standing there, Ted saw that the famously drink-intolerant Wainwright was already refilling his own glass. Away from the quiet of the car park, Gaston's soothing words appeared ever-more ridiculous. The churning in his stomach was reaching crisis point.

'Mon-sure Pres-coat!' exclaimed his old colleague, tapping the side of his nose and giving the group a delighted smile. 'Voulay voudray join us?' He pulled out a chair with a flourish, like a magician removing the swords.

Ted did not look at him. Lowering his ponderous frame into the seat, he instead turned his gaze upon Gaston who remained hovering above them. 'I'll ...' he began, before being silenced by a commanding wave of Gaston's arms, and a pointed cough from the mayor.

'Ssssshhh! Shhhhh!' joined in Wainwright. 'Shhhh!'

Ted shushed, but let his eyes do the talking.

'Eighty euro, Ted,' Gaston said in a very low murmur. 'Eighty euro. For to work twenty minutes.'

'Plus the booze,' said Wainwright, waving his hand at the contents of the table.

'But the eighty euro, it is not the goal. This is just the audition. If it is good, there will be more work. I know it.'

'More work? More?' Ted clenched his teeth, reached for the wine bottle, and filled his glass to the brim.

Twenty minutes later, the big Englishman was stood alone in the toilet, fumbling with his trousers with newly steady fingers. Two large glasses drunk at pace had done their bit to kickstart some form of calming process – the all-important calming process. It was now his task to balance this calming process with keeping his wits about him and not making a bloody fool of himself, if it were possible that the situation in which he had found himself hadn't already thoroughly accomplished that. Was it just him? His companions seemed to have no comprehension as to what was being asked of him; no sense that going up there to be exposed as some fly-by-night charlatan, mocking this region's most cherished cultural figure for the sake of a few quid, might be anything other than a normal evening's work for the average English guitar strummer. The mayor had even gone so far as to posit that Daisy would be proud of him, as if she wouldn't have lacerated them one-by-one, reserving her most barbaric slashes for her damnfool husband who had been talked into cheating these trusting music fans. Ted's stream petered out, yet he stayed where he was, clenching and re-clenching his fists, breathing in the chilly fumes from the urinal whilst trying to work out his best strategy for getting through the performance intact. Perhaps some noises, some grunts would be more convincing than keeping utterly mute between songs. The tiles before him were well polished; he practised frowns, gurns and nods in his reflection, grunting away in accompaniment; some of these antics seemed passably Gallic.

Ted physically jumped as a man pushed his way through the door, calling back at an unseen English friend to conclude a conversation. 'Or we could move to the table at the end? Hang on!' The man was in his thirties, well-dressed in a casual shirt and brown loafers. He wore black-rimmed glasses. Ted guessed that he was probably something in the media or television; the English people in the bar had seemed to have been from that sort of set: the well-to-do weekenders, always slightly smug that they were off the usual expat trail.

'Excuse me, may I squeeze through?' said the man in easy French, as he slipped behind Ted to position himself at a station further down. 'Thank you.' It took Ted a beat to realise that he was the target of this remark. Taken aback, he zipped up his fly with a yank.

'You're welcome,' he replied, striding out into the corridor without washing his hands.

The Englishman stared at his watch for the third time. There were fewer than five minutes to go. Monsieur Richepin had reserved them a table at the front, explaining that back-stage facilities were basic, and that the jazz band that would headline later had left little room to spare. Ted was very happy with this – it meant that he would not be forced into a conversation with other musicians, and at least a room with people and a bar in it contained some element of familiarity. Wainwright, chaperoned brutally by the mayor, had quietened a little, although he still offered periodic barks of manic laughter. Philippe had been sent to the bar for more wine, and a coca-cola for himself if required.

Ted picked up his glass, put it down, picked it up then put it down again. The calming process had reached a critical point. Breathing hard, he forced his hand away from the temptation of more drink, anchoring his palms together in his lap. They remained there for a microsecond before he lifted his arm to check his watch once more.

'Hey!' It was Philippe, at a swagger. He had returned to the table with two young women. Both were dressed up for an evening out. One stepped to the fore, one held back, both clasped goldfish-bowl glasses of white wine. Gaston fleetingly pursed his lips, before settling his face into that familiar hospitable smile. Wainwright nodded in appreciation, his eyes travelling up and down the short dresses.

Philippe thrust out his hand towards Ted. 'The ladies wanted to meet a musician,' he said, reaching out with his other arm to drape it awkwardly around the lead woman's shoulders. 'Do not worry, we speak English.'

'Pleased to meet you! I'm Janine,' she said, in the warm tones of the North-East of England. 'En-chantay,' her friend called from over her shoulder.

Ted mumbled helplessly, feeling as if he should stand but not at all wishing to. Gaston came to his rescue. 'Ah – Monsieur Prescôte, he is always embarrassed by the fans. He is …'

'We will get you the autograph after he plays,' Philippe nodded seriously. 'I will find you.'

'We were wondering if you'd dedicate a song to our friend Sara?' The girl addressed Ted slowly and clearly. 'She's thirty. Today.'

Ted felt his mouth open; he succumbed to the safety of his wine glass to quell any accidental speech. Gaston again. '*A song for their friend Sara,*' he explained in French to Ted. '*For Sara.*' Ted nodded as Gaston turned back to them. '*Oui,* that is arranged.'

'We have a drink for her birthday?' Philippe guided his new companion in an arc back towards the bar, not bothering to wait for an answer. Her friend gave them a happy, glazed smile and followed, Wainwright's eyes glued to her buttocks.

'I will join them,' Casimir whispered, nudging Wainwright hard in the ribs. Ted caught sight of Monsieur Richepin beckoning him from the side of the stage. The calming process threw itself screaming from the window.

Steps, why did there have to be steps? He stumbled on the top one, before almost falling flat on his face as he caught his foot on a trailing lead. A single chair had been put out for him centre-stage. In front of it were two microphones on stands, one bent lower than the other. He sat down, cradling his guitar. A man appeared and adjusted the bottom stand, so that the microphone peered into the soundbox of his guitar. He had forgotten that they would need to do this, and was thankful that he'd become familiar with the process back in that shabby studio. Ted pulled the second microphone so that it was level with his mouth and muttered a cough to test it. The gravelly sound burst from the auditorium's speakers.

Beside the stage, Monsieur Richepin reached for a third microphone and waved it at Gaston, who bounded up the steps, a joyous beam across his face. Ted felt a sick feeling in his gut as the Frenchman waved for quiet from the front tables. Gaston was enjoying this just a little too much, he thought.

'Ladies and gentlemen!' The café owner's smooth voice and immaculate attire failed to dispel the whiff of PT Barnum. Ted regarded him from his seat, desperate that the man should not build him up. Brief, Gaston, BRIEF for pity's sake! Gaston began a valediction which Ted lost track of immediately. He recognised 'chansons,' and he recognised 'Frédéric Debreu,' and he recognised 'Édouard Prescôte!' And he realised that Gaston had stopped talking and that those facing the stage were applauding.

'Now,' continued Gaston. There was more. Hell's Bells! Ted's gaze turned to machine guns. 'Now, I know there are many of our English friends here tonight. And I will just translate, the songs that you will enjoy are by Frédéric Debreu, a hero of this region. The man singing is Édouard Prescôte. Édouard Prescôte!'

There was more applause as Gaston turned away with a wave; from the corner of his eye Ted saw Wainwright stand and yell 'hooray!' He took a deep, sickly breath, arranged his sweating fingertips in an A major chord on the fingerboard, and realised that he had completely forgotten to check whether his guitar was still in tune. It would have to—

'Pardon, pardon! I forgot to say, this first song is a dedication to our friend Sara, it is her birthday. Happy birthday Sara!'

A small cheer erupted from near the bar. Ted jerked his gaze upwards at the café owner and bashed his nose on the microphone, prompting a muffled crack through the speaker system. Faces turned from him to look for the birthday girl; there was another cheer and a cry of 'over here!' He took the opportunity to pull his guitar away from its microphone and stroke the softest of chords; it sounded all right. Shifting back into position, he felt his body rocking back and forth ever so slightly. So this was it.

Bom-de, dom-de, bom-de, dom-de ...

The nylon strings were amplified loud, but it was not a harsh sound that filled the room. Bom-de, dom-de. His thumb and forefingers worked over and over, until the movement was automatic. Bom-de, dom-de. He kept it going, again and again, waiting for his head to stop spinning, waiting for the breathing and the beating and the adrenaline to settle, bom-de, dom-de, using the rhythm as a mantra to calm him until he could face the final judgement of singing. As he played the motif, he became aware of his vision seeming to clear. The audience was now not one abstract mass, but had resolved itself into people: men, women, old, young. The ten or so tables in the front row were now all occupied; further back there were more empty spaces. Some people, mainly men, had not moved from the bar – those ones looked like locals, dressed down, here mainly for the beer. He spotted the party of English girls, five of them, three champagne bottles gracing their table. Bom-de, dom-de. His gaze switched back to his own table, to Wainwright, the mayor, Philippe, Casimir and the re-seated Gaston. Casimir was waving a glass of red wine aloft in time to the beats; Wainwright gave a thumbs up. Ted's eyes swiftly moved on. Bom-de, dom-de. He realised suddenly that his extended introduction had quietened the room; it had done everything that he'd wanted Gaston not to do, and created a tension and expectation. His eyes swept the room. They looked up at him and—

> ♫ Marg'rite she is my long adored-for woman
> Her face it is the sunshine in my life
> I cry for her, I'd die for her, I'd have her for my own
> If it wasn't for the fact I have a wife! ♫

Ted almost leaped into the air as his own voice boomed from the speakers to either side. He stared at the microphone as if it were the first time that he had ever seen such a thing, and for a dangerous moment his mind teetered on the brink of conscious thought and analysis before slipping back into the mechanical safety of the song. He felt his fingers shift to the minor chord.

♫ *So Father hear my simple cry for pity!*
I've said my prayers and done my duty ... ♫

The volume and the natural reverb of the big space gave the sound a majestic, churchy quality and Ted seemed to find himself floating above the performer on stage; although he had listened to his own CD, it was as if he was hearing himself sing and play for the very first time; experiencing the song as other people would. And what a song it was! Debreu – he was a master of simplicity, of creating something uncomplicated and direct that nevertheless seemed to have a uniqueness about it. It was, it was – the ebb and flow of the story, the musicality of the intonation, the pacing of those punchlines that Ted knew by heart from the English translations – it was perfect. To say that this was a bloody good song was so much an understatement as to be risible. It was as good as any piece of popular music can be.

With shock, Ted realised that he had finished and that people were clapping.

It wasn't wild applause. It wasn't whooping and hollering – although there did seem to be one character at the front who was attempting wolf-whistles – Ted did not dare look across to see. But it was genuine, appreciative, spontaneous clapping. He shook his head in confusion. There was a lady at the front whom he'd noticed previously for her severe attire: her silver hair clipped up, a cold string of pearls across her breast, a dress so black and formal that it might be mistaken for mourning wear; it all sat ill with the very jovial setting. Well, this lady was clapping. And her husband was clapping. The people around them were clapping. The group at the bar were clapping.

Terrified, lest the spell be lost, Ted played the introduction to 'The Vengeful Widow,' his fingers working down the fretboard in a descending pattern, a slower pace than that of his opening song. He winced as he hit the fifth note, his finger tripping and covering the fret rather than nestling in the correct position just behind it; the resulting sound was mute and dull and he hastened on. The applause died out quickly, leaving only the sound of guitar notes in the air, the clinking of glassware upon table, the murmur of conversation from those at the back.

♫ *Forty years of marriage to a faithless lying hound*
A smile it passed across her lips as he passed in the ground
'I'll pay him back, I'll pay him back for being such a beast'
She chucked the soil into the pit and copped off with the priest ♫

There was a ripple of laughter.

♫ *Let us not begrudge this ancient widow her revenge*
They say the one laughs longest who is laughing at the end
No, let us not begrudge this ancient widow her revenge
They say the one laughs longest who is laughing at the end … ♫

He had never appreciated it before. After all, Ted had been drunk when he had reached for the guitar at Gaston's café all those weeks ago. He had been drunker at the festival. Making those recordings had been a technical, analytical process that had been enjoyable but essentially solitary. But as the end of the second verse was met by a bellow of laughter from the French workers at the bar, he suddenly understood. The joy, the absolute, utter, unbeatable rapture of being at one with a crowd of people, of leading them, of drawing them into your own world. Ted risked a proper glance across the room. There were still some people chatting at the back, moving between tables to get drinks, but many more were leaning forwards, studying him, nodding along with the music. His hand followed the well-trodden pattern, no more mistakes, hopping around the fretboard in a skilful tap dance.

♫ *The mourners heard the panting emanating from the nave*
The widow was cavorting with the lad who dug the graves ... ♫

Laughter, laughter and applause. He glanced over to his own table. His friends looked delighted, even Philippe seemed to have supplanted his youthful scowl with a look that verged on pride. Only Wainwright did not seem to be paying attention; he had collared a passer-by, no doubt to claim some sort of reflected glory.

He finished the song, near-shouting the final line as he wrenched his left hand from the guitar in a flourish. The clapping was louder this time, longer and enthusiastic. It fed itself as it bounced around the room, the French audience captivated by this bashful fat man who had come to life before them, the English and other tourists aware that something had happened which they didn't quite understand. Ted was stunned. They seemed to be clapping somebody who was not him. Feeling his face a deep crimson, he nodded his own appreciation of this other phantom man.

'The Mouse' ended like this also, and then he took an insane risk. He knew that the twenty-minute deadline left him time for one more song. But they would give him an extra one, they must give him an extra one. An encore, Gaston had said, French for encore. It was not ego that told him this. It was plainly and simply obvious. Ted stroked a few random chords as he got his breath and then, out of the blue, launched into 'When We Were Young,' Debreu's ballad of simple longing for days gone past. His confidence wobbled during the first verse; the lazy pace would allow him no place to hide his vocals, no hurrying on from a rogue Anglo-Saxon inflection. But he had played this song a hundred times, possibly a thousand. He was bewildered to find his eyes welling up as he sang, his mind drifting away to the times that he had sung this song to Daisy, a young couple cosying down of a winter's evening in their sitting room above Matlock, he pretending that this was merely casual practice for his own benefit, she buried in a crossword, affecting not to

165

listen. And then to earlier, a youthful man alone in his bedroom hunched over a big reel-to-reel tape that had arrived in the post, a half-dozen simple melodies painting pictures of his older brother in a foreign land. Ted forced his mind back to the task in hand – he could afford no slip-up now – and blinked once, twice, three times to try to clear his embarrassment. He felt a tear drifting down his cheek, but his hands were occupied; he had to let it go on its way.

He finished the song. There was utter silence, then a roar. Unaware of anything but his own inner thoughts, Ted reached into his trouser pocket for a handkerchief. With shaking hands, he dabbed his eyes and gave his nose a trumpeting blow, remembering only at the last minute to pull his face away from the microphone.

'*Édouard Prescôte!*' Monsieur Richepin near-leaped onto the stage, clutching his microphone and gesturing towards the Englishman. '*Édouard Prescôte! Frédéric Debreu!*' Ted felt himself start to squirm and burn. He realised that he was still holding his hanky over his nose and mouth and dropped his arm accordingly; he forced his face up from his feet to meet the applause, half rising from his seat in an awkward bow. Richepin said two or three more sentences, leaning forward to speak to the audience conversationally. For a horrible moment Ted thought that he was being asked a question; for a response he scratched his ear and bowed his head. But then, there it was, one more '*Édouard Prescôte!*' and one more flourish of the compère's hand, more applause, more shouts of appreciation and encouragement. Ted breathed, once, twice, three times, and launched into Debreu's masterpiece: the song of 'The Pretty Goat'.

> ♪ *Won't you let me guard your savings*
> *Said the banker, said the banker*
> *My reputation shows they're watertight*
> *I'll spend them on my women*
> *Thought the banker, thought the banker*
> *Though his conscience told him something wasn't right …*

166

Tra la, la tra-la-la
La la la la la
Tra la, la tra-la-la
La la la la la ... ♫

Ted almost forgot to sing as he gaped at the men at the bar chanting along with the chorus. One of their number was conducting, waving a Heineken bottle aloft, an ursine giant in workman's dungarees, with an enormous, dopey grin across his bearded face.

♫ *Tra la, la tra-la-la*
La la la la la ...♫

He could play that chorus over and over and over. He did not want it to end.

*

Sleep took an age to come. Ted's bulk sagged into the camp bed, his feet poking out through the open doorway into the corridor, staring with wide-open eyes in the half-light at the woodchip of the ceiling. He wondered whether this buzz would ever leave him. This was what it must be like: the envelope torn open at the Oscars; the ball sailing past the 'keeper in those last minutes of the cup final. At one point he threw off the blankets and crept out of the room to take a pee; before returning he poked his head around their bedroom door and watched Daisy as she slumbered alone in the double bed. He wanted so much to wake her and to share this feeling, to bring her in to the evening's triumph, to somehow make her understand the thrill that had consumed him and that he wished would never leave. But even had he found the unkindness to rouse her, he realised that he could never explain and she could never comprehend. Nobody could. He would tell her about how it had been a far bigger deal than he had expected, and that it had gone very well, and she would nod and smile and tell him 'well done' and be genuinely, honestly pleased for him. And if he tried to take it further, to try to articulate the love and the warmth that he had felt from all those strangers then it would become – what? A vulgar boast, the self-regarding anecdote of a boorish non-celebrity. The impotence filled him with a bottomless sense of loss.

He bit his lip. One thing that he could not possibly admit to was the fiasco around the reappearance of 'Édouard'. The journey home had been a blur of wine and glory, but he did recall impressing upon Wainwright the utter necessity of withholding this aspect of the evening from reports back to Daisy. Thinking further, Ted was sure that he had seized his fellow Englishman around the throat at some point. Best to have a quiet word with his old colleague in the morning, just to reinforce the point.

Daisy gave a little snore; her hand reached from under the covers to grasp at something imaginary in the night. It was time to level with her; to tell her about David and their money; to have the dreaded talk about their future. He could not avoid it forever. But when? After their guests departed? Or leave it a few days whilst they settled back into a normal routine? And what could he yet tell her that would not expose her to the uncertainty and anguish that he'd been bearing on her behalf for the past weeks? No. It would have to wait until he knew more. Business as usual, propped up by Gaston's money. He realised that the elated feeling had slipped away. He was Ted again, a fat old bugger dithering in his underpants, his clumpy bare feet cold on the floorboards. Exhaustion swept over him. He pushed the bedroom door closed and padded the three paces back to the living room to lower himself back into his makeshift bed.

13

Eloise Dufrénoy

The Wainwrights loaded up their car to the early morning birdsong. Stan Wainwright maintained a constant grouse about the cost of using the major roads, punctuated with abrupt giggles and bursts of cod-French that mystified the women and caused Ted to glower with menacing eyes.

They helped Daisy onto the verandah and breakfasted outside. She made sharp remarks about the charcoal edges that Ted had allowed to form on her toast. 'Well make some more yourself, ungrateful woman,' he retorted. 'I'll sit and watch you hobble to the cooker.' And she said that she had a good mind to, and he said that he was sure she would as well, and they both chuckled as Daisy rolled her eyes at her own incapacity.

'Thinks he's a big star, now he's in with his musician friends,' she said. 'Too important to pander to the likes of me.'

Ted puffed out his chest and adopted his American accent. 'I'll have my people send you up breakfast in future.'

'Ooh – his "people".' Daisy pronounced the word with exaggerated scorn. 'Gaston, would that be? Or that crooked old man from the festival? Still, show business has always attracted its sharks. I don't trust your people. They're all on the take.'

Ted reached for a new slice. The conversation had suddenly become uncomfortable.

'Why don't we tell them now?' said Wainwright.

Ted's head shot up. But his old colleague was addressing his own wife, oblivious to Ted's unease.

Wainwright leaned in. 'We weren't going to say anything until it was all done and dusted.' His voice was confidential. 'But we've also decided to emigrate!' He smiled at each of them in turn, a satisfied, knowing smirk.

The toast almost fell from Ted's mouth. He breathed heavily, staring at his old colleague who gave him a portentous nod in return.

'Cornwall. We're moving to Cornwall.'

'Cornwall.'

'Mmm hmm.' Wainwright continued his nodding, solemn, as if he were a gentleman detective building up to the name of the murderer.

Ted stole a glance across at Jenny. Her gaze was fixed on the plate in front of her.

'Cornwall! That'll be nice,' said Daisy.

'Well, you know. Better weather. Close to the sea.' Jenny spoke out without looking at them.

'Less of our immigrant friends,' said Wainwright.

Daisy beamed. 'We liked Cornwall, didn't we Ted? The little smugglers' bays?'

'Hmm,' Ted took a chomp.

'So there you go,' said Wainwright. 'You've set a trend.'

He watched the Mercedes disappear around the oak tree just as it had before. He pictured it creeping down the track, skirting the shell of his old car, out through the village, across the river and away into the countryside. But this time there was no cheer in their departure. He found a melancholia settling upon him – that these were his friends, or the closest things to friends that he'd maintained over the decades. And here he was, relieved that they'd buggered off now for good, that they'd left him to his own devices in his adopted new world. Out of the blue, it occurred to him that – whatever happened – he might never see them again. The wind gusted and he watched the leaves ripple and rustle; he gave an enormous snort to clear a build-up in his nose, and by the time he had followed this up with some throaty contortions around his sinuses his train of thought had been lost. There was a pair of partridge hopping and flapping in the grass beside the track. Ted watched their unfathomable routine in fascination before turning and trudging back indoors.

*

The social worker was younger than Ted had expected. At least he assumed that she was a social worker; she had been sent as a follow-up to one of the 100,000 forms with which he'd wrestled as he'd fidgeted beside the hospital bed that terrible afternoon. Ted had never actually seen a social worker before. She was a short woman with tightly curled hair and a pudgy face that exploded into a smile of delight as she produced an ID card from her cardigan pocket. 'Mister Press-cot?'

'Come in, love.' He did recall that they had promised him an English speaker. He beckoned her in to the kitchen, chaperoning her past the hole in the floor and on through the tiny corridor into the lounge. She edged cautiously through the narrow spaces, her head darting constantly as she went. Ted could feel himself being assessed.

Daisy was standing as they entered the room. She swayed and tottered, her left hand clutching her stick with white knuckles, her right grasping a wing of the armchair for support.

'Will you get back on the sofa?' The social worker gave a start as Ted barked at his wife; he almost knocked over their visitor as he strode forward in irritation.

'We've got a visitor,' Daisy said.

'Missus Press-cot. My name is Eloise Dufrénoy. I have your information from the hospital.' She patted a green document wallet whilst simultaneously flashing her ID card once more and beaming at the elderly lady.

'Eloise. That's a lovely name.'

'Will you sit down?'

Daisy shot her husband a glare, the movement involved in turning her head almost sending her careening sideways into the chair. Steadying herself, she addressed the visitor once more. 'Would you like a cup of tea?'

171

'No, thank you, Missus Press-cot.'

'You're going to really bloody hurt yourself if you don't sit down.'

Daisy's lips disappeared to nothingness. 'It won't be said that I'm a bad hostess and don't offer visitors a cup of tea.'

'Well who's going to say that? You're disabled, for pity's sake! She can see that – she works with the disabled all day! She doesn't expect you to start waiting on her hand and foot!'

'I am not disabled. It's common politeness, that's all. I notice that you didn't offer the lady.'

'Because she's come here to see you, not to sit around drinking tea!' Ted glared back at his wife before turning to the social worker, who had edged backwards to stand against the wall. 'Would you like a cup, love?'

'No, thank you, I am happy, thank you.'

'See?'

Daisy regarded them both with suspicious eyes before lowering herself back to the safety of the sofa, her arms trembling as they supported her slight weight. As her bottom neared its intended resting place she gave up the struggle and allowed herself to fall in a tiny heap on the cushions. Ted looked to the ceiling before remembering himself and indicating the adjacent armchair, which Eloise Dufrénoy perched on the very edge of. 'You are very weak,' she observed.

The social worker focused on Daisy, asking questions in careful English: about the accident, about what had happened in the aftermath, about what she was able or unable to do. She asked in more general about their wellbeing, about what they ate, about how they got down to the village to shop, and of course what they were doing here in France away from family and friends. To Ted's exasperation, he felt himself pushed to the periphery of the conversation; their visitor was perfectly nice and polite, and it might have been the language thing, but she seemed to be talking rather than listening, and it dawned upon him that she regarded them as 'the elderly'. She asked whether they were using the wheelchair that had been loaned to them;

Ted butted in to explain that it was being kept under the verandah due to space constraints.

'It was queer going round the garden with him lurking behind me all the time,' Daisy said. 'Like Rod Hull and Emu, we were.' The social worker's fixed expression failed to conceal her bafflement at this reference, and there was a short, awkward silence. 'Look, are you sure that you wouldn't like a cup of tea?'

'She does not want a cup of bloody tea!'

'No, no,' Mme Dufrénoy widened that smile even further. 'And using the toilet? You can manage?' The social worker half-stood before lowering herself once more in a physical demonstration that made Ted grimace.

'Perfectly well on my own, thank you. There's a shelf in there I can lean on. I won't go into details.'

'She won't let me help anyway,' said Ted.

'You should let your husband help.'

'She could help herself. Drink less tea to start off with.'

Daisy's look could have wilted the crops. 'I can manage.'

Mme Dufrénoy turned her relentlessly cordial face to Ted. 'I have brochures that I will leave. You do not qualify for a *carte d'invalidité*, but here you may qualify for subsidised prices.' She pulled some sheets from her folder and handed these to Ted. 'Brochures' was a grand term; the second- or third-generation photocopies were inky, and Ted had to peer hard at the illustrations to make out what they might represent. Here were some handles and grips – they were clear enough. Here was a mobility scooter, some alarms, and a thing that – after turning the sheet left, right and upside-down – Ted concluded was some sort of hoist apparatus for getting people into the bath. It reminded him of something that he'd seen on a documentary used to help farmers wash sheep. He squinted at the image, trying to work out the mechanics. Sifting through, he reached the last page.

'These are the subsidised prices?' he yelped.

'A scooter. I need one of those scooters. One that goes across

173

the grass and over the track. Otherwise I'm stuck here without him, even when he does get the car mended.'

The social worker and Daisy started discussing scooters – the practicalities, and whether it would be cheaper to buy or to rent one. Ted opened his mouth but closed it again, watching his wife, serene in her cluelessness, prattling away about sums of money that might as well be in the billions.

He could feel himself starting to perspire. Ted pulled himself to his feet, murmured an excuse and left the room. Sitting on the toilet, he panted hard, nestling one hand in another over his mouth, on his chest then waving his arms about helplessly, not knowing what to do with his limbs. He could still hear their voices through the flimsy wooden wall that separated them. Daisy was wittering on about David now. A grip. He had to get a grip. He clenched his fists, forcing himself to concentrate on the feel of his nails pressing into his palms, counting slowly, 1-2-3-4... A bloody scooter! Stop it. 9-10-11-12.

At twenty-four he stopped and stood, yanking at the flush as he made his way out. The visitor was standing ready to leave; he walked her the three paces to the kitchen with a smile that he hoped conveyed appropriate sincerity and gratitude.

Mme Dufrénoy paused and turned as she stood at the door to the verandah. Her beam wavered ever so slightly. 'She will have help here, but you understand that it may be better for Missus Press-cot to return to your home in Great Britain? I do not wish to cause offence, but ...' she tailed off as she looked around the shambolic kitchen, allowing her eyes to finish her sentence for her.

'No, no, no offence. Soon. We will go soon, but she is happy here.' Ted felt sick at his own words. Thanking the lady for her help, he watched her little city car pootle off around the oak tree. He paced around the meadow before returning indoors to make some lunch.

Patenaude's daughter dropped by in the afternoon, bringing with her a sack of coloured wools and a book of knitting patterns: jungle animals and other toys for young children. Daisy was delighted. The other woman had brought her own needles, and offered to sit with Daisy if Ted wished to do some shopping. Needing nothing, but grateful for the opportunity to get out, Ted made drinks before near-trotting down the track to the town.

There was something different as Ted passed through the square. The empty shop next to the florist's – the door was open, and figures were moving around inside. From across the street, Ted recognised one of the workmen from when he'd helped with the festival preparations. There was the mayor himself, wrapped in outsize dungarees and waving a chunky tenon saw as he spoke. Already, the front windows had been cleared of the tourist notices and maps. Despite his preoccupation, Ted was pleased that the building was being done up; even a lick of paint on the exterior would smarten the square. Waving his hand, he strode on to Gaston's.

The café was forlorn when he arrived. An elderly man slouched at one table with his newspaper. Marie and Celine sat in the corner, the younger girl facing the entrance; she registered Ted as he walked in and rippled her fingers in a girlish wave before resuming a whispered conversation with her sister. Gaston was expected back at any moment, explained the young barman, shooting the clock an exasperated look. Taking a cloth from underneath the bar, he gave the surface a desultory wipe.

Ted hesitated, asked the barman for a coffee and then, sensing the reluctance with which the youth approached the machine, halted him with a friendly 'would you rather I wouldn't?'

Philippe dropped his shoulders helplessly. 'Nobody uses it for two, three hours? It is bad when it is not used. The pressure, it gets big.'

'Ah. Shall I have a quick glass of wine instead?'

Philippe said nothing in reply to this, but reached for a bottle of red and poured. Ted was about to turn for the large round table, when the barman surprised him by continuing the conversation. 'Gaston, he spends nothing on this place.'

Ted put down his glass and rested his elbows on the bar. The lad's expression? For the first time since he'd met him, he looked like he cared. 'Well, times are a bit tight you know,' he said. 'For all of us.'

'It could be good here, Mister Prescott. Modern, you know? Gaston, he complains about no customers, but he does not do anything to get customers except the people who are always customers.'

'Well, I'm new in the big scheme of things,' said Ted. 'Although to be fair I'm probably not the sort of customer you're talking about.'

Philippe gave him a mirthless chuckle. The telephone rang, and he drifted to the other end of the bar to answer it.

Ted remained where he was. The boy was right. Without the hubbub of conversation, the building did have a tired air. Behind the bar, especially. Veneer was peeling off the wine shelves; the row of mirrors that rose up behind the spirit and liquor bottles had long since lost their lustre; the stretch of non-slip rubber that ran the length of the floor was in an indescribable state. Plus that coffee machine was from the ark. He felt guilty for even considering asking another human being to operate it. He sipped at his wine as Philippe mooched back. The booze was all right, anyway.

The barman glanced across at the girls in the corner. 'I can ask you something, Mister Prescott?' he said, startling Ted for the second time in one day.

'Go on, lad.'

'Philippe!' Celine hollered across the room, prompting the youth's skin to transform from sallow to a deep crimson in an instant. Mumbling excuses he scampered across. Ted watched him at work, hopping from foot to foot as they made an order. At one point he laughed loudly, to be met by silence from the girls; as he returned to the bar they resumed their whispering and Marie let loose a high, musical giggle. Philippe fled back to Ted, grabbing a bottle of Pepsi-Cola along the way.

'Ah,' said Ted.

'Mister Prescott?'

His elbows planted on the bar, Ted sunk his jowls into the palms of his hands. His voice was low. 'We have an expression in England called "punching above your weight." But I admire you for it, lad. May as well aim high. Mayor's daughters, and all that.'

Philippe leaned in and spoke in an angry whisper. 'Yeah, the mayor of a poxy small town. They think they are, you say, God's gift.'

'But the thing about women like that is that men usually agree with them.'

Philippe stood upright as if to turn away, but changed his mind, grabbing his cloth and wiping furiously. 'They will not look at a *monkey* who cleans glasses at a bar.' He dropped his voice once more. 'But in Paris ... in Paris there are the rich girls who search the bars to go to bed with working class like me. It is to cause anger for their parents.' The barman nodded his head at his revelations.

'Yes. We used to think that about Chesterfield, you know.'

'I go to Paris one day. I screw my way around the city and I earn money to come here and buy a proper bar. Then we see who will be fighting to be with me! Ha!'

'*Philippe!*'

'*Oui!*' The barman poured the cola so hastily that the rising froth cascaded over the rim of the glass. He wiped with shaking hands as his face glowed once more.

'You got to follow your dreams, lad,' called Ted, as the boy scurried away with the drink. 'Follow your dreams!'

Gaston stepped in through the double doors, an enormous smile upon his face. 'Ah! You are just in time!'

Ted had never seen the cellar. The stone chamber was sparse and disorganised, like a junk room. He took the weight of the crate as Gaston passed it down through the opening, then let it settle comfortably in his hands. It was full of cans of Fanta

177

Lemon. He scanned the shadows for a logical place to set it down and, finding none, simply pushed it to the corner of the room. The pair repeated the process eight more times, building up a tower of soft drinks and snacks. The finished construction was oddly pleasing to Ted; it was the result of – finally – the beginnings of a proper job.

'OK,' called Gaston's voice from above. 'Wait.' The café owner let the iron trapdoor fall with a clang that echoed around the underground room. Ted found himself in near-darkness until his companion reappeared at the interior door, wedging it open to draw in some dim light from the hallway beyond.

'I've got another ten minutes or so, Gaston. Let me change some of those bulbs for you.'

'*Lightbulbs, lightbulbs. Oui,* there may be lightbulbs in the room upstairs. I am sorry. Usually here it is just me or Philippe.' The wooden staircase creaked and groaned as Gaston picked his way down. '*Oui,* more light would be good.'

'More wine would be good.' Ted indicated with his head towards the towering racks on the wall. One was perhaps one-quarter full; the others were all but bare.

'Ah. These are filled, next year, the spring. Until then, we finish the good bottles together. You, me, the people in the town. We will get more when it is needed, but just the good bottles.'

'Sounds like a plan to me.'

The café owner sat himself down on a crate, his usual scrupulous demeanour out-of-place amidst the dust and debris of the cellar. 'Madame Kerharo, she is old. She stays for the winter, then I have a new chef here, one who will not one day fall dead in the *galette*. Philippe: he works, but he is simple, a dreamer. He thinks of bright lights and golden streets; he will be here when he is Madame Kerharo's age, crying about too many customers and dribbling about the young girls.' Gaston shrugged his shoulders. 'I thank you for your help.'

'It's me that should be thanking. You saved me a ...'

'Next year, Ted. Next year. Always next year. But this time. Next year, Ted, we have plans. Problems – we beat them.'

'Like the airport?'

'The airport, *oui*. No matter. Plans. I have plans. Bernard has plans.' Gaston rose to his feet, energised by his thoughts. 'Next year.'

Ted picked his way through the boxes, following the café owner towards the staircase. 'What's Bernard up to?'

'Ah! I let him tell you. You will be excited. The big work, good work for you, I think.' Gaston sprung up the flight two at a time, pausing at the top to look down upon the big Englishman.

'And also, Ted, you have already been important to the plans, to the town. You play a great show at the club of Richepin; people talk again about Frédéric Debreu; there is interest; there is excitement. If people talk about Frédéric Debreu, they talk about our town. It is the big, wide picture, Ted. Big picture.'

Ted clambered after the Frenchman. He could feel the stairs sagging and shifting under his weight. He gripped the handrail; it wobbled in his hand. 'Well, I'm pleased to help out on bits and bobs ...'

Gaston pushed through the doorway into the bar. There was an explosion of steam and a shriek.

Ted stood perplexed when he eventually made it outside, peering left and right as if confused by the geography of this familiar place. Gaston had finally given him a proper job to do, but had then started wittering about plans and big pictures. Everything seemed to be happening around him, to a man that looked and sounded like him but that wasn't. He rubbed his palms up and down his cheeks as he tried to salvage some grip on what entirely was going on.

He'd been interrupted once more as he had tried to resume the conversation with the distracted Gaston; to get some sort of sense out of the café owner about what precisely was expected from him on top of odd jobs in the cellar. Philippe had been livid as the men had shepherded him away from the care of Marie and Celine and into the back of an ambulance, only to discharge him a little later, the boy's hands bound and wrapped in swathes of white plastic. Ted had mopped the drenched bar area; Gaston had disappeared to his flat to telephone for a repair man.

He looked at his watch. Philippe's mishap had caused Ted to be away for longer than he had expected; he started walking at a stride towards home. A refuse lorry drew around the corner, its workers jogging abreast, shouting calls to each other. Ted remained on the near side of the square to give them a safe berth, and consequently found himself alongside the florist, and then the empty store. The mayor and his helpers had departed and locked the premises; glancing through the window it appeared that they had cleared the space entirely and begun to erect shelving and cabinets. As he passed the entrance, a single typewritten notice taped to the door caught his eye. Despite his haste, he paused to study it. Translating word-by-word, the message was simple:

'LOCAL LEGEND
HERO OF FRANCE
FRÉDÉRIC DEBREU
MUSEUM AND SHOP
OPENING THIS WINTER.'

14

The Photograph

Daisy was a bloody difficult patient. Stoicism and the spirit of 'I can manage' was all very admirable and all that, but stoicism in the face of the common or garden winter ailment was one thing; 'I can manage' in the face of a sudden catastrophic disability quite another. The water from the tap was ice-cold as Ted rinsed the mugs; he left them on the side to dry themselves before relenting and reaching for the tea-towel. When he was done, he plodded through to their room to make the bed, puffing the pillows and stretching out the blankets as best he could. It was good enough but still not perfect. And if it were not perfect then at some point during the rest of the day she would attempt it herself, hobbling in shuffle-by-shuffle as she clenched her stick and clung to the furniture, defying the world to stop her as she did her 'managing'. Ted squeezed himself to the far side of the bed and yanked at the covers.

Well at least she was just about self-sufficient once more. Enough for him to fret a little less about leaving her on her own, which had been his main concern as he had begun to run more errands for Gaston. But was this 'it'? His presumption had been that she would get better, but perhaps this was her 'better'; perhaps the social worker had been right and they were now officially 'the elderly'. It had fallen upon her in the blink of an eyelid with that bloody stupid accident; would the same thing be his fate, or would it come in a more gradual process, a gentle descent? He left the bed in frustration and stomped back through to the kitchen for no particular reason, trying to focus on his own body as he went. His heart, his lungs. The pressure on the soles of his feet; the slight throbbing in the muscles in his thighs. He flexed his big hands and bent the fingers into claws, holding them tightly there until the muscles felt like they might explode. He couldn't say that he felt old; he felt exactly as he had done the day before, and the day before that, and last year, and a decade ago. But that was the thing with gradual deterioration: you don't notice it happening. One minute you're leader of the pack, the next minute people are patting your knee and calling you 'dear'. Ted filled his cheeks with air and let fly with a contemptuous raspberry. The childish gesture startled even himself. Shaking his head, he padded through to the living room. He needed to get away from these four walls.

Daisy's needles were clicking away as she worked on her giraffe. Ted paused to watch, ever-fascinated by the skill involved. Being cooped up like this, stuck in this little place with only her own thoughts – it actually seemed to suit her. It suited her as much as it had been driving him bananas. Pulling open a drawer of the tiny dresser, Ted selected a brown envelope from the papers within.

'Are you OK if I go off for a couple of hours?' he said. 'I'll make you some lunch.'

She didn't look up. 'Another job for Gaston? You must be the worst retired person there's ever been.'

'I'm just helping him out. That's all. Anyway, it's not Gaston. I'm going to take Eric's photos into Maubette and see if I can find anything out.'

'Well I expect I can probably do without you for a bit. I might even be able to do without your gourmet services and make my own lunch. Or even go two hours without food.' She raised her eyes to his and formed the wrinkles of her lips into a shocked 'O'. 'Two hours!'

'It's no trouble to make you some lunch.'

'Just make sure you lock and bolt the door, in case the mad axeman gets me.'

182

Ted clamped his jaw shut, grinding his teeth around his mouth as he waited for the exasperation to subside. 'You're a bloody difficult woman to look after.'

Daisy looked up from her knitting, her needles barely pausing. 'Go! I'm perfectly all right, or would be without you hovering and bothering and under my feet!'

Ted pulled his jacket from the chair. 'It's just that Gaston doesn't need his car today, so it's a good opportunity.'

'Don't come home drunk, that's all.'

'Well I'll do my best, but no promises.' He paced out to the corridor, poking his head back round the door and shooting her a wolfish grin. 'You know what I'm like.'

He had parked outside a small parade of stores, each shabby and badly kept, the lettering on their signs faded and unloved. Looking up and down the street for a starting point, the scene reminded him of Debreu's 'Ironmonger of Vallières,' the song about the elderly shopkeeper who sells everything except the goods that customers keep coming in for. A smile spread across his face at the thought of this one. It had been on that initial reel-to-reel tape from Eric, right at the very end. Even now, he could picture himself hunched over the kitchen table, playing and rewinding word by word as he translated via a French dictionary from the town library; striving to nail enough in each line to allow him to make an educated stab at the rest; juggling with the alien grammar to produce some form of coherence so that he could sit back and guffaw at the tale that emerged.

♫ *Good morning, sir, how may I help?*
We have screws and bolts of every size
Stair nails to silence creaking flights
Should your home be troubled by rats
We have traps and bait to ease your blight
We have tile cement, and paint, and grout
Some string, good sir? I'm afraid we're out ♫

Ted could envisage Debreu on this street, wandering across the cobbles with guitar case in hand, casual on the face of it, but observing every detail, every person; his shrewd mind vigilant for the smallest item of interest that might open up a story to explore. In the vision there were fewer cars; there were more people in the shops; everybody was smoking. Ludicrously, he realised, the image in his mind was in black and white. Patting his inside pocket to reassure that the envelope was safely within, Ted set off at a saunter.

He passed two café-bars that he discounted: modern ones, or at least modernised, aimed too much at the young to be useful. The third was more promising. It crouched down a side street-cum-alleyway, a filthy cream frontage with smeared, dirty windows, one cracked fully from top to bottom. Looking into the gloom, Ted saw exactly what he'd hoped for, a smattering of elderly men crouched over mugs and glasses. With a burst of confidence, and calling upon his best language skills, Ted stepped through the door into the hush.

'Ah, no,' said the man, as he passed Eric's photograph to his friend who peered at it through thick, metal-rimmed spectacles. 'His brother,' the first man added, before turning back to Ted and pulling a sad face in lieu of words.

'He – uhm – he worked at the technical college many years ago,' said Ted, grasping for the words that he'd revised earlier with a view to sparing himself the embarrassment of having to produce his phrase book. The man continued to examine the picture, but gave no indication as to any familiarity with its subject. After an age he shook his head, offering the photograph back with a shrug of regret. Ted reached for it, but it was pulled from his hands once more, the first man limping unsteadily across to a corner table and speaking some words to its occupants. Ted sipped at his coffee, the harsh taste swamping his taste buds and lingering long after he'd set the mug back on the counter. Coming here had been such a long shot that he felt no disappointment at the blank that was being drawn.

Nevertheless, he stayed for a second drink at his new companions' monosyllabic bidding, the silence between the trio creating an odd comradeship that Ted found gratifying. They felt no need to change their routine to make this fellow old barfly comfortable; he had been recognised and accepted as one of them.

Ted felt a touch on his arm. Another man, stooping and bald, who had been slumped alone by the window. Ted had assumed that he had been asleep. The Englishman nodded thanks as his photograph was returned.

'The college?' The newcomer's voice was little more than a croak. Ted nodded again. The man pulled at his coatsleeve, saying words that Ted could not understand.

'Ah!' Ted's original companion slipped off his stool, beckoning Ted with his finger as he shuffled across the tired and nicotine-stained room. There was a small annexe on the far side, cold and empty of customers. Ted followed, the stooped man's hand still grasping at him as he puzzled as to what he might be being shown.

Hung amongst the dusty paraphernalia that adorned the wall were two photographs. Both had faded to a brown-yellow, and sat crooked in their frames. Ted saw once-proud men in jackets and ties posing in rows, a football and some sort of trophy on a pedestal in the foreground. He took a step forward to look closer. The name of the college was captioned on both, and the dates. Breathing heavily, he ran his eyes left to right, over each man, one-by-one.

There, on the second photograph. In the back row, directly in the centre. Ted brushed the stranger's hand away and leaned forward, his mouth half-open. He could feel his eyes straining and bulging as he stared at the grainy image from decades before.

The face of his brother stared back at him.

*

185

'It was spooky, so spooky,' Ted told Daisy, as they sat drinking chocolate, his eyes fixed on the low glow of the burner. 'I wish I'd taken it now. They did offer.'

His wife drew her blanket further up, so that only her mouse-like head was visible. 'Couldn't you go back?'

It was some seconds before Ted replied. 'No. I won't. It belonged there, if that doesn't sound funny.'

He did not mention how he had pulled in on the outskirts of the town; how he had sat rigid in the driver's seat for a good ten minutes, agonising over whether he should indeed turn round to retrieve the photograph. How he had been so shocked at his own reaction to that face from the past, that his whimsical little quest for some information that might put an episode of his life to rest had exploded into a yearning to find out what had happened all those years ago. And that he was afraid of this. Visiting places from his brother's past, making casual enquiries of old men, even writing that letter to a cottage owner who must long since have left or died – it had all been amusing armchair detective work until he had seen the photograph.

He could feel a draught on his neck, creeping through the gaps in the window frame, unencumbered by the flimsy material that served as a curtain. The late evening air was not icy yet, but it would surely get that way over the coming months. He had fallen in love with this ramshackle little cottage, with its run-down and make-do ways, its shabby rooms. But suddenly it seemed cold. He stared into the dark brown remnants at the bottom of his mug, tilting it around and around so that the remaining chocolate formed into rivulets, trickling criss-cross patterns up the inside of the china.

He looked up at his wife, and then back into his mug. 'The thing you said earlier about me doing odd jobs for Gaston. I'm just trying to give him a bit of a hand, that's all. He's been very good to us – they all have. But say if you can't manage with me being out a bit more. You will say, won't you?'

Daisy's face poured scorn on his concern. 'Four, five months

186

was it?' She held her bony fingers aloft and began to count showily on them. 'I knew you wouldn't stay retired.'

'Give over.'

'Why don't you do some work on this place instead? Lord knows it could do with it.' She reached out to replace her mug on the table. 'You're a soft touch, that's all. I know you like to be needed.'

'It's just that I owe him a bit of a debt, what with him being so good to us, and lending me his car and everything. And Bernard – the mayor – he's been very good to us; they all have.'

'What's he got to do with it?'

'Well, nothing really. But I'm just saying they've all been good to us.'

'What, like that man with no teeth at the festival who got you conning people out of their money? "Ed-oo-ard Pres-coat" the swindling guitar maker? That was good to us, all right.'

Ted could think of no answer to this, so he restricted himself to a muffled 'Mmm.' It did appear that the events of that day would be held over him for some time to come. It brought to mind the episode almost five years previously when he had eschewed professional advice in order to attempt his own repairs on their kitchen roof. There was silence between them now; he near-blurted to fill it: 'Anyway, I'm just checking that you're all right with it. Me being out.' He almost went on to make another request for reassurance that she could manage; wisely, he strangled the words as they formed.

Ignoring him, Daisy began the process of unravelling herself from the blanket. 'You need to sort out the car. You can't keep borrowing other people's.'

'Why?' Ted frowned. 'I can. Gaston doesn't mind, and half the time I'll be using it for him anyway.' He stroked his chin. 'You wouldn't believe all the paperwork if you want to buy a car over here. I'll hold off as long as I can.'

'Well you know best. I'm going to bed now.' Daisy lifted the blanket in folds from her legs and her lap. Ted watched hypnotised as she stood, her hands white and trembling as they took the strain of lifting her own trifling weight from the chair. She started to shuffle towards the hallway, lifting her stick and planting it forward inch-by-inch, reaching with her other hand for the support of the open door just slightly too soon and almost losing her balance, pausing to regroup before advancing on her dogged way.

Ted could feel his teeth biting into the end of his tongue. Breaking his trance, he rose and paced after her, guiding Daisy to the basin with one firm hand tucked under her armpit. When she was finally settled he returned to prod the fire, stoking it for the night with the largest log that the burner would accommodate. The envelope with his photos of Eric was still on the dresser where he'd set it down. He reached for it and, alone in the light of the single bulb, he leafed through the contents, dwelling on each image with moist eyes, one by one, by one.

15

The Barber

'Well, I've decided on one.' Daisy's voice possessed a disquieting note of triumph that caused Ted's eyes to veer up from his chisel. The autumn temperatures had made his workshop less practical; he had started on a new instrument a few days previously yet had found his chilly fingers less than willing to perform the intricate work that was required. So he had installed himself in the living room, ignoring his wife's pointed looks at the shavings that were collecting on the floorboards, his tongue poking from the corner of his mouth as he worried away at his remaining slab of ash.

'One what?'

She was waving something horribly familiar at him: the scrappy catalogue that the social worker had left.

'Right.' Ted made heroic efforts to look nonchalant.

'It's this one, if you want to know.'

Ted set down his tool and made a face that he hoped conveyed enthusiasm.

'When did you do that?' Her finger appeared to be jabbing at the biggest scooter on the page.

'Eloise came yesterday. She's a very nice lady once you get to know her. We had a chinwag. It took her ages to find the catalogue; it was in there with the paper to light the fire.'

'You didn't tell me she was coming. I'd have stayed in.'

'Yes, I imagine she'd have enjoyed you making your comments to her, and all your lavish hospitality. Perhaps you'd have baked her a cake.' Daisy withdrew the catalogue to study it herself, her eyes darting around the page with a sharpness at odds with her body. 'Besides, she came to see me. Not you.'

'So what did she say? And why was she here?'

'It was just a chat. To see how I was getting on. Because that's her job.'

Ted picked up his chisel once more and toyed with it, rolling it round and round in his big fingers. 'So which one do you fancy?'

'This.' Daisy thrust the papers at him. 'She says it's the best one for this sort of place, where we haven't got a proper road. Like having my own Land Rover.'

Business as usual. Ted took the catalogue with his other hand and pretended to study the blurb in great depth, making sure to nod in approval several times. She had picked out just about the most expensive one, not that it made a jot of difference. Daisy continued, oblivious. 'I could rent one, but we can take this with us when we leave. I'll need something rugged for back home.'

A nausea swelled around Ted's stomach. His face grew clammy; he could feel his eyes starting to itch. He tried to regulate his breathing, to stop the redness from rushing to his face, to look normal. His mind raced. For now, there was absolutely nothing to gain by manufacturing objections. 'Well, I don't know much about them, but it looks all right to me. I'll ring them up and get some more information when I'm in town. Or I'll get Gaston to.' He let the brochure fall to his lap and juggled with the chisel, passing it from hand to hand, his watering eyes fixed on the tool.

'Gaston?'

'Well it's bound to be a complicated conversation and they probably won't speak English, will they?'

Daisy had retrieved her knitting, and was now concentrating intently on her work, her eyes fixed at the end of her needles as they worked stitch by painful stitch. 'There is a problem though.' She paused. The room was filled with an immense silence. 'Isn't there?'

Ted felt his heart drop through the floor. His palm closed around the wooden handle, tighter and tighter until his grip seemed to be forcing the blood from his hand. 'Is there?' he asked, desperate to keep his voice even. His response seemed to echo in the room.

Daisy made an 'mmm' sound. She resumed her knitting, but absent-mindedly this time. 'We'll need somewhere to keep it.'

'You what?' The words came out in a blurt.

'We'll need somewhere to keep it,' she said. 'Eloise pointed that out. It can't come in here, and it'll get ruined outside in the winter. It needs a proper garage.' She fixed him with a stare. 'Which means your precious workshop.'

Ted almost exploded as the relief surged around him. 'A garage?'

'It's not just the scooter. There are spare batteries and bits and pieces.'

'But – but.' He found himself struggling to remember how to talk, as his senses put themselves back together. 'But that's not a problem. What's the problem with that?'

He could see astonishment written all over her face. 'I thought you'd kick up a fuss,' she said.

If Daisy had been further taken aback by the speed in which Ted emptied the outbuilding then she had done her best not to show it. And the self-reproach that she had been trying to conceal over commandeering his workshop had been quickly forgotten, judging from her complaints each time he reappeared in the house bearing more items to store. Within two hours, the second bedroom was piled high, with tools, wood and ironmongery strewn across the bed, on the chest of drawers, around the floor.

'You don't have to bring the whole lot in,' she insisted. 'It's only a little scooter.' Daisy craned her neck to see down the corridor. 'Don't get filth everywhere. You're going to have to clear up properly when you're done. Properly, I mean.'

Ted paused to lean against the door frame of the lounge. 'What we need to do is wait until it arrives, then park it in there with space around it. There's no point in having it if you can't get to it easily.' Even as he spoke, Ted was shocked at how easily he was running with this new pretence; how bullshit appeared to have become second-nature to him. How long would it be before he would have to tell her that there would be no scooter? 'Besides,' he said. 'There's all sorts of stuff that ought to go properly under cover for the winter. I need to make space for that.'

'Well you'll have to move it all outside again if we have more visitors.'

'But we're not going to have more visitors. We've had our visitors.'

'What about David if he comes? He did say he'd come. I wish he'd write.'

Ted turned his back to hide his expression. 'Then I'll move it all again.'

'Well you could sort out some of your other clutter while you're at it,' she said. 'That dead ferret. It's creepy.'

'It's a weasel.'

He shifted his box of records and the gramophone last. With nowhere else for them to go, he set them down upon the kitchen table, running the lead to the socket that sagged from the wall next to the hob. They had been hardly using this room anyway, forsaking formal meals for the ease of a tray in the lounge. It would be good to have music in the house once more.

*

Philippe opened a new bottle, performing the process with theatrical, sulky glances at his bandaged hands. Gaston pursed his lips and made coochie-coo noises as the youth kicked a stool from his path on his return to his station behind the bar.

'Next time we'll want cocktails,' Gaston called after him. 'With slices of lemon, cut delicately.' The mayor, sat opposite, snorted through his moustache.

'Ah – give the lad a break.' Ted took the bottle and began to pour. 'He makes a meal of it, but he's properly hurt.'

'Makes a meal, yes, makes a meal,' Gaston wiped an

imaginary tear from his eye. 'But his face, it is bad for business. Philippe!'

Philippe turned back to the group and leaned forward, planting his elbows on the bar and glaring. *It's not busy. And I can do without you today. Go to bed. Rest. Grow new skin.*

'Those hands will be no good for anything in bed tonight,' called out the mayor. *'What will you do, eh?'* He roared, looking at each of his friends in turn to share in the joke.

'You will have to get a girl to help you,' said Casimir, pausing to take a gulp of wine before he continued. *'I bet you can think of two.'*

The mayor's laughter tapered off. *'Anyway. Let us get on,'* he bristled.

Leaning back in his chair and toying with his glass, Ted realised how much he had missed his sessions in the café. He had not been a stranger to the establishment, but his visits recently had been perfunctory in the shadow of events, or simply functional in his new capacity as Gaston's hired hand. Pottering in the cellar, driving around the café's suppliers, even cleaning up around the bar: they had been cheerfully enjoyable ways of keeping himself occupied. But they had been nothing compared to the advent of the mayor's 'museum,' and the realisation that – for one afternoon at least – he was expected to pay off some of his debt by sitting with his friends, drinking wine, and chatting about Frédéric Debreu.

A planning meeting, they had called it. Well, if this was how they ran their meetings then it was all right by him. The mayor had seemed genuinely pleased by Ted's enthusiasm for his prospective venture; the Englishman had already been assigned a number of errands pertaining to Debreu's history. Ted made less effort to understand the conversation around him as the talk veered towards the logistics of opening, his mind wandering back to the man and the songs that were to be so justly celebrated. When Madame Kerharo appeared from the kitchen bearing two big platters of fried pike, he took a cube and savoured it. The fishy, buttery taste; the flesh that melted away around his tongue; it reminded him of why he'd fallen in love with this place so much. He looked past Casimir's shoulder, through the plate glass and on to the market place. The traders had all but packed away for the day. All the people out there, ambling about their daily business, living the snail's pace of life that might well be the most hackneyed of visitor-guide clichés but that had its foundation in solid truth. If he could get things sorted –

'You agree, Ted?'

Ted raised his eyes from the table to find faces turned to him. He blinked back at them, his mouth dropping open in confusion.

'Eh?'

'Eh?' Gaston aped his expression good-naturedly.

'He is dreaming.'

'He is more gaga even than you are, Casimir.'

'And his face goes redder than your nose.'

'Well they all seem good ideas to me,' Ted said, once the mayor had recapped the discussion that had passed him by. 'I'm hardly the world's authority compared to you lot, but you know how I feel about Debreu. Plus,' he stole a glance at Gaston, 'it would be good to lend a hand.'

'Mmm.' The mayor nodded, and recorded a satisfied tick on the clipboard before him. Behind the official, the double doors swung inward to admit the hulking Claude. The newcomer registered each of them in turn with a nod, adding an oily beam and a thumbs-up gesture when he reached Ted. He made no attempt to join them, waddling his way through to his usual far table. Gaston glided across to take his order.

'What else?' said the mayor. 'What else? Ted, what would you, the English, expect to see?'

Ted screwed up his face as he pictured himself walking through the door of this new place. 'Well I suppose most tourists wouldn't actually have heard of him. So I guess you want a big introduction right by the door in words of one syllable.' He saw Casimir's expression. 'Simple words,' he clarified. A thought

194

struck him. 'And how about a map? A big map. With all the places mentioned in his songs marked on it?'

The mayor scribbled. '*Oui, oui.* This is good. How about we have a big model of Debreu, he stands by the door to welcome people?'

'A model?'

'*Oui, oui,* a mannequin. We dress him, he has a *hairpiece,* and –'

'*That is a crappy idea.*' Casimir threw up his hands. Gaston eased back to join them, placing a freshly opened bottle on the table.

'OK, a statue. A statue. A big, big statue in the *market place.*' The mayor half stood, throwing his arms toward the windows. '*That would show them this is the true home town of Debreu.*' He glared at the street scene before resuming his position and scrawling again on his pad. He turned to Ted. 'A statue. My sister, she would be proud, very proud. She was Debreu's lover, you understand.' Pouring the wine, Casimir paused to grimace, making sure that the mayor saw his expression.

'We need the information in English, maybe in German also,' said Gaston. 'English is easy; you can write it, Ted?'

'Well, I'm not much of a wordsmith, but I'll give it a go.'

The mayor nodded. 'It will be good to have also a native English speaker in the museum.'

Casimir leaned in and brandished a bony finger. 'The problem.'

The mayor swung round to the old man, daring him to produce another barb. But his old sparring partner was oblivious. '*Ted must not work in the museum. Not soon. People come, they are tourists, but also there are the fans. They may have been at the big club.*' He turned to Ted. 'One day they see Édouard Prescôte play. The next day they visit and, zipppp! You are the English museum man.'

'Well, it'll be a while. I'm not sure they'll remember?'

'Casimir is right,' said Gaston. 'It is a risk. Too much risk. He cannot meet the customers. We speak English. It is OK.'

'Maybe we take the leaflets to the club?'

'*Oui,* they say "you remember that show, you discover more, you visit the museum."'

'There is perhaps a *discount. If they bring their leaflet they get one, two euro off anything that they buy.*'

'*Richepin could be an important guy to us. He knows lots of people.*'

'*Are there people here who speak other languages?*'

The conversation moved on to a discussion about one of the market traders who may or may not have worked in Belgium at some point in the distant past. Ted excused himself and made a break for the gents.

He bid his friends farewell an hour later. He was jaunty and rosy-faced as he pushed his way out through the doors, but by no means the tottering spectacle that those get-togethers had once habitually turned him into. He drunk in the outside air with a grin. Philippe's accident – whilst a shame for the boy – had created a ready supply of work for Ted, reassuring the Englishman that he was properly repaying Gaston's loan with honest labour. But this work with the museum! Brochures, explanations, annotations – all would need to be produced in English. Most would just be straight translation, but still – writing about Frédéric Debreu! As jobs went, you couldn't do much better. Perhaps an English booklet might sell by mail order, as he had bought those first records so many years ago. Surely it was possible that there might be people like Ted all over Britain, people who had somehow or other stumbled across Debreu, as he had via his brother's introduction; people who had fallen in love with the great man's work. All over the world, even. Gaston had talked of having a website designed. That would root them out.

Instead of heading directly home, Ted turned left to make a short diversion via the new museum. His breath steamed up the window as he peered through to see the progress that had been made. Frédéric Debreu! If there was to be a revival, fancy that he was here, right in the centre of it!

As he turned away, his eye caught sight of the barber's shop at the very end of the street. His own grooming – always sporadic – had been particularly neglected over the past couple of months. Returning to check his reflection in the shop window confirmed this; he was in danger of starting to resemble the old photographs of himself in the mid 1970s. Taking a sheepish look at the figure in the glass, Ted strode off to get his haircut.

He had been in the chair for ten minutes when he noticed Philippe, the youth peering and waving through the grime of the barber's window, thudding at the glass with his bandaged hands to prompt the Englishman to turn his semi-tidied head. Ted pulled his arm from underneath the orange cape, sending a cloud of grey-black hairs cascading to the floor. His first reaction was that this was a stroke of luck – a translator would be handy, given that he had no confidence that his request for the cheapest haircut possible had been understood. But this was all forgotten as Philippe burst through the door and stammered out the news.

'When? Just now?' Ted swung his chair around in his urgency, causing the barber to leap backwards and yank his scissors away in concern.

'*Oui, oui.* Five minutes! Monsieur Patenaude, he comes in, he says he sees you come here for your hair. I have a number.'

Ted briefly contemplated leaving there and then, throwing down his money and hurrying along the street sporting half a haircut. Instead he fidgeted and sucked his teeth as the barber continued, finishing off with ever slower and more meticulous snips, single hair by single hair, deliberating with each laboured jab of the scissors to reflect upon the exact accuracy of his cut. At one point the store's telephone rang; the shopkeeper ambled toward the instrument as if he were unsure and suspicious of its purpose, and Ted stewed and fumed as the resulting conversation meandered in languid Gallic from topic to topic. The Englishman felt the wine sweating out from his pores in the warm shop; his fingers beat a frantic tattoo on the arms of the barber's chair. What had happened? What was the news? And, more to the point, what would he say himself?

It was a full twenty minutes before he was in the café once

more, his friends looking across at him as he huddled in the corner at the end of the bar, fingers trembling as he punched in the number on the keypad before him. He wondered as to the origin of the dialling code; it was not one that he recognised. He prayed as the tone changed, pleading with the deity that he had so long neglected that the boy's shaky writing had recorded the digits correctly.

And then, after a hundred, a hundred thousand rings, a familiar voice spoke from another country.

'Hello?'

'David!'

There was an endless pause.

'Dad, I'm so sorry.'

16

An Intimate Setting

Ted was washing clothes when he heard a car draw up. The water poured grey-brown from his trousers as he lifted them from the sink and began to wring them out with his big paws, screwing each leg into a tight knot of old corduroy. Daisy had been right: they had needed a bit of a rinse. He would give them one more soaking before pegging them up outside.

Gaston poked his head through the kitchen doorway. 'I am interrupting?'

'No, no.' Ted reached for the tea towel to dry his hands before accepting the obligatory handshake. 'Chores.'

'Ah.' Gaston stepped into the room. He held aloft a small bottle of golden liquid. 'I have this. For Madame Prescott. To wish her better health.'

'You'd better come in then.'

'It is Calvados, the apple brandy,' Gaston said, having declined the offer of tea with his customary courtesy. 'To say to you "become well again," and to help as the evenings are colder.' He studied the bottle himself before setting it on the table next to Daisy. 'Although it does not say the word "Calvados," it is Calvados. You will know it as Calvados although the law says that it cannot say that. I am sorry that I have not been before to visit.'

Daisy peered at the gift. 'That's very generous of you, Gaston. I shall enjoy a little nip of that.'

'And you are feeling well, Madame Prescott?' Gaston beamed as he stood over her.

'Stuck indoors. But I won't grumble.'

'You have Monsieur Prescott working hard in the kitchen. That is good.'

'It would be better if he didn't carp on about it so much.'

'Ah.' Gaston waved his arm towards Ted, who was hovering in the doorway. '*Oui*, yes. The boy that works for me, you have met him, Philippe. He hurts his hands. He still works, but he complains. Complain, complain. But Ted, he is much older, he helps me kindly, he does not complain. Now I will teach Ted to work in the bar until the boy is less useless.'

'Well if you need some help on that front?' Ted said.

'Ah! Yes.' Gaston turned to the Englishman. 'You have free time this evening?'

'Yes, of course. It'd be no problem.'

'Good, good. There is an opportunity for you to play.'

'I only know today,' insisted Gaston, as Ted shepherded him out on to the verandah. 'It is a small bar. The owner, he rings me, I drive directly to your house.'

'Well you could have just told him "no" there and then.'

'But I must speak with you first. The opportunity, it is very good.'

'In what sense could it be "very good?"'

Gaston turned from the Englishman and began to pace the shabby decking, his head bowed, his hands cradling his chin. 'Ted, I realise that it is unusual to ask you, that you worry about your performance, you worry about being Édouard. I say before that you have already been important; if it is not for the *triumph* at Richepin's then perhaps Bernard does not have the confidence to do his plans.' The café owner paused, looked directly at Ted and gave the lightest of shrugs. 'We resurrect Frédéric Debreu, we resurrect Mailliot le Bois.'

Ted said nothing. He looked past his visitor to the rolling meadows beyond, listening to the wind as it ruffled the grass and hedgerow.

Gaston stepped forwards and laid his hands on Ted's

shoulders. 'It is small, Ted. I promise, it is small. I know of it well. Yes, you are nervous, but you love it very much when you play before. Remember! They clap, they cheer! In the car, a big, big smile on your face! You are, they say, king of the hill? And this evening – there is no time to worry, eh?'

'How small?' Ted brushed Gaston's hands away. 'Exactly how small? How many tables in the bar, for instance?'

Gaston stroked his chin as he considered this. 'Ten? Perhaps twelve? You see, small. I promise.'

'And it has to be tonight?'

'Tonight. We go in, we play, we go out, thank you.'

'We?'

'*Ah, oui,* I was sure that you would. It is arranged.' Gaston hopped down the wooden steps towards his car. 'Me and Philippe. We will collect you, seven o'clock.'

*

Ted examined his fingers. They were grubby and smelt of rust. Ideally he should change his strings before the evening's antics but he had no spares. The thought crossed his mind that Gaston should supply some – surely it was an employer's responsibility to provide tools for the job? He snorted to himself as he ran through some minor chords.

The conversation with David had been heartbreaking. Ted had wanted information; to know the practicalities. David had wanted to apologise, over and over, his voice cracking with the tears that he was holding back so ineffectually. The money that had been lost paled into insignificance against Ted's horror at hearing his son broken with guilt on his father's behalf. Twice Ted had hesitated when the conversation had turned to Daisy, the older man agonising over which approach would be kinder. Should he reveal to David that she was living in happy ignorance of all that had happened? Or would that be worse, implying that he had spared her shame and disappointment at her son, leaving an inescapable future revelation hanging over them as further punishment? He had said nothing, whether out of consideration or cowardice, although he had spoken of her accident, glossing over its severity and implying that she would soon be trotting down to the village to speak to him on the telephone.

The conversation had been heartbreaking, but it had been a conversation.

Ted pulled a sheet of paper from the sideboard and scribbled down an order of songs. 'Marguerite', 'The Vengeful Widow', 'The Forger', 'Thorigny Fields', 'The Pretty Goat'. He wasn't sure that he really needed a list, but he knew that his brain would fly out of the window later on. Best leave nothing to chance.

The facts, the bare facts, had been encouraging. This is what he should focus upon. The boy had a place to live, and the chance of a job, and a telephone. A telephone so they could keep in touch and get through this without the long weeks of wondering and speculation that had eaten away at Ted. Things had gone wrong, but David was bright. Given a bit of time, he'd get himself together and they'd be able to work out what to do.

Ted stole a glance at his wife. His list was twenty minutes' worth, easily. If they wanted more he could do any number of other songs. He folded the sheet and slipped it into his back pocket. His nerves were firing warning shots already.

'I'll be off,' he said.

'You changed your shirt then?'

'My shirt?'

'Your shirt was "too English". That's what you were muttering to yourself just then. What did you mean by that then?'

Ted picked at his lapel, staring downward to study the button on his cuff. 'Well the people there will all be French. You know what they're like with their sense of style and what have you.'

Daisy sniffed. 'That was a good shirt. You look scruffy now.'

'Anyway. Best not muck about.' Ted's hand hovered over his guitar case as he searched the room for an excuse not to pick it up. 'Are you sure you don't need me to do anything before I go?'

'I'm sure. Have a nice time.'

As he slipped through the doorway, Ted gave his wife one last lingering look. She was already reabsorbed in her handiwork. The remark about his shirt had rattled him; Daisy was not stupid, although his troubled conscience was now habitually causing him to read more than was probably warranted into the slightest remark of hers. Earlier, she had suggested that he might incorporate some Jake Thackray songs into his performance, her mention of the English songwriter seeming to confirm that she had no inkling as to the sham that would be involved. He had almost contemplated admitting to her about 'Édouard' there and then, but his mind kept returning to her ire over the festival stall. It was back to her principle of 'respectability' again. Ted had a fairly robust notion that Édouard Prescôte's continued existence had no place in this doctrine.

Gaston was alone when he arrived, reversing his big car onto the dirt track as Ted rose from the tree stump that had been his perch for ten chilly minutes.

Philippe would not be coming. Gaston's tone was abrupt. The barman was to have been cleared to drive once more, but his doctor had supposedly advised him to wait for a further fortnight. Ted pictured the scene as he heaved himself into the luxury of the front seat, the boy with his lips pursed and arms crossed, showing sulky, lion-hearted resolve as his employer shouted and threatened. He was a surprising lad sometimes.

Their usual easy conversation was absent during the first part of the journey. Gaston tutted and fumed at each negligible delay on the road; Ted devoted his mental energy on quelling rushes of agitation about the evening ahead. Nevertheless the Frenchman warmed as they neared their destination, his excitement seeming to rise in direct proportion to Ted's fear.

'You are ready?' he asked as they drove through the outskirts.

'As I'll ever be.'

'Humm.' Gaston nodded his approval.

'Very small, right?'

'Very small.'

Gaston parked in the street at the rear of the bar and they walked together through a urine-stinking alleyway towards the front of the building. Ted carried his own guitar.

There was a small window about halfway along the length of the wall. Ted paused to peek through. What he saw eased his anxiety a little. There were fifteen or so tables in the compact bar, with a microscopic stage on the far side that would raise Ted all of six inches above the customers. His eyes darted around the interior. Everything appeared to be zealously shiny, the fittings looking expensive if dated, all brass and mahogany and crystal. Ted was still learning to interpret the vernacular of this strange country, but his impression was that this would be a 'nice' place, frequented by 'nice' people. It looked all very middle-class; the sort of establishment that he might pass by as a punter, but for this evening's purposes safer than the buzzing den that had seen Édouard's debut.

The front of the building consisted of the ubiquitous plate glass folding doors. Before leading his friend inside, Gaston took a step back and beckoned Ted to look about him.

'See. Very small. Very small tonight. April, the doors open, tables everywhere in the square here, filled with tourists. Tonight, we play, we get perhaps some *publicity*, a little money, much *goodwill* from the owner. After April, many people are here, we use that *goodwill*. Big opportunity, heh?' Gaston rubbed his hands together.

'You know come April I probably won't be here, Gaston?'

The Frenchman shrugged. 'Perhaps no. I speculate. Come.'

Ted had been calmed by his first sight of the cosy room. But it transpired that the intimacy of the surroundings held a trap for him. Because whilst the audience may have been politer – attentive rather than rowdy, and less likely to hurl beer glasses should he mess up one of Debreu's cherished works, there was simply nowhere to hide from them. In the cavernous jazz club he had been shielded by friends. The surrounding hubbub had allowed him to talk softly in English. He had been able to move around the space without social interaction by pretending to catch the eye of an acquaintance on the far side of the room. Here, it was hopeless. As before, Gaston spoke for him, but Ted became convinced that his own attempts to appear mysterious were simply coming across as surly and rude. And when the promoter attempted to introduce him to a young couple who were to be the headline attraction for the evening, he was forced to manufacture a coughing fit, alternating desperate heaves and splutters into his palms with a repertoire of nods and thumbs-up gestures that he hoped conveyed an acceptable 'pleased to meet you' to the startled musicians. Feeling miserable, Ted downed his glass and withdrew to the car to await his friend's stage call, muttering words as he went.

> ♫ Dear Editor, Back after the war
> Young people respected the rule of law
> But now they behave like the apes ... ♫

A hip flask. He would need to bring a hip flask, lest ever again he needed to flee a bar in advance of a performance. A single large glass of red was woefully inadequate to calm his screaming nerves. Nevertheless, after some jitters during the expectant silence that accompanied his tuning up, he made a decent fist of it. This would never be a sing-along venue, but the well-bred people there rewarded him with gently tapping feet and orderly applause. He was playing without amplification, so there were no microphones to confuse him, and by the time he had charged through the last bars of 'The Pretty Goat' he understood that he had learned a great deal more about the act of performance. The reception for this final song was warm, but Ted felt none of the surge of shared joy that he had experienced before. He realised that he had been wrong about the bearpit of the jazz club. In that big room of cheerful drunks he had been part of a shared experience, leading the crowd along in appreciation of these wonderful songs, a conduit for their joy. It had been the same as that spontaneous time in the café at Gaston's, and at the pissed sing-along at the festival. Here? Well, here he had just played the guitar for them to listen to. The performing monkey. He willed himself to maintain eye contact as the customers clapped him off the stage, returning their appreciation with a forced smile of his own, hoping that those who had attempted to speak with him would take his earlier diffidence for simple stage-fright, and that the relief in his gait would pass undetected. The girl who was to perform next was unpacking her violin at the bar; she gave him a delighted wave and stepped forward as if to approach him. Ted returned her gesture with another thumbs-up, warm and confident this time, and continued walking, through the door and out on to the cold street, striding off into the alleyway and onto the car alone.

Gaston appeared five minutes later, having stayed back to sort out their payment. Speeding away through the outskirts and into the black night of the countryside, he was as buoyant as Ted had ever seen him. Perhaps it was the wine – in his regular driver's absence he had noticeably reigned himself in, but by no means could he be under the limit. Perhaps it was the conversation that he'd had with the venue's management. Ted reclined in the front seat, feeling his eyelids becoming heavier as the post-performance comedown began to creep over him.

Gaston broke the silence. 'It was good tonight, Ted. Very good.'

'Mmm.'

'No, you did well, to be sure.'

'Thank you.' Ted's head lolled against the side window; he regarded the blur of a seemingly endless stone wall as they pressed on past. 'It's a long way to go for the sake of so few people though.' There was a pause before he turned to Gaston and added, 'For you, I mean. You know – the cost of the fuel alone.'

'Ah. As I say, I speculate. I invest.'

Gaston slowed the car, but not appreciably, as they passed

through a hamlet. On the far side, he paused to give way to a logging truck before turning left onto the main road that would take them towards the ravine and thence to the river crossing and home. He reached for the dial on the air conditioning. A polar blast hit the two men.

'The big picture is my concern, Ted. Like I have said before always. When you play, all things that are not the music are my concern. You are very nervous, extremely nervous, when you go to play. It is my job to make you less nervous.'

'Thank you. It was – different tonight.' Ted cast his mind back. It was true. He had been anxious, and he had been stressed. He had sweated and his mouth had dried. But so much of this had been to do with the crazy deceit that he'd been forced to adopt in that close-knit environment. In terms of the playing, in terms of the sheer visceral terror that he'd experienced before – well, it didn't compare. In its own way, it was encouraging. He opened his mouth to speak again. 'But Daisy –'

'We need, what we need, is something to balance the costs.' The tone of Gaston's voice had changed subtly.

'What sort of something?' Ted asked, keeping his eyes fixed on the road ahead.

Gaston ran his hand around his billiard-ball chin. 'Hummm. I will think of the something.'

They drove the rest of the journey in silence.

17

The Lovesick Clerk

'"Meanwhile, *Le Rendez Vous* continues to host the acoustic musicians in an atmosphere of comfort and quality. Thursday's show featured the familiar players Andrée and Robert who delight regularly with the traditional music of the Bretons. On the same evening was the new discovery Édouard Prescôte who had the audience very attentive with his playing of the songs of Frédéric Debreu."'

Casimir pummeled Ted on the back. 'New discovery! You are the new discovery, Ted.' The ancient man threw his mouth wide open to let rip a rasping cackle.

'Very attentive? They were a bit stiff, but like bloody putty in my hand.'

Gaston resumed his translation. '"Prescôte is a farmworker who has performed in public never until recently; he is a simple man and obviously has nerves for the occasion until his music starts and he is transformed. His phrasing is eccentric occasionally but his music is from his heart and not calculated, and he has an – ahh – a pleased smile? A happy smile? And he has a happy smile to soften some of Debreu's sentiments of, ah, *misogyny*. It was notable how the audience enjoyed these classic songs. If this is the start of a *resurrection* of this man's music then that is welcomed."' The café owner lay down the magazine and nodded in satisfaction, oblivious to Ted's finger poking him in the chest.

'Where'd they get all that guff about being a farmworker from? A simple man?'

'The people who ask for you to play, I give them a *biography*.'

208

Gaston's tone was dismissive as he removed the Englishman's fat digit, smoothing down his shirtfront with his own manicured fingertips. 'You do some work. You live at a farm. You are simple. Next question.'

'It is good, Ted. A comeback for the great Debreu.' Casimir threw his skeletal arms wide, indicating the exhibits that were already adorning the visitor centre. *'So writes the authority of the magazine.'*

'Gaah.'

The photocopier's clattering fell silent. Gaston reached for a new ream of paper and tore open the packet. Ted stood to retrieve the sheets that had been spewing from the machine. 'Off we go, then,' he said.

'A new discovery.' Despite his show of indifference, Ted felt a giggle rising within him as he began to line up the pages three at a time, thumping a staple through the top corner of each batch. It was crazy, it really was crazy. He tried to picture himself back on that little stage, warbling those lines by rote whilst the reporter took her ever-so-serious notes. He felt sweat on his brow as his chuckle turned to one of his recurring glimpses of horror at what might have been. Stupid! He was stupid – stupid to have done it in the first place; stupid to be getting stage fright, here and now, on behalf of something that had occurred days before.

'I can't do more evenings like that, Gaston.' He tried to make his voice sound natural, final.

Gaston did not pause from his work. 'I understand, Ted. It was not a good place for you. Very small; you were not protected from the people talking to you.'

Ted put down his stapler. 'I mean, don't get me wrong. I appreciate all you're doing for me, and all the other stuff is fine, all the stuff in the bar, all that to do with this place. Even playing a few songs in your café. It's just the acting, the pretence that I can't do.'

Gaston set down a fresh pile on the table between them. *'Oui,* I agree,' he said. 'The next one is more organised. We go back to Django's club; we take lots of people to make you feel at home, to look after you. It is an opportunity that is very well-paid. Better paid now you are known, you do a longer performance.'

Gaston crossed the shop floor, reaching for some papers on the counter. He passed one to Ted, who recognised the logo right away. The page had been divided into three panels of enormous block type, each set beside a date and time. The middle section was entitled *'The Songs of Frédéric Debreu.'*

'See – your name it is bigger this time. Much bigger. Things happen, Ted. Things happen.'

The three continued their work to the accompaniment of the photocopier. Ted tried to occupy his mind by attempting to translate the quiz sheets in his head. He knew some of the questions already, as they had been his suggestions. 'One. How many bedrooms were there in *The Lodging House*?' The clack-clack-clack noise started up again as Gaston closed the cover of the machine. 'Two. What was *Monsieur Berlin's* final excuse to his wife, before she set his clothes on fire?'

'Hey hey!' The mayor's frame filled the front door. He set down a tray – a cafetière and four mugs, and shook the rain from his hair like a wet dog. Casimir thrust his work to one side whilst Gaston sat to join them. Ted, after a microscopic delay, did likewise. He would never understand this bloody country, or how they ever got anything done. Gaston set out the mugs and started to pour, nodding his head towards the open magazine on the table. The mayor took it and began to read, a delighted smile breaking out beneath his shaggy moustache.

'It's good,' said Ted, indicating the pile of quiz papers beside him.

'It is, *oui,*' replied Casimir. 'Thank you. You can write it again in English? When you have done the guide?'

Ted nodded. 'You'll have to check it. But even if I don't

210

understand each word, it's pretty obvious if you know the song what most of the questions –'

The thunderclap almost made Ted leap from his chair. The mayor had slammed the magazine into the table and had half-risen, glowering, shifting his gaze up and down from the article to his companions, his entire face quivering in outrage.

'Misogyny!' he spat. *'Misogyny!'* He took up the magazine once more, only to throw it back down in disgust.

'Classic songs, Bernard. They call them classic songs.'

'Like hell!' The mayor left his place and paced the room in an explosive fury, circling his friends in strides whilst waving and brandishing his clenched fists like a novice conductor rehearsing some Wagnerian climax. *'Misogyny!'* He swung round to confront the men. *'They have the nerve to call themselves critics, these people that know nothing of any culture but the lah-di-dah shit they pretend to understand!'* He turned away once more, his chest heaving as he breathed deeply to compose himself. *'Gaaaah!'*

Ted caught Casimir's eye. The old man was chortling silently.

There was an awkward silence before the mayor spoke again. 'Ted, I am sorry.' He reached for the article one more time, thrusting it down at the Englishman as he loomed above him. 'I am sorry. It is a good story for you. You do a good show, and it is recognised. But Frédéric Debreu will not be said to have *misogyny* just because this *bimbo* writes it in a magazine. Not!'

'Non, non.' Gaston's words were soothing.

'Hmmmm?' The mayor's tone became dangerous once more, yet he paced steadily back to his seat, lowering himself softly and reaching for his coffee. Ted avoided his eyes. 'Debreu ... Frédéric Debreu, he was a hero to the region. He was, he should have been a hero to France. Yes, he was not a perfect man. He was a human being. But he was also a genius, and some of his genius was that he writes songs about the men and the girls and love, and they are beautiful and they are with much warmth and humour. And I know he loved and he respected the girls. After all, my sister was Debreu's lover.'

Casimir opened his mouth but his interjection was quelled

211

with a warning wave of Gaston's palm. Ted downed his coffee and took up the stapler. 'Shall we get on with these?' he said.

The visitor centre was taking shape nicely. The talk of mannequins with wigs had caused Ted to fear the worst type of half-baked tat. But as he beavered away, the big Englishman reflected that the mayor had backed up his passion with some proper, hard brass. Although these quizzes were being knocked out on the photocopier, a glossy pamphlet had been professionally designed and printed; three big boxes of them were stacked beside the door. Ted's proposed map had been created by a local artist, an enormous sheet of ink and watercolour, each of Debreu's haunts marked with a black silhouette of a guitar and lovingly annotated in hand-drawn lettering. It had been installed in place of the previous, tatty affair from the days of the tourist information office; it covered fully one third of the wall and looked magnificent there to the Englishman's eyes. Beneath it was a display case with a glass front and top. Here, Ted found things getting a little problematical. A duffel bag and guitar took centre stage in the exhibit, the neck of the instrument resting casually across the bag as if Debreu had set them down momentarily before popping outside to check on the bus times. The bag was threadbare and battered; Ted could quite envisage the musician lugging it from town to town on his endless tour of those dead-end venues. The guitar was rudimentary in construction but a fine-looking instrument, just as much so as when Ted himself had presented it to Gaston some months earlier. Surrounding this little exhibit were pinned a number of sheets: pages torn from notebooks and restaurant pads. They featured snatches of writing: lyrics, couplets, ideas. All pertained to Debreu's early works, although the handwriting may have struck a chord with any tourist who had previously requested a written receipt from the café along the street.

'It is to just make an atmosphere. Until we have enough of the true ones,' the mayor had reassured him, and it was true that they were beginning to collect a stock of more authentic material, brought in by various townsfolk and acquaintances of the undertaking's prime movers, all logged by hand in an exercise book, a stamped receipt issued to their owners. The care with which each donor had presented their item; their eagerness to see it displayed – it newly impressed upon Ted the special position that the master musician had held within this community. What particularly struck him was how widely Debreu's memorabilia had found itself scattered. It seemed that every household in the region, every business, had been left with one reminder of the great man, however small.

Ted stapled his final sheets together. Leaning back in his chair, he felt a numbness in his right hand from the repetitive process. He flapped it vigorously to restart the circulation. 'Are we done?' he asked.

'Done,' said Gaston, miming a drinking motion.

'I'm out this afternoon, Gaston. Remember?'

'Time for one, just one. I have something. *You guys tidy up here. I have something to show Ted.*'

Philippe glowered at them as they walked in through the doors. The barman said nothing, but looked pointedly across to the gaggle of customers.

'*Yes, yes. Five more minutes. You can manage,*' snapped Gaston.

'*I can work at half my usual speed.*' Philippe held up his hands. '*I have to use a tray to carry. And I am not touching that machine.*'

'*Five minutes.*'

'*The doctor says –*'

'*The doctor seems to say a lot. Perhaps I should speak to him, eh?*'

Philippe scuttled through to the kitchen as Gaston glided to retrieve a bottle from the bar. After a brief hesitation, Ted plodded across to the round table and sat down.

'One small glass, Gaston. I'm driving.'

'*Oui, oui.*' Gaston thrust a sheet of paper at him. 'Here!'

Ted took the sheet. It was the output from a laser printer; a black-and-white photograph around four- or five- inches square of an unknown man staring awkwardly into a camera in what appeared to be a photo he'd taken of himself. Superimposed on the image were the names 'Édouard Prescôte' and 'Frédéric Debreu'.

'What is this?'

'CDs. We make CDs.' Gaston looked up from the corkscrew, regarding the Englishman with evangelical eyes. 'We have the recordings that you have already done. We make CDs from them and we sell them at the shows, we sell them at the information centre, we maybe sell them here at the café?'

Ted stared at the sheet once more.

'Alain. He is Bernard's younger brother. You recall Bernard he says that Alain will take your car away? No matter. He has designed a cover on the computer. This is Alain's face here, for the demonstration. He will come to photograph you.'

'But we can't do that.'

'Why not?' Gaston shrugged, an enormous, expansive gesture that bore the hallmarks of pre-rehearsal. 'It is what the musicians do.'

'No.'

'Ted ...'

'Look, Gaston.' Ted pushed the image across the table towards where his friend was filling his glass. He could feel himself getting annoyed. 'Did you not hear what I said back then? It's one thing turning up and playing a few songs, and people enjoy it, and they have a few pints and go home and have nice memories. It's quite another taking money from them for something that's –' he said, turning away – 'properly dishonest.'

'What is dishonest?'

'It's not me, is it? It's not bloody me!'

'But what is the difference between the CD and the show?'

'Well, because.' Ted rose from his chair and started waving his big arms about. 'Because one is transient and one is permanent! Because there is a difference when you – when you put things in writing, to last! It's like, when I play it's like, well it's over when it's over – it's like tomorrow's chip paper and –' Ted caught the Frenchman's nonplussed look at this last phrase. 'Never mind. It's different, and we're not doing it.'

'Would Missus Prescott not be proud? A bestselling CD with your face on it?'

'A bestselling CD with my fat mug on it, faking it? No she would not be bloody proud. She would be bloody unproud. In fact she'd be bloody cheesed off.'

'But you sell those people your guitars? They are permanent?'

'And she was bloody cheesed off with that as well, and keeps reminding me. Anyway, that's different, of course it is. They were good instruments.'

'And they will not be good CDs?'

'They didn't have my name on. There was my name at the stall, fine, yes. But not on the instruments.'

Ted resumed his seat and glared at Gaston. The Frenchman seemed unperturbed by this challenge to his plan, pouring a generous measure into his own glass. 'No CDs,' said Ted, in a calmer tone. 'Nothing with my photo on.' He glanced at his watch – nearly midday. He should have taken the car straight after finishing at the visitor centre. But who knew what this lunatic might get carried away with if Ted did not keep tabs on him?

'Look, look.' Gaston's voice was sugar-coated. 'I understand. I do understand. But I think, 'Édouard Prescôte' – it is your *pseudonym*. That is a very common usual thing. That is what the musicians do. Elton John? That is not his real name. It is on his CD, all his CDs, his posters. It says 'Elton John'. It does not say 'Elton John but this is not my real name.' They all do this, all the big stars. Elton John. The English guy – Cliff Richards? Elvis Presley. Now see this good design again. You call yourself 'Édouard Prescôte'. The CD, it says 'Édouard Prescôte'. Does it say 'Édouard Prescôte, I am a French Man'? *Non.*' Gaston's head shook nineteen to the dozen.

'But Elvis Presley was his real name.'

'Pffft.'

'No CD. And nothing with my photo on it.'

215

Ted's sense of exasperation lingered as he drove to Saint Ouen-de-l'Éléphant. The skies darkened further as he approached the town and parked the car. He was apprehensive as he plodded through those canyons of apartment buildings that would lead him to the centre. It started to drizzle: nothing that could be called good honest rain, just an overarching and dismal wetness to add to the feeling of gloom. The architecture of this town was cheerless on the best of days, he thought, as Ted passed by walls of stained-grey and faded-beige shutters that had rotted closed. Things didn't automatically become pretty just because they were old and abroad. He pulled his big coat around him as he sloshed through the puddles.

By rights he should be excited to be revisiting the old museum this afternoon; certainly he was keen to see the shrine to Frédéric Debreu again, to study those remaining papers. But the background was different this time. His initial discovery had been burnished by the joy of serendipity, and crowned by his determination to make those songs live again. But today he came with a less straightforward agenda. Yes, to confirm his years-old transcriptions against those original lyrics would be helpful, and there might be entire songs in that drawer that would otherwise never see the light of day. And whatever his beef with Gaston, if he was going to perform those songs, he was going to perform them properly. Any chance to immerse himself in Debreu's life would be valuable, and this was surely a genuine reason for him to be there.

On the other hand, the mayor's letter to the trustees of the museum here had been frostily rebuffed. The official had offered to safeguard the unseen Debreu papers in his town's own display, so that they might be enjoyed by as many lovers of the great man's work as possible. Whatever the reason for the snub – Bernard had railed against historical rivalries and political conspiracies, although Ted had an inkling that the request had been worded with a certain absence of tact and humility – it cast a small shadow over Ted's presence here in Saint Ouen, and he fretted that he would be repaying the goodwill of that otherwise dour lady curator with an underhand act.

Ted stepped into the street to avoid a filthy lake that had spread wide around a blocked drain on the pavement. He was not about to steal anything, he reminded himself. And, at the end of the day, when all was said and done, he was, first and foremost a fan, a lifetime fan. He repeated this in his mind as he approached the town square, the towering black church appearing from behind the tenements to loom over him in the murk. He turned towards the forbidding doorway of the museum. If it was gloomy outside, heaven knows what it would be like within.

If the curator had connected Ted with the unwelcome approach then she did nothing to show it. Indeed, when she poked out her head from the door of her office, her face seemed to brighten ever so slightly, as if somebody had switched on a ten-watt bulb at the far end of the corridor. Ted had memorised some French sentences to open up with and the lady seemed content with his efforts. She followed him up the stairs, her bunched keys jangling against her hip as she took each step. Ted paused for breath as they reached the top room, allowing the curator to unlock the display as before. He thanked her with a nod and a smile.

'A *coffee?*' she asked, performing a wooden mime to ensure his comprehension.

'Ah. Thank you. *Thanks.*'

Ted had stowed a canvas chair in the boot of Gaston's car, but had decided at the last minute not to carry it to the museum – it would have been presumptuous, especially given that he had been unsure as to the reception that he would receive. As he retrieved the stash of papers and lowered himself to the ground, he fleetingly thought of returning to fetch it. Yet he had been forced to park further away than before, and much as his bones were ill-suited for a morning on the hard floor, his preference was to get through his work as quickly as possible and leave. He reached for his inside pocket and produced his notebook and a pen. He left Philippe's mobile phone in his coat. Earlier, they had shown him how to use it to take a photograph. Just in case that would be useful.

There was a bashing noise on the stairway. He looked around. The curator was hauling a dining chair up the flight; the effort was clearly troubling her, and she had paused to rest. Ted heaved himself back to a standing position and hurried to help, murmuring embarrassed thanks as he took the weight from her. She gave a tepid smile, turned and glided back to the floor below, presumably to fetch his drink.

Ted had not expected any dramatic revelations from the remaining papers. These were, after all, items which were considered not worthy of the display. But he felt a mounting sense of disappointment as he worked his way through. There were no new songs to discover here; many of the sheets contained merely a line or two of Debreu's scrawl, and some were completely blank. An autograph on a menu might be a prize for some fervent collector, but it spoke little to Ted, and as far as he could ascertain, such things were two-a-penny anyway. Nevertheless, he logged everything in his notebook, transcribing anything that could possibly be of interest and, in particular, noting down any dates and places as they cropped up. An idea was forming that he might map the movements of the great man's life and perhaps produce a definitive list of appearances, to tie in with all the 'Debreu Trail' material that was being worked upon back in the village. He did pull out Philippe's phone at one point, thinking that it must surely be quicker than making his longhand notes. But his big fingers fumbled around as he tried to recall the instructions, and he was still unsure as to whether the device had captured a readable image even after the flash had irradiated the gloomy chamber, the tell-tale 'click' reverberating about the walls. Ted secreted the phone back in his coat as he heard the curator on the prowl downstairs, returning to the honesty of pen and paper as he started upon the final pile.

There was one thing that bothered him as he examined the first item of this new set. It appeared to be an early draft of

'Monsieur Berlin', complete with amendments and crossings-out. Yet he was sure that he had already seen this particular sheet; it had been part of the batch that he'd examined on his initial visit. His shoulders sagged as he regarded the papers strewn about the floor in front of him; either he had got in to a muddle and mixed up the piles, or some other person had disturbed their order in the meantime. Either way, if he were to be thorough, he would have to sift through everything again to ensure that nothing had been missed.

There were no more anomalies as he ploughed his way through the remainder, his own handwriting growing more and more slapdash with his declining enthusiasm. He took a deep breath after completing the final sheet, willing himself to do that necessary reassessment. He lifted himself from the chair and paced the room momentarily, exercising his shoulders in circular motions and feeling some life returning to his arms and legs. His belly rumbled from neglect.

He found it a mere three sheets into the very first pile. Ted looked hard to ensure that there was no mistake. But no. He hadn't messed up, and there had been no interference with his system. It was a duplicate. Hand written, with the same changes, the same deletions, the fully-transcribed lyrics of 'Monsieur Berlin', all six verses in their tragicomic splendour. He stared at both sheets side-by-side. One was not a later version than the other; both had their basis in the same words – it had given Ted much joy to glimpse the history of the song's progress, from Debreu's dark original, which had concluded with the murder of the incompetent lothario, to the more playful account that had finally seen the light of day. Ted could not fathom why the musician had sat down to rewrite the same song two times, on both occasions alighting upon identical final lyrics. He pondered. Perhaps Debreu had lost the first rewrite. By all accounts, the musician had led a chaotic existence, although his earlier years – the period of the work in question – had been relatively settled. There would be an explanation.

'You eat?'

The lady's voice made him physically jump in his chair; he was astonished to hear her giggle, a tinkling, musical sound, utterly unsuited to this austere woman. He rose and turned to her. 'Ah. Finished. *Finished,*' he said. 'Ahh. I'm going.' He made a walking movement with his fingers. 'I tidy up and go.'

It was as if her thin smile had never been there. 'Oh,' she said.

'So, yes. I tidy.' Ted searched for a suitable mime, before realising that it would be just as expressive to begin tidying. Gingerly, he lowered himself to his knees and started to gather the papers together in neat piles.

'I help.' In a trice, she was on the floor beside him, sweeping up the sheets with her spidery fingers, throwing them together with none of the care that Ted had been so scrupulously applying to the historic documents. Their shoulders touched as she leaned forward to toss a mishmash into the open drawer; she froze and read in a robot voice from a single sheet that she'd retained in her hand:

♪ *In her life of numbers, stark digits on the page*
All she wants is the warmth of a soft touch on her face ♪

It was a couplet from 'The Lovesick Clerk', a couplet that Ted knew too well. Lifting his head, he found her pallid face just inches away; behind the wire frames of her spectacles, grey-green eyes were boring into his. To his horror, Ted realised that she was going to try to kiss him. He hurled his own pile of papers into the cabinet and pushed his palms urgently against the floorboards to try to heave himself up into a standing position, but all his strength seemed to have evaporated; his legs, suddenly those of an old man, refused to obey all instructions; his knees – oh Lord, his knees! – were numb and immobile, paralysed by the hard floor, incapable of shifting even one-hundredth of the weight that he'd promised himself that one day he would lose. Her eyes were half-closed now, that odd-shaped face angled to one side as it closed in, her non-existent lips parting to expose the teeth and tongue within. Ted clawed at the floor with his hands, pleading with his arms for one burst of strength. He could feel the muscles in his neck scream as he craned back his head; his nose caught the scent of her perfume mixed with a trace of alcohol. With one Herculean effort, the Englishman flung his kneeling body backwards, wincing as his arse hit the floor, followed by the entire weight of his ill cared-for frame. Scrabbling over to his knees once more, he took one, two, three humongous crawls towards the staircase, heaving himself upright on the fourth, staggering and nearly toppling, grabbing at the corner of a winged armchair to steady himself, sending a cloud of dust billowing from the fabric.

'Ahh. I leave now, go home,' he gabbled, his fingers a blur as he made the walking motion nineteen-to-the-dozen. Thank God he had kept his coat on to mitigate the chill of the old building, although he would have quite happily abandoned it as a small price to pay for his flight. Ted took the top few stairs with as much dignity as he could muster, making huge efforts to keep a neutral expression on his face, daring his head not to turn to see if she was watching him or, indeed, whether she had risen from her own knees with a view to pursuit. Then, when his head was safely below the level of the floor above, he took the steps two at a time, hurtling through the oaken entrance doors at a lope, a pace that he did not lessen until he was locked within the steel cage of Gaston's motor car.

18

The College

There was a single envelope for them at the farmhouse the next day: a change of address from Stan and Jenny Wainwright. Daisy's hands shook as she read, holding the card so close that it almost touched the end of her nose.

'December,' she said. 'They'll be gone by mid-December.'

'Yes?' Ted worked hard to ensure that his tone conveyed the appropriate level of disinterest.

'He's put a P.S. "Come to Cornwall on your next tour, Edd-oo-ard." What's he mean by that?'

'Thinks he's funny.' Ted toyed with his biro. 'Be bloody joyous Christmas parties this year round their area.'

'Don't be nasty.' Her eyes turned to the card once more. 'Camborne – where's that? I don't think we went there.'

Ted pursed his lips. 'One of the old tin mining towns I reckon. Probably on its uppers these days.' His gaze returned to his writing. 'Like it hasn't suffered enough.'

His page was so full of deletions that it was about time to start afresh. Setting his ruler on the original sheet to mark his place, he tore the top leaf from his pad and started to transcribe the sentences that he'd settled upon. Free from all the scribbled corrections, this version ran to eleven lines of his deliberate, draughtsman's script. He read it through again, his brow furrowing as he progressed. 'No good,' he said.

'It isn't?'

Ted scratched his head. 'Well it's all right,' he said. 'But it's ... literal. Too formal. But that's how the French are sometimes, I suppose. The thing is that the English readers – well, hardly any of them will have heard of him at all. This is all too – academic. And then when I try to change it to be a bit more approachable it just reads like, well, the sort of guff that the marketing people use.'

Daisy lifted a half-knitted monkey from its resting place on the coffee table between them. 'Well write it from scratch yourself, then.'

'But I'm not sure if that's what they want.'

'But would it be better?'

'Well, yes. I think so.'

'And how would they tell, anyway?'

Ted frowned once more at the page.

This is the story of Frédéric Debreu, or at least as much of the story that can be told about this brilliant, mysterious genius. As custodians of his legacy we invite you to visit the places that he once visited, the market village of Mailliot le Bois, the green fields of Thorigny. To see places off the tourist trail that you might otherwise walk past, the everyday street scenes, the bars and the clubs. But the real Debreu might remain elusive, his essence only to be found in the wonderful and magical songs that have outlived him.

'I know what I want to say.' Ted scratched his chin. 'I'm just not very good at putting it down on paper.'

'It sounds very good to me. You've always had a way with words.'

Ted bounded to his feet. 'I'm due down there anyway,' he said. 'I'll see what they think.'

'Will you ring the scooter people? Find out what the delay is?'

Ted pulled on his jacket. 'I will.'

*

Ted looked at his watch, pointedly. It was hopeful, possible even, that at some point within the next twenty minutes or so his friends might finish laughing.

The mayor roared and bellowed. Philippe, hanging back between the table and the bar, chortled into his bandaged hands, biting away at the fabric in an attempt to control his sniggers. Casimir took a little longer to catch on, Ted's recount of his trip to the museum requiring translation for his benefit, Gaston spluttering out jagged bursts of French as he mopped away tears with his snow-white handkerchief. The ancient man's face exploded as he understood, hooting through his smattering of yellow teeth, showering the table before him with a spray of foul spit.

Ted regarded them in turn. 'Are you finished yet?' he demanded.

'I am sorry. I am – I am...' The mayor erupted once more.

Ted pulled himself to his feet and plodded down to the urinal, allowing himself his own little private smile as he relieved himself. The incident had provided him with, when all was said and done, a fine after-dinner story. But he would not be returning to the museum any time soon.

The faces were more composed as he re-entered, although this appeared to have been achieved via a deliberate consensus, judging from the agonised glances that the mayor and Casimir were exchanging; the official's moustache quivering with the threat of new spasms.

Ted stood beside Gaston, placing his palms on the back of a chair in order to lean forward, looming over the pair. 'Just don't tell my wife,' he muttered, prompting the mayor's fragile defences to crumble beneath a wave of further guffaws. 'Oh now, now, come on.'

Gaston laid his hand on the mayor's shoulder. *'Bernard, we must get on now.'*

'Yes, yes, yes. Ted, I am sorry.'

'Like hell you are.'

Gaston passed the car keys to Ted.

They had tried, but no amount of tacked-on glass foyer would make the old college building anything other than what it was: a run-down mess of futurism, modernism and whatever other isms its third-division architect had been minded to employ when he had first scribbled out the design on a cigarette packet at some time between the wars. Ted pulled into the car park, coming to rest in one of the scores of empty spaces. The signs had been in several languages: 'Luxury Hotel and Spa' was the English version. Ted wondered how long this place had been thus, and, looking at the peeling walls and the unmown green spaces, how long it might have left.

He was here to take photographs, and to formulate a few dozen words about this place, once so central to the wider region, and the setting for no less than three of Frédéric Debreu's songs; minor works, admittedly, if there could be such things, but all would be featured on his map and in his English guide. Of course there was another interest. This was where Eric had been for that period of time when he had called this region home. He had worked here, he had boarded here for a while, he had played for their football team.

Ted felt little urge to announce himself at the reception desk, so he took a path that led him into the grounds. Away from the public facade, the building grew even more shabby. The white walls took on a rising dirty green hue, as if algae was taking hold of the structure; the windows were filthy; two on the ground floor were boarded up. The facility was nothing like he had expected, although he realised that the hazy image that he had maintained over the years of a stout British municipal institution was always going to be far from the truth.

He had not thought to come here when he had undertaken his initial burst of detective work, having figured that any old colleagues of Eric must have long gone, to other institutions, or perhaps upping sticks for Paris when the educators had finally abandoned the place. But as the building became real to him, it occurred to Ted that there could still be people around from that era: caretakers, or maintenance men perhaps. He had not brought his photograph. But there was no harm asking.

225

♫ *When we were young*
We lay together on the green
We listened to the birdsong
To the song of the stream
The day was warm
There were butterflies in the sky
I stroked your hair, we had few cares
When we were young ♫

If the song had indeed been inspired by the college then this must be the green in question, a quarter-acre or so of grass that panned out from a patio spanning the rear of the building, the terrain roughly tidied where it met the concrete slabs but becoming ever more overgrown as the ground fell away in a gentle slope. As Ted strolled across, he was astonished to hear the faint sound of running water. 'The song of the stream.' This was the place! He followed the noise, ambling downhill into the longer grass. At the foot of the green there it was, a small brook, overgrown with bushes and nettles, a resting place for tin cans and crisp wrappers, the litter bleached and faded. Clearly it had been here for years. Ted turned back, fingering the camera in his pocket. Even if he could find some angles from which he might take acceptable shots of the old college, he was unconvinced that he should be sending eager visitors to such a sad and neglected destination. He paused to re-examine the rear of the building.

A man in a blue suit was advancing across the grass towards him. *'Can I help you, sir?'*

At least the patio windows had been cleaned. Ted looked out across the stretch of grass where he had been apprehended. The duty manager had been content to talk once he had ascertained that Ted was no vandal or trespasser with ill-intent. But he was uninterested in Debreu, and knew nothing of the history of the building. No workers remained from the old days; the ancillary staff were generally foreigners or uneducated locals who might stay six months until something better came along. He had wished Ted well in his quest, and steered him towards the bar. Ted sat in the empty room, nursing a coffee of eye-watering expense. Before he'd set out, he had considered stowing the wheelchair in Gaston's boot and bringing Daisy with him. He was pleased that he had not made the suggestion. She had asked him about that scooter again: how long would it take, what was the delay? Sucking at the froth at the bottom of his mug, he started to formulate strategies by which he might explain away the machine's future non-appearance: that they were made to order, that the factory had gone bust. But even as he rolled increasingly fantastical ideas around in his mind, he knew that this was all trivia, all window dressing, a trifle that dwarfed the deckchairs on the *Titanic*.

'*One more, sir?*' The barman's approach startled him.

'*No. No thank you.*'

He needed answers. He had betrayed Daisy to protect her from the dread of the unknown; now he had taken things this far, he had to go through with it. When the time came to tell the truth, it would need to be the whole truth with no ambiguities to eat away at her. He knew now that David was all right, and this was the most crucial part of that reassurance. It would be good to have more details about his job, about the life that he was starting to rebuild. Ted had been so flummoxed by his son's first contact that he had neglected to ask all but the most basic of questions.

So then there was the money. What would they live on for the next twenty, thirty years? He would need to be able to tell her that. Where to start? His state pension, fine. What about benefits? He was sure there must be benefits, but there would be forms, and questions, and assessments and explanations. Where would they live? He wanted to stay put until he had answers, but how could he get answers whilst they stayed put? How could he do it? Pretend he was popping out for some milk and nip over to Britain on the ferry? He –

The smash sent him shooting bolt upright in his seat.

Ted's stared at his fingers as they clutched at the remains of the mug's handle. Froth-coated china was strewn across the table and floor. He realised that he must have slammed his drink down ferociously, yet had no recollection of doing so. His face flooded with crimson as the barman hastened over. '*Sir?*'

He had to get things sorted out.

*

His chance to move things along came two days later. He had agreed a time to ring David again, and made the call dead on eleven o'clock, having hovered in the empty bar for ten minutes, his eyes darting between the telephone and his wristwatch.

As ever, their conversation began with the awkwardness of the superficial. But over the following ten minutes, Ted began to learn what he needed to know. David would be starting on the rigs in a few weeks' time; he had found a place to stay in Aberdeen and would be moving what remained of his things shortly. Ted questioned him intently, wanting reassurance upon reassurance that the past was now the past. Yes, it was a good job, a steady salary. The flat was small, but the area was pleasant. Too cautious to be optimistic, Ted strained his ears to discern any hint of sugar-coating in his son's explanations.

'How's mum?'

'Good, good.' Ted shuffled at the telephone. 'Not walking too well. But getting better.'

There was a pause. 'How has she taken – things?'

Ted tried to keep his voice even. 'Fine. She's fine. Don't worry about your mother. She just wants to know you're OK. Can I tell her that you're OK?'

'You can. Honestly you can. Give her my love.' Another pause. 'Dad – is there anything I can do?'

Ted took a deep breath and started talking.

19

The Final Bow of
Édouard Prescôte

Ted was more on edge than he could ever remember. He was due
to be taken to Django's for the second time. He paced from
room to room, sometimes muttering to himself, sometimes
babbling random thoughts and observations to his increasingly
irritated wife. He picked things up, put them down, picked them
up again, toyed with them. When Daisy told him to sit down, he
barked at her before relenting in immediate shame, asking her for
the thousandth time if he could get her anything. 'I don't know
why you're doing it,' she had demanded in the face of his agitation,
but of course she had no idea of the scale of things, of what was
being demanded of him, why he could not simply pull out, stay at
home, drink cocoa. Finally, he grabbed his things, bent to kiss his
wife on the cheek and stomped outside to loiter in the dusk.

He was underprepared. He knew he was underprepared.
In the run up to his previous outing there he had practised and
practised, going through his chords, his lyrics, his vocal
inflexions, knowing that whilst he knew these songs so
intimately, his brain could let him down at any moment under
the terror of the stage lights. Granted, he had been immersed
in Debreu all week, he knew more about the great man's work
than he had ever done. But this had been as a writer and
researcher, not as a musician. Lingering on his verandah perch,
he cradled his guitar case as if the physical contact with it might
lead him to absorb some of its wisdom.

The car that eventually drew up was unfamiliar, a grumbling
Range Rover of at least three decades' vintage, its body scratched

and bashed, its dull ivory hubcaps blistered with rust. The passenger door was open before the vehicle had spluttered to a halt, Gaston hopping out with a beam, his ever-immaculate blazer and trousers in sharp contrast to the agricultural carriage.

Ted recognised the driver's face. He had seen a photograph of it previously, CD-sized, with his own name plastered across it. This must be Alain, the mayor's younger brother. Ted watched him warily as the driver heaved the car into reverse. Gaston grasped his hand and shook vigorously, his smile spreading wider and wider even as Ted bit down upon his bottom lip.

Ted felt himself physically double-take as the Range Rover clattered in to the town square. A cream-coloured minibus was parked outside the café, a dozen or more people milling around it. Ted could see Casimir, the ancient man swigging from a hip-flask as he leaned on the tailgate. He saw Bernard the Mayor, Philippe, also Marie and Celine, the gargantuan form of Claude. Even his barber was there, chatting to two or three of the market traders that he recognised, along with some strangers who had also been included in the party. Alain blasted his horn as he swung in to the kerbside, sending bodies hopping on to the pavement. Casimir waved. Claude held both thumbs aloft, two podgy globes of fat, almost as broad as they were long.

'All of them?' Ted spoke out loud, his voice incredulous, the question aimed at nobody in particular. He felt a hand on his shoulder.

'You say that you are not comfortable without the big support,' Gaston said. 'These people, they come to support.'

'Blooming heck. How much did you pay them?'

'It is not a charity for you, Ted. They want to come for to enjoy a good concert. We have the minibus from the school; they share the money for fuel.'

'*Good evening!*' The rear door was pulled open and the mayor eased himself in beside Gaston. The pavement began to empty as the remaining people climbed aboard the minibus. '*Go, Alain. They can meet us there.*'

Gaston had reserved them the four tables at the right of the stage. It was a canny move: they would be close to the performance, but they would also be able to box Ted in to their own territory; he could be sat where no member of the public might casually walk past and overhear the Englishman or, worse, try to engage him in conversation. Despite his tension, Ted was quietly impressed once more at Gaston's aptitude for his role.

The stage seemed to be bigger than before, looming over him, casting a deep shadow despite the pervasive lighting. It was probably an accident of perspective, some visual trick dependent on where they were sat. Nevertheless, Ted was sure that last time he had been required to trot up a mere couple of steps to take his place at the microphone. Tonight, the act of taking the stage appeared to require massive strides up a towering and near-vertical cliff-face. He cemented himself to his chair, his back to the auditorium, trying to focus on nothing but the songs that he would soon be performing. The big posters in the foyer, the ones with his name on them, hadn't helped.

Alain returned from the bar. He was much younger than the mayor; a half-brother rather than a brother, it transpired. He had proved surprisingly good company on the journey, down-to-earth and with a wry appreciation of the ridiculousness of Ted's position. No words were said about the CD that wasn't, but Alain had clearly not taken offence that his services had not been required. He parked himself next to Ted.

There was a flurry of noise from the rear of the room: exuberant voices, calling out, the chanting of a familiar chorus. Ted kept his eyes fixed straight ahead. It was Alain who glanced around to register the scene, before turning to Ted with a look that the Englishman interpreted as concern.

'The minibus has arrived,' he said.

The villagers might have clubbed together for petrol money, but it seemed to Ted that they had invested heavily in booze, also. The venue's doors had barely been thrown open, but as the minibus party took their seats, pummelling him on the back as they came through, there was already a hint of late-night rowdiness in their raised voices and laughter. Soon, the four tables were jammed with carafes and beer. Casimir, in particular, appeared to be well on his way to intoxication, the glass barely leaving the old man's lips except on the frequent occasions when refills were offered.

Marie and Celine were the last to join them, Philippe almost upsetting the table in his haste to demonstrate the chairs that he had saved. The smiling girls accepted, but turned their backs to chat between themselves. The barber leaned in to comment; Ted judged from Marie's expression of mock-outrage that the intervention had been lewd. Behind her, the young barman glared as if he were about to gut the interloper with his own scissors.

Well, he had wanted support and he had got it. Ted took a hefty swig of wine himself. He would have to be careful to strike the right balance.

It should have been less busy this time, in the off season, the townies holed up in their city homes, the fair-weather weekenders sitting it out until the Christmas holiday. Ted forced himself not to repeatedly scan the room in his nervousness, but the hubbub behind him said it all, and when he did weaken and turn his head it appeared that the venue was all-but full. On his first visit, the club had only recently opened; obviously it had taken time for such a place to build up a clientele. He returned to the conversation that Bernard was having with Claude. Claude's off-white T-shirt was shabbier than ever, threadbare around the folds of his neck, shrunken so that it left exposed a good three inches of pale gut. For the first time, Ted noticed that there were dark splatters of dried blood down his left side. Perhaps another woodland creature might be coming his way.

'Ladies and Gentlemen!' Monsieur Richepin's voice boomed from the speakers. 'Two fantastic artists here at Django's tonight for your entertainment. Bringing us two sets, we will enjoy the music

232

of the Gaëlle Cot trio! In between, with the songs of Frédéric Debreu, we are excited to welcome back for a full set Monsieur Édouard Prescôte! So first, sit in comfort and enjoy –'

But Ted did not hear the rest. He was reeling, stunned, from the cheer that had erupted upon the mention of his ludicrous pseudonym. Not the cheer from his friends, holding their glasses aloft, reaching across to slap his shoulders. But the cheer from the strangers behind him, from the full tables at the front of the stage, from a pocket of men clustered at the bar.

A double bass and drums set up a beat; the pianist, presumably Gaëlle Cot, stabbed out the first bars of a jazz tune. The notes were vaguely familiar to Ted. They drifted in and out of his mind as he clutched his wine glass in stupefaction.

Over the next hour, Ted attempted to lose himself in Gaëlle Cot's music, switching his eyes between the blonde woman hunched over the piano, to the walking fingers of the old man on the double bass, to the swarthy drummer, detached and mechanical as he plonked away with his brushes. Gaston and the mayor took their turns on sentry duty beside him, the latter drifting away as further carafes arrived. The Englishman found himself studying the band on stage with a professional eye. They were fine musically, he thought, no better nor worse than a thousand others who knocked out this sort of thing every night across the world. But they seemed so at home up there, utterly blasé about the surroundings. They were totally comfortable on that stage, in a way that he would never be if he were to play there every week for the rest of his life.

Gaston tugged his forearm. 'Not long,' he murmured tapping his wristwatch. 'You are OK?'

Ted nodded. 'I'd better have a piss.'

The pair rose, Gaston gesturing to the others to allow them to pass through. Alain and the mayor stood to make room; Claude waddled to one side, sweating and puffing from the exertion. Casimir tottered to his feet, lifting his glass in a toast before stumbling forward and making a haphazard grab at the edge of a table for support, his hand crashing into the bottles and glasses and upending a half-litre of Amstel. The beer flooded across the table, cascading over the sides in a golden waterfall.

'Shit!'

'For Jesus' sake, Casimir!'

'You stupid old cretin!'

Ted affected not to notice as he pushed past the geriatric, who was swaying forward and back, regarding the devastation with serenely glazed eyes. The Englishman pressed on, following Gaston towards the toilet, the hammering inside him swelling up as the music on stage drew to a close. Behind him, Gaëlle Cot thanked the audience for their appreciation.

'Psssst!' The low noise caught Ted's attention as the dryer completed its howl. He glanced around. There was nobody there.

'Psssst!'

The door to one of the toilet cubicles was ajar. Ted could see the very edge of a figure within; the tips of a pair of pointed shoes on the wet floor; a sallow hand waving and beckoning. Frowning, he took a step back so that he could see. Philippe was pressed against the cubicle wall, flapping his arms, mouthing words that the Englishman could not decipher.

'Édouard?' Gaston called from the outer door.

'You go. Two minutes.'

Ted waited for the thud of the closing door before turning back to the young barman, who had poked his head from around the cubicle door and was craning his neck to see around the chamber. 'In here,' the boy hissed. 'Need your help, Monsieur Prescott.'

'I'm not joining you in there. I've had more than enough misunderstandings as it is. There's nobody else out here. Come out, but quick.'

Philippe shuffled into view, his head darting left and right. 'Monsieur Prescott, you wish to leave directly after you play?'

'Get out of here quick. That's the idea.'

234

'*Oui, oui.*' The barman leaned forward. 'Alain, he is driving, he is happy to go early. Gaston, Bernard, they stay to get more drunk. Marie, Celine, they have a visit tomorrow for their college. They also perhaps leave early.'

'I think I can see where this is heading.'

'I carry your guitar to the car, you are in the front, I am in the back with them. Boom, boom!'

'Blimey, lad, you've got it all worked out.'

'They are very sad to see the scars on my hands.'

'Women always do love a hero.'

'You tell them that they go with you?'

Ted looked to the ceiling. 'I tell them.'

'Yay!' Philippe gripped both his arms and blessed him with a look of such puppy-dog gratitude that Ted felt himself starting to laugh. The outer door opened and a man trotted in, nodding to them both before positioning himself before the urinal.

The young barman snapped to attention. '*Ahhh – thank you, Monsieur Prescôte. I am very excited to have the opportunity to hear a fine musician like you play the great songs of Frédéric Debreu.*' Ted winced at the wooden performance as he strode back in to the auditorium. If the lad was to ensnare those two then he'd need to put on a better act than that.

The stage was higher. Surely it was higher.

Thumps and bangs came from the loudspeakers as the technician adjusted Ted's microphones. But these sounds were augmented by another rumbling: a rapid and hoarse panting, like an immense prairie beast, chased and wounded, alone and lying down to die. The man stepped back, satisfied. Ted's grunt of thanks rang round the room. He realised that the other noise had been his own breathing.

He could not discern an empty seat in the entire venue.

Ted ran his tongue round his lips and tried to collect what thoughts he could muster. Tune, he had to make sure he was in tune. His shaking hands fiddled with the pegs: clockwise, anticlockwise, clockwise again. That was right. No, it was not right.

Clockwise again. Now the D-string was flat. Or was the D-string fine, and the others all sharp? No. That was it. He strummed two chords with the soft flesh of his thumb; the noise from the speakers silenced the remaining chatterers in the crowd. Below him, Gaston hovered at the foot of the steps. Ted gave him a small nod and the Frenchman bounded onto the stage beside him.

'Ladies and Gentlemen, my fellow connoisseurs of great French music and culture! Some of you have seen him before, for some of you this is a new experience. From Mailliot le Bois, the true home of the great genius, presenting the music of the legendary Frédéric Debreu, please will you make your appreciation heard ...'

Ted didn't hear the rest of the introduction. His horrified eyes were fixed upon one table near the back of the hall, where a familiar face was staring back at him. Even at this distance, even with all the stage lights directed at him, he could make out her angular nose, her puritan hair. The wave of applause passed him by as he saw her rise carefully to her feet, her pasty features as clear as stones in an icy pond. For an instant, the curator stood deathly still; Ted, in turn, frozen to his chair, arms dangling across his guitar, his lips and tongue working to form the shapes of words that were rising from somewhere in his subconscious. Then, with one rapid pounce, she swept up a sheet of paper from the table – Ted could discern that it was one of the club's handbills – brandished it before her in both hands and ripped. Allowing the torn paper to flutter down from her grasp, the lady from the museum whirled around and pushed her way from the room.

It took some moments for Ted to register that there was a dead silence around him. He forced his gaze from the door at the back. The people, they had stopped clapping, they were looking at him. He felt the silky-smooth wood of his guitar in his hands. He strummed an E-chord to try to jolt his brain into action. What – where – how was he to start? He looked to the floor for his set list, but he had left it in his back pocket; he could feel the folded paper in there against his buttock. Another E-chord. He raised a clammy finger to the audience – wait! –

forcing a watery smile for their benefit as he fumbled around with his other hand, pulling out the sheet to unfold and uncrumple it, setting it down beside his chair where he could glance at it at will. 'Marguerite,' of course – he started with 'Marguerite.' He took one further look at the list, the security of the familiar titles providing reassurance.

Bom-de, dom-de, bom-de, dom-de ...

He could almost hear the audience breathe as one as the tension was lifted. Ted stole a look towards his friends at the side of the stage. Gaston had his head thrust forward with expectation; Claude was bobbing his head in time; the mayor was conducting an imaginary baton. Casimir was slumped back, his eyes open but his head lolling about randomly. Philippe was leaning in between Marie and Celine, whispering something in the older girl's ear.

Bom-de, dom-de, bom-de, dom-de ...

It was time. Ted took a deep breath and pushed his head towards the microphone.

Bom-de ...

Something was wrong. He could feel it. He jerked his head back.

Bom-de, dom-de ...

'Marguerite!' 'Marguerite' was in A-major, yet his fingers were still locked in to the E-major chord! Even as he realised his mistake, he was engulfed with dread at the thought of the humiliation that had so nearly become his fate. He would have – it would have – no. He could not think about that. Keeping his bom-de's going, he switched his left hand, passing through several chords before alighting on the A, forcing his face into a mask of nonchalance even as his heart pounded, bluffing that his horrendous error had been merely part of an extended introduction.

Bom-de, dom-de ...

Now it was really time.

> ♫ *Marg'rite she is my long adored-for woman*
> *Her face it is the sunshine of my life!* ♫

A murmur of recognition passed through the crowd as the words boomed from the PA system. And suddenly, it was just Ted, there with his guitar, singing and playing this old song as he had a million times before, wallowing in the joy of the melody, the rising and falling of each word and syllable, sharing a secret smile with himself at the perfection of those comic lines in that tongue that he barely understood.

> ♫ *I cry for her, I'd die for her, I'd have her for my own*
> *If it wasn't for the fact I have a wife*
>
> *So Father hear my simple cry for pity*
> *I've said my prayers and done my duty*
> *And in your wisdom and your beauty*
> *Won't you bring my Marg'rite to me!* ♫

When he reached the last chorus, he did not let the final notes ring out, but clapped his hand across his guitar strings to climax with a percussive slap that echoed with the natural reverb of the concrete room. Time stood still for one instant, and then the clapping started.

Ted breathed hard as he sat looking out at these people, his first test complete, eight, perhaps nine to come. 'The Vengeful Widow' was to be next. Ted allowed the audience's response to die back. He grinned as he wiped his forehead with his handkerchief, nodding back at the crowd to indicate his own gratitude. He shot a wary eye at the door at the back of the auditorium, and at the seat that the potty woman from the museum had vacated. It was still empty. Now. Get it right this time! Ted's left hand shaped the first chord in preparation as the room fell into a dead hush of anticipation.

There was a lurching, heaving sound from his right as Casimir's guts emptied into his lap.

Ted's jaw dropped open as the commotion unfolded, four of the old man's immediate neighbours leaping to their feet, others on the tables around them peering and pointing and murmuring to themselves. A glass or jug hit the concrete floor with a heavy smash; Ted could hear Philippe's nasal voice muttering *'Jesus, Jesus,'* over and over again. More people were looking now, from the tables immediately in front of him and from further away in the hall, some people semi-standing to satisfy their curiosity.

Ted's mind galloped as the scene unfolded. He could not possibly ignore the furore that was taking place just yards from him and that had claimed the attention of a sizable proportion of his audience. Gaston was working his way around the village party now, organising, calming things down. With consternation, Ted comprehended the fact that he should say something to the audience. That was what a proper act would do in the circumstances: reclaim the initiative with some witticism, some deadly one-liner. Already faces were turning back to him in anticipation of his response to the disturbance.

'Ah – OK?' Ted heard himself adopting a bottomlessly deep voice ladled with Gallic butter. He craned his neck to see what was going on. Two of the stallholders were assisting Casimir towards the toilets, the older man crashing from side to side as he stumbled and lurched, drips of vomit forming a zig-zag trail behind him.

The mayor rose to his feet. His face appeared even redder than usual as he clutched his wine, shifting his feet to control an apparent compulsion to sway. 'Sorry. Please continue, Ted,' he called, in English. Almost before the words were spoken, the official's crimson hue deepened at his howler. Behind him, Alain stood and grabbed the mayor's shoulders, using both hands to force his older brother down to his seat.

'*Ah,*' said Ted, turning back to the audience and summoning his finest French accent. '*The English.*' He jerked his thumb towards the mayor, who was deep into a series of hissed protestations with the people around him.

The audience roared. Their laughter made him chuckle also, more so when he saw faces turning back to direct their hilarity at the mayor himself, who was by now the intensest shade of beetroot. On a roll, Ted raised his hand to his mouth to perform the universal mime of taking a drink; he was rewarded by a fresh gale from the newly-energised people before him. He paused for the noise to subside, holding up his palm in a gesture for quiet. '*OK,*' he said. '*OK.*'

> ♫ *Forty years of marriage to a faithless lying hound*
> *A smile it passed across her lips as he passed in the ground*
> *'I'll pay him back, I'll pay him back for being such a beast'*
> *She chucked the soil into the pit and copped off with the priest* ♫

'Is she gone? For pity's sake tell me she's gone.' Ted covered his mouth as he hissed at Gaston, the two men pushing their way around the side of the room, Ted's urgent glances at the café owner alternating with wordless smiles of gratitude at the customers who were waving, giving him cheers, patting his arms as he passed by. He grabbed Gaston's hand and forcibly pulled him; the Frenchman appeared to want to linger, to milk the moment, transfixed by the reception that the crowd had given Édouard's concluding songs.

'Who?' Gaston replied finally, as the pair reached the bar area.

'The mad woman.' Ted poked his head round the side of the door. 'I think it's OK. Let's get out of here.'

'*Hey!*' a trio of young men approached them, grinning. One offered his hand to shake. Ted gave a cordial thumbs up and turned away, but Gaston appeared to be freshly smitten by this new attention, and held his arms out wide as if greeting new friends.

Exasperated, Ted locked his arm around Gaston's shoulder and dragged him towards the door. The Frenchman's beam was seemingly glued to his face as they fell outside, Ted wrestling him towards the darkest corner of the car park.

'My God, my God,' Gaston was almost gibbering. Ted had never seen the man so lose the sangfroid that had always seemed so central to his being. *'Did you see them, Ted? Did you see them?* Did you see them, Ted, they sing, they dance, they ... yeah!' The Frenchman threw his arms aloft like the most awkward of uncles cheering at the school sports day.

'Yes.' Ted allowed himself a single smile. The immense buzz that remained within him was strangely at ease with his calm at what he was about to say. He released his hold on the café owner and they walked further, Ted at an amble, Gaston skipping and tripping in his exultation.

'You deal with the problems that take place – Ted, you are natural. A natural.'

'Yes, yes.'

'You see from the stage how they –'

'Yes, yes.' Ted halted his progress, grasping Gaston's shoulder to force him to do likewise. The two men faced each other, Ted's features set firm, Gaston's sweating and bubbling.

'That's my lot, Gaston,' said Ted. 'No more.'

'Ted, Ted did you see them? Jesus! Sky is the limit. The sky!'

'No. That's my lot.'

Gaston's contortions arrested themselves as the Frenchman stared into Ted's face. From the club came the noise of whooping and shouting as a group of revellers fell out of the doors and made their way to their cars. Ted started walking again, further into the darkness. Gaston hastened after him.

'Ted –'

'Thank you, Gaston, for all that you have done for me. Thank you, genuinely. I'll carry on working to pay my debt to you, I'll

241

help out with whatever you need, whatever Bernard and the others need. But that's my lot for playing things like that. I can't do it.'

'We could –'

'All the Édouard nonsense. I know it's not a big deal in the great scheme of things. And it's the best feeling in the world, going up there, believe me. The best feeling. But I can barely do it as me. Let alone him. And you know it's only a matter of time, anyway; look what happened tonight. Daisy was asking questions earlier; saying I could bring her in her wheelchair next time. I can't do it anymore, Gaston. It's just not me. So. That's my lot.'

He reached the threshold of the car park, where the shingle petered out into scrubland. Ted turned away from the blackness of the countryside, looking back towards the lights of the club. Gaston faced him again. He said nothing, but the Frenchman's face registered his acknowledgement. Composure appeared to be regaining its grip.

'Quit while I'm ahead,' said Ted.

Gaston nodded. 'Quit while you are ahead.'

Side-by-side, the two men began to drift back towards the building. More people were leaving now. They could hear the hubbub from the bar through the open doors.

'Ted, it is important to tell you.' Gaston's voice was deliberate, as if he were choosing each word carefully. 'What I have done, Ted, I always try to do what is good for you.'

'I know, Gaston. Thank you.'

They reached the concrete paving. The room beyond the glass was still packed. A thought occurred to Ted. 'Philippe wanted to carry my stuff,' he said. 'One last service to Édouard, eh?'

'One last service, Ted.'

'He is not in a good state, Gaston.' The two traders stood either side of the old man, their burly arms preventing him from sinking to the floor. *'We've cleaned most of the puke off him and given him some water.'*

Casimir's eyes rolled around in incomprehension as a plastic bottle of water was inserted between his dribbling lips. *'Hey! Drink this!'* said the larger of the men.

'He stinks, Jesus he stinks. We tried to get him to the urinal but he couldn't sort his cock out in time.' The charcutier screwed up his face.

Ted regarded the scene from a safe distance. He bore a contented smile as he supped up the remains of his glass. He should still be on his way, but it seemed less important now. Whilst he had no wish to find himself collared by any of those members of the audience who had skipped Gaëlle Cot's final set in order to linger at the bar, shooting him glances and nodding and whispering to themselves, Édouard's retirement had freed him from any sense that his inevitable exposure would somehow betray his friends. He suddenly viewed the antics of the past weeks as they must have done: as a game, a drawn-out joke, a chuckle without malice at their fellow Debreu worshippers. Well if the secret of comedy is timing then he had delivered the punchline at the right moment. Time to drink up and go.

He cast his eyes around. Alain loitered on the periphery of the group, swilling around ice in his empty glass, lifting his arm to check his wristwatch. In front of him, Marie and Celine stood with Philippe. He was talking and they were laughing, their perfect faces lit up, their young eyes dancing. Celine swayed to one side and Ted watched her shoulder come to rest against the young barman's. Seeing this, Ted felt his own heart do something he couldn't quite put his finger upon. He knew that Debreu's music had affected people in many different ways over the decades; might he be witness to these songs' greatest achievement?

'OK, outside everybody.' Gaston glided about the villagers, grasping arms, nudging people towards the door. *'Let's sort this out.'*

It was cold in the car park and it had started to spit with rain. Alain, who had led the party through the bar and outside, jogged off to fetch his car. Several of the friends had left clutching unfinished glasses or bottles to the clear dismay of the club's door staff. A furious exchange ensued, which Ted ignored as he swung his guitar about in its case.

The mayor was deep in his own animated conversation with the minibus driver, waving and pointing at his watch. *'The bus goes – thirty minutes,'* he called out eventually, his own words slurred and stuttering. A handful of his companions immediately cheered and turned back for the door. Through the glass, Ted could see them striding towards the bar.

Alain's Range Rover shuddered to a halt beside them, the coughing and rasping of its old engine belching oily smoke into the night. *'Let's go, Ted,'* the driver called through the open window. *'Who else?'*

Ted felt the instrument wrenched from his hand. *'I will go,'* said Philippe, making a beeline for the car whilst glancing over his shoulder towards where the mayor's daughters were standing. *'I'll look after Monsieur Prescott's things.'*

'Thank you, lad.' Ted pulled open the front door and planted his boot on the sill to heave himself up. 'How about you girls? It's getting late.'

'Yes, come on,' called the young barman, bouncing on the old springs of the rear seat.

Gaston was nudged to one side as the charcutier manhandled Casimir forwards, the ancient man's wizened head lolling from one side to the other, his spindly legs dangling uselessly behind him. *'He cannot go in the minibus. The children have to ride in it tomorrow.'*

'Alain, will you take Casimir?' Gaston took one side of the unconscious geriatric, visibly wrinkling his nose at his soiled and fetid clothing.

'I've had worse on the back seat. I'll keep the windows open.'
'Hey!'
'No, Philippe. In the middle! Casimir must be by the window in case he vomits again.'

'But –'

'*Who lives closest to him?*' Gaston turned his back upon his barman's aghast protestations. '*Someone who can make sure he gets home?*'

A massive shape lumbered forward. '*I can.*'

Claude's bulk had filled the doorway before Philippe could spring for safety. '*OK!*' said Alain.

The others turned for the comfort of the bar. Only Gaston remained. He took a step forward and thrust his arm through the open front window to shake Ted's hand.

'Édouard Prescôte,' he said.

'Gaston.'

The engine bellowed as Alain swung the Range Rover around on the gravel, wrestling with the gear stick as he made towards the exit. Ted stole a glance backwards as they left the orange glow of the car park light and turned left onto the road. On one side, the old man's head had fallen to rest on the barman's shoulder, a trail of drool sliding down his cadaverous cheek into glistening smears upon the arm of Philippe's leather jacket. On the other, the youth was enveloped by the overspilling fat of the gargantuan taxidermist, smothered by the excess of his stomach and arm. Philippe himself was contorted into some squashed, sideways shape, glaring with livid and frustrated eyes into the dark of the footwell.

Switching his glance to the wing mirror, Ted watched the illuminations of Django's recede and disappear. His driver reached to put the car into top gear, and Édouard Prescôte retired into the night.

20

Centre Frédéric Debreu

'*Centre Frédéric Debreu*' opened to the public two weeks later, the mayor performing his duties in a ceremony attended by perhaps one hundred of the townsfolk. Ted watched from the back of the crowd as the official made his speech, tottering on an upturned soft drinks' crate, the smile that spread out beneath that hedge of a moustache childlike in its enthusiasm and pride. The Englishman could not help but feel pleased for this man who had invested so much of his energy into a project so personal to him.

Daisy listened patiently as the French words passed her by. Ted had been running some last-minute errands in the morning, and had picked her up in Gaston's car. It was her first trip into the town for many weeks.

'Has he finished now?' she said, as a new ripple of applause spread through the crowd.

'I think that's it.' Ted looked down at the figure nestling in the wheelchair. He reached to adjust the blanket that lay across her knees. The mayor started speaking once more. 'Or perhaps not.'

'Will you just leave that blessed blanket alone for one minute?'

He wheeled her around the market whilst he waited for the crowd to thin, and then took her into the visitor centre itself, pointing out the big map, and the photographs, and the piles of English brochures that he had agonised over for so many days. Just in time, he spotted that one of his own handbills had been pinned up in a corner; he pulled her chair around and away lest

246

her eyes alight upon the telltale print. 'The Pretty Goat' rang out from loudspeakers set into the ceiling, Debreu's best-known works having been burned to a CD by Alain, to be looped from morning until night. Ted wondered how long that even he could have maintained his love of the music should he have found himself working here.

The mayor bounded out from behind the counter to greet them, engulfing Daisy in the shadow of his bulky frame as he stooped to kiss her on both cheeks.

'Madame Prescott! So good to see you!'

'Likewise.'

'Your husband, he has done much work to make this a big success.'

'Well it's very impressive, I must say.' Daisy shifted in her seat, causing her blanket to slip down her legs. Ted bent to rearrange it, but Daisy yanked it from his hand, flinging it with some exasperation onto one of the stools at the counter. 'Does he treat all of you gentlemen as cripples as well?'

The door to the back room pushed open and Casimir edged his way through, tottering under the weight of a box of paper. '*Madam*,' he grinned, allowing his load to drop down onto the counter with a thump.

'Mmm.' Daisy returned a curt nod.

The mayor clapped his hands. 'So now we open. *Centre Frédéric Debreu*.' He leaned in towards Daisy, his face suddenly deadly serious. 'It is like in Paris they have *Centre Georges Pompidou*, a place of important culture. This is our *Centre Frédéric Debreu*.'

A hooting noise came from behind him. '*Centre Georges Pompidou? The worldwide national ...*'

The mayor flapped his arm in irritation but the smile remained fixed to his face. 'Anyway, it is very good to see you in the town again, Madame.'

'Well I thought I'd be coming down on my scooter. But I expect I'll have grown a new pair of legs by the time it arrives.'

'Yes, anyway,' Ted reached for the handles and swung the

wheelchair around towards the door. 'We're going for a drink together. We need to discuss a few things.'

Backing through the doors with the wheelchair, Ted did not notice Gaston until the café owner had planted his hand on the Englishman's shoulder.

'Madame Prescott! Welcome!' Gaston's voice was laced with cheer. The room about them was busy following the earlier ceremony; it brought to Ted's mind the joyful buzz of the summer months. 'Come!' Their host indicated the round table.

Ted held up his hand. 'No, no. Not today. We're just here for a small drink together. Things to discuss.'

Gaston's face grew grave. '*Oui*. I will get you a table. We move these chairs to allow you through.'

'I'm perfectly capable of walking.'

'Don't be silly.' Ted swatted her hands away from the armrests, which she was already exploring, searching for the best leverage to push herself up from the wheelchair.

'I am perfectly capable.'

'You push Madame Prescott to the window, there. I will take the chair away.'

'Right.'

Gaston walked ahead clearing a path as Ted wheeled the still-protesting Daisy to the empty table. When she was in position, Gaston turned to the Englishman. 'You have one minute to talk? For a favour.'

'Sure,' said Ted as Gaston beckoned Philippe over. 'Afternoon, lad. Go through the cocktail list with her, would you? I'll just have a frothy coffee.'

'What is it, Gaston?' said Ted, bemused by his friend's furtive air as the two men huddled in the corner by the telephone.

The café owner stroked his chin. 'First, you say that you are here to discuss things with your wife? Things are OK?'

Ted inclined his head as he thought. 'They are OK.' He shuffled his feet on the floorboards. 'Gaston, the conversation

248

that we had the other day – well, it's time. Time to think about leaving. David has sorted some things, and he's all right. So I have to prepare the ground for telling her what's happened. Just start talking about things in general.'

'I understand. That is good. It is sad for us, but it is good for you.'

'Yes. Thank you for asking. And thank you for understanding.'

Gaston looked across to where Daisy was sitting. Ted followed his eyes. Marie and Celine were with her, leaning on the table as they shared some joke. The elderly lady was laughing with them; Celine patted her forearm in affection. A stranger might mistake them for two nieces and a favourite aunt. The hiss of a hundred angry geese revealed that Philippe had started up the coffee machine; Ted glanced over to see the youth bustling around with mugs and a milk jug. Something had clearly blessed him with new courage.

'You will tell her also about Édouard?'

Ted blew air from his cheeks. 'I think that it's very unlikely that she'd see the funny side. Very unlikely.'

Gaston nodded. His voice grew purposeful. 'A shame. Ted, I was wondering, if for one more time –'

Ted took a stride backwards. 'No. I have said no. No more times, Gaston, you must –'

'Wait, wait, listen to me.' Something in Gaston's tone prompted Ted to yield; this was not the usual bewitching purr that he had come to grow so wary of. 'For here. There is no pretending. That is finished.'

'Go on.'

'Robert at the market. He is the stall with olives, chilli pepper? You know him?'

Ted nodded. He had rarely paused there to shop, but he had a picture of the stallholder in his mind, a beanpole, dark-complexioned man under a grey-green cap.

'He has a nephew, he is *handicapped*. I speak with Robert this morning. His sister and her husband, they worry about money. There is a school for the boy that is good and they try to get money. We talk, and I have an idea: perhaps we do a show here in my café? No pretending, no fooling, goodbye to Édouard, hello to Ted, we have a party, we have a good time, we get him some money.' Gaston shrugged. 'An idea.'

'A farewell show?' Ted chewed the end of his thumb. 'What, just as me? No messing around?'

'Farewell show. Proper farewell, even more if it is true that you are leaving. We do it soon, for the people in the village only, a few euro to come, all goes to Robert's family. Remember, many of your friends here have not seen you as you were on the stage. They deserve this opportunity. It would be a great evening. Easy and fun, as it is at the festival.'

Ted wrapped his friend in a hug. 'You know what, Gaston? I'd be honoured to.'

'OK. I will arrange.'

'They want me to play another show.' A grin erupted across Ted's face as he returned to his wife at the corner table. 'Here, in the café.' His left hand reached out to grasp an imaginary guitar neck, whilst his right strummed up and down his belly. 'Bom-de-dom-de-dom-de-dom.'

'Well it's nice to see you so happy about it for once. Normally you're a nervous wreck.'

'Yes, well.' Ted whisked up his coffee with vigour. 'There's a disabled lad in the town. Autistic, he is. They're trying to raise some cash to help the parents. So – you know.' Ted brushed froth from his top lip with his finger. 'They've all been good to us, as I've said before. Nice to put something back.'

'Preparing the ground' he had told Gaston; Ted had no intention of doing any more than that in this public place. He told Daisy of David's latest call; that his restaurant business hadn't worked out; that he had taken the job cheffing on oil rigs. He mooted that he might head for home sooner than their plans had anticipated, citing David's schedule: they would surely wish to see him, and would need to fit in with his off-shore postings.

250

Ted made some noises about speaking to the bank, but this was lost amidst Daisy's concern about the new job: would he be out at sea for long? What would he be doing? Surely it was dangerous? Ted filled in the gaps as best he could, and soon they were reminiscing about David as a boy, about his early days at school, about defying the horizontal deluge to watch him stomp around a field in his first rugby match. Their hands found each other across the table and squeezed.

'I'd like to go now,' said Daisy, when she had finished her tea.

'We could stay for a bit longer? Have another one?'

'No. I'd like to be home before I need to use the ladies.'

'What's wrong with going here? They're all accessible and all that for disabled people.' Ted scrunched up his mouth in thought. 'Well, I think the ladies might be.'

Daisy pushed her empty mug to the middle of the table. 'I would just like to use my own lavatory, if that's not too much to ask. I am not a disabled person. I just don't want to – well, it's a production.'

'Right ho.' Ted rose to his feet. 'I'll pay. You sort yourself out. Where's your blanket?'

Centre Frédéric Debreu appeared to be abandoned as Ted peered through the front windows. No visitors, no staff, just the sound of music from within. He pushed at the door and it yielded.

The opening verse of 'The Lovesick Clerk' was pouring from the loudspeakers, its cascading minor chords bouncing around the empty room, Debreu's voice, even at this low volume, urgent and commanding. Daisy's blanket was not on the stool where she had left it. He scanned left and right. Perhaps they had found it and stored it somewhere.

The whoosh of a toilet flushing came from the back room. Ted paced over to the desk; there it was, resting on a shelf at the back. He rounded the counter to fetch it as Casimir appeared from the interior door, his claw-like hands still fumbling to arrange his flies.

'Thanks.' Ted held up the folded blanket.

251

'No problem.' Casimir made a show of staring into every corner of the room. 'Perhaps busy at the weekend.'

'Afternoons are always quiet. And in the summer, I'm sure.'

'*Oui.*' The old man threw out his arms as Debreu hurtled into his chorus. 'The world comes here! French, British, *Germans*, from America, *Australia, Africa, the Africans* they forget their problems, their *famine*, they come, *the Arabs, the Israelis* … eh?'

Some primal instinct, some lightning reaction that his old body had somehow dredged up from his youth had caused Ted to hurl himself to the old man's feet at the first glimpse of the woman who had stepped into view beyond the plate glass at the front of the shop. The Englishman stared up as Casimir gawped down upon him. Ted threw his index finger over his mouth, his eyes pleading for hush, his other hand flapping and waving as if shooing away an imaginary mosquito. Above the sound of the sublime music, Ted could hear the door open and close.

'*Madam?*' Casimir had turned from him. Ted closed his eyes as Debreu's words were interspersed with the sharp crack of footsteps pacing the room.

'Fake.' Her dead voice was unmistakable even as she spat the words. 'Fraud.'

'*Madam?*' There was further pacing.

'*This, stolen. Also, this. This, taken from us.*'

Casimir said nothing in reply, shuffling his feet around the Englishman's prone body. Ted risked a glance upwards to see Casimir's cadaverous head peering forward, presumably following the woman around the room. Too frightened to shift his own weight, Ted wondered if he would be able to maintain his silence should the flyweight old man plant a boot on his hand.

'*This, fake. This, copied from us.*'

'*Perhaps you would like a brochure, dear lady?*'

'*This, this.*' There was more pacing. '*This!*'

'*You would be very welcome to take one.*'

'*This, the liar Englishman on the internet, the liar Englishman who visits to copy my exhibits.*'

Ted could see Casimir's head incline toward the corner in which Ted had spotted his own poster. A crazy thought crossed his mind that he should simply leap to his feet and face this woman, his already-galloping heart screaming into an extra gear as he fought his own suicidal impulse. He had no wish to be like one of those poor mad buggers carried from the zoo in little pieces, having been convinced that they could befriend the lions. There had been no firm evidence that the woman might turn violent if confronted, but it seemed not beyond the bounds of probability. Worse, she could follow him back down the road and introduce herself to Daisy. He clammed his eyes shut once more.

'We have many good value souvenirs for you, Madam? Pencils, erasers, a postcard?'

'Many false souvenirs. Fake souvenirs.'

'Perhaps you would leave your name in our visitor book?'

♫ *In her life of numbers, stark digits on the page*
All she wants is the warmth of a soft touch on her face ♫

Silence seemed to swamp the room as Debreu's final chords died away. As Ted's ears adjusted, he tuned in to the gentle crackling and hissing between the tracks of the old recording. There was something else, too: rapid, panting breaths, like a creature in the wild exhausted after a long chase. Casimir's boots shuffled once more. Then, a scraping sound, and footsteps hurrying away from him. The sound of the door opening and closing accompanied Debreu's next introduction.

The two men waited for what seemed like minutes, Ted slumped in the dust at Casimir's feet, the older man resting his elbows on the counter, his shoulders beginning to quiver with mirth. Finally, Ted started to manoeuvre his arms and legs to begin the process of hauling himself up.

'This is your girlfriend?' Casimir's glee emphasised every crack and crevice in his face.

'Bloody hell. Help me up.'

'Very angry lady. Also, phew!' Casimir wafted his hand around his nose. 'Her breakfast, it is vodka.'

Ted straightened his shirt. 'What did she mean?'

'What? She is very angry.'

Ted shook his head. 'No. The Englishman "on the internet". Even I understood that bit. What did she mean?"

Casimir screwed up his face. 'She's crazy. Her head is crazy.'

'She said "on the internet". She said that. What did she mean?'

'Me, I don't know.' Casimir waved his arm towards the old laptop plugged in at the end of the counter. 'There: the internet.'

The double doors crashed as Ted flung them open. He paused on the threshold of the room, his eyes scanning the café for its owner.

'Oh, so you did decide to come back for me then?'

Ted held his fingers up towards Daisy. 'Two minutes. Give me two minutes.' The big man strode forward towards the bar where Philippe was going through the motions of wiping glasses. 'Gaston?'

The young barman took a half-step backward at the barked tone, before jerking his thumb towards the door to Gaston's apartment. Marching across, Ted shoved his way through without knocking.

'So how did they get that photograph then?' Ted turned his back on the café owner and began to pace, up and down the neat lounge, kicking and scuffing his boots on the floorboards.

'I send it. When I send the recordings. I wish that the man is reminded of you. So I send him Philippe's photograph from the studio.'

'What about a contract?'

'Pardon?'

'There must have been a contract. You don't do things like this on a handshake. There must have been a contract.'

'He sends me a contract, I sign it, I send it back. I assume it is just the formalities for his money.'

Ted whirled round. 'You assume?'

Gaston threw his arms out wide. 'Ted. The contract is long, very long. It is in English. I speak English well, but?' He gave an extravagant shrug. 'I am not a lawyer. Should I pay money, lots of money for a lawyer to see it? I think no. I think "this is the paperwork for the money he leaves me." I think "I must return this right away".'

'So you had no idea what they were planning?'

'Ted, whatever has happened with the misunderstanding, I confess I do not understand your difficulty. Especially now Édouard Prescôte is no longer with us. Why should you not be proud that they sell your songs on the internet? But I will contact the American and I will fix it.'

There was a tentative tap on the door. Philippe's head poked its way around. 'Missus Prescott, she is very agitated. Says she will go home on her own if you do not come.'

*

♫ ... *I told him there was nothing I could do*
The rude fellow then spat down upon my shoe!
Editor, Editor see what they're doing
Dear Editor our country's gone to ruin ♫

The sound from the gramophone in the kitchen was crystal-clear, or as crystal-clear as the hiss of the old recording would ever allow. Ted tapped along with his biro, rapping the pen against his knee in time with one of those five masterpieces that he had re-recorded himself on that strange and marvellous day at the studio. Now that he had recovered from the shock of seeing his own face gawking back at him from the computer screen, Ted afforded himself a wry inner smirk at the morning's discovery. He had not met the American, but from his friends' description had taken him for a genuine individual, a kindred spirit who had been touched by this music, as opposed to some huckster after a quick buck. But a record executive! He hoped that it had been a misunderstanding rather than any deviousness on the American's behalf. 'Transport from ferry' he scribbled on his list.

He was already regretting raising his voice at Gaston. The café owner had been atypically naive, but what could have been expected from him? Gaston might have the gift of the gab, but Ted's 'manager' had just been a man who ran a bar. Perhaps they should speak again; sort things out with the American; explain the joke that had got out of hand. Perhaps his company would agree to keep the music on sale under Ted's own name. From nowhere, the big Englishman found a new spark of enthusiasm – downloading his songs from the internet: it might be miles away from a physical record that you could hold in both hands, but it was surely what all the big names did these days? But just as this daydream fluttered through his mind, another part of his brain brought him back to reality. Stopping the sales was one thing; admitting they'd taken the money under false pretences quite another.

'Help for Daisy' he scrawled, glancing across at his wife as she dozed.

Leaving his paper and pen on the table, he hauled himself from the armchair and padded from the room to the kitchen. The speakers were blaring out here in this tiny space and he reached for the knob to adjust the volume.

Sliding the bolt to one side, Ted took two steps out onto the verandah, folding his arms across his chest as a barrier against the cold that hit him. Dusk was already approaching. The burner was keeping the cottage warm and cosy – certainly warmer and cosier than he had anticipated – but they were getting through firewood at a frightening rate. How had he possibly thought that this would be a good place to spend the winter? Ted cast his eyes across to the diminished pile of fuel. What about making woodwork or the like for the markets? He would add that to the list.

♬ *When we were young*
We sat together you and I
You daydreamed of the future
The joy of living in your eyes
The feel of the grass
There was no place ever greener
I stroked your hair, we had few cares
When we were young ♬

Debreu's baritone hung in the air. For a second or two there was just the crackling of the run-out groove and then a sharp click as the gramophone turned itself off and left Ted in silence. He stood for several minutes, looking out across the farmland, searching for the detail of the trees and hedges in the fading daylight. He and Daisy might be as poor as church mice now, but they would be happy; they would always be happy.

He registered a faint noise just as he was turning for the warmth of the kitchen. A car on the road at the foot of the track. It was probably the farmer returning home, but for some reason Ted paused, listening as the vehicle began to climb the hill. As it got closer to him, Ted could ascertain that it was not his landlord's old banger; this was a smooth, big engine. He rested his elbows on the railing and waited.

'Monsieur Patenaude, he is in the café, says he has a letter for you.' Philippe seemed breathless, as if he had just made the journey up here on foot. 'Gaston, he reads it and writes it in English.' The youth handed over an envelope and a sheet of paper.

Ted took the items, nonplussed. Why had Gaston opened his post? There must be something that he had recognised about it; something that had told him that the Englishman would want a translation. The writing on the envelope was neat and slightly childish; the lower-case 'i's had been adorned with small circles rather than dots and the last line of the address had been underlined with a ruler. Whatever Gaston had spotted, it must have been important to send Philippe all the way up here, rather than waiting for the farmer to finish whatever he was doing in town.

For some reason Ted pulled the letter from the envelope before looking at Gaston's translation. It was brief; less than a single side. 'Dear Mr Prescott,' he could read, and some of the words within. 'Thank you,' he murmured, as an afterthought, as Philippe looked up at him with expectation.

Gaston had composed his translation on the back of one of the Édouard Prescôte handbills. His pseudonym confronted him in accusatory type as Ted unfolded the sheet. Ted held it up to his eyes, his big hand quivering as he digested the English words in Gaston's elegant hand.

'Dear Mr. Prescott,
    Thank you for your letter. I am sorry I have been late to reply. I remember very well your brother Eric living with our family, but I was a child at that time. He was a good man. I am happy to talk about him more if you are to visit. I live at this address here until Christmas.'

There was a telephone number.

Ted could feel tears filling his eyes. He tried to blink them back without drawing attention, but it was too much. Philippe was still standing there, hopping from foot to foot in embarrassment at the older man's reaction, keeping his eyes steadily fixed on the cottage's sagging guttering.

'Thank you,' Ted said once again. 'I – er – I ...' he jerked his head towards the kitchen door.

'OK Mr Prescott,' replied the boy, turning in relief and crossing the grass to the track at a near-canter. Ted watched Gaston's car round the oak tree and disappear down the hill. Daisy's voice called him from inside, but the words passed him by as he lingered on the verandah, staring out across the darkening landscape, his eyes drifting across the trees and the sky and the grass, but registering nothing aside from a mishmash of images and memories from long ago.

Then he read the note again, and then again.

21

Eric

'Are you sure you are able to do this?'

'*Oui, oui*. It is no problem, no problem.'

There was a chill on the morning wind as it gusted in from the northern hills, tumbling autumn leaves and litter across the potholes. Ted had arranged to meet Casimir outside the tenement that the ancient Frenchman shared with his sister. The two men were leaning on Casimir's old Ford, which had been abandoned at a slapdash angle in the shadow of the run-down building, dust and birds' mess accumulating on its windows and bodywork.

Ted grasped the door handle, but held back from climbing in. 'It's just that it's a bit of a journey.'

'*Non, non*.' The nimble octogenarian was already at the wheel, urging the starter motor into action. Ted hesitated before lowering himself into the seat beside him, brushing away sweet wrappers with the back of his hand.

'Sorry, I do not drive often now.' Casimir leaned over to gather more debris from the shelf above the glove compartment; elbowing open his door, he allowed the rubbish to fall from his hands into the street. 'It is more clean since I stop the smoking. For good health. Eat *sweets* now.' He patted his chest then activated the windscreen wipers; creamy streaks of filth smeared the glass in front of them. 'Drink wine.'

'Thank you. I appreciate your help. Really.'

'Perhaps I am not the most good translator.' Casimir tugged furiously at the washers. 'I try.'

'No, I appreciate your help.' Ted's voice was a murmur, faraway and absorbed.

His antiquated driver had apologised for his linguistic skills, but it was his performance behind the wheel that caused Ted the most concern as they passed through the town. Casimir used the throttle enthusiastically, maintaining a speed that was invariably too high for the gear being employed, and his understanding of braking appeared to be that the mechanism could either be 'on' or 'off'. As the lurching and swaying of the vehicle dragged Ted from his own preoccupations, he started to wonder whether the Frenchman could discern any aspect of the road ahead through those feeble and decrepit pits that he called eyes. Casimir's adoption of highway protocol appeared to be utterly random. At one point the clamour of a truck horn made Ted grab for the dashboard in alarm; the old man had pulled out in front of an articulated lorry that was rumbling away from the petrol station on the edge of town. It did not help that the beat-up old hatchback embellished every jolt and bump of these ill-maintained roads. Why had he not postponed this morning's arrangements until Gaston's car had been available for Ted to take the wheel himself? Ted gripped his safety belt and gave a sigh of relief as they crossed the ravine and turned left onto the straighter and less populous main road.

'Your brother, he was the lover of her mother?' Casimir asked, as their transit had settled in to some form of equilibrium.

Ted shrugged. 'Yes. No. Perhaps.' He wrinkled up his nose as he thought, rubbing his palms around his face, massaging the flesh of his chin and jowls. 'My own mother said that. It would probably be best not to say that to the lady.'

'Not say that, no.'

'He lived there with them. That is all I know. It was her pet theory, the stuff about the lovers. Mainly because he was always writing about this woman or that woman. It was her guess.'

'But what is your guess, Ted?'

The Englishman looked out upon the farmland that rose up beside the road. It seemed dour under the grey skies. Perhaps it had just been the vibrancy of the spring and summer months that had sprinkled this landscape with that peculiar magic; that had convinced him that he had found the most beautiful place on Earth. Whereas a field was a field was a field. Wherever he and Daisy were going to end up living on their return – and he knew that it would not be a picturesque country cottage – it would never be improved by the Derbyshire rain.

Ted realised that Casimir was looking across to him. 'Oh,' he said. 'Well perhaps he was? But no guess, really. Like I say, he lived there with them. And then, well, he didn't. He moved on.' Ted turned his eyes back to the road ahead. 'He just disappeared from view.'

The men drove on in silence.

The road diverged from the river as it drifted into the heart of the countryside, but the landscape remained rocky and primitive; wild without any great magnificence. Casimir appeared to be more comfortable as a driver without the distractions of a built-up area around him. Ted sat staring ahead, rigid, in his own world. The whine of the engine was monotonous and did nothing to take his thoughts from the meeting ahead. Ted glanced down; there was a litter-packed gap in the dashboard where a radio might have been fitted. He bit his lip and looked out of the window, forcing his mind on to anything but the meeting ahead.

Bom-de-dom-de-dom-de-dom ...

The snatch of melody brought something to mind, and he spoke. 'There was something that I did not understand. When I went to see Debreu's papers in Saint Ouen-de-l'Eléphant.'

'Oui?'

Ted frowned as he recalled that morning in the museum, surrounded by the remnants of the great musician's life, scratching his head over those two identical documents. In the cold light of day, he could not quite believe that he had not made a silly error; his recollections of the event had been made hazy by the subsequent indignity that had exposed the dusty chamber as some sort of monstrous love trap.

He searched for words that would explain his perplexity to Casimir. 'You see – I found two documents. Two.' He held up two fingers accordingly. 'They were old lyrics; the words to "Monsieur Berlin," as he'd written them. They were early versions, when he first wrote the words, do you understand?'

Casimir bobbed his head as he drove. 'Two. When he first writes, I understand.'

'Well the thing is – he had corrected them. Made changes. He had changed them both. But the changes were the same. Like he'd copied the changes from one to another for some reason. So I did not understand.' Ted drummed his fingers on his knee as he began to think out loud. 'I did wonder if they were a fake – a fraud – or if one of them was. But they seemed genuine, and why? If you were going to go to the trouble to –'

Turning to the driver, Ted was astonished to see his gummy mouth stretched wide in a grin. 'What? What is it?'

'You did not ask your *lady paramour* about this?' The Frenchman mimed two kisses at the road ahead.

'No I bloody did not.'

Casimir reached for the gear lever in an eleventh-hour anticipation of the junction that was almost upon them. Swinging the car to the right, he turned to regard his companion with eyes that twinkled despite their age. 'Non, the documents are not fraud. Not big fraud.'

'Not big fraud?' Ted's frown grew deeper as he attempted to second-guess the riddle, all the while hoping that Casimir would return his fickle attention to the main road.

'OK. Debreu, he has no money. He drinks. Women, girls, lots of drink. No money.'

'Broke.'

'Broke, *oui*, broke. Very broke. But he is also *a celebrity*.' Casimir gave a skeletal shrug. 'Small region, big star. He has – ah – power? Power. People, they want to know him. Even the police, when he has his big trouble, he does a concert for the police, there is no more problem. So. He goes to the café, the bar, to eat. No money. Says "I sing a song," one dinner. "I give you this *autograph* or document," some wine.' The Frenchman sniffed, a rasp, heavy with snot. 'The words for this song? Who knows? Not big fraud.'

'He bloody wrote it out twice deliberately.' Ted blew air from his cheeks. 'There might be dozens of the same out there. Hundreds.'

'Oui.'

Ted tried to picture the musician sat – where? A café? A bedsit? On a park bench? – painstakingly scratching out couplets; scribbling and revising to alight upon words that he had already written and performed so many times before; hoarding them about his person so that at any time he might be able to produce this valuable authentic document: the original lyrics to one of the region's most beloved songs.

How did that other song go? The one about the forger?

> ♫ *Although the law may misconceive*
> *It is no crime if you believe*
> *Although the law may well lament it*
> *It is no crime if you're contented* ♫

Those people had wanted a tiny slice of the great musician, and he had bloody sold it to them. Ted had sung those words himself so many times without twigging that there was more to them. Somewhere, up there, Debreu had been laughing at him.

Casimir poked his arm. 'Here. We are here.'

There was a baby 4x4 parked up on the grass verge at the nearest point on the road to the isolated cottage. They left Casimir's car nose-to-nose with it and traipsed up through the field via a gap in the stone wall; Ted could feel the first spots of rain on his face as he walked. There was no path, so they simply took the shortest route across the field, as Ted had done when he had first been here all those months ago.

He hung back, intending to collect his thoughts before

committing himself to knock, but this was not a place that you could approach unseen and the squat green door swung open when he was barely twenty yards away.

It was an incongruous figure that appeared from within the primitive stone building. The woman had chic rectangular glasses and a bob of blonde hair; she bore one of those smiles that makes a whole neighbourhood light up. Her top and jeans clung to her figure as she ducked her head underneath the lintel and waved to them; Ted waved back, an automatic gesture. He was already comforted by her ready air of warmth. She beckoned them in and turned; Ted could not help but watch her bottom as it withdrew back into the cottage. He surmised that she must be fifty – perhaps older – but one of those women who seemed to be of the younger generation, like the impossibly glamorous mothers on the American television shows who were always best friends with their daughter. He felt a claw on his forearm and looked down. Casimir was gurning up at him with his cadaverous face screwed up in lechery. Brushing off the revolting old man, Ted stooped forward into the house.

The stylish woman had seemed out of place outside the tumbledown old cottage, but she had clearly made her mark upon the interior. It had been completely renovated, and expensively so; whereas the outside was a jumble of cold weatherbeaten stone and decaying timber, here was a revelation of pine floors, white walls and stainless steel. The doorway opened directly into a large open-plan sitting room. It was a warm and airy space; a multitude of small spotlights were strung from steel wires, their starry pinpricks defying the gathering skies outside. Minimalist leather chairs and a sofa clustered round glass coffee table; the paintings on the wall were of subjects that Ted could not recognise aside from being able to describe them as 'modern'. To Ted's discomfort, the woman turned and kissed him on both cheeks before bounding one step back to examine his face carefully.

'Ted. Ted Pressscott.' It was a statement rather than a

question. She patted her breast. 'Christelle.' She waved him to one of the armchairs. Ted kept his eyes averted so that he need not witness any physical contact she made with the ancient degenerate.

'No English!' Her voice was cheery as she bustled round a cafetière. '*Non,* very bad English. *German?*'

Ted realised the question was addressed to him. 'Er – no German. Sorry.' He pointed at the old man. 'Casimir. He is my translator.'

'Ah.' Their hostess aimed a delighted smile at Casimir whilst she arranged mugs of black coffee for the pair. Ted put the mug to his lips; the taste was strong; he guessed that the coffee was expensive. Fetching her own drink, the woman sat down to talk.

The subsequent few minutes were maddening for Ted. Courtesy demanded that he could not simply wade in with questions about his brother. Her manner implied that she had no shocking news to reveal, whether dreadful or joyous; this realisation lifted much of the anxiety that had been building since Ted had crawled from bed that morning. She was a garrulous sort, which relieved him of the burden of niceties, but he fidgeted as she told them lengthy anecdotes about her life which Casimir constantly forgot to translate anyway. Ted drank his coffee, feeling like a spare part as the old man lapped up her company.

'Umm – she is sorry she did not write in the summer.' Casimir had grasped his responsibilities and was speaking directly to Ted, his wizened face grave and formal with the solemnity of his task. The Englishman smiled at the woman to show his understanding, waving his hands in what he hoped would be recognised as a 'no problem' gesture.

'This is the house of her family, but she does not live here. She works in Limoges, she lives there. Comes to this house on vacation, for the quiet.'

'It is a very nice place.'

'It is a very nice place.'

'Thank you.'

Casimir took a swig from his own mug, noisily swilling the liquid around his mouth and between his teeth. 'She says you look like Eric,' he said, pointing at Ted's face. 'You have a nose like his. But it is a long time since she has seen him.'

Ted could feel his heart pound at the mention of his brother's name. He nodded hard to gee the old man up.

'Christelle, she remembers he arrives with her brother one day. Her brother, his name is Roger. Eric lives in this house with the family. She is maybe eight, ten years. She calls him *"Tonton"*, means "Uncle".'

The woman nodded happily on hearing this, and spoke again.

'Before he comes, she is lonely. But he is very much fun for her. He plays games, he makes her laugh. Her brother Roger is older, he is more serious to play with a little child. There is not a father in the house; her mother is on her own.' Casimir paused at this point; Ted caught his raised eyebrow. The Englishman held up his palm in warning. 'This is in 1970s, when this house is not – ah – not made good inside the rooms.'

'Tell her that it is nice to hear that she has good memories of him.'

Ted sat back as best he could in the spartan armchair as the pair began to confer in French once more. He tried to picture Eric, here in this cottage, a guest but soon one of the family, delighting this lonely little kid living out here in the middle of nowhere. He had always been good with children, Eric had. Ted was filled with a longing to nose round the house, to see the room where his brother had slept; the place where they had shared family meals. But even as his restless eyes scanned the room, he realised how foolish he was being. Quite apart from the discourtesy of demanding a tour, the place would be unrecognisable from those days; the fleeting image in his mind of his brother, in boots and leather jacket, stood before those fashionably sparse bookshelves, was as false a memory as it is possible to have.

'Ah. Not so good memories, I am afraid.'

'What?' Ted could feel a pit opening in his stomach.

'No, no. It is not something bad with Eric.' Casimir spoke hastily. 'It is her brother Roger. He is in an accident on the *motor scooter*, ahhh – the motorbike. He dies.'

'Oh. Christelle, I'm so terribly sorry.'

Seeing Ted's expression, Christelle shrugged, a careless gesture. But the life was gone from her face; her reply was the merest hint of a nod.

'After that, the memories were not so much fun.'

Ted ran his hand through his hair, his eyes darting around the room to find anything to look at but the woman sitting opposite. He felt the weight of all his years pulling him down, as he perched on this ridiculous armchair dredging up this lady's grief for the sake of his whimsical little quest. They could not possibly walk out at this point, but he suddenly longed to go. He thought of Daisy pottering away back in their own cosy cottage, busying herself with crafts and knitting despite her frailty. He needed to be back with her, surrounded by the security of feelings and emotions that he could explain.

Christelle clapped her hands together, her smile returning. But it was half as broad, and certainly not enough to quell the fog of awkwardness that had enveloped the room.

'She says you will want to know about your brother,' said Casimir.

Ted bit his lip. 'If...' he began.

'I will ask her?'

Ted bowed his head.

The woman appeared to recover her vitality as she reminisced to Casimir. The glow returned to her face and her gestures once more became tactile and animated; whatever she was recalling, there were clearly some happy moments amidst that dreadful event. Ted drummed his fingers as his translator appeared once more to be sidetracked into chit-chat. He wondered about this cottage. She came here for her holidays; she had spent much money on improvements – obviously her love for the place had not been tarnished by her lonely childhood or the awful tragedy

268

that had struck her family. Her mother must be dead now, surely. He thought of his brother becoming the man of the house. Suddenly, overnight, in such extreme emotional circumstances. Perhaps that salacious speculation was more accurate than he had ever supposed.

'Your brother stays for a short while. He loves the outside. He walks in the fields, he makes archery. He is good at making wood for the fire. All the time he plays with her, Christelle. He builds a *treehouse* for her. There is a *treehouse* in the wood on the hill. It is still there, very broken.' Casimir waved his bony arm in the direction of the window.

Their hostess bounded to her feet to fetch more coffee, her recollections again in full flow as she busied herself with the cafetière. What she said made sense: Eric had always been out there on the peaks, rain or shine, restless for the wind on his cheeks even as brother Ted badgered him to listen at the wireless. Perhaps that was why they had drifted apart; it had certainly been no surprise when his older brother had started travelling.

Christelle screamed with laughter, jolting Ted from his introspection and causing his jaw to drop open in bemusement. 'Non, non, non!' She waved her hands at the two men, crossing and uncrossing her raised palms at speed before composing herself to wipe a tear from her eye.

Ted caught sight of Casimir's expression. He felt his own face flooding with crimson as he realised that his companion had posed that question which had been specifically forbidden. 'I ...' Ted tried to butt in, to formulate some words of apology, but the woman had already resumed talking, her tone more serious. He cursed the old fool upon whom he had been forced to rely for this most sensitive of encounters, his helplessness mounting as the pair conversed. Once more his thoughts turned to the familiarity of his own sitting room. It was time to bring this to a close.

Looking up from his watch, Ted became aware that the others were staring at him as they spoke. The woman appeared to be biting her bottom lip; Casimir, normally such a riot of

269

impishness and decrepitude, was squatting rigid in his chair, seemingly lost in some quandary. The two spoke again, questioning each other, all the time looking across to Ted. The Englishman felt that pit reforming.

'Ted.' Casimir's voice was hesitant. 'Ted, I say to the lady the guess that your brother is the lover of her mother. She is, she laughs very much. The guess is not correct.'

Ted felt his embarrassment returning in waves; he held up his hands to show his mortification.

'Ted, the guess is not correct. Your brother is the lover of her brother, Roger. That is why he is living here.'

Daisy would be making her lunch now, faltering around the tiny kitchen to fetch bread and meat, clinging to the table, the chairs, the cooker as she defied her near-useless legs, peering at the dial as she lit the hob beneath the pan of water that Ted had left so that she need not wrestle with its weight.

'Christelle, she is sorry if it is news that you do not want. Her thought was that you know already, as he always speaks of his family well.'

'No, no.' Ted's breath wavered as he inhaled deeply. A squall of rain blattered the windows. 'I – we – did not know.'

'When Roger dies, it is his tragedy also. He realises he cannot remain here in this house. She is very unhappy when he goes. They do not see him again. Never see him again.' Casimir clasped his hands together, his crab-like fingers whiter than ever before as they knotted amidst each other. 'That is the story.'

They finished their drinks. Christelle produced some old photos of Roger; she pulled out a buff envelope to show them a yellowing newspaper clipping from the time of his accident. Standing at the front door, the woman kissed Ted once more, and then grasped his forearms with both hands, speaking directly to his face.

'She says Eric is a good man.'

Ted nodded, then found himself wrapping his big arms around the woman, enveloping her in a hug, ensuring that her face was buried in his shoulder so that she would not see his expression. He held her there for what seemed like minutes, breathing hard into her hair, nodding gently at the questions that were arriving unseen from his own thoughts. Then he turned and trudged off into the drizzle.

They found the treehouse in a small copse above the field; a platform of sodden grey-brown planks topped with a pitched canopy. The wood was rotten but the structure had held, wedged into a fork in the trunk of an ash tree, perhaps ten feet from the ground. Ted circled, peering upwards to see every detail.

'He did a good job,' he said at last. 'I knew he would. Properly mitred joints, see? Bit of a faff to lift everything up there.'

Casimir had loitered at the edge of the grove. He stepped forward, craning his scrawny neck to follow Ted's finger.

The Englishman kept his eyes fixed to the branches. It was dry in their shelter; the patter of rain on the leaves was beginning to abate.

'He was heartbroken. In the depths of despair. And he couldn't talk to us. He thought that we wouldn't understand,' he said.

'You would understand?'

Ted turned to his companion. 'No. We wouldn't have done. That's the thing, isn't it? That's why he left in the first place. That's why his letters were full of ladies this, ladies that. He was still playing the big brother he thought I wanted.'

Casimir inclined his head.

'I would understand now, of course I would now. But there we were in our small town.' Ted breathed deeply. 'Jesus, Jesus Christ. He must have been so bloody lonely.'

'What do you do?'

Ted said nothing as he stood looking past the old man into the horizon beyond. He shook his head gently, an almost automatic movement. 'Nothing. Just nothing.' Ted shrugged, a hopeless, empty shrug. 'He made his own new life. He didn't think that he could share it with us, and he was probably right. Which is shameful. Our shame, not his. But he had a right to his new life, his privacy, and me coming here ...' He returned to the trunk of the beech tree, looking up once more at the remnants of the monument to Eric Prescott, picturing the young man perched in the branches with his hammer and nails whilst a small girl stood watching expectantly below. It was a good memory to leave it on. 'Casimir, he'd decided that he didn't want me to know all this. It wasn't my place to seek it out. Would you – well, I'd like all this to remain with us.'

'One more secret.' The old man nodded. '*Oui*, it is no problem. Maybe you find him still? Tell him – uhh?' Casimir held out his arms in an air hug.

'I think I've blundered around enough in other people's lives.' Ted gave the trunk a pat, feeling its steadfastness against his palm. 'He's out there somewhere. But he could have found me easily over the years and he decided not to. I think I have to respect that.'

The rain had stopped as they emerged from the wood, looking down towards the shining wet slate that roofed the cottage. Tramping their way through the grass, the two men made their way back to the car.

22

A Last Goodbye

Ted's boots glistened as he ambled towards the gap in the hedge. Months of his size twelves had flattened the beginnings of a track where once there had been a faint line of discoloured grass; he wondered how many years and how many men it would take to create an actual proper path in the landscape. Hundreds and hundreds, he supposed. Perhaps somebody would come here after him, a new old fool with romantic ideas of living simply in the countryside, a fresh pair of feet to continue his work.

This morning's rain was a misty spray, fresh but no challenge to one who had spent his boyhood in the drizzling High Peaks. Instead of heading towards the village, Ted turned left after he had eased himself through the hawthorn. He followed the arse end of the lane before it petered out, first into a trail of earth and stones and then to simple nothingness as it curved and rose and met the hills. This was a patchy moorland of granite and heather, one that nobody had ever thought worthwhile to farm, certainly not the lazy bugger who owned the land next door. Despite the chill, Ted began to sweat as his route took him further up, each step chosen carefully to avoid a turned ankle on the inhospitable ground.

He wanted to do this walk one last time. There was a beauty in this particular craggy scenery that was very similar to that of those slopes so familiar to him from his English home. But it had not become a regular route, being a little too far from the village and the comfort of post-ramble refreshments. He had never been one to pack a sandwich.

Perhaps they might find an hour or so to bring David up here.

Their son was due at the end of the week. All the way down through the British Isles to pick them up. They had argued about it on the telephone together, Ted incredulous at the time and expense that would be required, but unable to come up with any alternative plan.

And it was better that they would be able to talk to Daisy together.

At the very crest of the hill Ted turned to survey his route. The fine rain blew about his face, cold and crisp, invigorating him after his climb. Ten feet to his left was a table-like slab of granite that rose up knee-high above the other stones. Tramping over, he planted one boot onto the mirror-grey surface and, after taking a furtive look in all directions to check that he was not being observed, lifted himself up to stand atop the rock, king of this historic landscape in the face of the wind and the spray. Glancing left and right again, and then three hundred and sixty degrees just to be safe, Ted coughed to clear his lungs, raised his head to the horizon and bellowed:

♫ *O'er the mountains, through the streets*
From the eastern borders to the western seas
Across the world
For wherever I go
I long for my Thorigny girl ♫

He stood there for some minutes before he moved on, the words lingering with him on his trek.

The commotion started as he pulled the front door closed and clattered around the kitchen kicking off his boots. He paused to listen. His name. Daisy was calling his name from the living room. No: it was less a 'call' than a 'yell'. He took one rapid stride and then hesitated as the noise recommenced. His first thought had been that his wife was suffering pain or distress, but the tone was something quite different. Rounding the doorframe, he inched down the corridor to investigate.

She was waving something at him; something that he recognised but could not quite place. 'You're back? Did you get your morning exercise? Stop and have a booze-up at Gaston's? Pretend to be a Frenchman again in order to fleece some more people?'

Ted took an involuntary step backwards, blinking in bewilderment at her expression. Then he registered the piece of paper in her hand. It was the handbill from the club, the sheet upon which Gaston had written when translating the letter about Eric. She brandished it at him, its half-inch high lettering confronting him like a smoking revolver. He gawped at it with horrified eyes.

'"Edooard Pres-coat, Guitar?" You! What do you think you're doing? What in the Lord's name do you think you're doing? Have you gone stark staring mad?'

Daisy forced herself up, her limbs whitening as she pushed at the arms of the winged chair. Taking no more than the briefest of pauses to steady herself, she started shuffling towards him, still waving the paper, her face convulsed in a cocktail of fury and incredulity. For an instant, Ted thought that she might be about to bodily attack him.

'Love ...'

'I'm thinking, have you gone crackers? Completely crackers? All that flannel about helping Gaston, about playing some music with your friends? With your "too English" shirt! I know I can't get out, but did you think I wouldn't find out? Do you think those people who paid to see "Edooard Pres-coat" won't find out? Are you selling them things as well?'

'I ...'

Ted grabbed at her as her leg gave way and she toppled towards him, his right hand shooting out to seize her under the armpit, his big paw fully rounding her tiny ribs from her breast to her backbone. Taken by surprise, he staggered forward, throwing out his other arm to regain his balance, cracking his knuckles hard against the door frame, causing him to swear in pain.

'Put me down!' she shrieked.

'But I've just caught you! You need your stick, you didn't have your stick.'

'Put me down!' Her voice was furious. He bundled her around and onto the sofa. 'I know what I need my blooming stick for!'

'Now, now.' They were both panting hard as they eyeballed each other, Ted towering above his sprawled-out wife. Her face screwed up in pain as she made a useless attempt to shift her torso; the threat of disembowling had passed. He stooped down to build the cushions into a proper support; she complied as he eased her into a semi-sitting position.

*

'Go on. Why don't you come?'

Ted reappeared in the living room, his big paws fumbling at the cuffs of his brand new shirt. Silky white, with prints of scarlet roses, he had acquired it from the second-hand stall on his earlier round trip. The man had sold it to him for a token euro, on learning that he wanted to wear it for the show that night. Ted worked around his midriff, thrusting the tails down to his underpants and then buttoned and belted his corduroy trousers.

They had sat in silence for much of the afternoon: initially icy, then thawing through frost to chilly with occasional outbreaks. After all these years he knew better than to try to engage her in conversation before she was ready. He knew his gambit was a risky one.

'How, precisely?' she said. 'You're going to drive me, are you? Or wheel me down the hill? Sit me at the back with a specimen bottle for when I need the lavatory?'

He had played too soon. 'We could sort something –'

'No I am not coming on your scam. I am staying here, and I am going to bake a cake for our son.'

Ted stared at her. 'How are you going to bake a bloody cake? You can't even lift the teapot without me.'

'I am perfectly able to bake a simple cake without your master

276

chef skills, thank you.' Daisy returned her attention to her knitting, before raising her eyes once more to meet his. 'Unless you're really a French pastry chef and have just been posing as my husband for the last four decades.'

Ted ground his teeth. 'Well tell me what the ingredients are and I'll get them ready for you.'

'No. I don't trust you in the kitchen. I've hardly been out of this room all day. For all I know you could have opened a nuclear physics laboratory out there.'

Ted blew air through his cheeks, emptying his lungs as he contemplated defeat. She was ignoring him entirely now, her focus on each meticulous twist of the wool on the tips of her needles. He hovered for a while in the doorway.

'Do I look a little snazzy in this shirt?'

She didn't raise her eyes. 'You look like a nincompoop.'

That was better. He wasn't forgiven, but they would laugh about it one day.

*

Gaston's café had been transformed for the evening's event. Most of the tables had been stowed in the cellar to make room for extra seating; the large round one had been hauled outside to spend the night on the pavement. Gaston had blocked off the main doors to create a stage area from where Ted could perform to both halves of the room, with one of the French doors serving as a temporary entrance. Celine and Marie stood guard here, the younger girl rattling a tin for admission money, smiling and laughing with the customers who were already trickling in from the chilly market place. Philippe's eyes bored into her from behind the bar, lingering on the raven hair that cascaded to her snug jeans. The youth jumped as he felt a sharp dig in the ribs; Casimir was lurking beside him, pressed into casual service for the night despite the debacle of his previous occupancy. The ancient gave a rancid smirk before returning to the beer pump to continue filling glass jugs.

Robert, the olive trader, introduced Ted to his sister and brother-in-law. Both seemed overwhelmed by the occasion, the woman gaping in wonder as people started to file into the room. Her husband gave Ted's hand a timid shake before hanging back, obviously awkward in his suit and tie. In turn, Ted was embarrassed by their appreciation, and was relieved when the couple withdrew to the front-most table, where Gaston presented them with a carafe of wine. It occurred to Ted that there was something strange going on with his own emotions, or rather something strange that was not going on. He was not frightened, not in the slightest. Even as the handful of tables filled, as more faces pushed through to the back of the room to find a place to stand in view of the makeshift stage, he could find no trace of the fear that would normally be gripping him. Sidling to the very end of the bar, he parked himself on the stool that had been reserved for him, to find that his glass had been clandestinely refilled. Casimir winked as Ted raised it in a toast.

Beside him, the interior door opened and Alain pushed his way through, a cardboard box under each arm. He set them down on the stainless steel bar. 'You managed to do them?' Ted attempted not to appear too eager, his eyes searching the contents within.

'All the afternoon.' Alain reached down and removed an item, passing it to Ted who examined it with reverence.

There was no cellophane wrapper, no plastic case, merely a six-inch square cardboard sleeve adorned with the watery colours from a home printer. But a smile of gratification burst its way across Ted's face as he looked at his own picture, an Englishman clutching his guitar in the recording studio, and he drank in the words:

TED PRESCOTT *guitar*
The songs of Frédéric Debreu.

'Ted!' The mayor took his hand, and then enveloped him in a bear hug. 'It is fantastic, brilliant.' The official waved around the packed room, his voice close to a shout to compete with the rising noise.

'Oh you know. I haven't played yet.'

'Ha! Philippe, Casimir, ensure his glass is full.'

Ted held up his hand. 'They're ahead of you on that one.'

'I am the master barman.' Casimir leaned across to speak in confidence. 'I pour him one, I pour me one. I pour him one, I pour me one.'

'*Well pour me one also.*' The mayor beckoned Ted to resume his seat, then slotted himself in beside the Englishman, his elbows planted on the bar, his chin spreading into folds as it nestled in his palms. 'Ted, thank you for all you do. For this town, for Frédéric Debreu.'

'For Bernard.' Casimir set down a glass of wine.

The mayor shot the old man a look. 'It does mean very much to me to make this town good again. Very personal to me, as is the reputation of Debreu. After all, he –'

'*He was your sister's lover, oui oui.*' Casimir planted a newly opened bottle between them. 'Have this, Ted. For the nerves.'

'No nerves tonight, funnily enough. But don't take it away again.'

'*But indeed, he was my sister's lover!*'

Casimir threw up his hands. '*He was not your sister's lover! She was besotted with him as they all were, and he gave her one because he needed a bed, though even then she was three times as old as his usual –*'

The mayor rose up to his full height, looming over the ancient old man behind the bar. '*You have no clue! No damn clue! You –*'

Ted felt Gaston's hand on his shoulder. 'Perhaps five minutes, Ted?'

'Suits me. I'll go and tune up.'

'*Ladies and gentlemen!*' Gaston had twice called for quiet now; he waited for the remaining hubbub to die down before continuing.

279

'Fresh from the most prestigious venues across the region, great performer, recording star, top interpreter of the songs of Frédéric Debreu, for one night only here at Café Gaston, I ask you to bid welcome to the one and only, our own – Ted Prescott!'

Gaston beamed as the room erupted in whistles and applause, the Frenchman taking a stride to one side and throwing out his arm to indicate the stage area, which remained resolutely unoccupied as the clapping died down. Frozen in the gesture, the café owner's smile wavered very slightly, before he turned to scan the bodies at the bar, unaccustomed confusion etched across his face.

'Me? My name is Édouard!' The voice that broke the silence appeared hurt and affronted.

'Ah.' Gaston turned once more, his composure returning in a flash. He gave a small cough. 'Ladies and gentlemen. Édouard Prescôte!'

Holding his instrument before him, Ted pushed his way across, past Bernard, past Claude, past Mme Kerharo from the kitchen, past strangers, past familiar faces, held aloft on their goodwill even before he had played a single note. Reaching the front, he turned to face the crowd, held his free arm aloft to quieten the fresh tumult, lowered his rump to the chair and attacked his guitar.

♫ *Forty years of marriage to a faithless lying hound*
A smile it passed across her lips as he passed in the ground ... ♫

Why had he ever been bashful of this experience? Ted wallowed in the applause, casting his gaze around the crowd, seeking out faces to nod to and people to wave at. He stroked some idle chords as the noise subsided once more, before clearing his throat and blessing everybody with the most enormous of happy grins.

'Good evening!'

There was a smattering of whooping, which he raised his hand to acknowledge. Philippe pushed his way forwards with the glass that Ted had left on the bar, setting it down to one side on the floor.

'Ah! Ladies and gentlemen: Philippe! Thanks, lad. Bring the bottle as well, will you?'

Cheers pursued the youth as he scuttled for the anonymity of his station. Ted lifted his glass and took a long, long swig.

'Now. Um. Je swees Édouard Prescôte, le legend de France! This song – um – cette chanson – est about un homme, um – well, it's about a man who writes to the newspapers. I hope you enjoy it.'

♫ *Dear Editor, Back after the war*
Young people respected the rule of law
But now they behave like the apes
Why it was just the other day
I told one to kindly mind his language ♫

The evening galloped past as Ted worked his way through the repertoire that he'd been learning for all his life. He charged through 'Marguerite', he bounced in his seat to the up-down rhythm of 'The Forger'. He stopped playing entirely during 'My Old Bicycle', waving his fat fingers to conduct the audience as they bellowed out that 'la-la' chorus. He paused to mention Maurice, sponsor of his shirt for the evening; the old man from the clothing stall stood and took a modest bow from the back of the room. Ted completely forgot the words to 'The Mouse', improvising on the same chord whilst people shouted prompts from the crowd. When it was time to slow things down, he introduced 'When We Were Young' with a stumbled English dedication to his brother Eric, before lifting people to their feet with 'The Pretty Goat', which grew so raucous and shambolic by the end that he repeated the final chorus once, twice, three times.

As the cheering crumbled into laughter, Ted slipped his hand into his trouser pocket to draw out a crumpled envelope. Peering at his own writing, he waited for the room to compose itself. Then before he began to recite the words over which he had racked his brain earlier, when he had chewed away until the end of his biro splintered, thumbing furiously through his phrase book and dictionary as he went through pronunciations in his head.

'*My friends.*'

Everybody was quiet now. Ted cleared his throat, feeling his face beginning to redden.

'*My friends, thank you for coming tonight to support Mr and Mrs Dionnet. I hope that your evening was enjoyable.*'

Applause spread through the room, a ripple of claps and murmurs of appreciation building into a wave of hollering and foot-stamping. Ted began to speak again but had to wait. Thrown by the interruption, he buried his face in the scribbled words whilst he waited for quiet.

'*My stay here is almost over. From my heart I thank you for the kindness and generosity you have demonstrated to my wife and I. We will not forget you, and I know that we have found friends here that we will remember for the rest of our lives.*'

The crowd clapped once more. Ted raised his eyes from the envelope to see faces that were nodding and serious. Mme Kerharo was dabbing her eye with a tissue. With dismay, he realised that his own eyes were filling with water. Stupid. Shaking his head and blinking hard, Ted hastily concluded his speech.

'*I would like you to please use your glasses to toast the man who gets us together tonight with his songs and his genius. Ladies and gentlemen: Frédéric Debreu!*' Ted held his glass aloft as the room resounded with cries of the great man's name.

'Right.' He stroked chords for one final time. 'No. Wait. There's a CD! It is – there, look, a CD.' The mayor had pushed his way to the edge of Ted's stage area and was holding the item triumphantly in the air. 'The CD, um, it's ten euro?' He searched for Alain's face in the crowd, the mayor's brother giving him a nod of assent. '*Ten euro to buy, all for Mr and Mrs Dionnet.* It's – um – well, it's quite short but I think it's all right. *Ten euro.* Right.'

♫ *Into the cloisters he passed*
A stranger just passing he claimed
He walked with the Father and asked
What is that monk just there named?
Just there, his face lined with cares?
He keeps to the shadows, leaps at the slightest sound?
He stares around, So gaunt and pale
'Brother Jerard?
There hangs a tale ♫

It took Ted all of ten minutes to make the twenty-foot journey to his place at the bar. Each time he managed to shuffle forwards there was another hand to shake, another pair of lips to surrender his cheeks to, another babbled commendation to which he could only respond with a confused *'thank you'*. He stood nodding in consternation as Mme Dionnet maintained a limpet-like grip on his forearm, tears falling in rivers down her cheeks as her breaking voice repeated 'thank you, thank you' over again. Finally, Gaston stepped in, placing one arm around the Englishman's shoulder, the other held aloft in a polite-yet-firm signal. *'Come on, come on, let Monsieur Prescôte have his drink.'* Ted suddenly found himself dying to throw some cold water on his face, and Gaston showed him through into his apartment, where the Englishman revelled in a few minutes' solitude amidst the sterile tiles and chrome even as his ears drunk in the pandemonium from the bar downstairs.

He walked the long way round by starlight, his swaying strides becoming ever-more laboured as he pulled himself up the track that wound to the farm. His pocket torch threw flickering amber onto the grass and weeds that lined the edge of the road; his panting breaths were the only sound aside from the scuffing and stumbling of his boots in the dirt and stones. Ted had no clue as to the amount of wine that he had consumed – it could have been no less than two bottles, and probably more – but it was the euphoria of the evening that caused him to start giggling as he paused at the half-way mark to rest his lungs.

There was the faraway sound of a car door slamming, an engine revving. Swaying in the darkness, he listened to the vehicle pull away, pausing, pulling away once more towards the village, fainter and fainter until the sound evaporated into the night. He strained his ears but there was nothing but the rustling of the trees. Mailliot le Bois was asleep. His breathing was near-normal again now. Time to carry on.

A dull glow lifted the blackness as he approached the oak tree, blowing and puffing with the effort once more. Daisy had forgiven him enough to leave the kitchen light on. On level ground at last, Ted loped the final few yards to the cottage, its familiar silhouette promising the welcome of a comfy chair. Reaching the back wall, he edged unsteadily round the side of the building, clutching at the woodwork to guide him towards the point where the steps would take him up onto the verandah. Something tripped him with a metallic crash that cut through the stillness and resounded across the night. Ted swore as he hopped and swayed; it was the bucket that lived with the floor mop. Up at the farmhouse, a dog barked but lost interest immediately, the stony silence descending once more on the countryside. Ted steadied himself as he planted his boot on the step. The wine would surely wear off soon. One. Two. Three. Ted shoved open the door and stepped in.

She lay so still on the floor before him.

Later, he found it impossible to recall the moment. He sat, stunned and empty, his hands welded to the arms of his chair. He did not think that he had moved her, although he might have done. He could not remember any blood, or whether he had checked her pulse or just known, or whether there had been a delay before he had stumbled to the farmhouse, battering at the door and bellowing until Patenaude's face had appeared at the window. He looked blankly through the big rural gendarme who was asking the questions in halting English, and made no response when the man arose, laying a brief hand on his shoulder to show that the interview was over and that a human being lived inside the uniform.

Belatedly, Ted got to his feet and shuffled like a robot after the departing officer. In the kitchen, the farmer's daughter was scrabbling about on the floor, brushing flour and raisins and shards of broken pyrex into a dustpan. Ted framed the doorway, clutching the woodwork with both hands to prevent him from falling. He opened his mouth to say some words of thanks, but he could not remember the girl's name, and so he just nodded, hoping that this would suffice even though her back was to him. Through the room, the outer door was still open. The ambulance had gone but the police car remained, its blue lights washing across the trees and bushes, their cold illuminations offering no respite from his despair.

23

David

Ted listened to the sound of the car as it rattled nearer. He had been sat on the verandah steps all morning, waiting.

An old estate rounded the tree and pulled to a halt. His son climbed from the driver's seat, stretching and grimacing from the journey. Ted rose, and the pair regarded each other across the ten feet of scrub, both unsure as to what to do or say. Then Ted strode forward and clutched his son in a hug, thrusting his head over David's shoulder so that the lad would not see the tears that were engulfing him. He clung on wordlessly for some minutes until he could dredge some composure from within, blinking the water away, furious at letting himself be overcome.

'It's good to see you,' he managed to say at last.

It took them no more than the rest of the morning to load up the car. Ted had taken his son inside, showing him around the cottage in a one-minute tour. But each room prompted a moment of agonising past tense. 'That's where we slept.' 'That's where she used to sit.' 'That's where she was.' He saw David's glance at his bedding, still strewn across the lounge from the previous night, but realised from his son's expression that he did not have to explain.

When they were done, Ted plodded to the farmhouse. Thankfully there was nobody to be seen. He pushed open the door to the kitchen and left the key on the windowsill without a note.

The Vauxhall was piled high with Ted's things: his clothes, his tools, his personal items and the paperwork that he had kept back from the previous evening's bonfire. He had rescued a wooden apple box to keep his records safe. Otherwise there was little that he was bothered about. So they left it. A single car load representing the best part of seven decades. Ted cradled his guitar between his legs as he lowered himself into the passenger seat.

He caught sight of the cottage in the wing mirror as David fiddled with his seat belt. It seemed to be distorted, an alien place. He kept his eyes fixed on the building as his son started the engine; he studied the verandah, the side window, the kitchen door. And then the car drew forward, they rounded the oak tree on to the track, and the little house was no more.

24

An Englishman's Home

It was springtime according to the calendar, but the battleship skies and damp chill told a different story. The Frenchman poked at the button for the lift and then examined the tip of his index finger, as if his eyes might eradicate the colonies of foul germs that had doubtless been transferred.

He stepped in, the door stuttering shut with the grating of metal on metal. Even within the isolation of the lift, he was too controlled to allow himself to gag at the smell of stale piss. Nevertheless, he placed a well-manicured hand over his nose and mouth in defence. At the top floor, the door ground open once more, but halfway only, so that he had to edge sideways like a crab to make his escape. He paused to take several breaths of city air, feeling the exhaust fumes swill into his lungs and around his body.

His hand-shined shoes glided across the stained concrete as he followed the numbers on the indistinguishable front doors. Almost at the end of the walkway he found what he was looking for. Extending that finger once more, he pressed the bell.

There were noises from inside, but it took four more rings before the sound of bolts being drawn assured him that he had made himself heard. The door opened inwards and held on the security chain. An old man in a dressing gown peered round.

'Gaston!' said Ted.

The Frenchman paced in the drizzle whilst Ted found his clothes. He watched some young teenagers riding bikes along the fourth floor of the adjacent block, hooting and shouting as they went. A young woman with her hood up left an apartment further up the walkway; she seemed to spend an age fiddling with the locks on her door. She noticed Gaston and looked at him with suspicion and hostility before hurrying away. He smiled politely at the shapeless mass of her retreating fleece top.

'Are you sure you don't mind if we go somewhere else?' Ted said, reappearing in his familiar old shirt and jacket. The garments seemed to sag on him as he half-pulled the door shut so as to obscure Gaston's view of the hallway. 'It's just – well, it's a bit untidy for visitors.'

'No no,' said Gaston, taking a step back and turning his face tactfully away from the entrance. 'I suggest that we use the stairs?'

The pair said little as they walked, negotiating the rubbish-strewn verge of the dual carriageway in single file as the traffic blasted inches past them. Despite the greyness of the weather, the low-rise blocks still appeared to throw shadows across them. The two men reached a pedestrian underpass and hastened through, their footsteps echoing around the concrete tomb. Gaston held his peace as they followed cycle-path signs for the city centre.

'How did you find me?' Ted had to raise his voice to be heard over the shouting. He had fetched them drinks: red wine from a box for Gaston, a pint of John Smith's for him. 'I'm sorry about this place. It looked all right from the outside.'

Gaston shook his head – no matter, although his face hinted that the pub had confirmed all his prejudices about English drinking. It was a cavernous, open-plan barn that appeared to be both boisterously crowded and yet sad and empty all at once. The bar was several yards long and lined with beer pumps, but the badges on most had been removed or turned to face away from the customers. A big screen hung on the far wall, although the picture was restricted to a flickering 'no signal' message in the bottom corner; a group of a dozen or so men in football tops milled before it laughing and swearing, keeping a non-stop flow of lager to their throats lest its temperature should rise in the heat of their mitts.

'Your friends from England,' said Gaston, raising his eyebrows as his glass reached his mouth. 'We have their *cellphone* number still from when we have to call them to help.'

Ted took a swig of his beer, and then a deeper one, so that when he replaced his glass on the table fully one-half of it had been consumed. He looked around the pub. He might have been in here before, once, but that had been years ago, possibly decades, before the individual bars had been knocked out, certainly before the days of the karaoke that was advertised on the fake chalkboard opposite. Perhaps once it had been a locals' place, he thought, although there were no locals left around here now. It was probably frightening in here of an evening; at this time of day all there was were the sports fans and the occasional shopper killing time before they were needed at the bus station.

His pint was almost gone now. 'I should ring them,' he said. 'They did invite me down to Cornwall, but – well, it's a long way.'

Gaston nodded his understanding. Ted felt as if he should say more, but to his relief the Frenchman spoke to fill the gap, recounting his experiences of the past two days: of the Tower of London, of the river, of St. Paul's, of his adventures purchasing a ticket and travelling north by rail. 'I am happy you are at home!' he said. He had enjoyed his vacation. He would do it more often.

Ted toyed with his pint glass. Looking across the empty tables he watched a couple of about his own age take a seat, the man resting a clutch of supermarket bags about his feet as his wife set down a pint in front of him. They sat gazing around and about the room, nothing to say to each other after all these years. The man caught Ted's eye as he watched; Ted, embarrassed, looked away.

'One more beer?' said Gaston.

For some reason the question startled Ted. 'Yes. I mean, I'd like one.' He refocused his attention on Gaston. 'Are you sure you want to stay here?'

Gaston smiled at him, his own drink almost untouched. 'This is the real England, eh? Yes. We will stay.'

'I ...'

'Do not worry. I have money.'

The football lads drank up and filed from the bar to catch the match elsewhere. In the absence of their row the sound of human speech was all but absent and Ted realised that music was being softly piped in to the background, the tin beat of a drum machine making forlorn attempts to bring some spirit to the sparse room. Gaston returned with Ted's bitter, a half-pint glass and a bottled beer for himself.

It took most of this second pint for Ted to feel comfortable enough to speak. He told Gaston about David, cheffing on his oil rig. He hoped that he would get to see the boy again in the summer.

'Thank you for the money you send, Ted. You should stop now.'

Ted avoided his gaze, supping down another enormous mouthful to empty his glass once more. 'Sorry they were all such pitiful amounts. But I've always paid my debts. Tried to, anyway.' He drummed the base of his glass against the tabletop. 'I should have sent my address and everything with them, Gaston. I'm sorry.'

'No problem. I have it now.'

'I might not be there for long. I don't really know.'

How long had it been since he had drunk beer in a pub? A year? This stuff was gassy and bland, but he had forgotten just how well a pint hit the spot when you fancied one. Perhaps if he rooted around he might find a better place in this neighbourhood. Down one of the back streets, most likely.

'How is it in Mailliot?' he asked.

Gaston rose to his feet. 'I will tell you, with another beer.'

The Frenchman was lingering in conversation with the barman, so Ted left the table himself, plodding past the mute couple

291

towards the gents. The heavy stench of disinfectant hung in the air as he relieved himself. It was peculiar, he thought, how Gaston had so quickly come to seem at home in this new environment. He realised how much he had missed talking with his friend.

'OK. Well, what news have I?'

Ted leaned in as Gaston told Ted about the winter back home, about the sixtieth birthday party that they had hosted for the mayor. He smiled and nodded as the Frenchman talked about *Centre Frédéric Debreu,* and clapped his hands together in delight as Gaston filled him in on some early ideas that had been put forward for the coming summer's festival.

'Hey!' Ted's head shot up. The sound was unmistakable. His own guitar playing was ringing out from somewhere in the room, the plucked arpeggios descending through the introduction of 'The Vengeful Widow'. Ted's eyes searched the room for the loudspeakers, as if by finding them he might deduce an explanation for this surprise.

'I ask the barman,' said Gaston, a beam written across his face. 'He says that he is not concerned as the television is broken.'

Ted's own voice boomed across the pub:

♫ *Forty years of marriage to a faithless lying hound* ♫

Gaston studied the Englishman as he gawped. 'I did not know whether you took a disc,' he said. 'You did not collect one from me.'

Ted shook his head. 'No. I didn't.'

'Your music was good for the town.' Ignoring his glass, Gaston lifted the bottle to his mouth and swigged, a gesture so uncharacteristic that it made Ted stare. 'Lots of enthusiasm this year, to do things, to get more tourists. There is hope about the airport again; maybe it happens and suddenly "boom!". We will have musicians in the café over the summer. So I will be busy, so I have a holiday now.'

'You left Philippe in charge?'

'Philippe?' Gaston raised his eyes to the ceiling, pursing his lips until all the colour had been squeezed from them. 'Philippe has gone, Ted. He pisses off to Paris with the girls Celine and Marie. "Follow my dreams! Follow my dreams," he says! He abandons, runs away, leaves me without my barman after all I do.'

Ted's jaw dropped open. 'Both of them?'

'Bernard, he is furious. Furious with them, furious with him. He says "where do you get ideas like that?" Follow your dreams! Hah!' Gaston banged his fist against the table, rattling the empties that had accumulated.

Ted suddenly found his beer mat very interesting. 'Do you want some crisps?' he said.

Gaston told him about the little cottage at the farm. It had suffered, unoccupied in the harsh New Year weather; Monsieur Patenaude had talked alternately of demolishing it and rebuilding properly to let it out as an official *gîte*. Gaston suspected that the farmer would get round to neither, and that the building would remain as a gathering ruin until the wood disappeared into the Thorigny soil. Casimir had rescued the possessions that Ted had left behind; the smaller items were being kept in his sister's spare room; the furniture had been sold in aid of the Dionnet family, if that was acceptable to him. Ted nodded. 'Again, I'm sorry I didn't give you an address,' he said. 'I should have done.'

Ted excused himself to visit the toilet once more. His mind still could not process the disparity of his own singing resounding around this room. The shopping-bag couple were still there, the woman without a drink, the man still nursing his undrunk pint. Perhaps they would spend the rest of their lives waiting there. He should ask them for the name of their taxi company, so that he might avoid them.

♫ *No, let us not begrudge this ancient widow her revenge*
They say the one laughs longest who is laughing at the end ♫

The big Englishman's eyes couldn't express more gratitude as he returned to find one more newly filled glass in front of him. He was plucking the introduction to 'The Pretty Goat' now. Ted took a pause to lean back in his chair and listen. It was good.

'Come back, Ted,' said Gaston, out of nowhere.

'What?'

'Come back. To Mailliot.'

'What?'

'Come back. Why not?'

Ted stared at Gaston across his beer. 'Well I can't.'

'Why not?' Gaston held out his arms. 'There is Philippe's room. There is his job. You started to understand the work in the bar; maybe you will be a good barman? There is music to play in there, and the festival, there is *Centre Frédéric Debreu*? Why not?'

Ted shook his head. 'Things here …'

'Things?' Gaston turned his head left and right, peering into each corner of the bar. Ted stared down at the table, his fingers toying with his pint glass. There was silence between them, neither man willing to speak first.

Gaston stood up. 'Now, I go to the washroom,' he said.

♫ *Won't you let me guard your savings*
Said the banker, said the banker ♫

It was eerie, it was properly eerie. He had made a small mistake at the conclusion of this first verse, tripping over the words in a way that threatened to lose the metre of the final line. Ted pictured himself sat in that tiny studio, recalling that he had suggested rerecording the whole song, to be persuaded that the error was so slight that it would not be worth using the precious time. He listened hard as the song reached that point. They had been right; it was hardly noticeable. Perhaps the man Ric had been able to make some correction with his equipment.

♪ *Tra la, la tra-la-la*
La la la la la ♪

Ted gazed around the pub once more. Over towards the gents, the lonely couple sat, now the only other customers in the bar. Three-and-a-half pints had made Ted less shy of staring. He looked hard at the old man, thin and gaunt, a shabby sadness about him as he sat his life away in this soulless waiting room. His eyes were elsewhere, his grey head bobbing, very slightly but still very noticeably, up and down in time with the music.

♪ *Tra la, la tra-la-la*
La la la la la ♪

On the far side, Gaston stepped through the door. From across the room, Ted caught his eye and the faintest of smiles crossed the Englishman's face.

Epilogue

In the heart of Charles de Gaulle, a man paused amidst the surge from the baggage reclaim into the main arrivals area. The river of travellers jostled and bumped past him, peering into the crowd for relatives, hastening for the first cabs. But he had nobody to meet and nowhere in particular to get a cab to. The man waited until the final straggler had passed through before shifting the backpack that held all that he had retained for his new start, wriggling so that the weight of his possessions was borne equally by both shoulders.

He resumed his progress at an amble. There was a coffee bar directly opposite, but he was too sensible to touch plastic airport coffee after all these miles. He would bear that bag a little further, out into the hot city to find somewhere a little more authentically French. To stretch his legs, to breathe in the air – however polluted – to sit down and refocus his thoughts on what might lie ahead. That was what he needed.

It had been a long way from Tennessee.

He might have got away with it. It would have been an embarrassment, but he might have kept his job if he'd done things a little more quietly. If he hadn't cajoled his ultra-conservative bosses to take a shot at the modern world; if he'd used an American artist for his foray into music downloads; if he'd been less superior in the wood-panelled boardroom when confronted with a die-hard sea of redneck dismissal of those glorious and unexpected songs.

If, if. If he'd queried the illegible signature from the artist when he'd sent out that contract. If he'd been there in the office to intercept the long and rambling email from the crazy lady, with its allegations about the music's origin in a jagged rage of pseudo-English.

If, when it came down to it, he hadn't thrown several hundred dollars of the company's money at a man whom he'd met in a field.

A bus pulled up and Roy boarded, heaving his bag ahead of him as he picked his way towards the rear.

*

Although Roy thought himself alone in Paris, he might have found one familiar face just a few miles into the city. Out of the airport and across the industrial zones, past the sink estates and the rundown suburbs, into a cheap apartment in a backward area of the city that had somehow been overlooked by both gentrification and decay.

Philippe pulled his T-shirt up over his head. Letting his jeans drop to the floor, he kicked them off to one side of the room. Lifting the duvet, he sunk face-down into the double bed, burying his pock-marked nose in the pillow. The cotton smelled of Marie, lovely, luscious Marie – her perfume, her hairspray. He snuggled down like that for some minutes before turning onto his side. He hadn't planned to sleep, but found himself drifting into a doze, impervious to the din of the traffic three floors below, a week of shifts into the small hours catching up with his exhausted body.

Perhaps he had slept for two hours; perhaps it was two minutes. But the next thing he comprehended was the dreadful turn of the doorknob, the arresting squeal of the hinges. A familiar silhouette stood framed against the light pouring in from the landing.

'Philippe! What are you doing, you animal? Get out! Get out! Get off to your own bedroom! Don't ever come in here again!'

In mortified horror, his eyes still fighting his slumber, Philippe bounded from the perfumed cocoon and bolted, stumbling past the figure at the door, and silently howling as he scrabbled for the safety of his own bedroom door. A few seconds later, his trousers came flying out after him, slapping

297

against the wall opposite and falling gently, crumpled and dead upon the cold linoleum.

*

His suitcase had almost fallen apart on the journey, but Ted would not need it again if everything went to plan. But, of course, when did everything ever go to plan? He paused momentarily to regain his puff, reached for his handkerchief to clear the sweat that was pouring from his forehead and, with one final effort that caused his face to glow purple, hauled the luggage up onto the bed. The frame sagged and creaked in protest. Ted had planned to unpack there and then, but what was the hurry? He left the buckles fastened and made the single stride to the window. The catch came away easily and two strong bashes released the frame in a cloud of dust and paint flakes. Fresh air crept in to the box room.

Ted stooped to see through, his big palms flat on the sill, his head moving this way and that as he took in the comforting scene of the market square. He saw the remnants of the traders as they cleared and swept; he heard the vans, a car horn, somebody shouting across the road to an unknown person.

A pushchair came into view from the street on the right; he recognised the young mother who he'd often encountered on his walk from the farm. His eyes followed her progress as she trotted down the kerb and diagonally across the street. The child was bigger now; her mother seemed less weighed down by the world, more upright, a small spring in her step. Halting when she reached the far side, she leaned over the back of the pushchair, gave her hand a small kiss, and planted it on the upturned forehead of the infant.

Ted watched the street cleaners as they clashed their bins, then turned back to the yellowing walls of his new lodgings. He would do some sprucing up, perhaps find a new eiderdown, at least get Gaston to replace the other light bulb. His eyes fell back upon his unopened suitcase. For the briefest of moments he wondered whether he was making just one more stupid move in his recent history of stupid moves; whether he should grasp the handle and lug it back down the stairs to seek out a more conventional old age for a foolish old bugger from the High Peaks.

Something caught his eye on a gloomy shelf in the far corner: an odd shape that he couldn't discern in the shadow. Stepping around the bed, Ted reached for the object: a weasel mounted upon a wooden block. 'Weasel. For Ted,' he read, and read once more.

Replacing the animal on its perch, Ted slipped off his jacket and draped it across the suitcase. Then he stepped out through the door that led to the stairs, the bar, and a big, big glass of red wine.

Le Pâturage de Thorigny
(Thorigny Fields)

I have travelled far
Just a working man and his guitar
Up and down this land of ours
From the smallest country route to the great cities
Yearning I feel
For wherever I go
I long for the Thorigny fields
I've made my choice
Just an artisan, my tool is my voice
I have met the people from every region
The world is my village, France is my family
The earth is my bed
For wherever I go
I long for my Thorigny bread
It has been so long
Just a simple fellow with his songs
O'er the mountains, through the streets
From the eastern borders to the western seas
Across the world
For wherever I go
I long for my Thorigny girl
I long for my Thorigny girl

Frédéric Debreu
Translation: J. Bonny

Acknowledgements

Many thanks as ever to my friend and sounding board Andrew Viner. To Damien Cabanis for his patience with my daily questions. To Clare Christian. Above all, to Catherine Sanderson, without whom this would have remained just another idea.

And for the inspiration of Georges Brassens and Jake Thackray, who tower above everything in this book and, indeed, most other things in life.

About the Author

Photograph: Tori Hancock

Alex Marsh was born in 1971 in Essex. His parents had worked in publishing in the fifties and sixties, and he grew up in a house piled high with books. These competed for space with paraphernalia from Australia, his Victoria-born grandfather having been known as 'Mister Melbourne', a baker and local celebrity on Hampstead's South End Green.

His childhood coinciding with the microcomputer revolution, Alex's first professional writing job was as a teenage columnist for *Spectrum Adventurer* magazine. Since then he's written short columns for the *Guardian*, jokes for BBC Radio and guest-edited one of the UK's biggest satirical news sites.

Alex's alter-ego blog 'JonnyB's Private Secret Diary' achieved internet fame with its eccentric snapshots of English rural life, gaining him an unexpected cult-status amongst US gun enthusiasts, a letter of apology from a national newspaper editor, and the distinction of being set as a text to 'discuss' in a mock A-level exam.

He lives in Norfolk.